THE MAGIC PO

THE FIRE
WITHIN

AN UNOFFICIAL GRAPHIC
NOVEL FOR MINECRAFTERS

CARA J. STEVENS

ILLUSTRATED BY SAM NEEDHAM

SKY PONY PRESS
NEW YORK

Sky Pony Press books may be purchased in bulk at special discounts for sales
promotion, corporate gifts, fund-raising, or educational purposes. Special editions
can also be created to specifications. For details, contact the Special Sales
Department, Sky Pony Press, 307 West 36th Street, 11th Floor, New York, NY
10018 or info@skyhorsepublishing.com.

Sky Pony® is a registered trademark of Skyhorse Publishing, Inc.®, a Delaware corporation.

Minecraft® is a registered trademark of Notch Development AB.

The Minecraft game is copyright © Mojang AB.

Visit our website at www.skyponypress.com.

10 9 8 7 6 5 4 3 2 1

Library of Congress Cataloging-in-Publication Data is available on file.

Cover design by Brian Peterson
Cover and interior art by Sam Needham

Print ISBN: 978-1-5107-6661-7
Ebook ISBN: 978-1-5107-7117-8

Printed in China

#2

THE MAGIC PORTAL
THE FIRE WITHIN

INTRODUCTION

Once upon a time there was the world, and in the world were creatures who did their best to get along with each other and find their place among their neighbors. The path was not always easy, and it was not always clear.

Time passed and people arrived. Villagers and miners tamed, ate, and battled the creatures and called them mobs. The mobs often got in the way, stopping game play, messing with competitions, and causing a lot of people to say "ouch" far too often.

Our story begins as Keri and Omar, rivals in their teams but fellow travelers in time, are setting out once again to uncover ancient secrets. Their mission is to discover the origins of the creatures who cause them the most ouchies, and to see if they can use the knowledge they gain to make their world a better and safer place. In this adventure, their mission is clear, but their return home is much more complicated than they realize.

Chapter 1
Floor Cakes

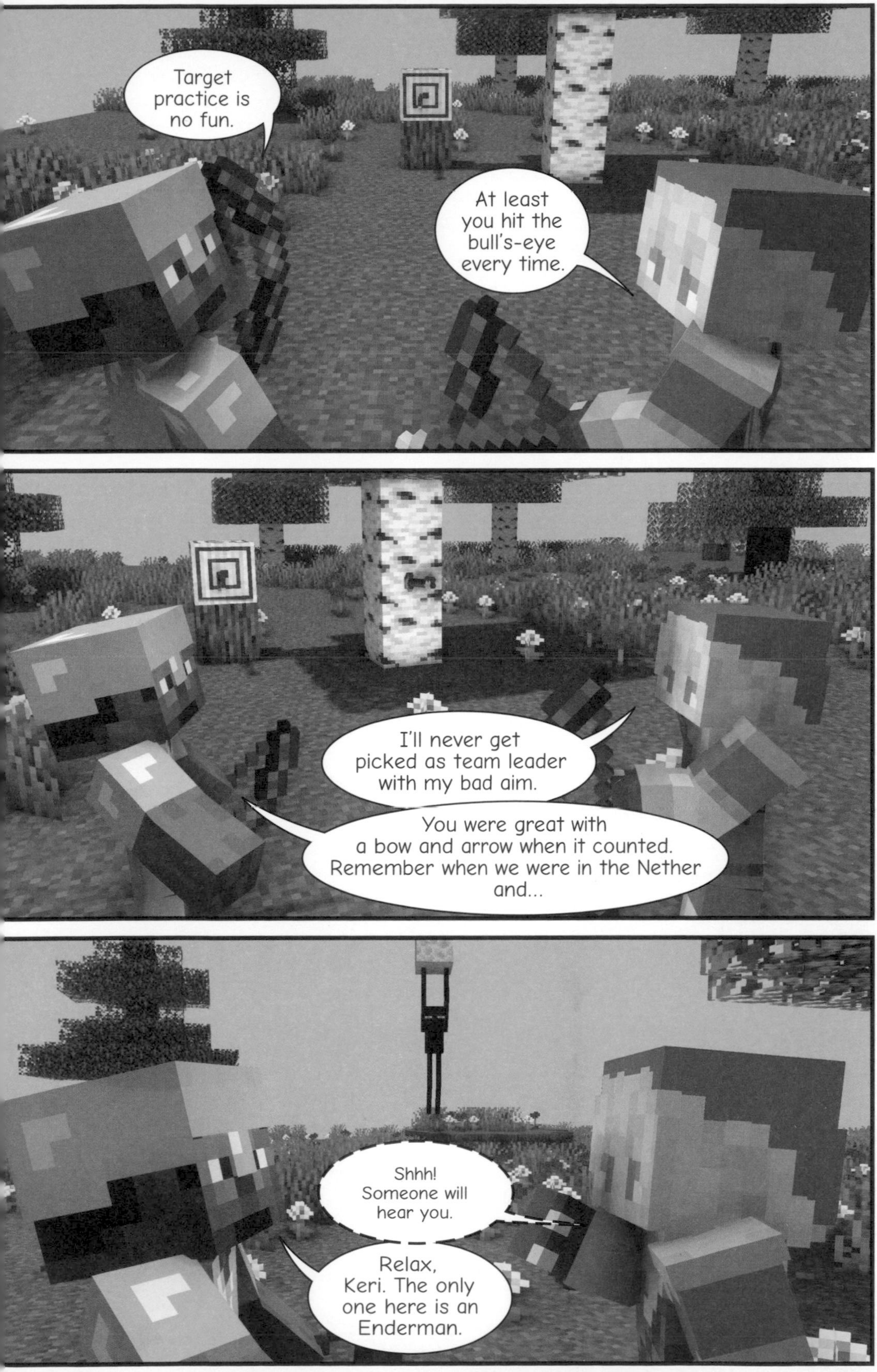
Target practice is no fun.
At least you hit the bull's-eye every time.
I'll never get picked as team leader with my bad aim.
You were great with a bow and arrow when it counted. Remember when we were in the Nether and...
Shhh! Someone will hear you.
Relax, Keri. The only one here is an Enderman.

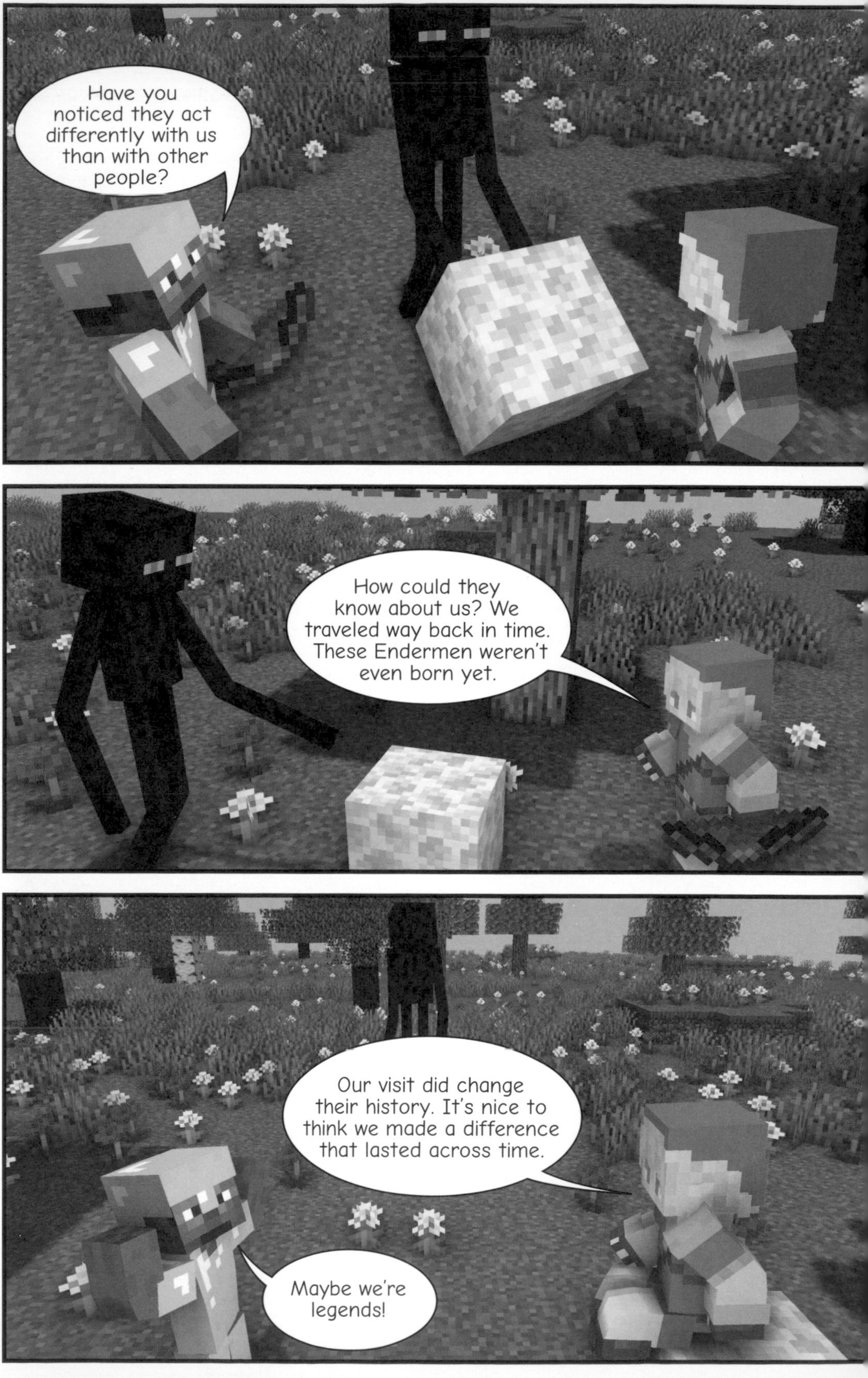
Have you noticed they act differently with us than with other people?
How could they know about us? We traveled way back in time. These Endermen weren't even born yet.
Our visit did change their history. It's nice to think we made a difference that lasted across time.
Maybe we're legends!

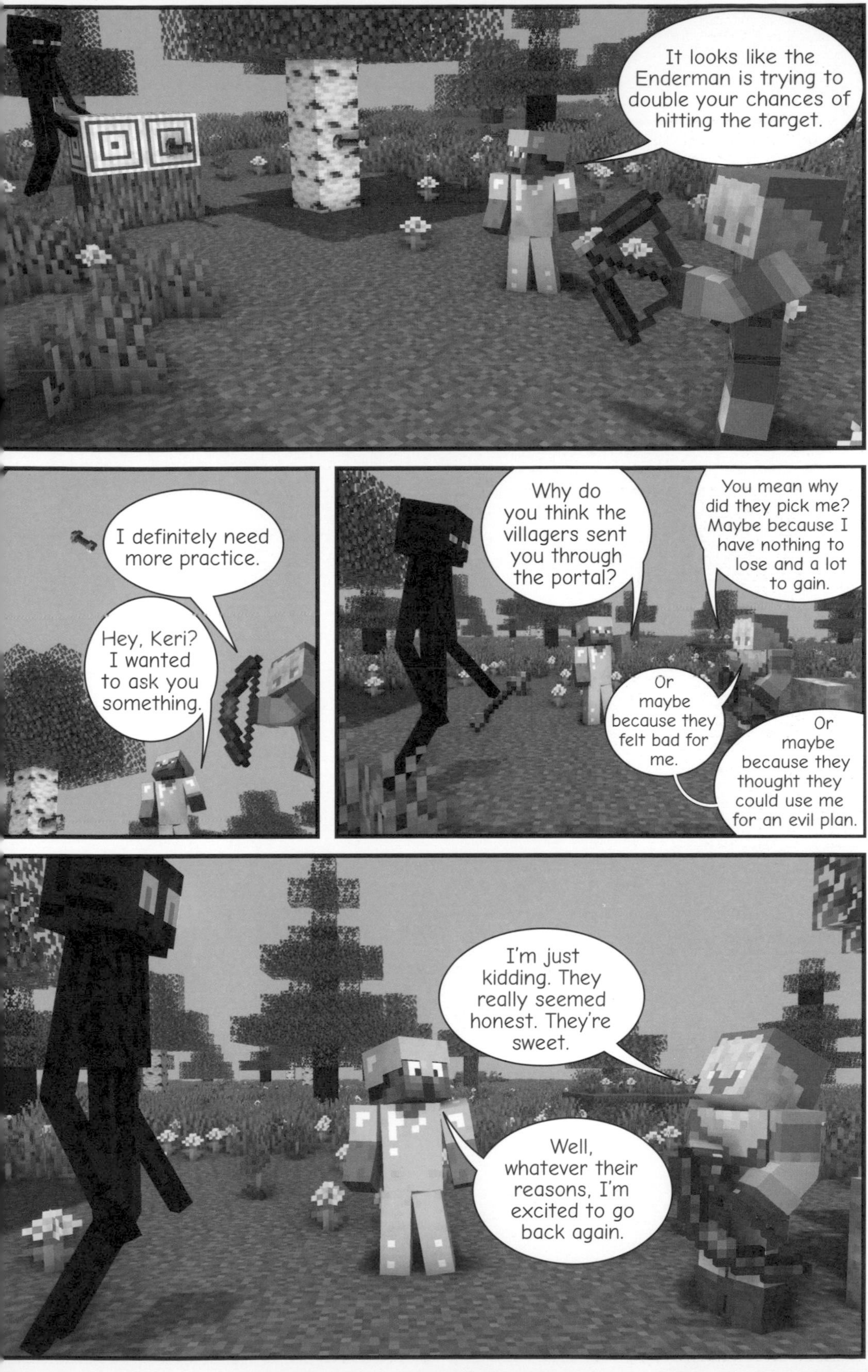
It looks like the Enderman is trying to double your chances of hitting the target.
I definitely need more practice.
Hey, Keri? I wanted to ask you something.
Why do you think the villagers sent you through the portal?
You mean why did they pick me? Maybe because I have nothing to lose and a lot to gain.
Or maybe because they felt bad for me.
Or maybe because they thought they could use me for an evil plan.
I'm just kidding. They really seemed honest. They're sweet.
Well, whatever their reasons, I'm excited to go back again.

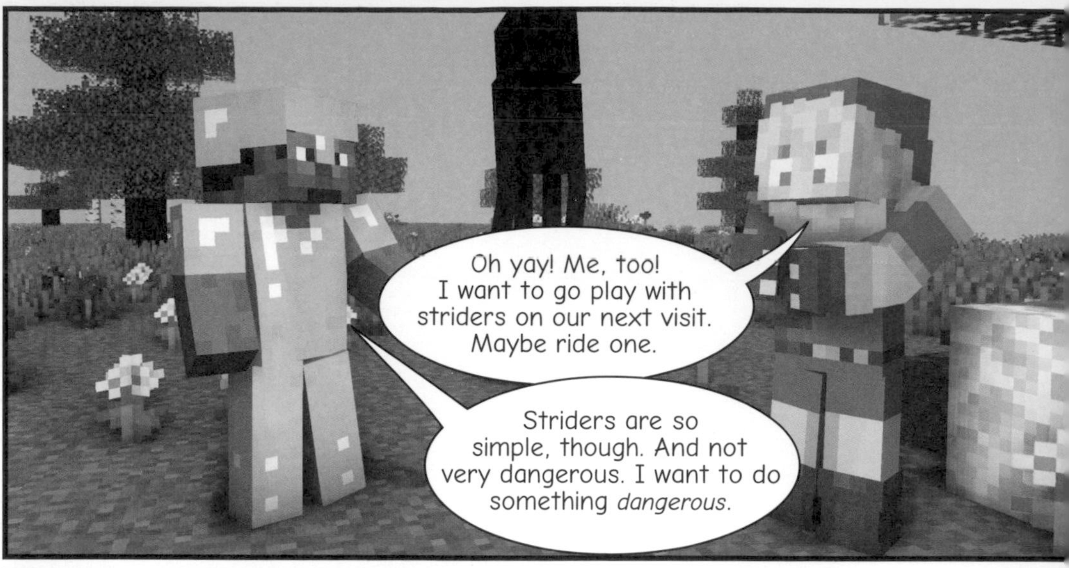
Oh yay! Me, too!
I want to go play with
striders on our next visit.
Maybe ride one.
Striders are so
simple, though. And not
very dangerous. I want to do
something *dangerous*.

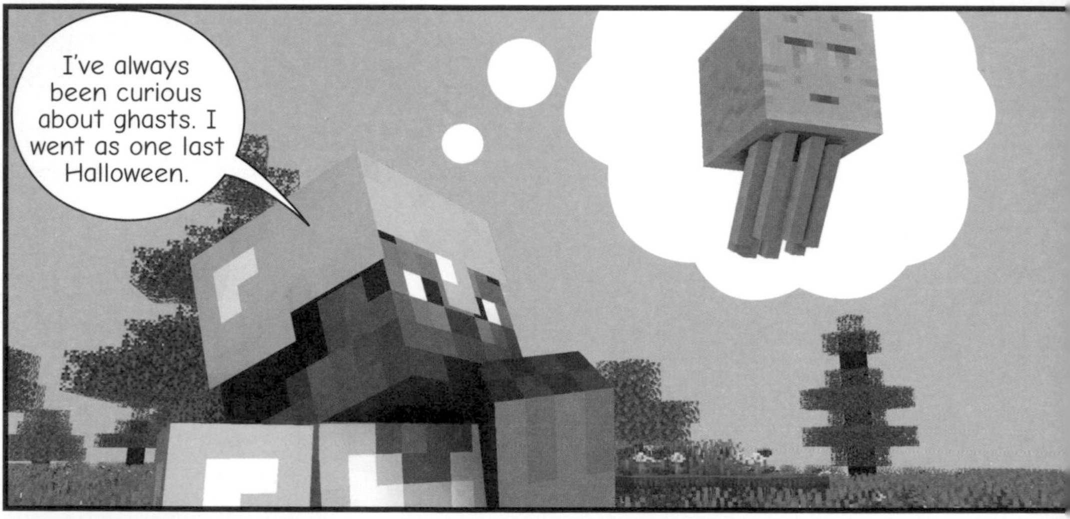
I've always
been curious
about ghasts. I
went as one last
Halloween.

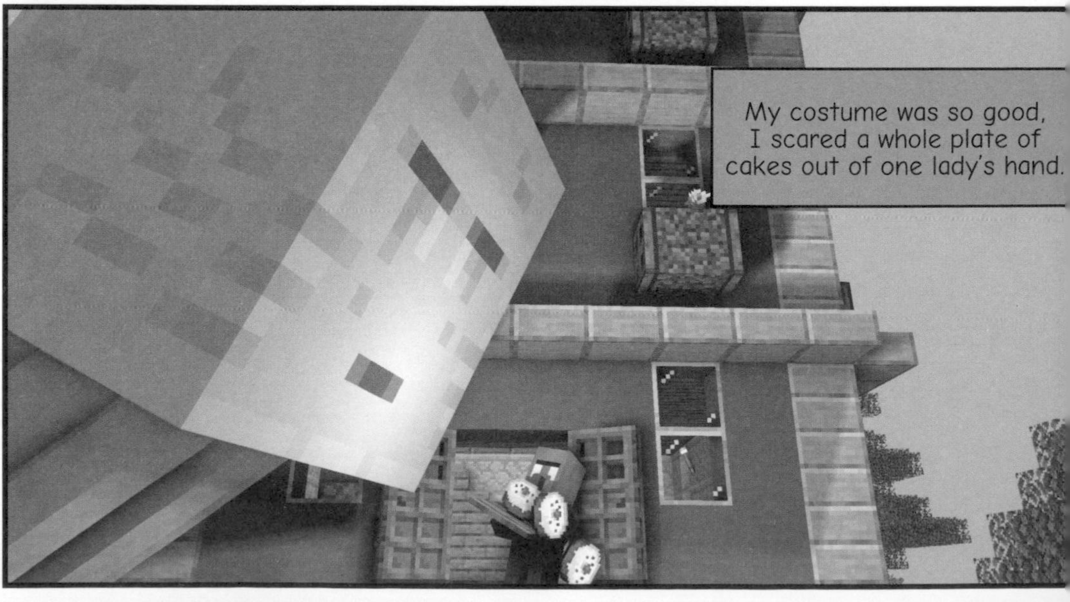
My costume was so good,
I scared a whole plate of
cakes out of one lady's hand.

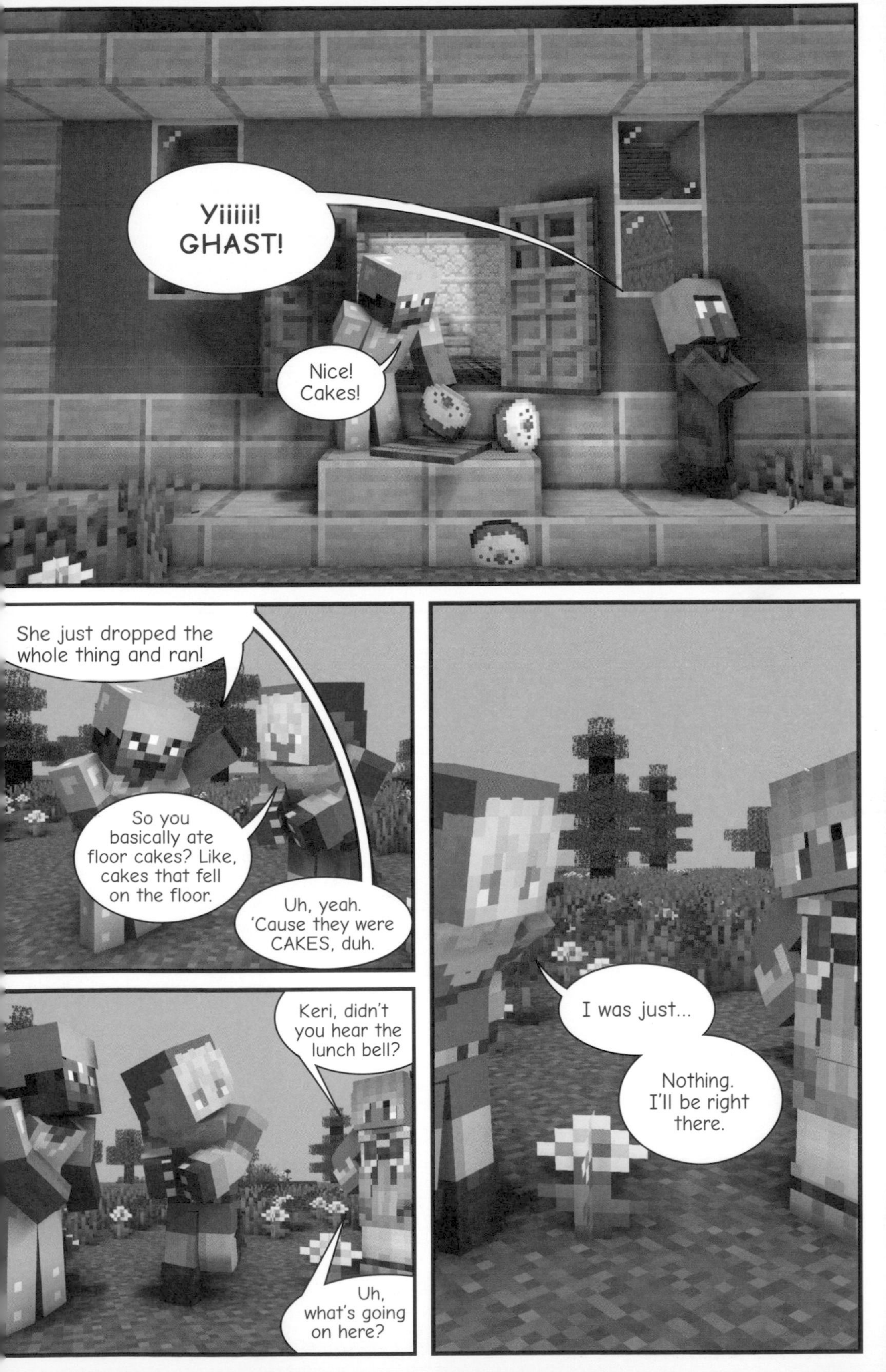
Yiiiii! GHAST!
Nice! Cakes!
She just dropped the whole thing and ran!
So you basically ate floor cakes? Like, cakes that fell on the floor.
Uh, yeah. 'Cause they were CAKES, duh.
Keri, didn't you hear the lunch bell?
Uh, what's going on here?
I was just...
Nothing. I'll be right there.

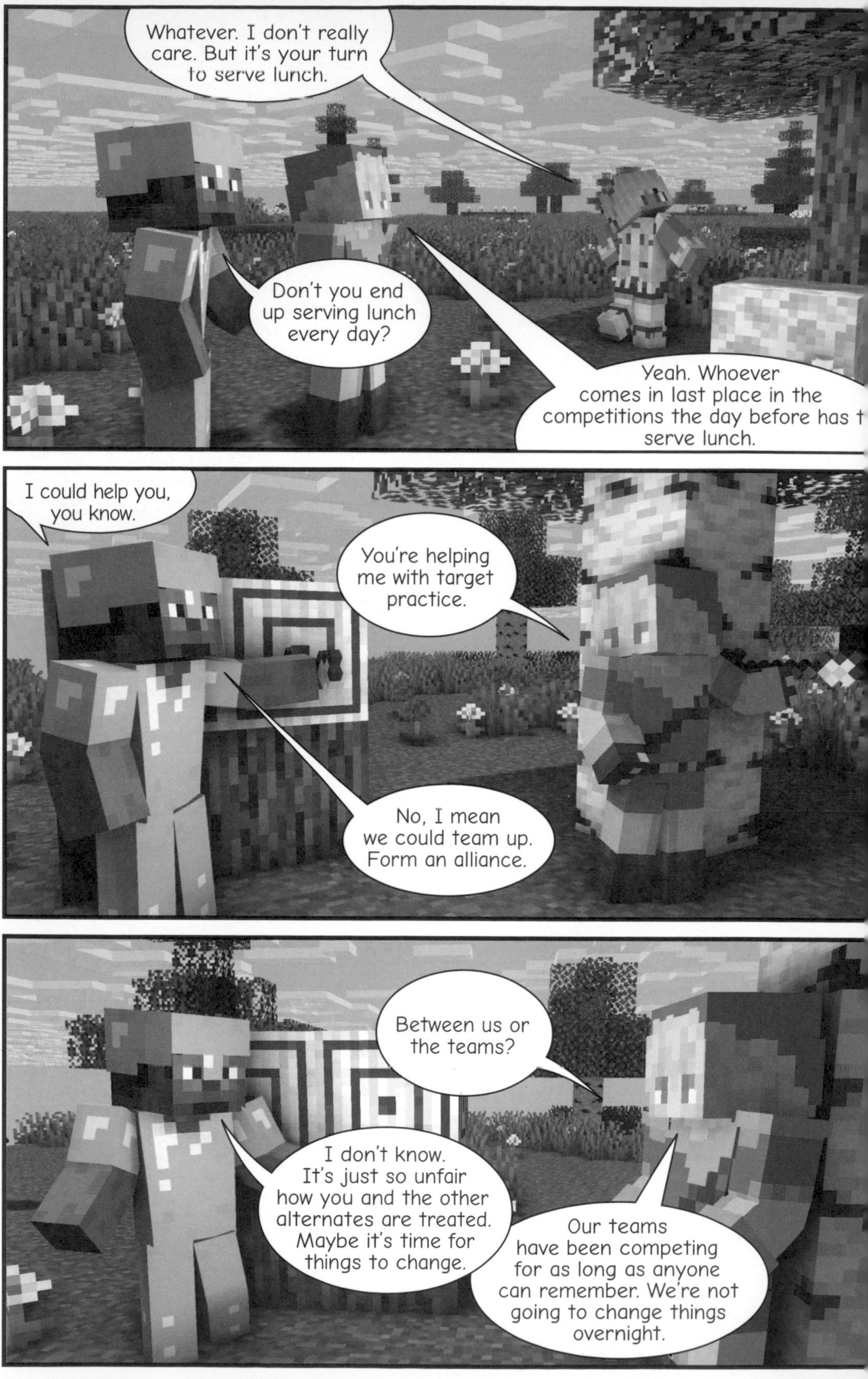
Whatever. I don't really care. But it's your turn to serve lunch.
Don't you end up serving lunch every day?
Yeah. Whoever comes in last place in the competitions the day before has t serve lunch.
I could help you, you know.
You're helping me with target practice.
No, I mean we could team up. Form an alliance.
Between us or the teams?
I don't know. It's just so unfair how you and the other alternates are treated. Maybe it's time for things to change.
Our teams have been competing for as long as anyone can remember. We're not going to change things overnight.

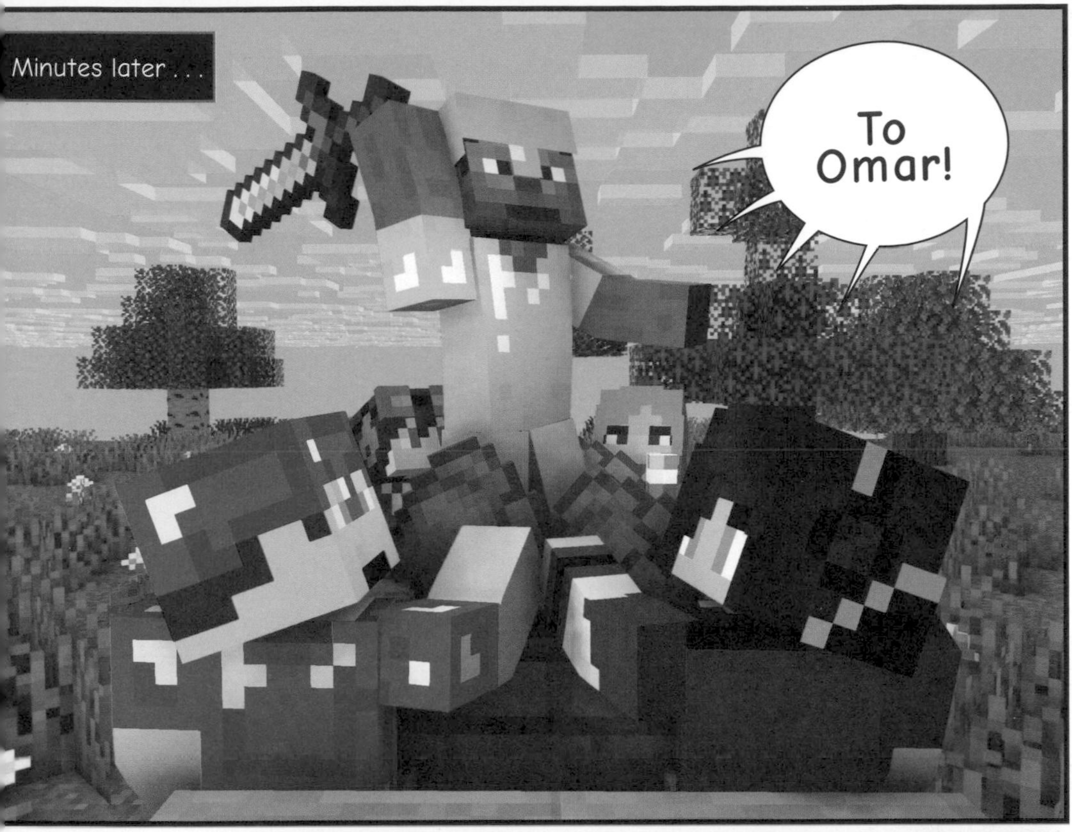
Minutes later . . .
To Omar!

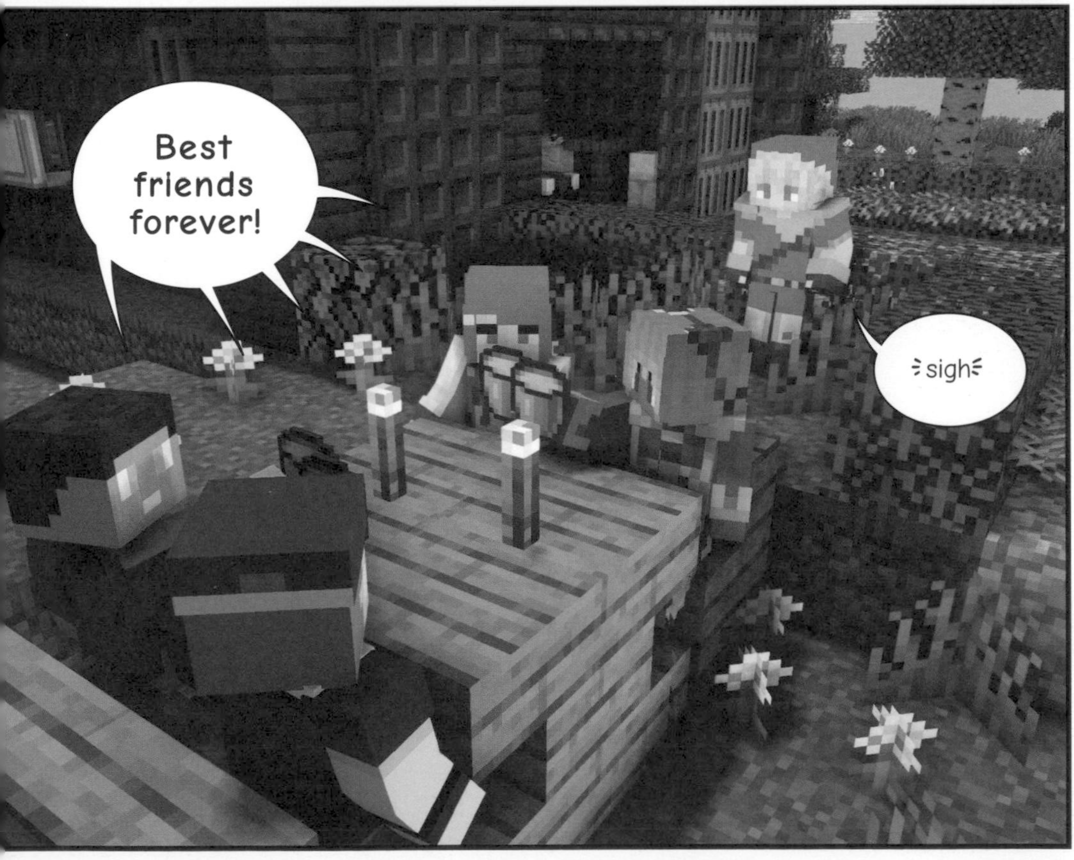
Best friends forever!
sigh

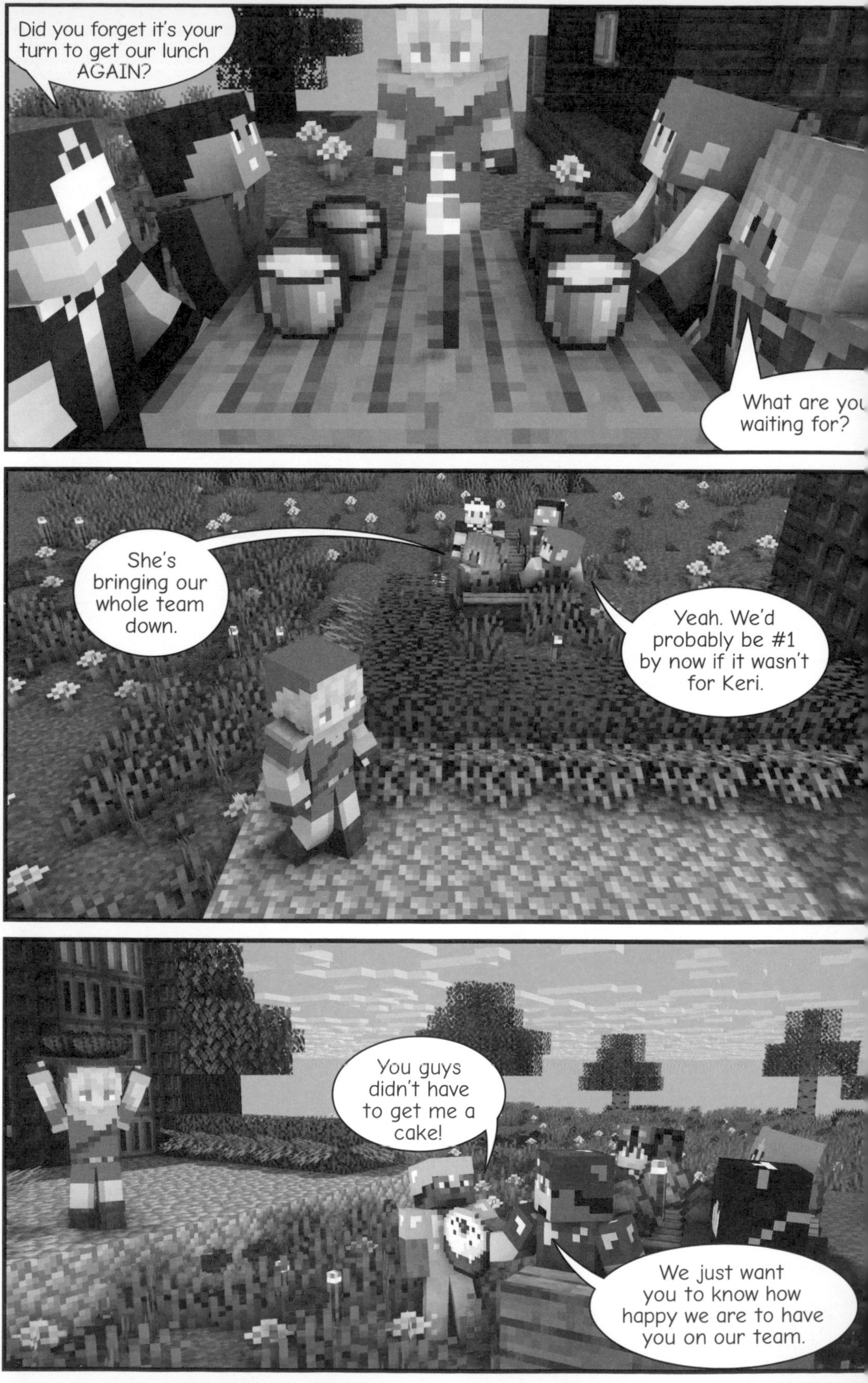

Did you forget it's your turn to get our lunch AGAIN?
What are you waiting for?
She's bringing our whole team down.
Yeah. We'd probably be #1 by now if it wasn't for Keri.
You guys didn't have to get me a cake!
We just want you to know how happy we are to have you on our team.

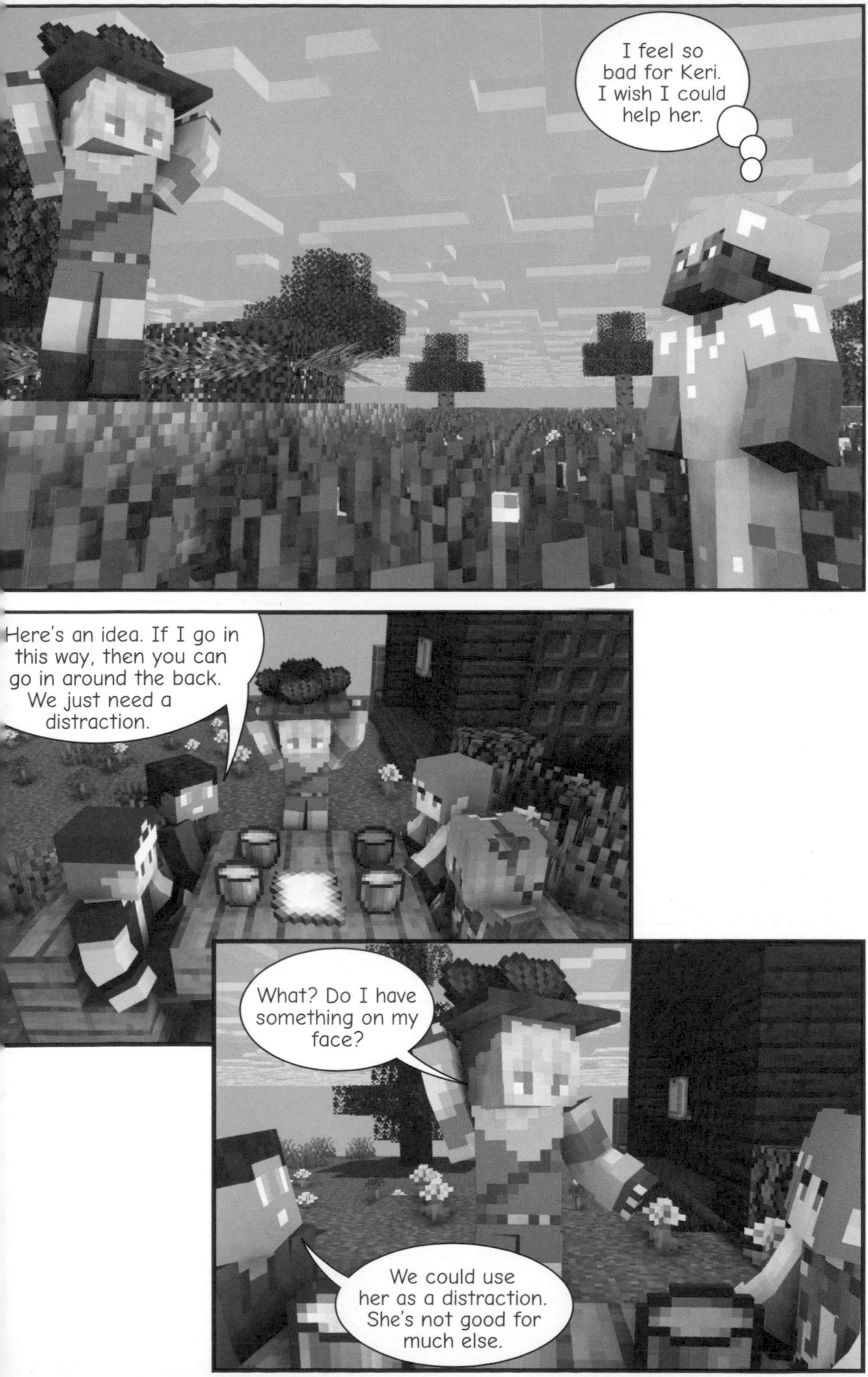
I feel so bad for Keri. I wish I could help her.
Here's an idea. If I go in this way, then you can go in around the back. We just need a distraction.
What? Do I have something on my face?
We could use her as a distraction. She's not good for much else.

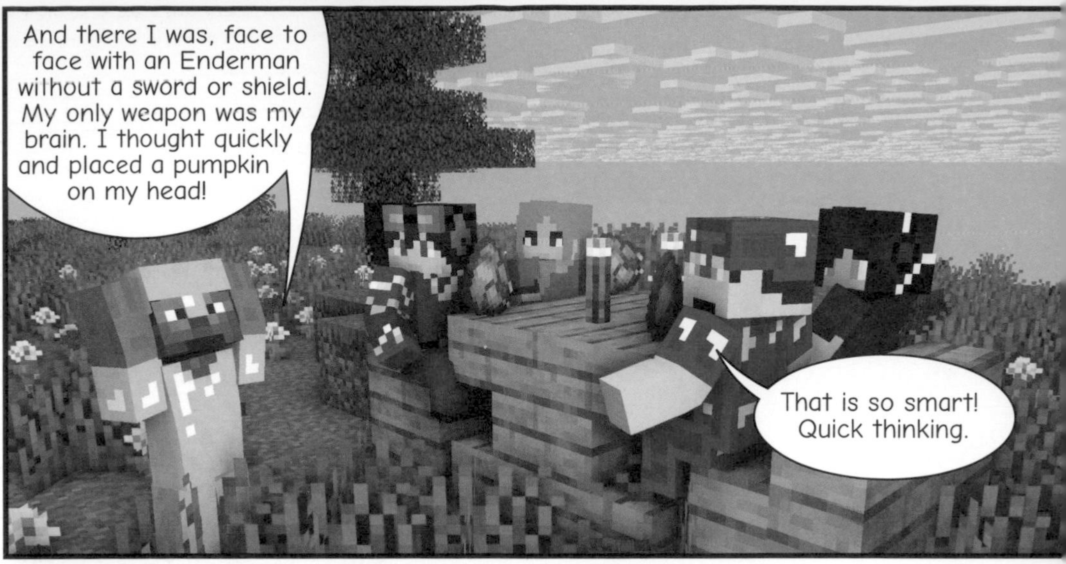
And there I was, face to face with an Enderman without a sword or shield. My only weapon was my brain. I thought quickly and placed a pumpkin on my head!
That is so smart! Quick thinking.

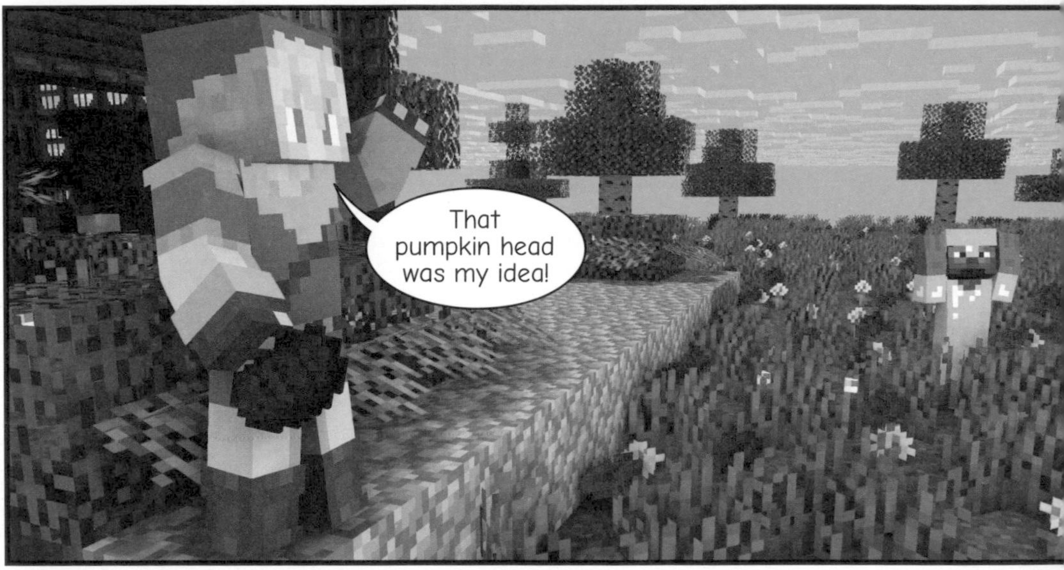
That pumpkin head was my idea!

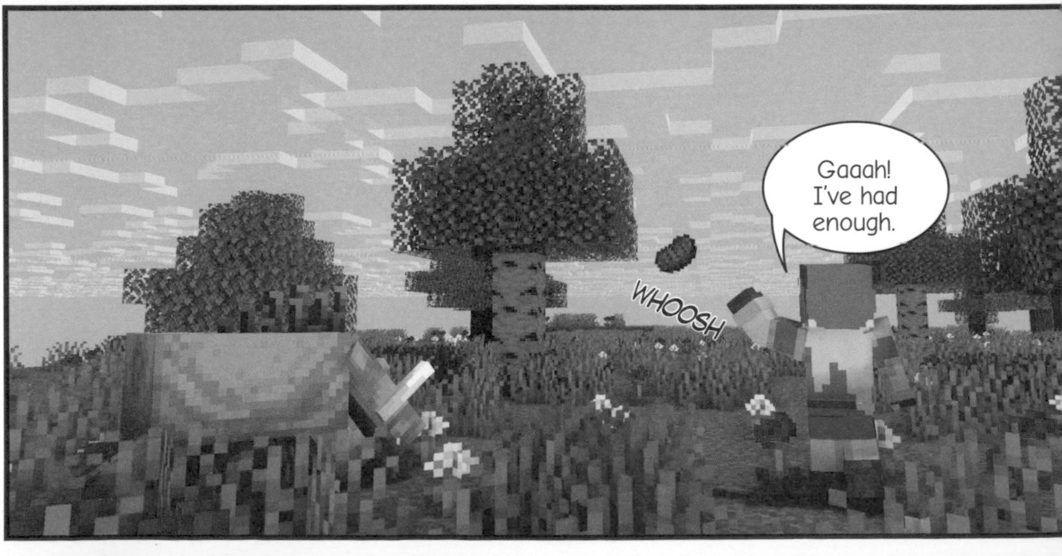
Gaaah! I've had enough.
WHOOSH

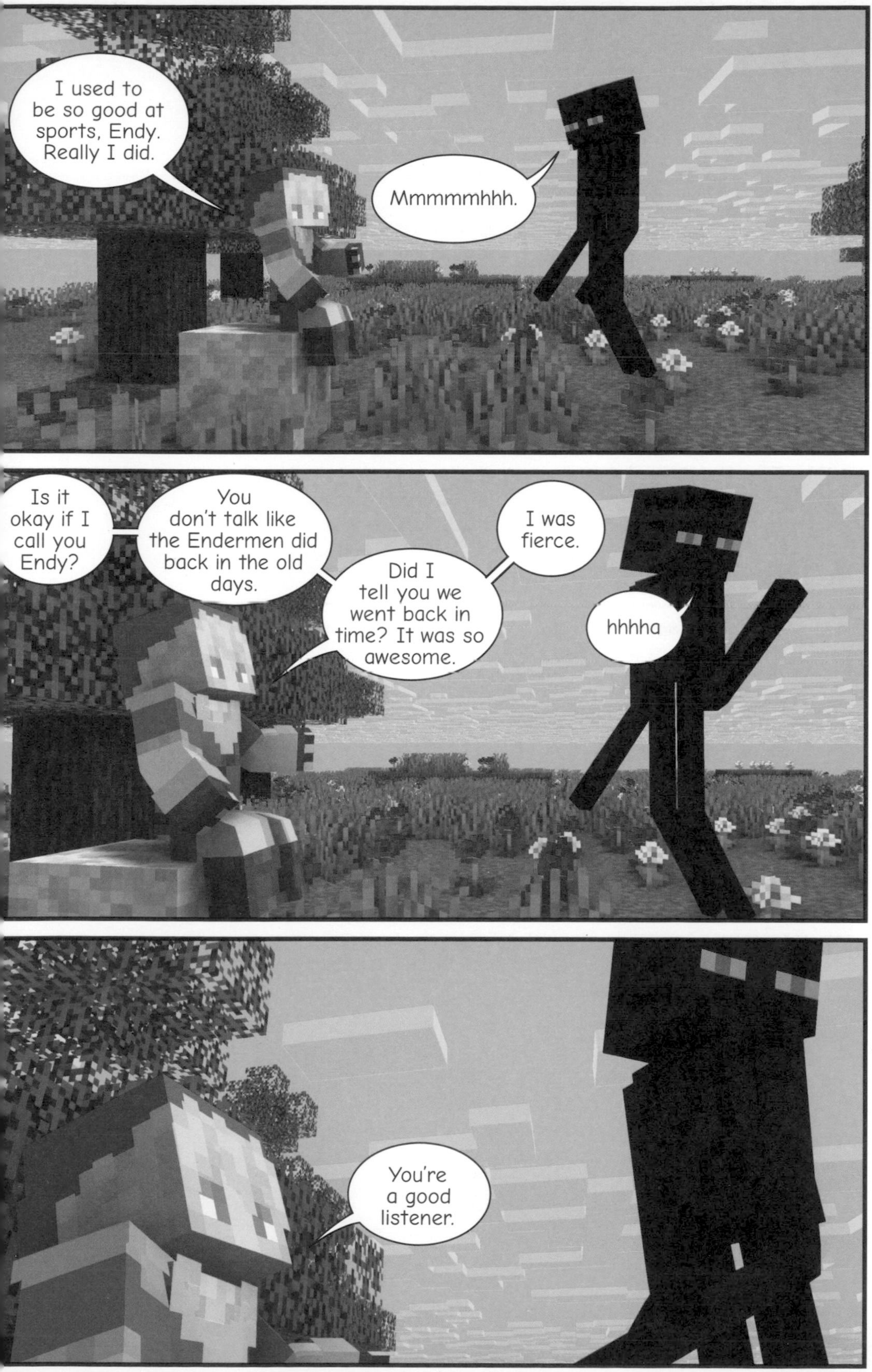
I used to be so good at sports, Endy. Really I did.
Mmmmmhhh.
Is it okay if I call you Endy?
You don't talk like the Endermen did back in the old days.
Did I tell you we went back in time? It was so awesome.
I was fierce.
hhhha
You're a good listener.

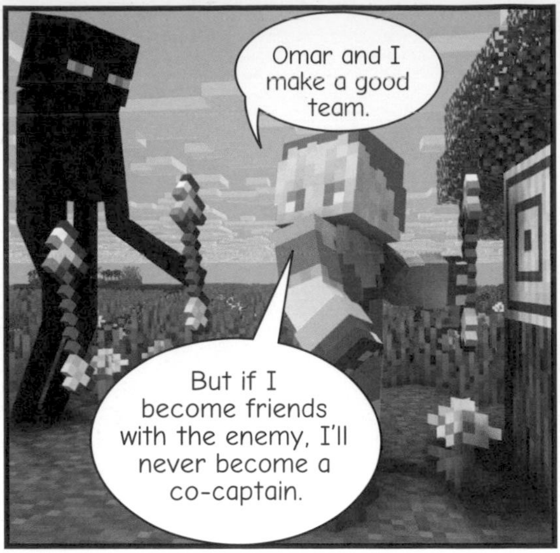
Omar and I make a good team.
But if I become friends with the enemy, I'll never become a co-captain.

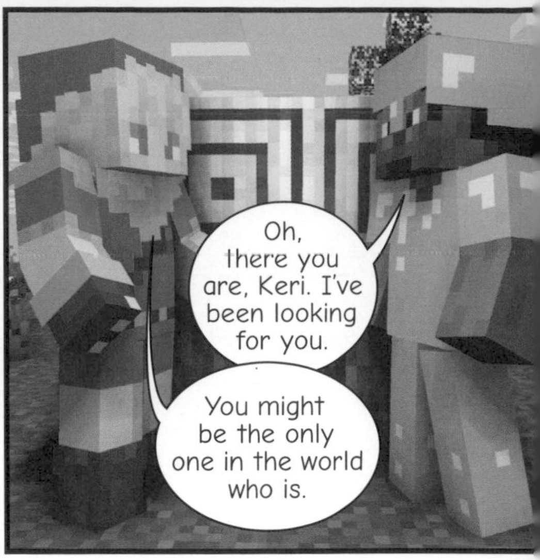
Oh, there you are, Keri. I've been looking for you.
You might be the only one in the world who is.

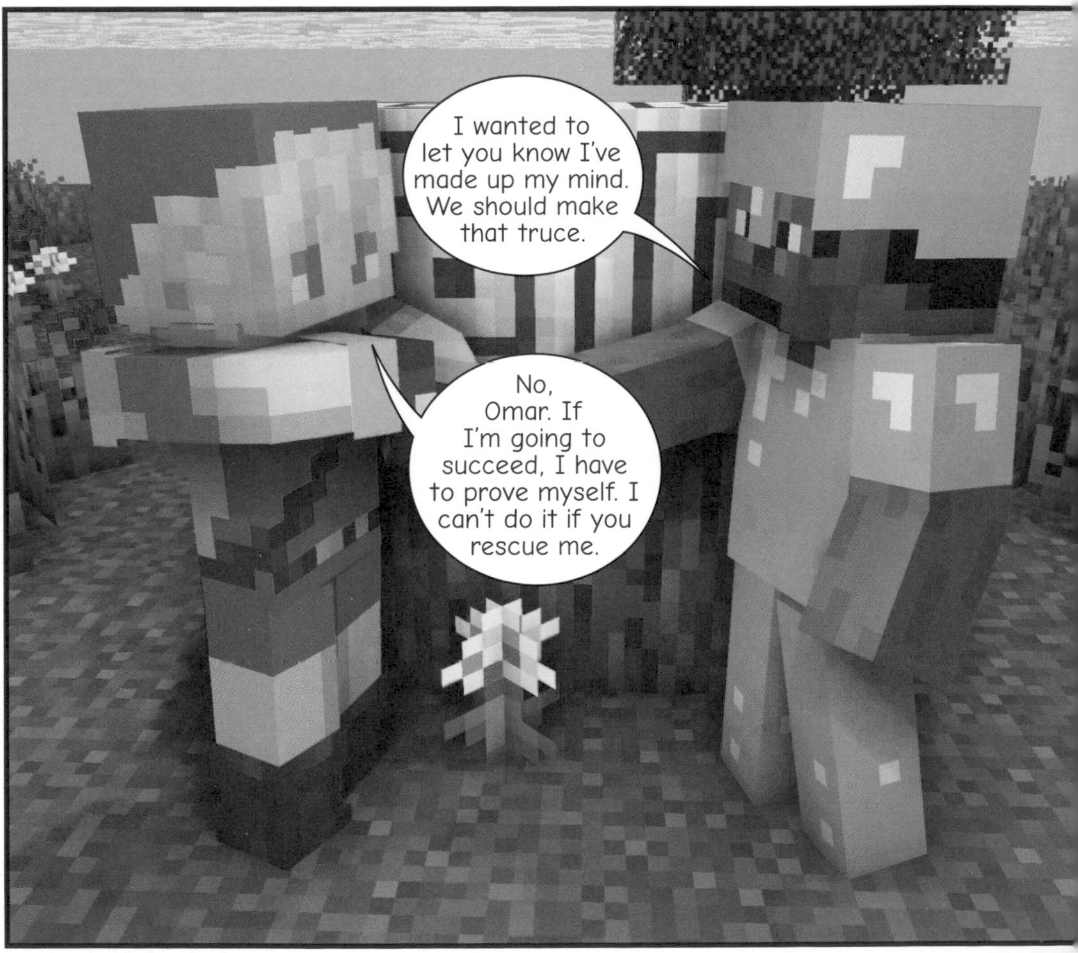
I wanted to let you know I've made up my mind. We should make that truce.
No, Omar. If I'm going to succeed, I have to prove myself. I can't do it if you rescue me.

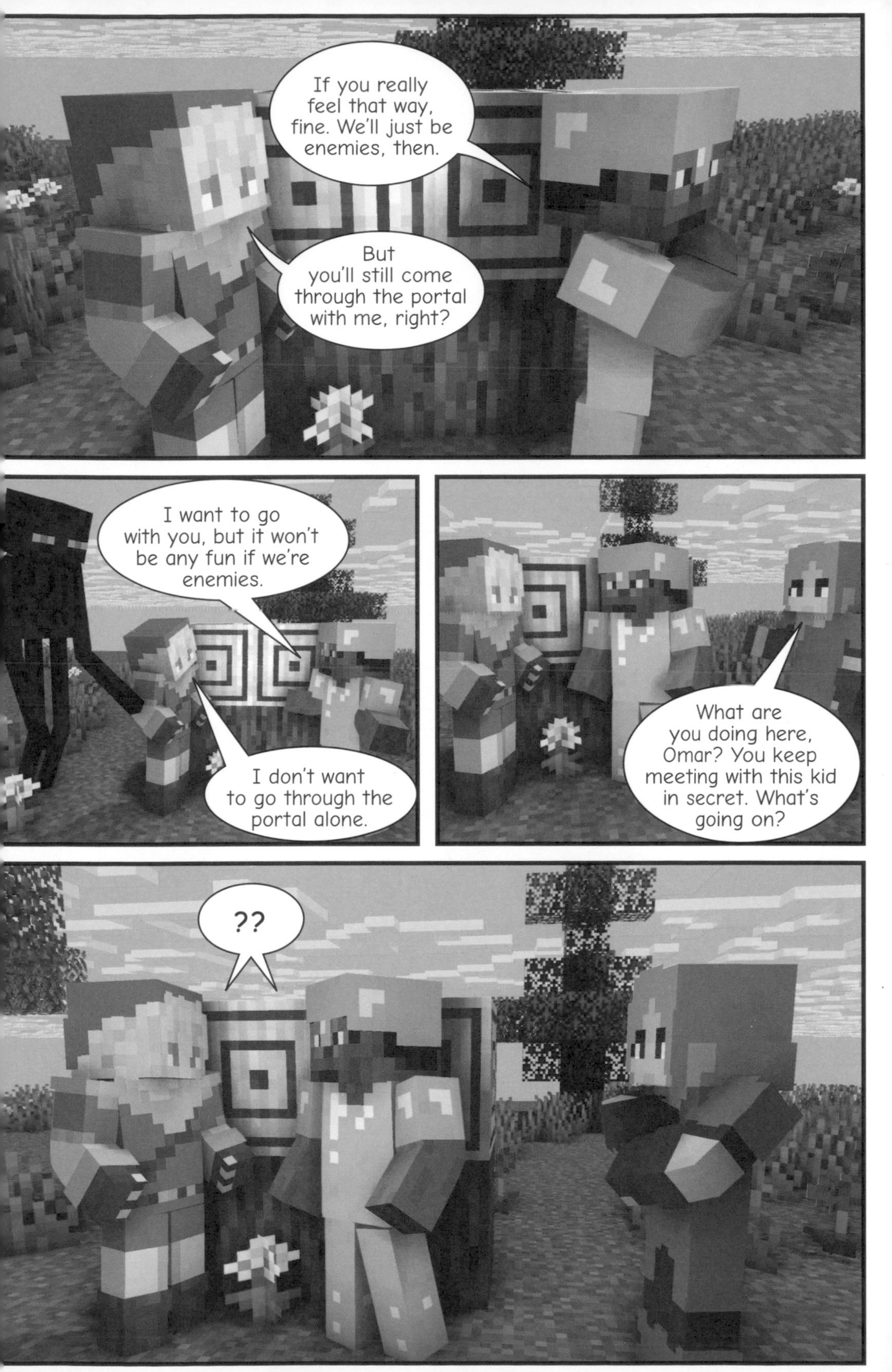
If you really feel that way, fine. We'll just be enemies, then.
But you'll still come through the portal with me, right?
I want to go with you, but it won't be any fun if we're enemies.
I don't want to go through the portal alone.
What are you doing here, Omar? You keep meeting with this kid in secret. What's going on?
??

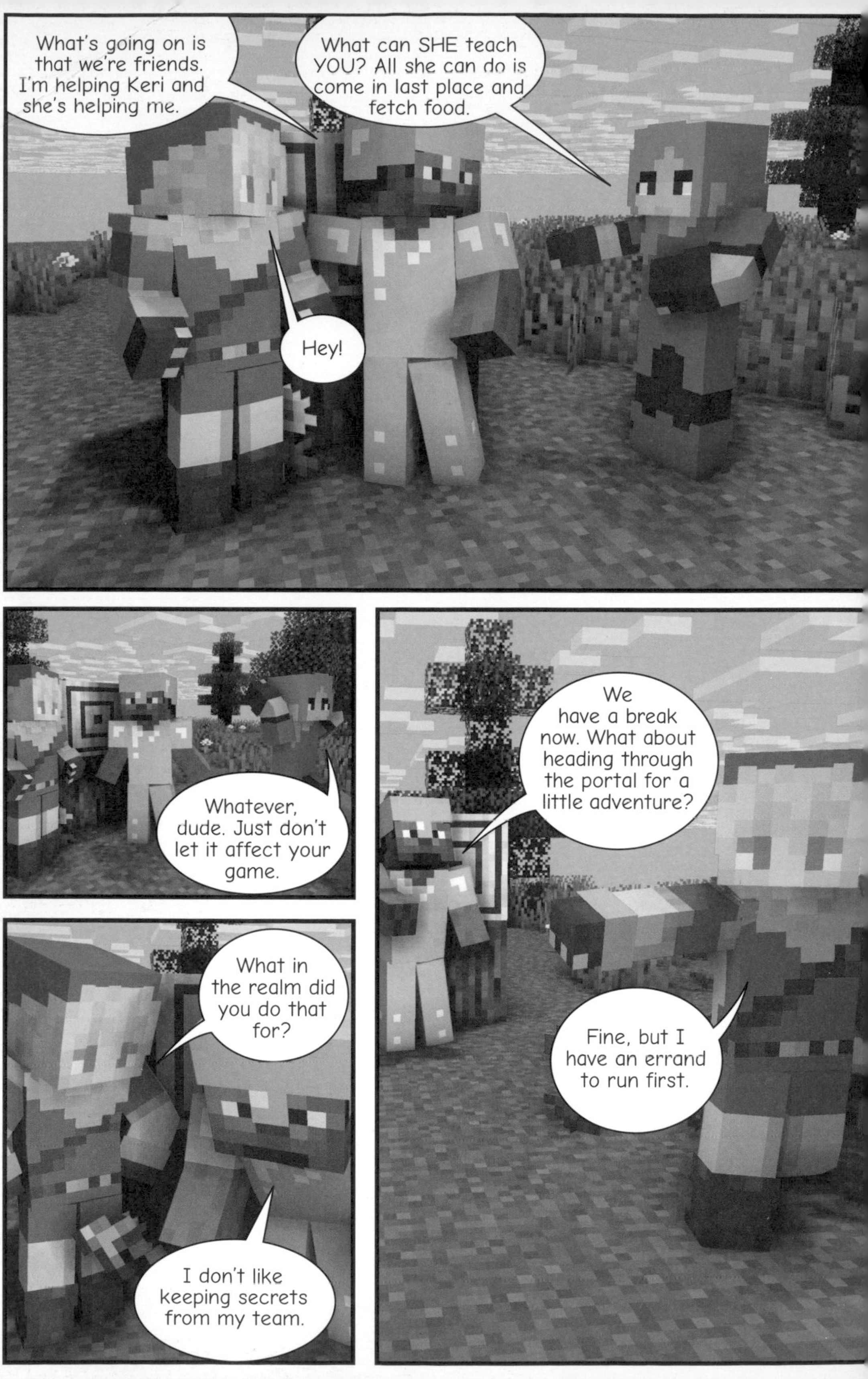
What's going on is that we're friends. I'm helping Keri and she's helping me.
What can SHE teach YOU? All she can do is come in last place and fetch food.
Hey!
Whatever, dude. Just don't let it affect your game.
What in the realm did you do that for?
I don't like keeping secrets from my team.
We have a break now. What about heading through the portal for a little adventure?
Fine, but I have an errand to run first.

Chapter 2
Control

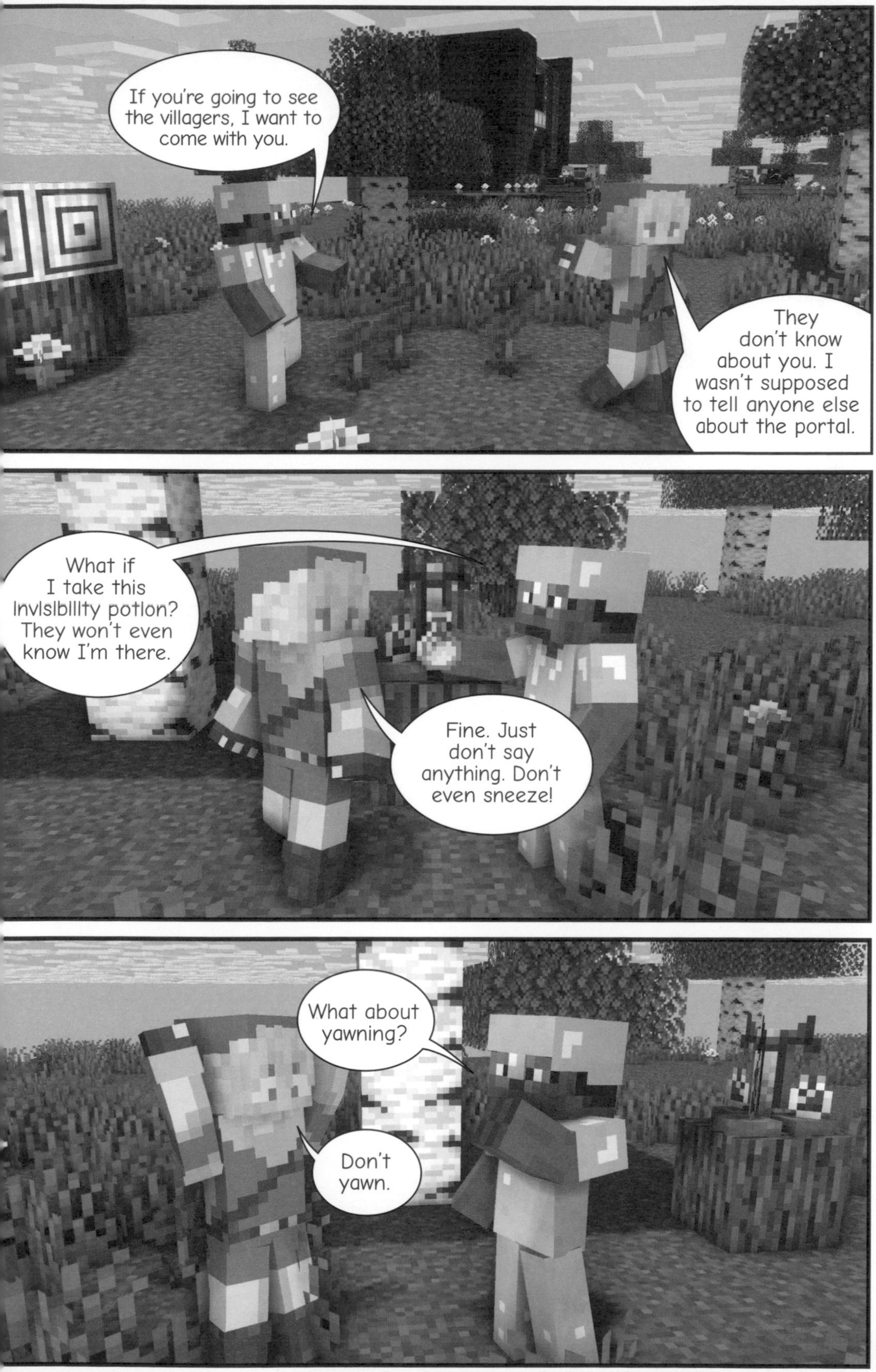
If you're going to see the villagers, I want to come with you.
They don't know about you. I wasn't supposed to tell anyone else about the portal.
What if I take this invisibility potion? They won't even know I'm there.
Fine. Just don't say anything. Don't even sneeze!
What about yawning?
Don't yawn.

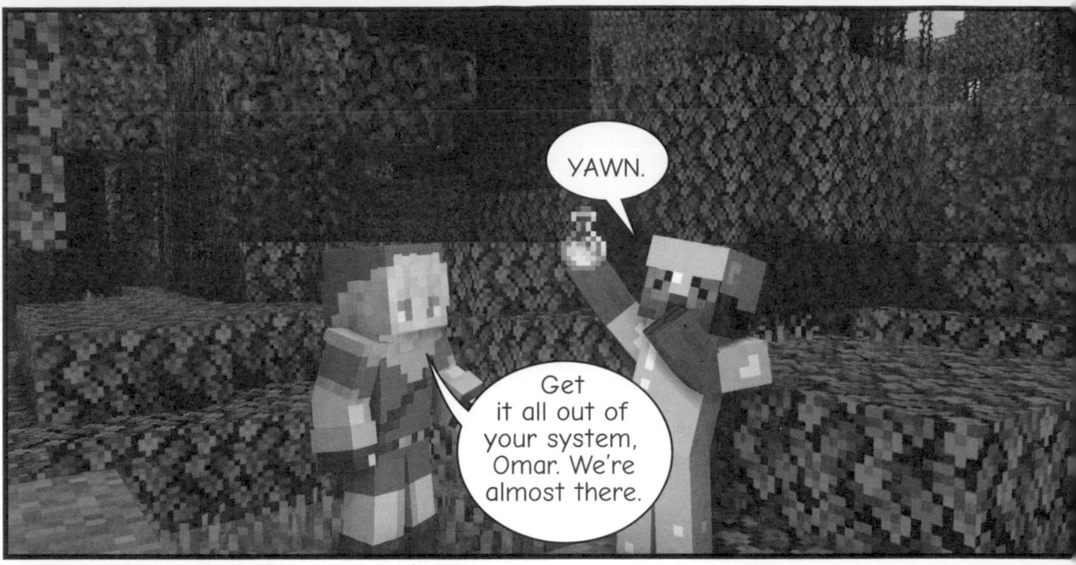
YAWN.
Get it all out of your system, Omar. We're almost there.
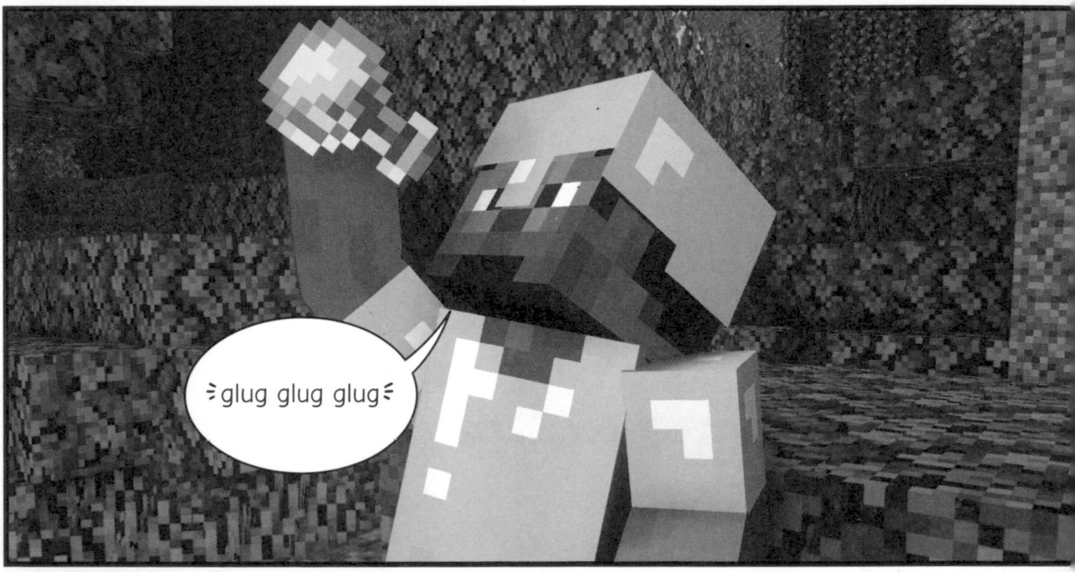
glug glug glug
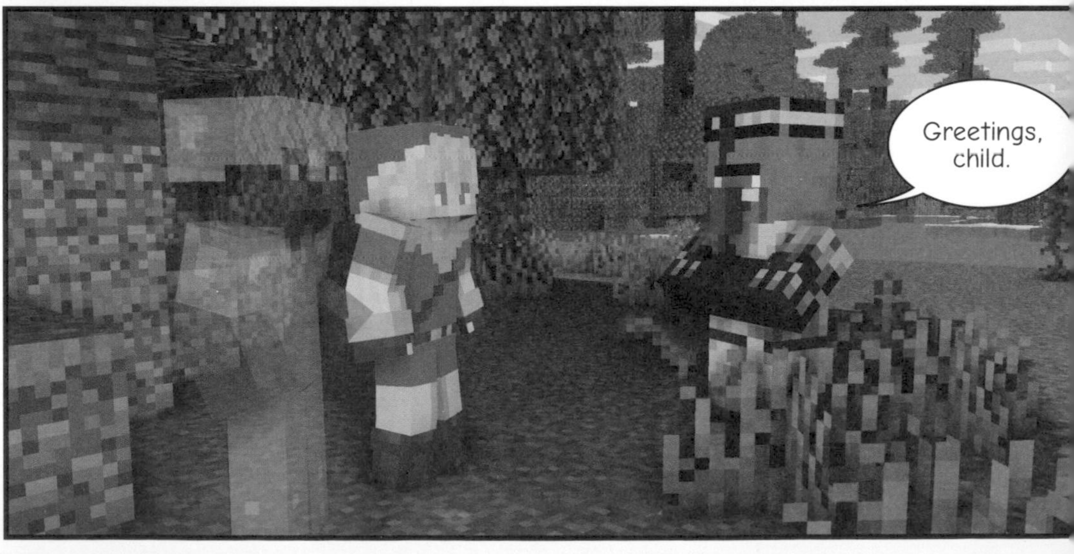
Greetings, child.

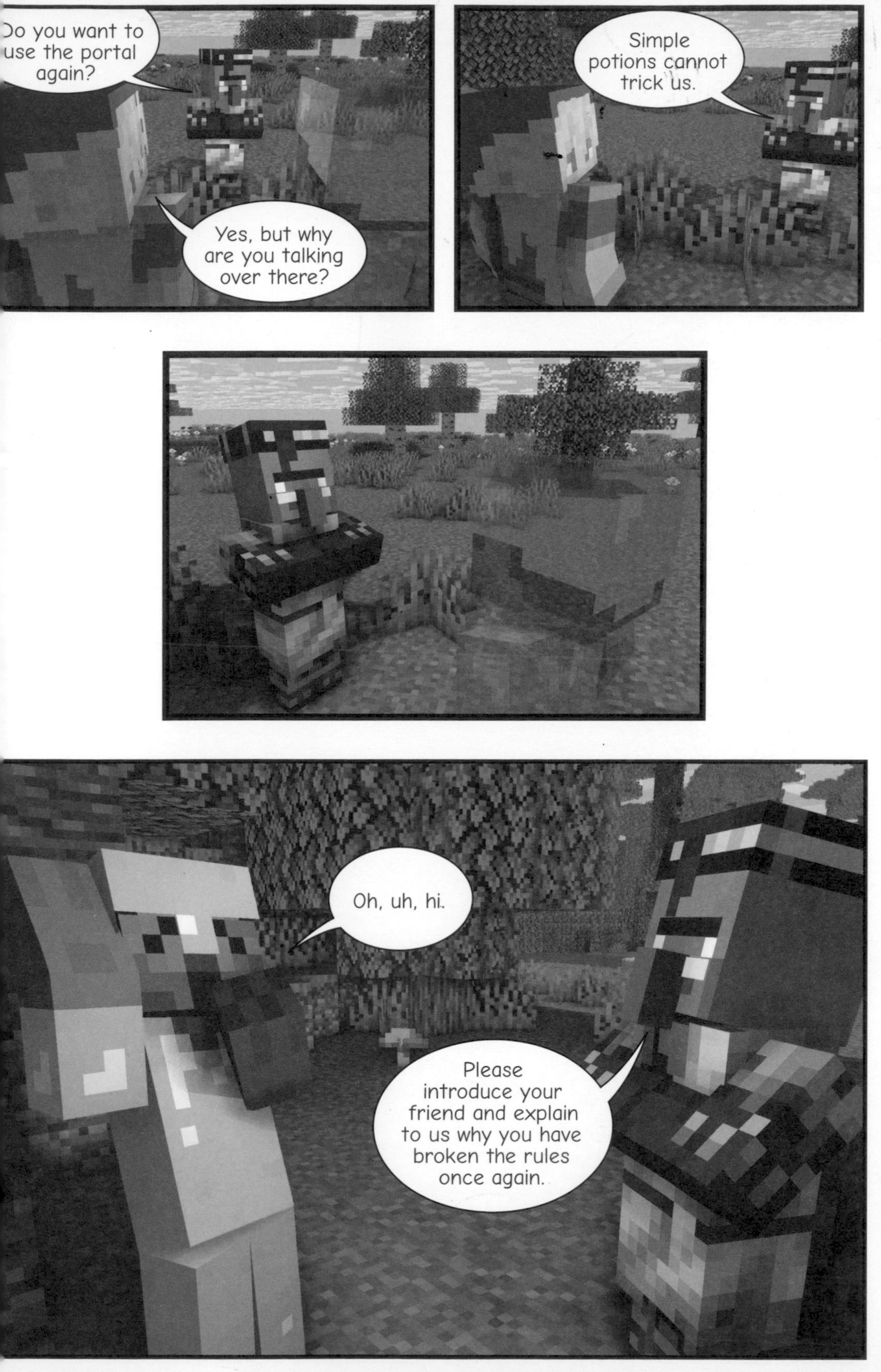
Do you want to use the portal again?
Yes, but why are you talking over there?
Simple potions cannot trick us.
Oh, uh, hi.
Please introduce your friend and explain to us why you have broken the rules once again.

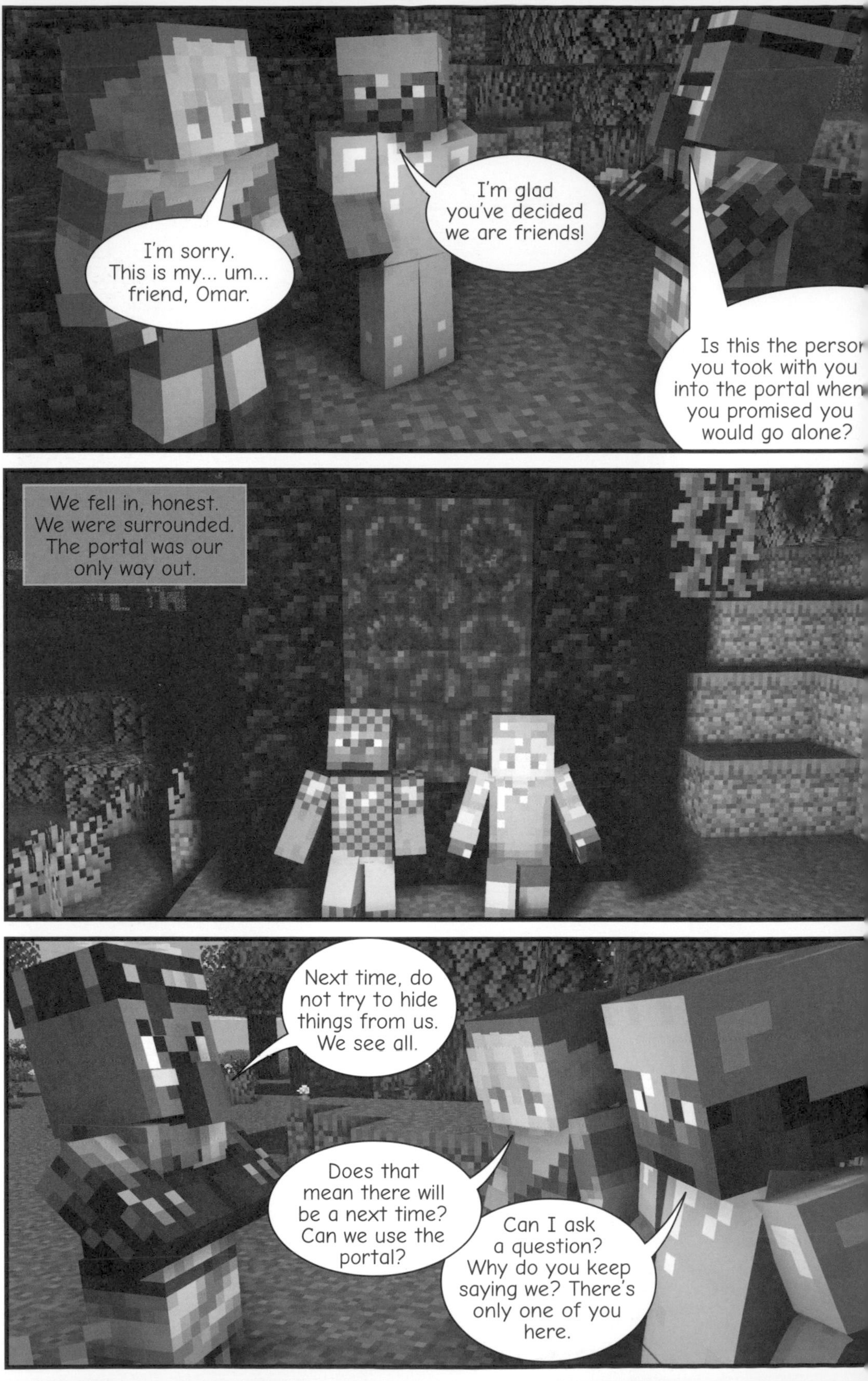
I'm sorry. This is my... um... friend, Omar.
I'm glad you've decided we are friends!
Is this the person you took with you into the portal when you promised you would go alone?
We fell in, honest. We were surrounded. The portal was our only way out.
Next time, do not try to hide things from us. We see all.
Does that mean there will be a next time? Can we use the portal?
Can I ask a question? Why do you keep saying we? There's only one of you here.

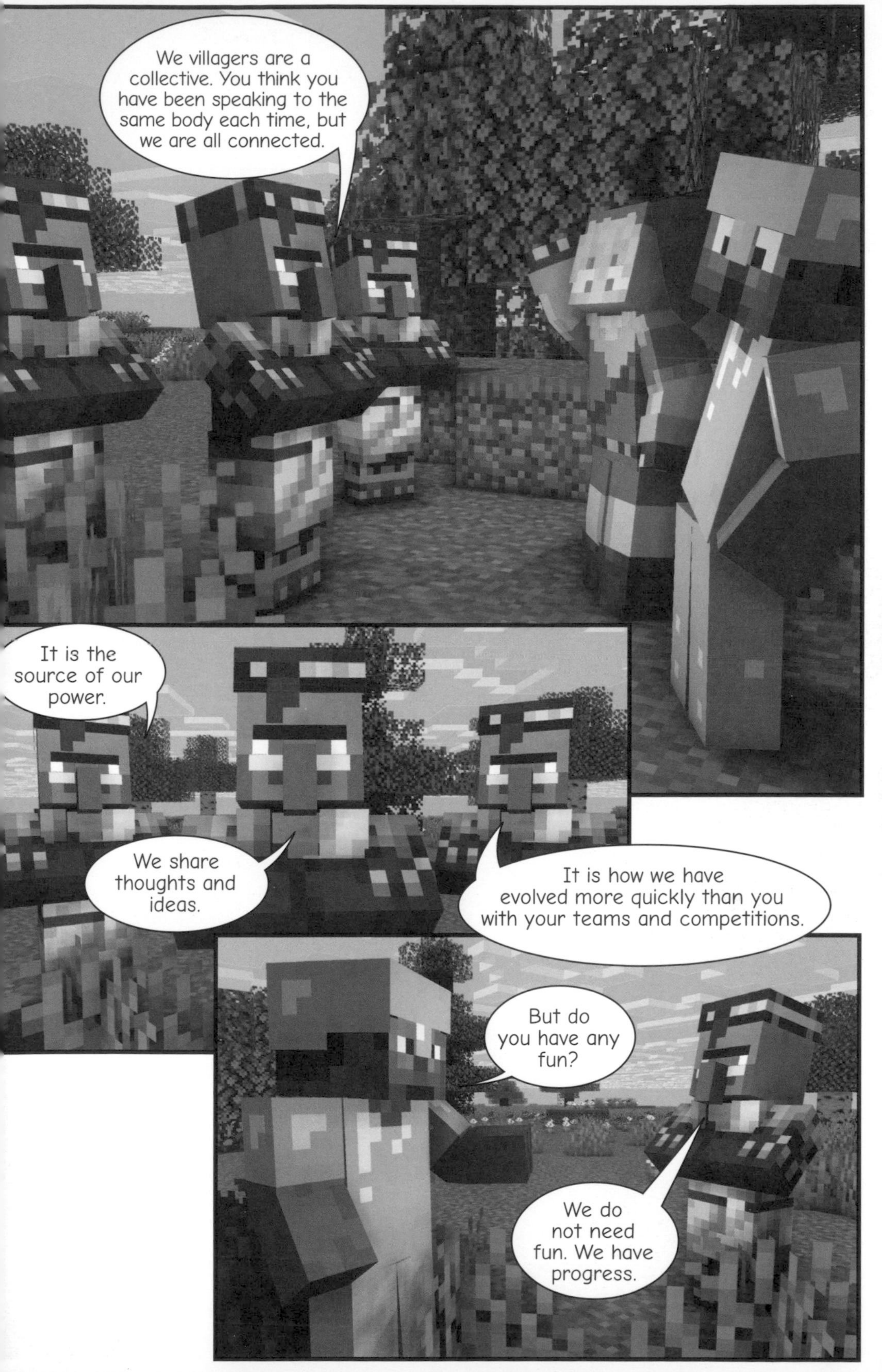
We villagers are a collective. You think you have been speaking to the same body each time, but we are all connected.
It is the source of our power.
We share thoughts and ideas.
It is how we have evolved more quickly than you with your teams and competitions.
But do you have any fun?
We do not need fun. We have progress.

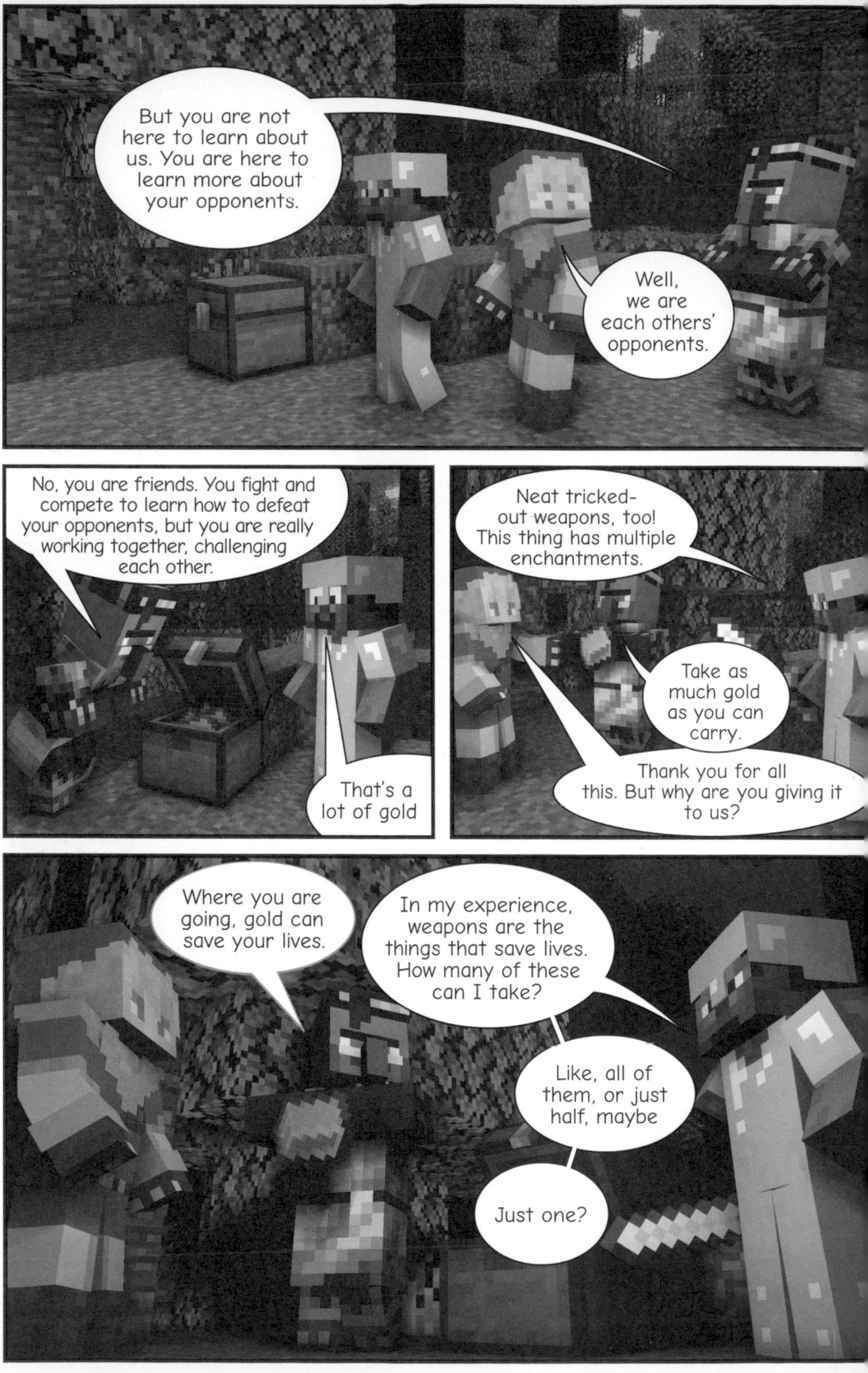
But you are not here to learn about us. You are here to learn more about your opponents.
Well, we are each others' opponents.
No, you are friends. You fight and compete to learn how to defeat your opponents, but you are really working together, challenging each other.
That's a lot of gold
Neat tricked-out weapons, too! This thing has multiple enchantments.
Take as much gold as you can carry.
Thank you for all this. But why are you giving it to us?
Where you are going, gold can save your lives.
In my experience, weapons are the things that save lives. How many of these can I take?
Like, all of them, or just half, maybe
Just one?

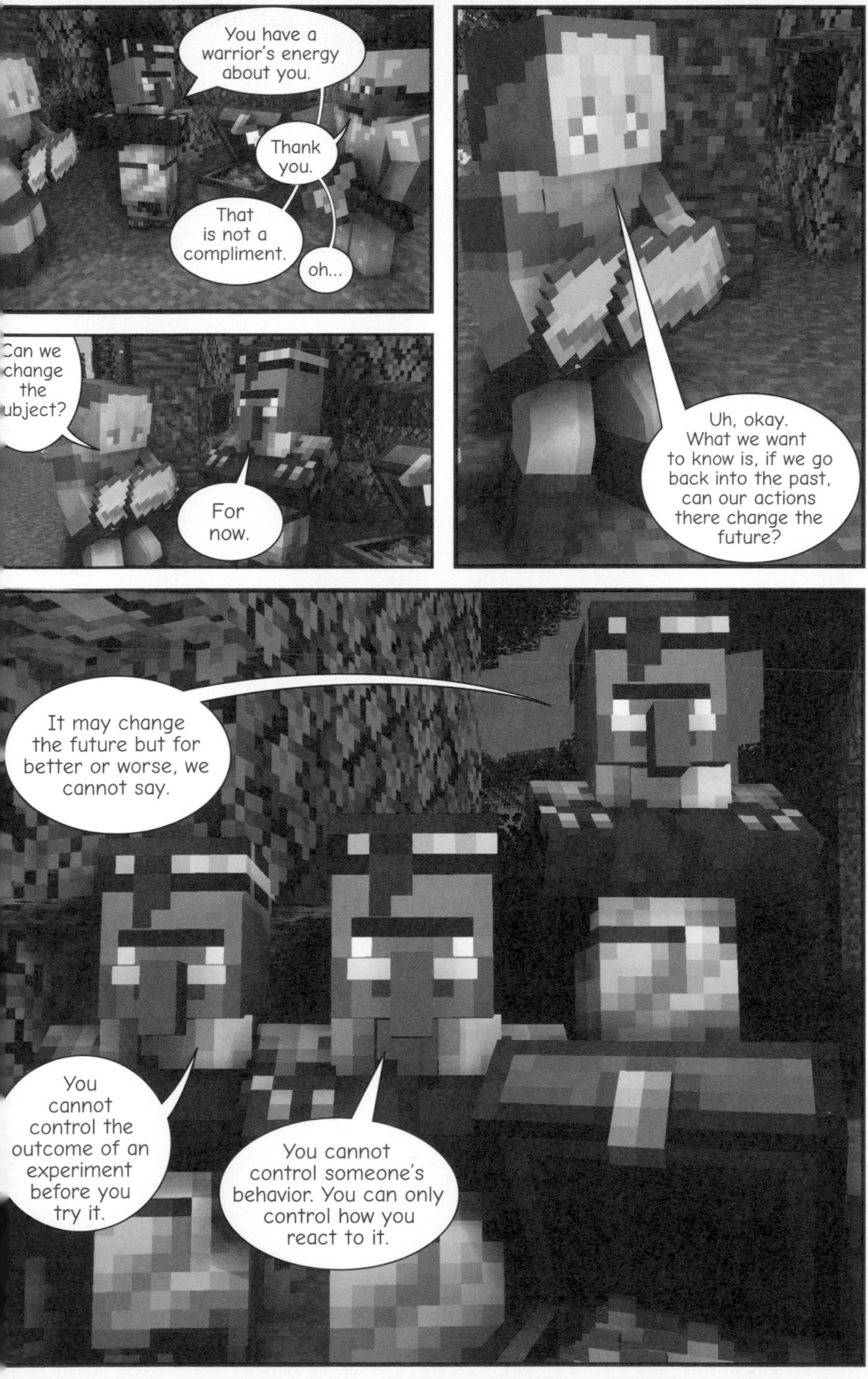
You have a warrior's energy about you.
Thank you.
That is not a compliment.
oh...
Can we change the subject?
For now.
Uh, okay. What we want to know is, if we go back into the past, can our actions there change the future?
It may change the future but for better or worse, we cannot say.
You cannot control the outcome of an experiment before you try it.
You cannot control someone's behavior. You can only control how you react to it.

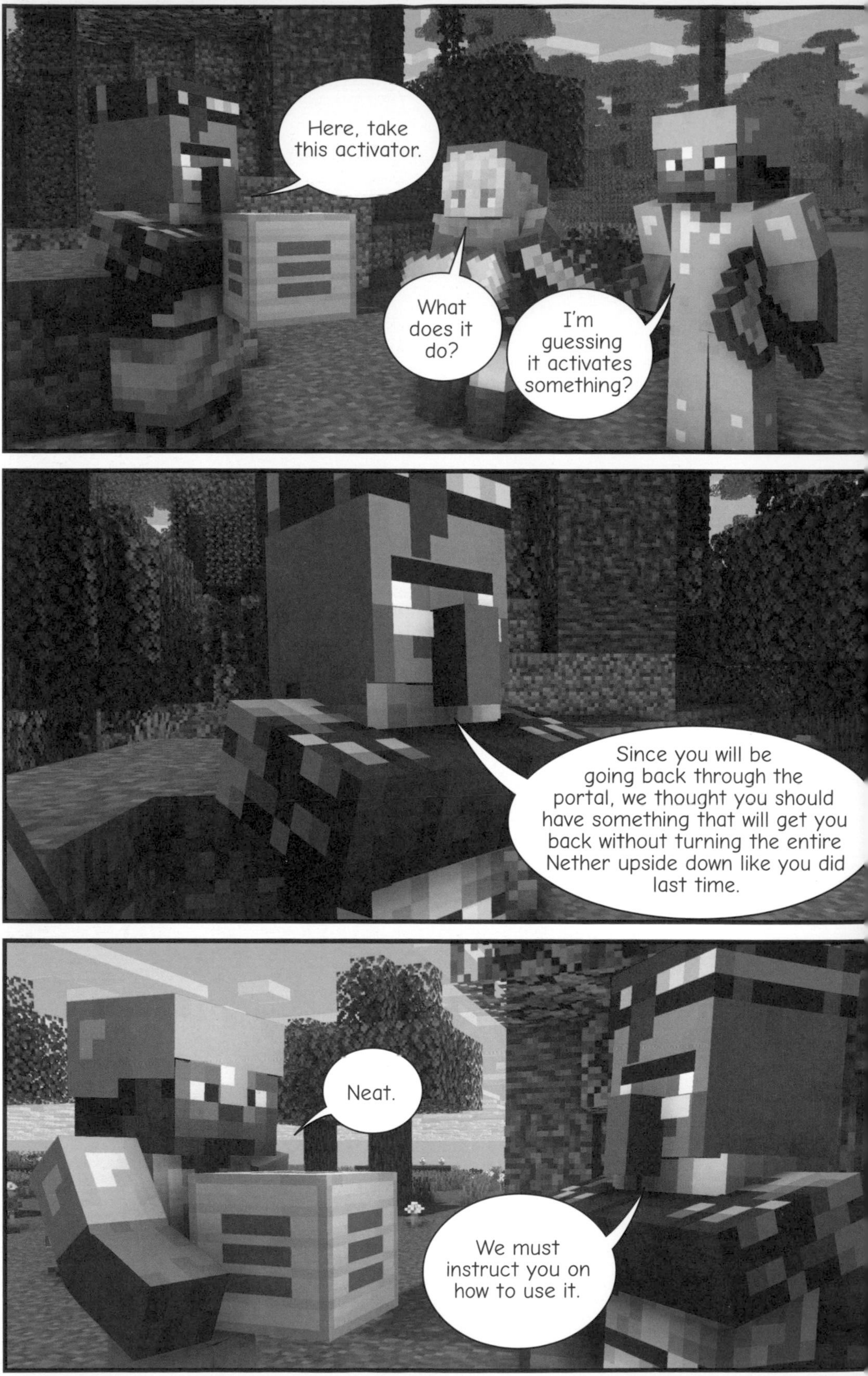
Here, take this activator.
What does it do?
I'm guessing it activates something?
Since you will be going back through the portal, we thought you should have something that will get you back without turning the entire Nether upside down like you did last time.
Neat.
We must instruct you on how to use it.

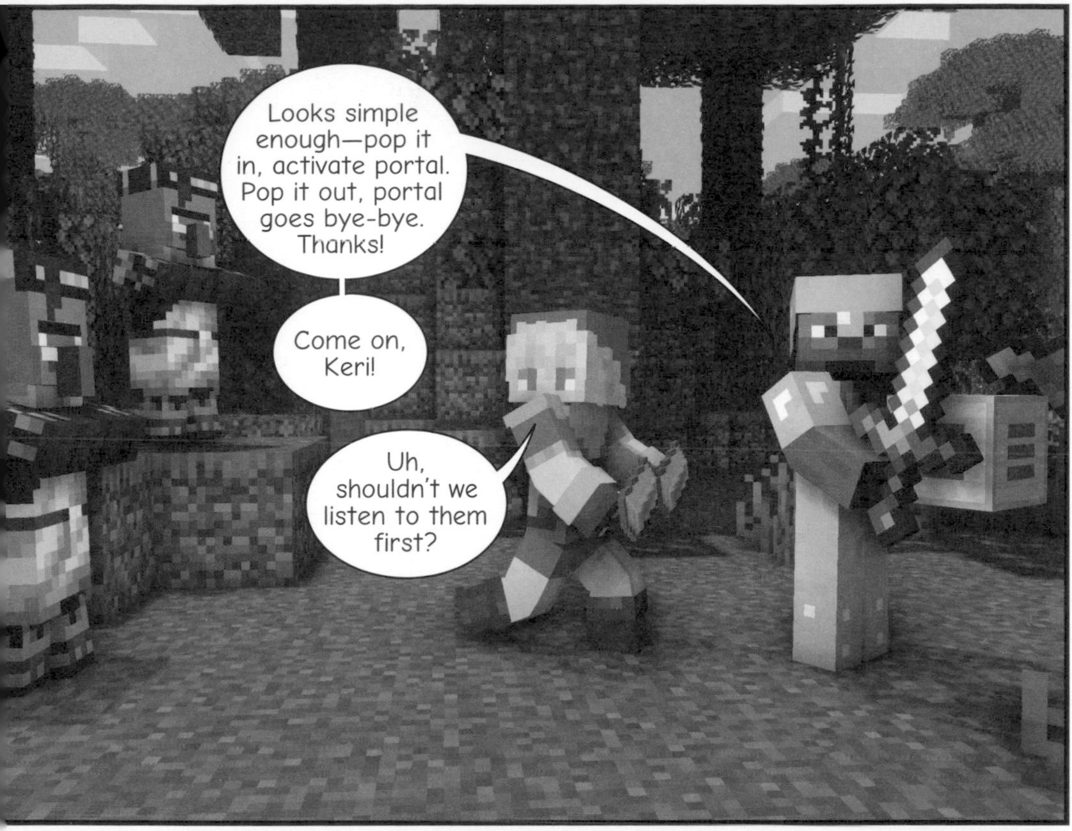
Looks simple enough—pop it in, activate portal. Pop it out, portal goes bye-bye. Thanks!
Come on, Keri!
Uh, shouldn't we listen to them first?

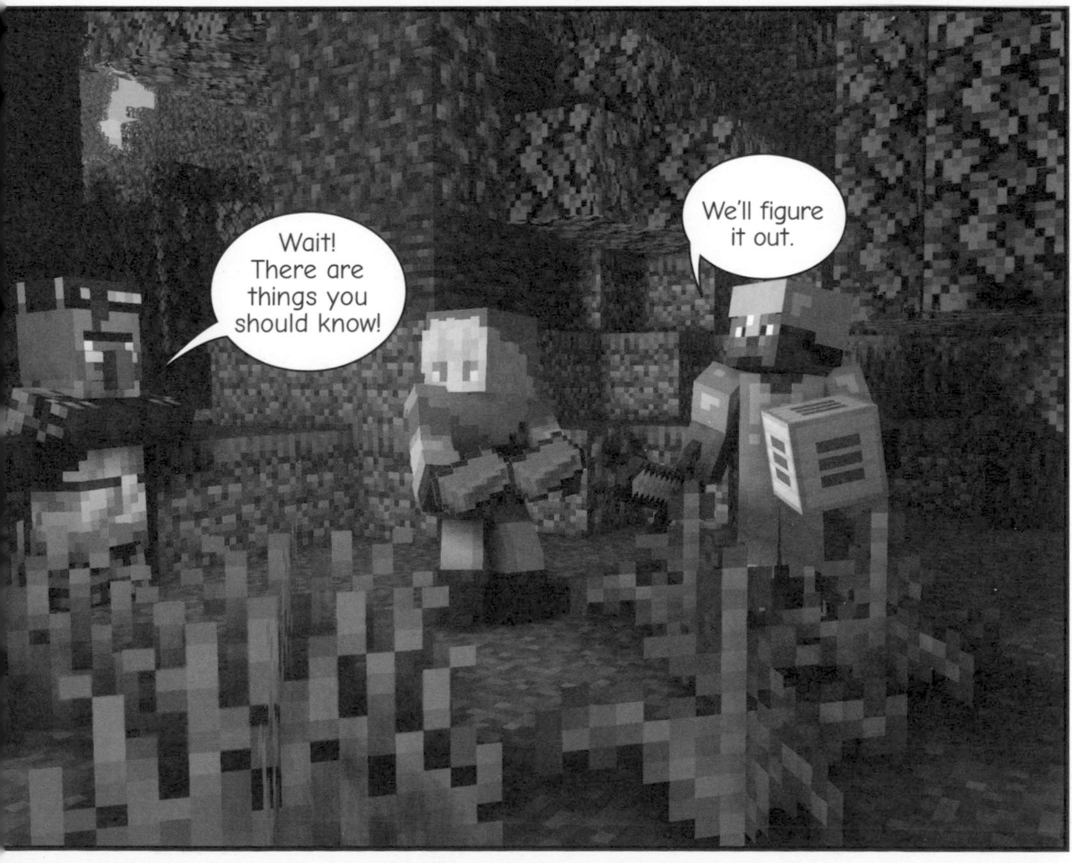
Wait! There are things you should know!
We'll figure it out.

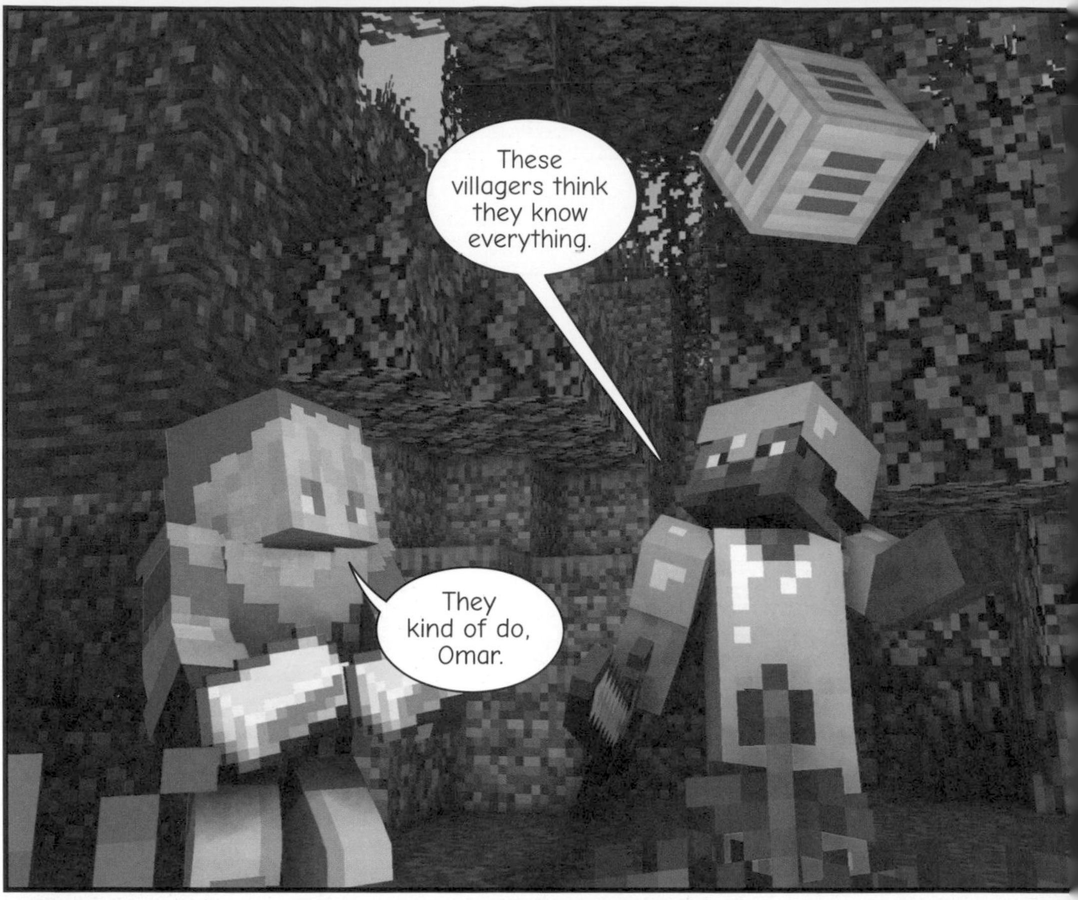
These villagers think they know everything.
They kind of do, Omar.

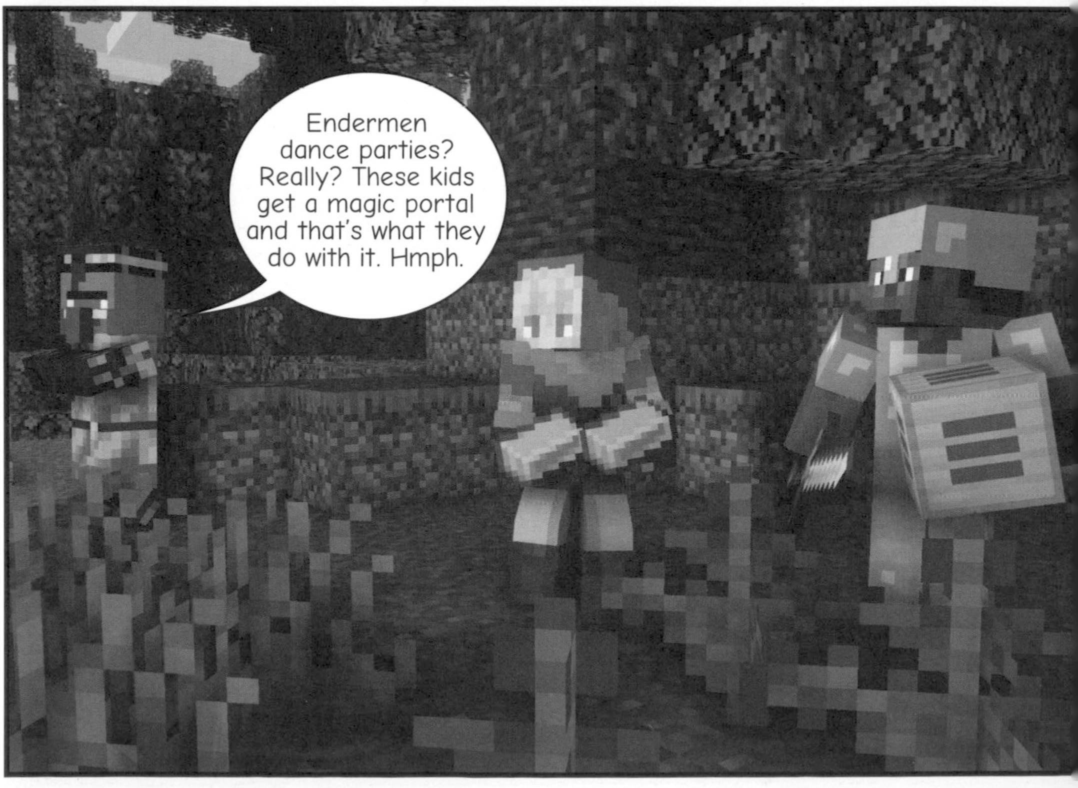
Endermen dance parties? Really? These kids get a magic portal and that's what they do with it. Hmph.

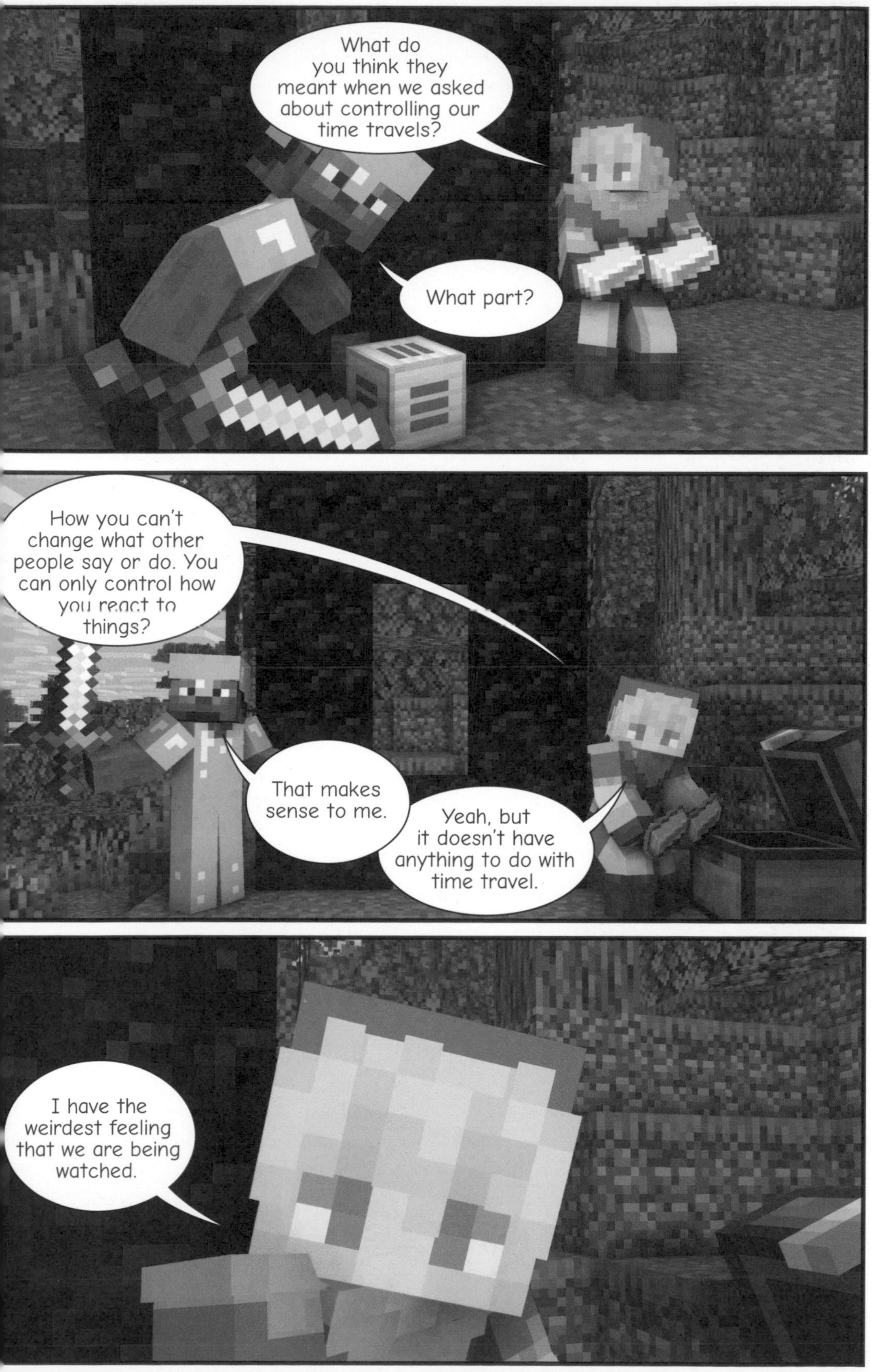
What do you think they meant when we asked about controlling our time travels?
What part?
How you can't change what other people say or do. You can only control how you react to things?
That makes sense to me.
Yeah, but it doesn't have anything to do with time travel.
I have the weirdest feeling that we are being watched.

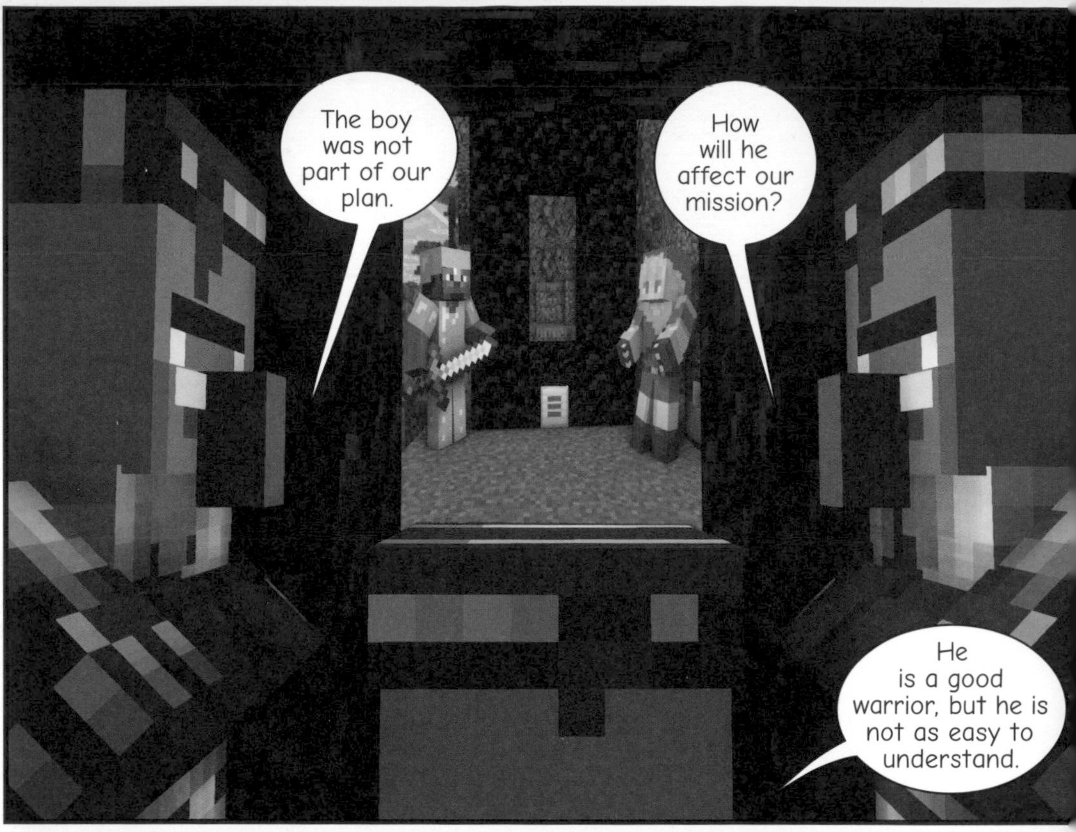
The boy was not part of our plan.
How will he affect our mission?
He is a good warrior, but he is not as easy to understand.

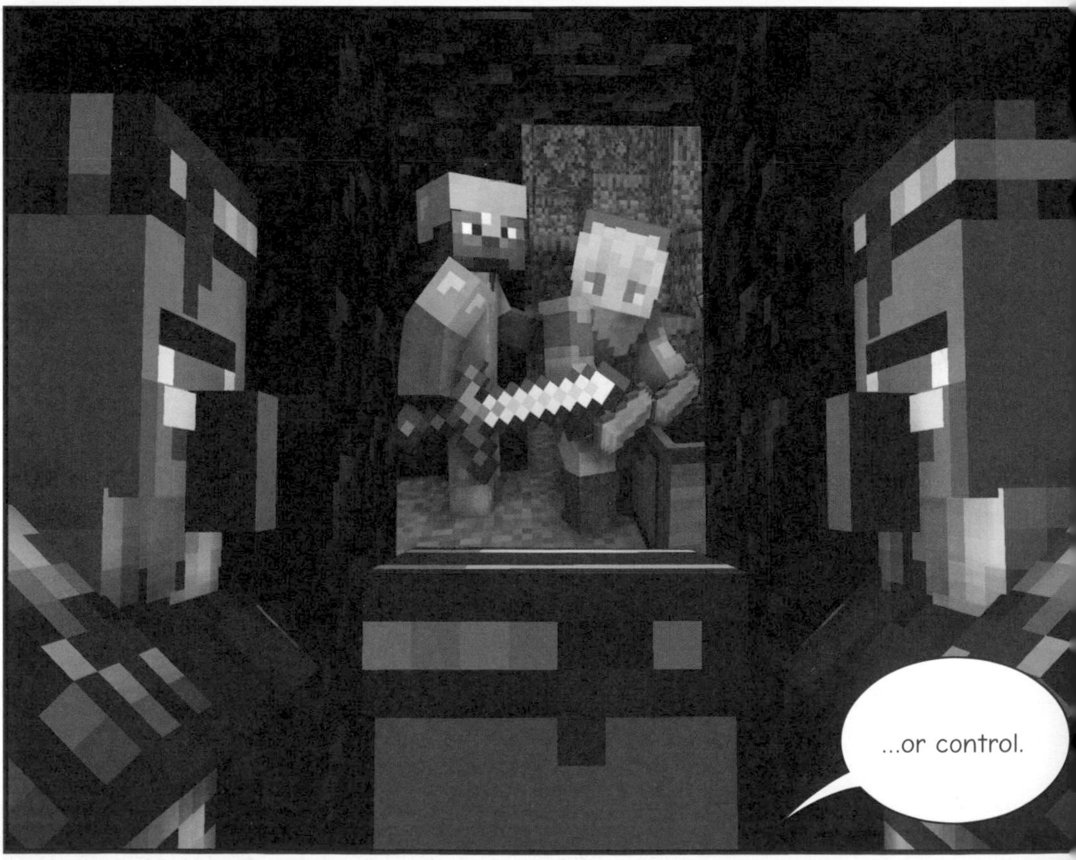
...or control.

Chapter 3
Ghast Tears

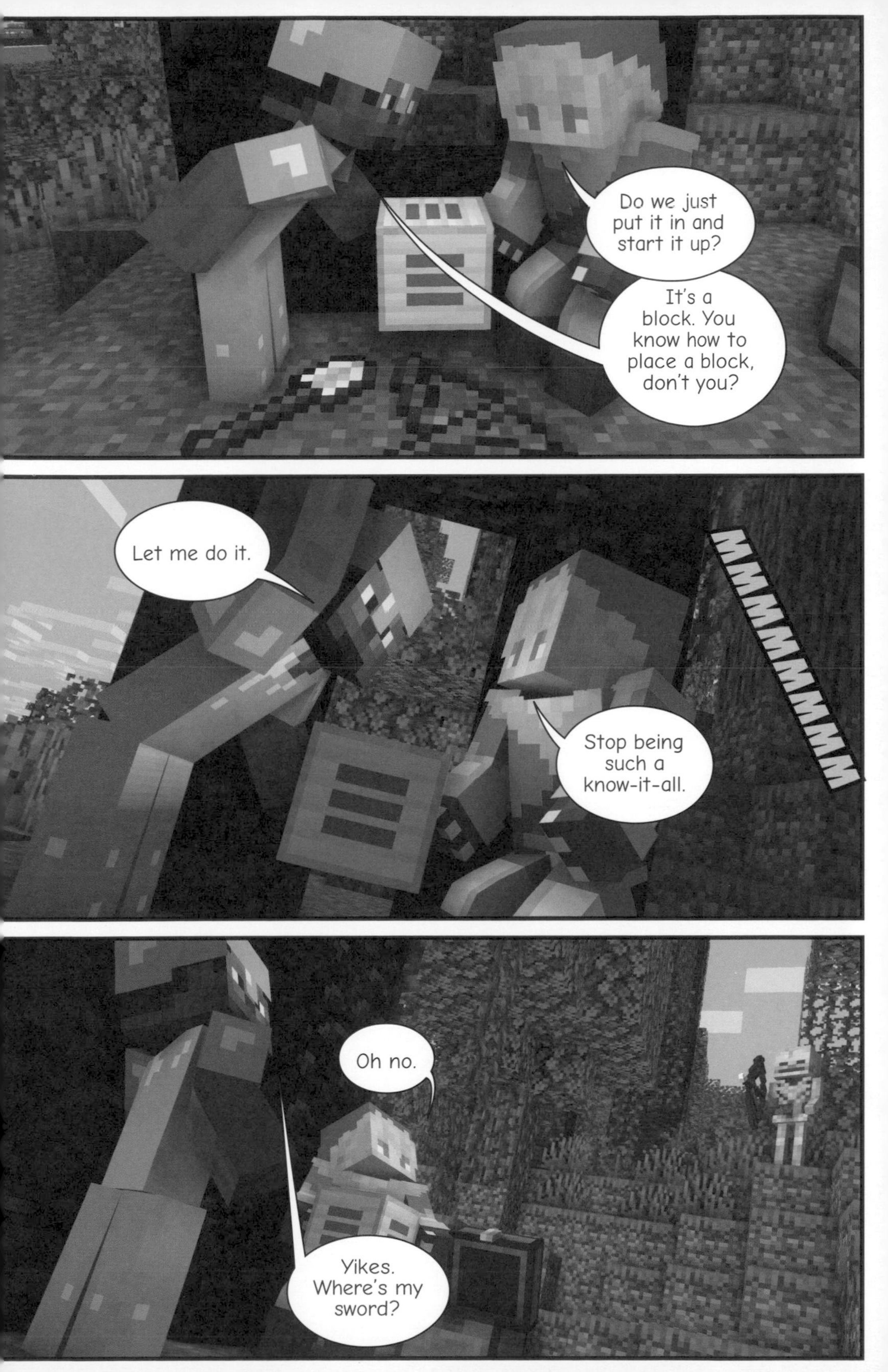
Do we just put it in and start it up?
It's a block. You know how to place a block, don't you?
Let me do it.
Stop being such a know-it-all.
MMMMMMMMMM
Oh no.
Yikes. Where's my sword?

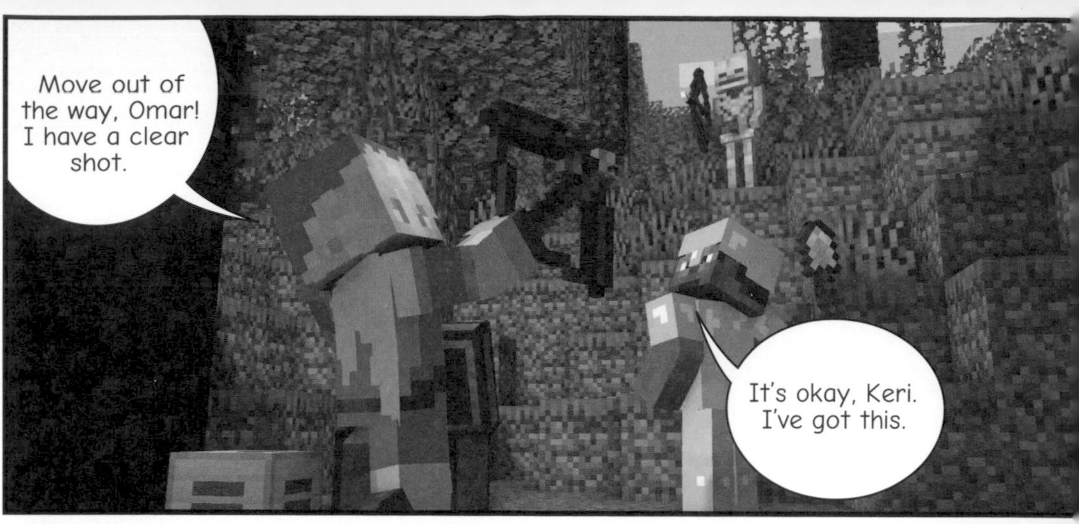
Move out of the way, Omar! I have a clear shot.
It's okay, Keri. I've got this.
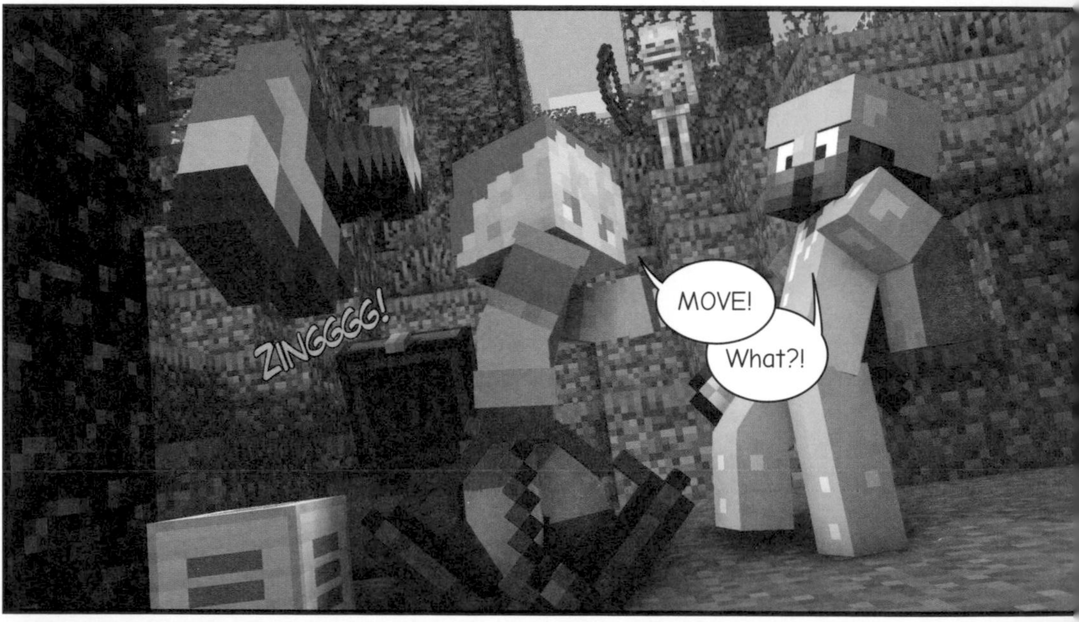
ZINGGGG!
MOVE!
What?!
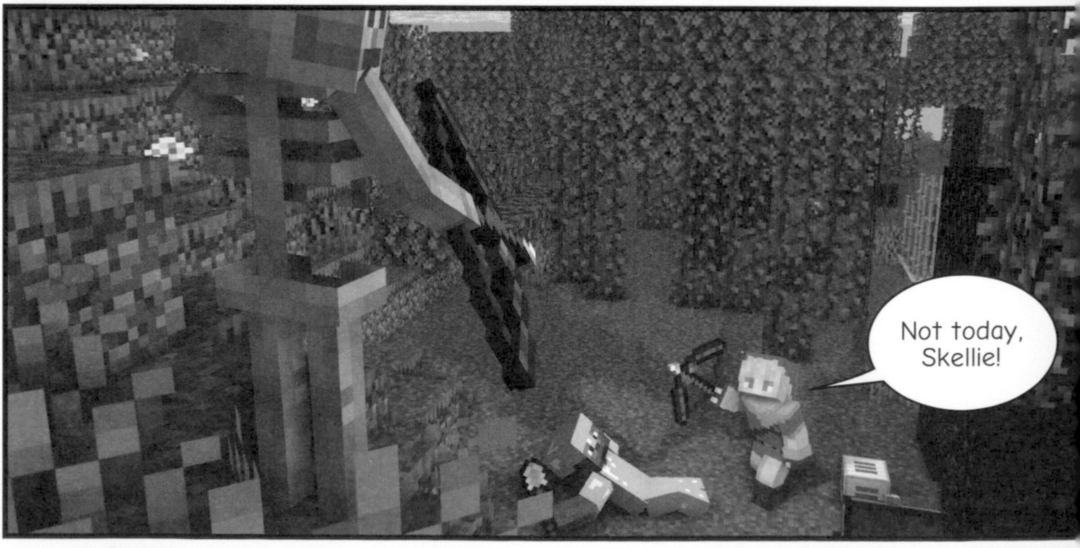
Not today, Skellie!

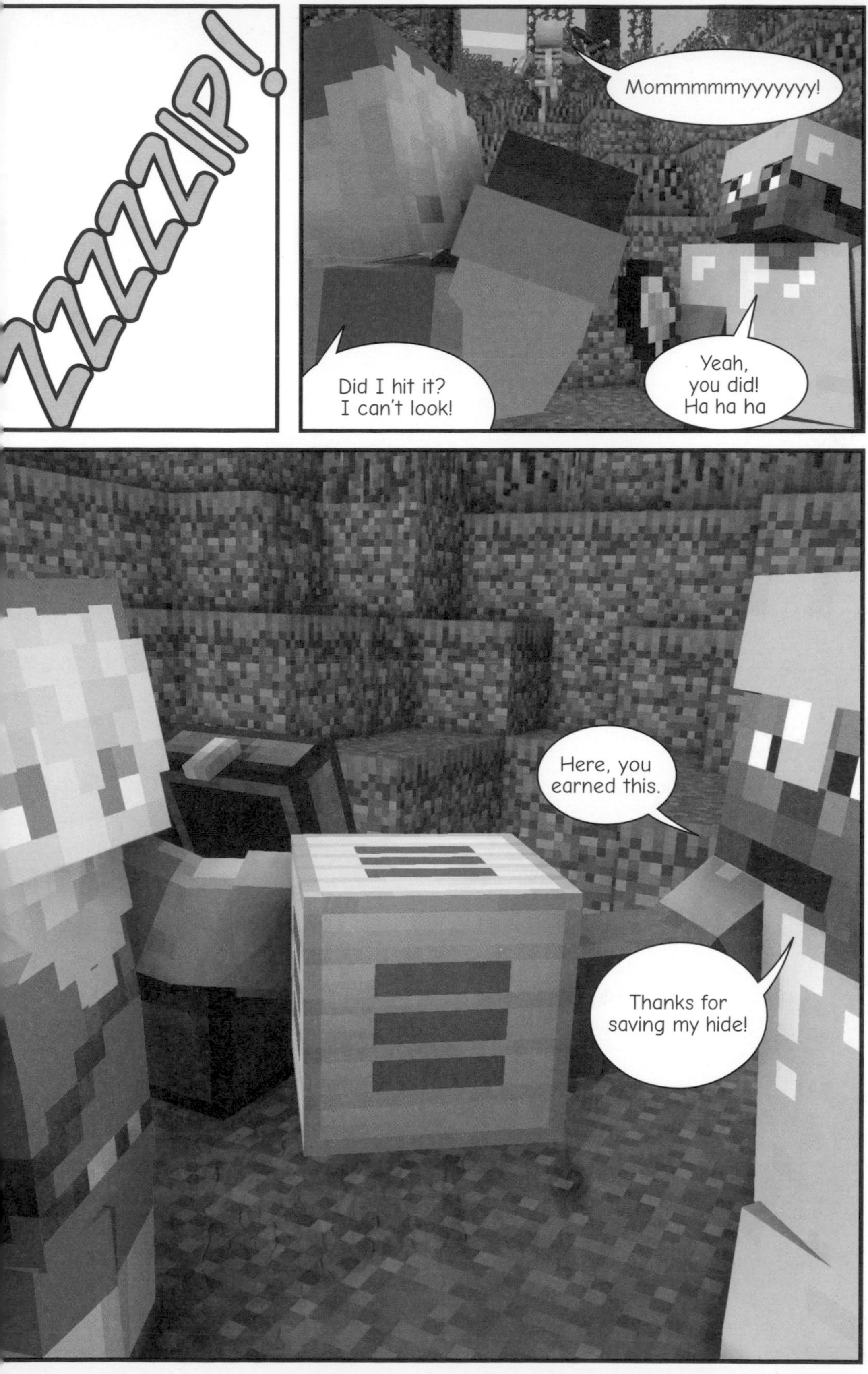
ZZZZZIP!
Mommmmmyyyyyyy!
Did I hit it?
I can't look!
Yeah,
you did!
Ha ha ha
Here, you
earned this.
Thanks for
saving my hide!

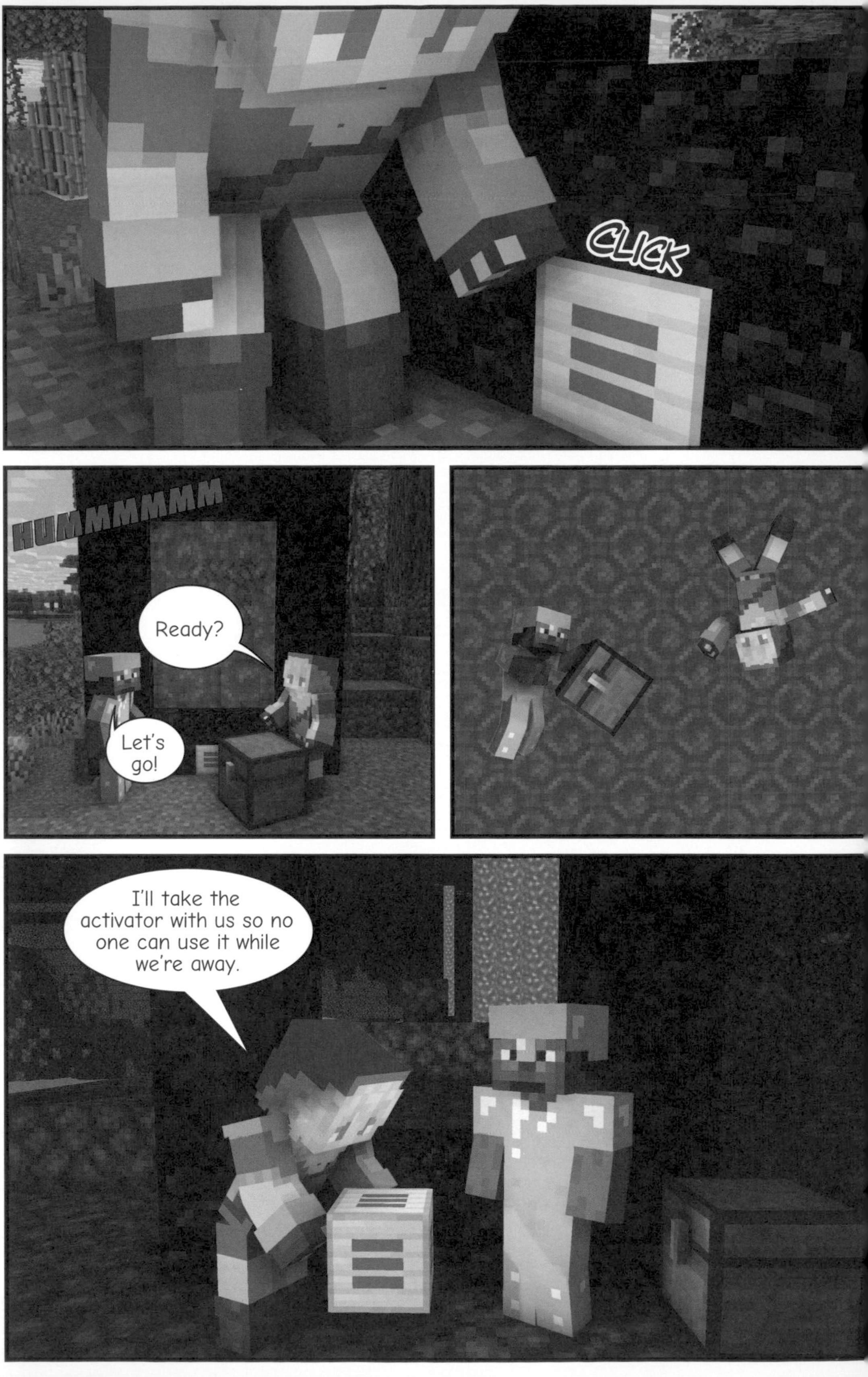
CLICK
HUMMMMMM
Ready?
Let's go!
I'll take the activator with us so no one can use it while we're away.

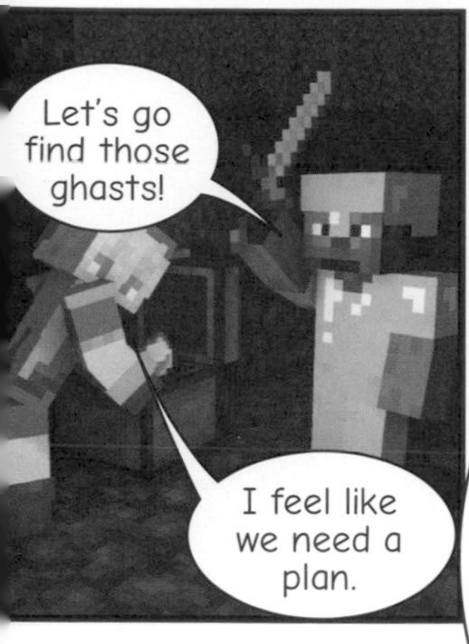
Let's go find those ghasts!
I feel like we need a plan.

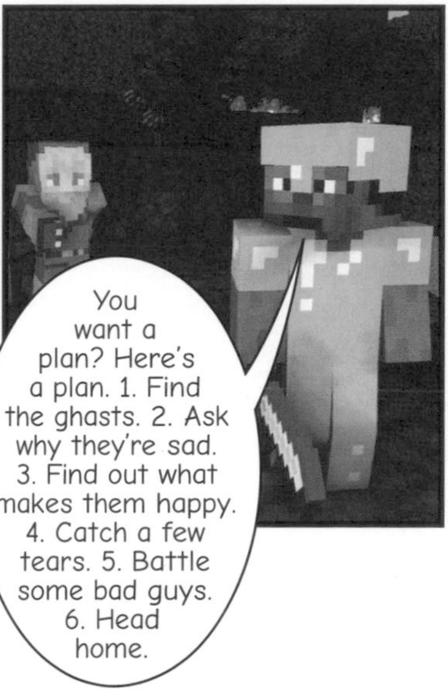
You want a plan? Here's a plan. 1. Find the ghasts. 2. Ask why they're sad. 3. Find out what makes them happy. 4. Catch a few tears. 5. Battle some bad guys. 6. Head home.

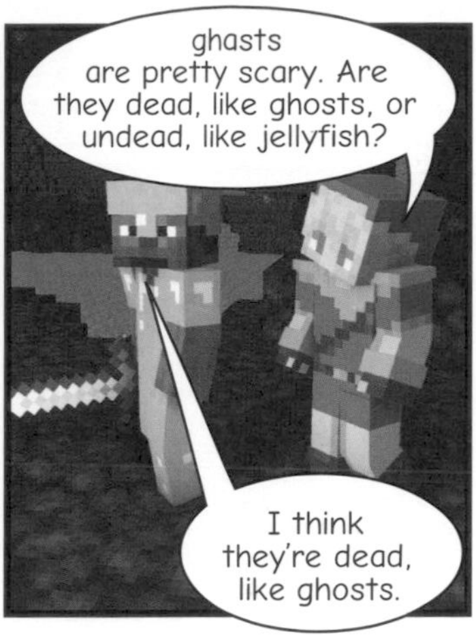
ghasts are pretty scary. Are they dead, like ghosts, or undead, like jellyfish?
I think they're dead, like ghosts.

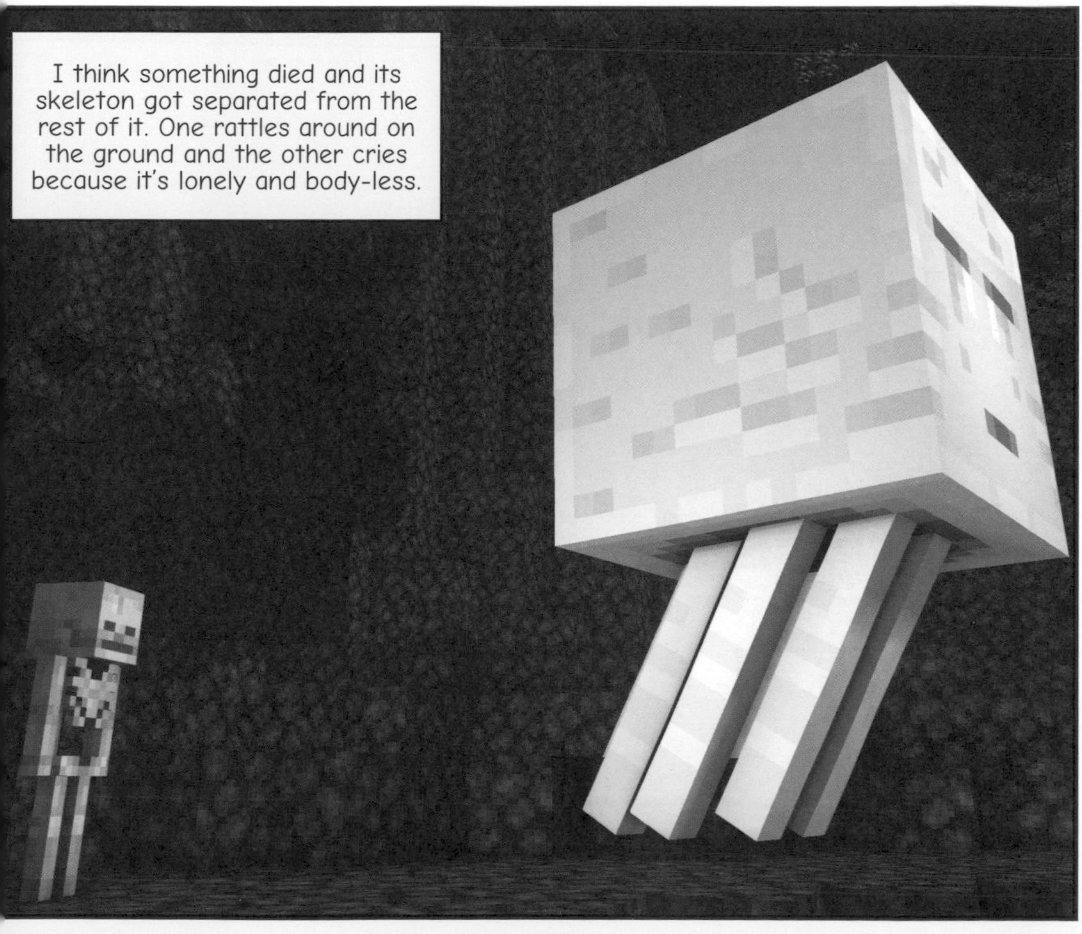
I think something died and its skeleton got separated from the rest of it. One rattles around on the ground and the other cries because it's lonely and body-less.

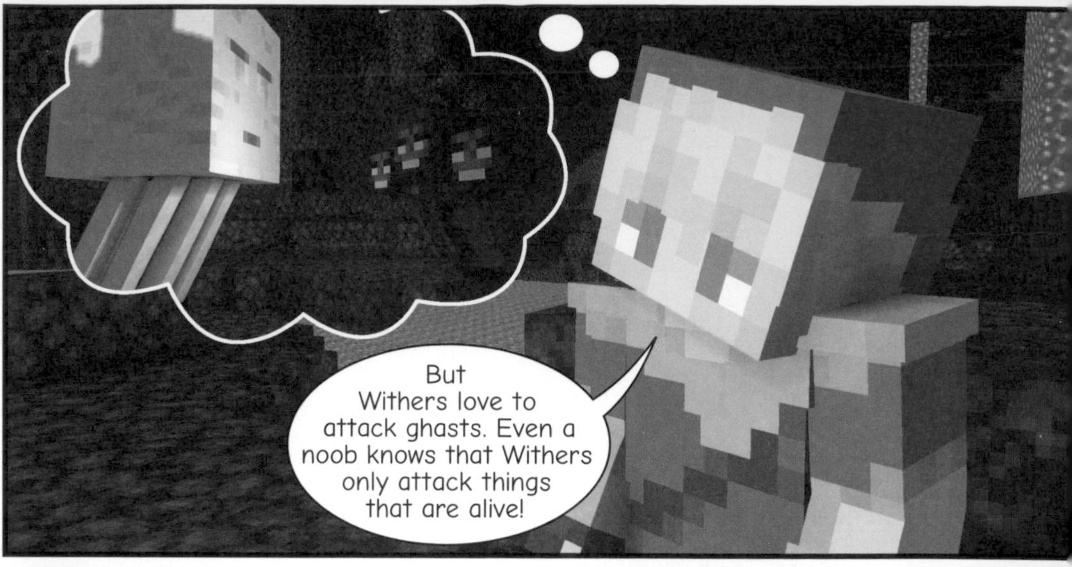
But Withers love to attack ghasts. Even a noob knows that Withers only attack things that are alive!

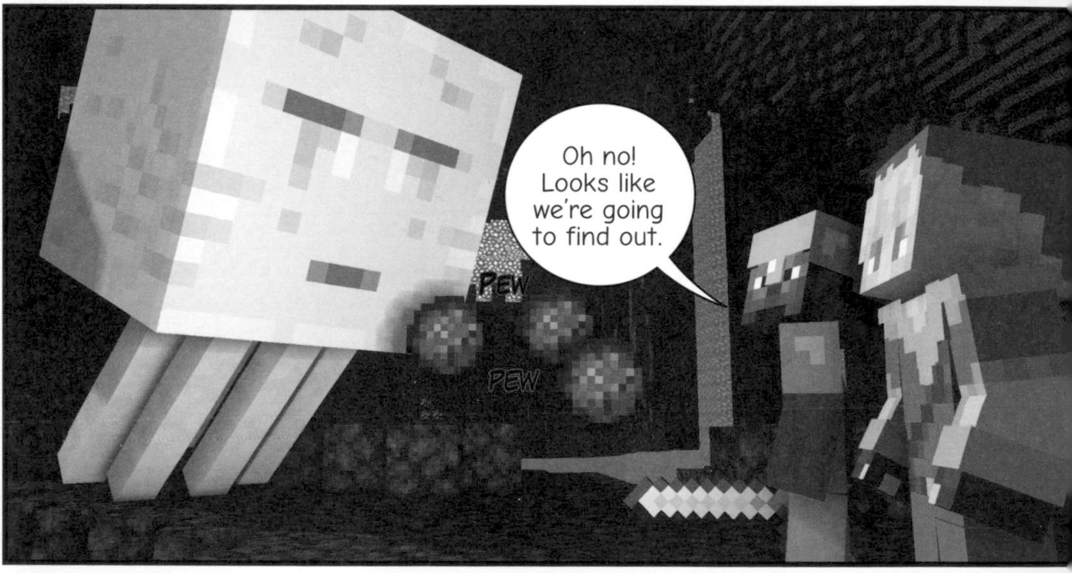
Oh no! Looks like we're going to find out.
PEW
PEW

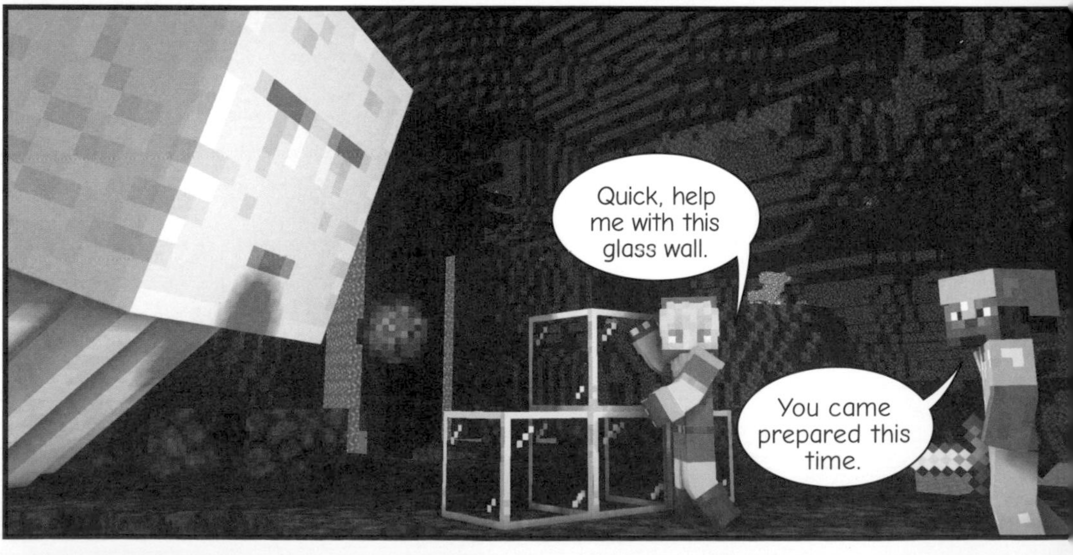
Quick, help me with this glass wall.
You came prepared this time.

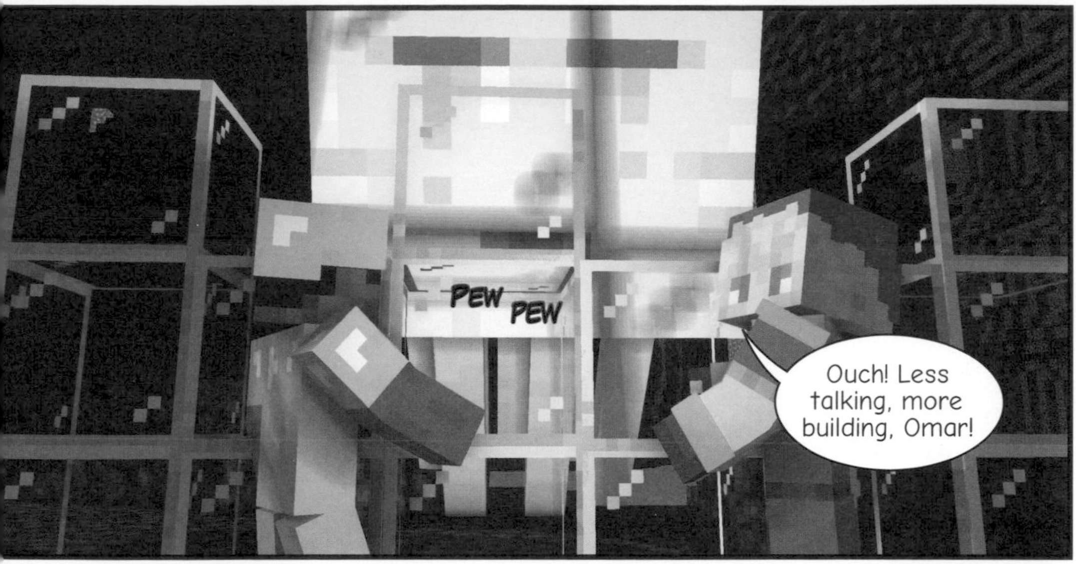
PEW PEW
Ouch! Less talking, more building, Omar!

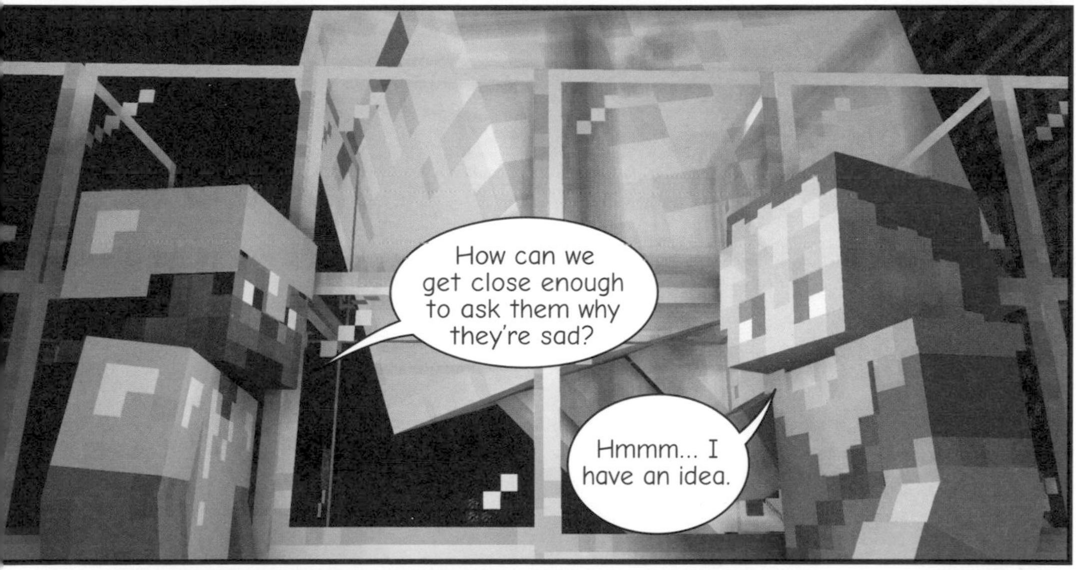
How can we get close enough to ask them why they're sad?
Hmmm... I have an idea.

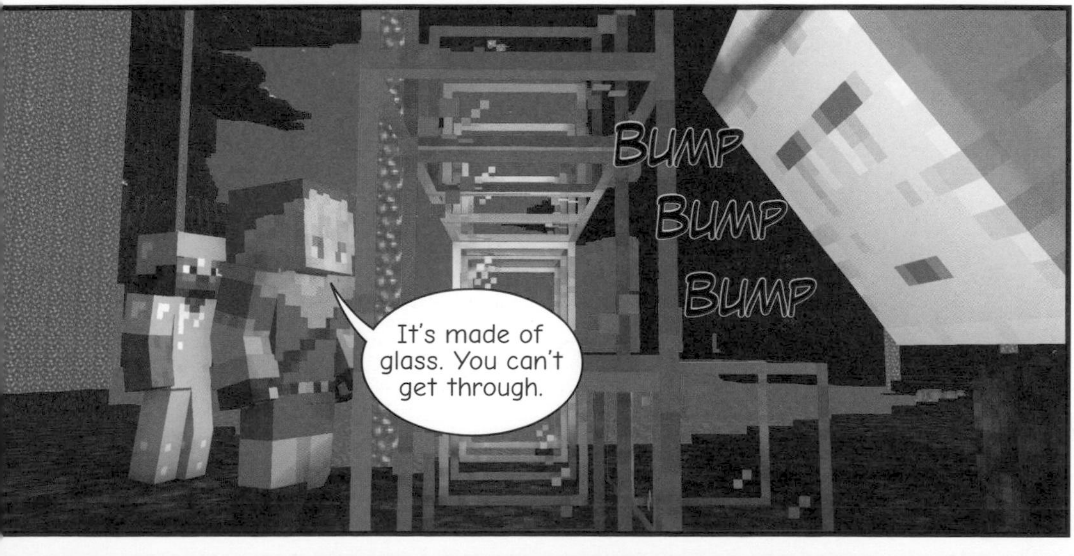
BUMP
BUMP
BUMP
It's made of glass. You can't get through.

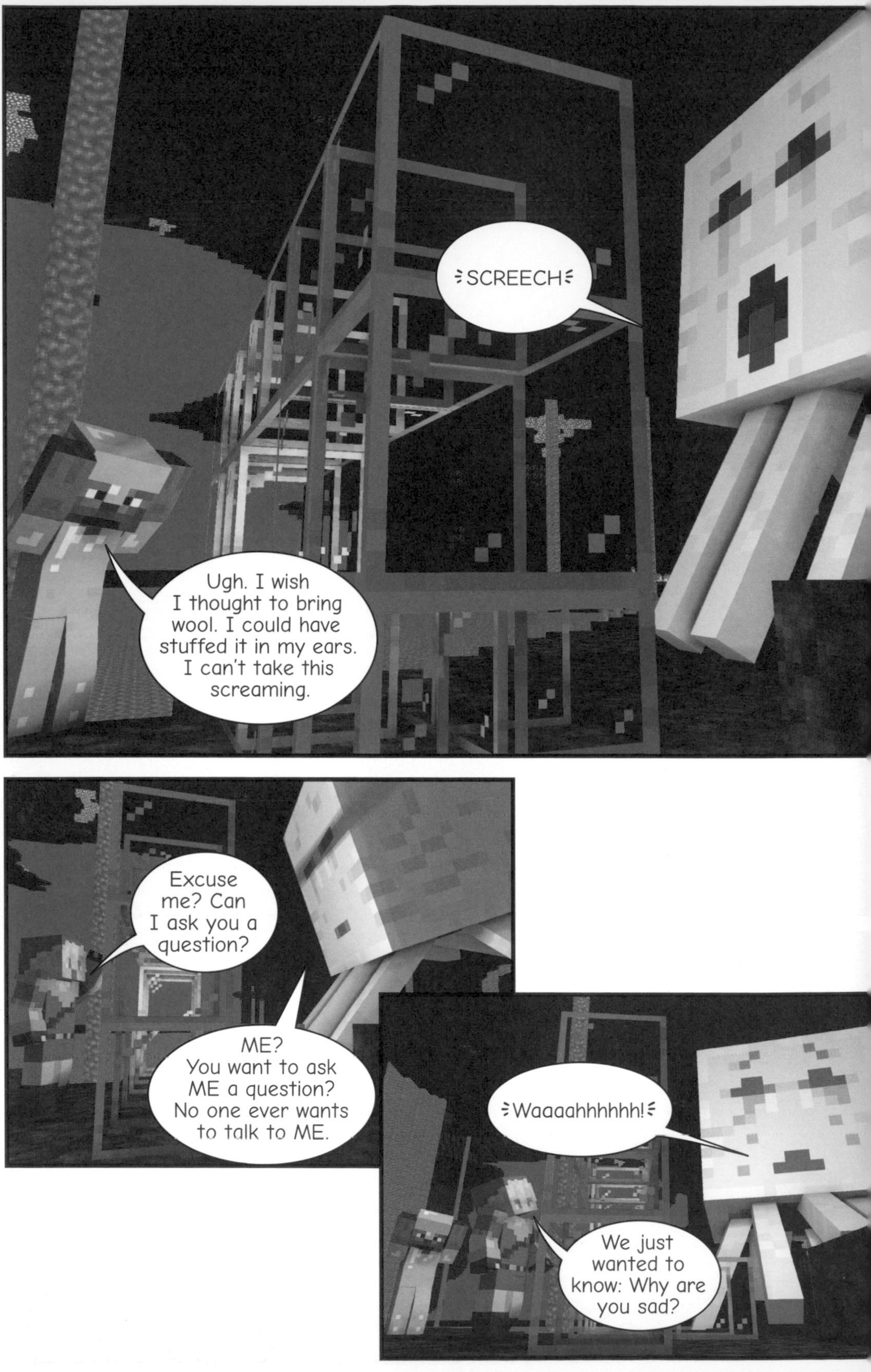
SCREECH
Ugh. I wish I thought to bring wool. I could have stuffed it in my ears. I can't take this screaming.
Excuse me? Can I ask you a question?
ME? You want to ask ME a question? No one ever wants to talk to ME.
Waaaahhhhhh!
We just wanted to know: Why are you sad?

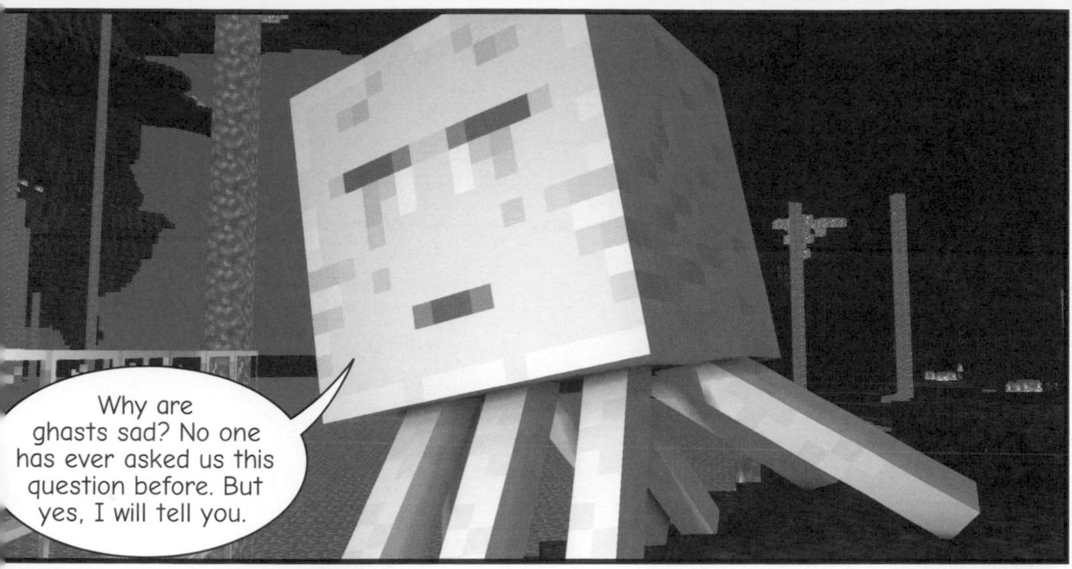
Why are ghasts sad? No one has ever asked us this question before. But yes, I will tell you.

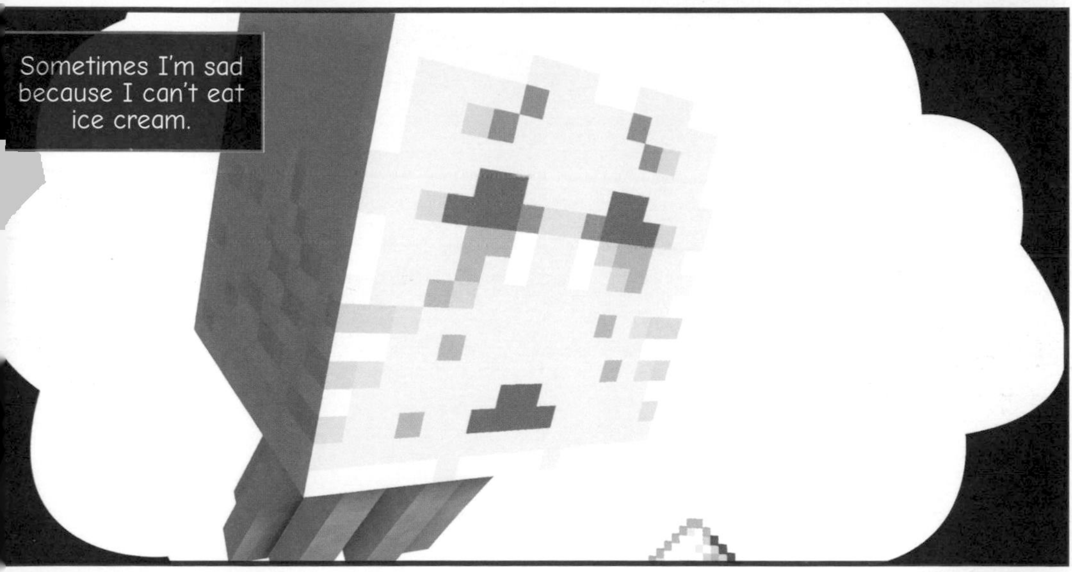
Sometimes I'm sad because I can't eat ice cream.

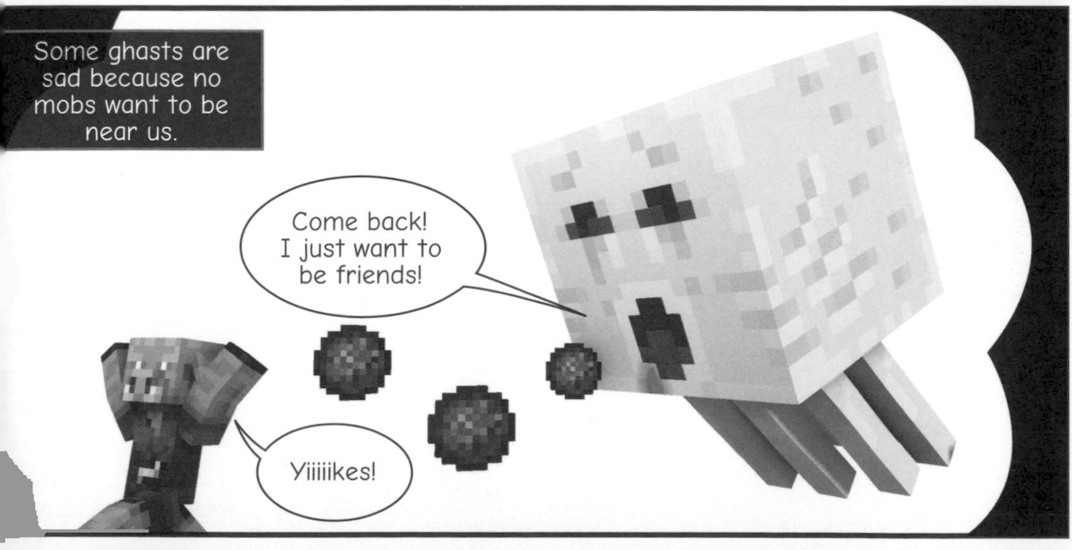
Some ghasts are sad because no mobs want to be near us.
Come back! I just want to be friends!
Yiiiiikes!

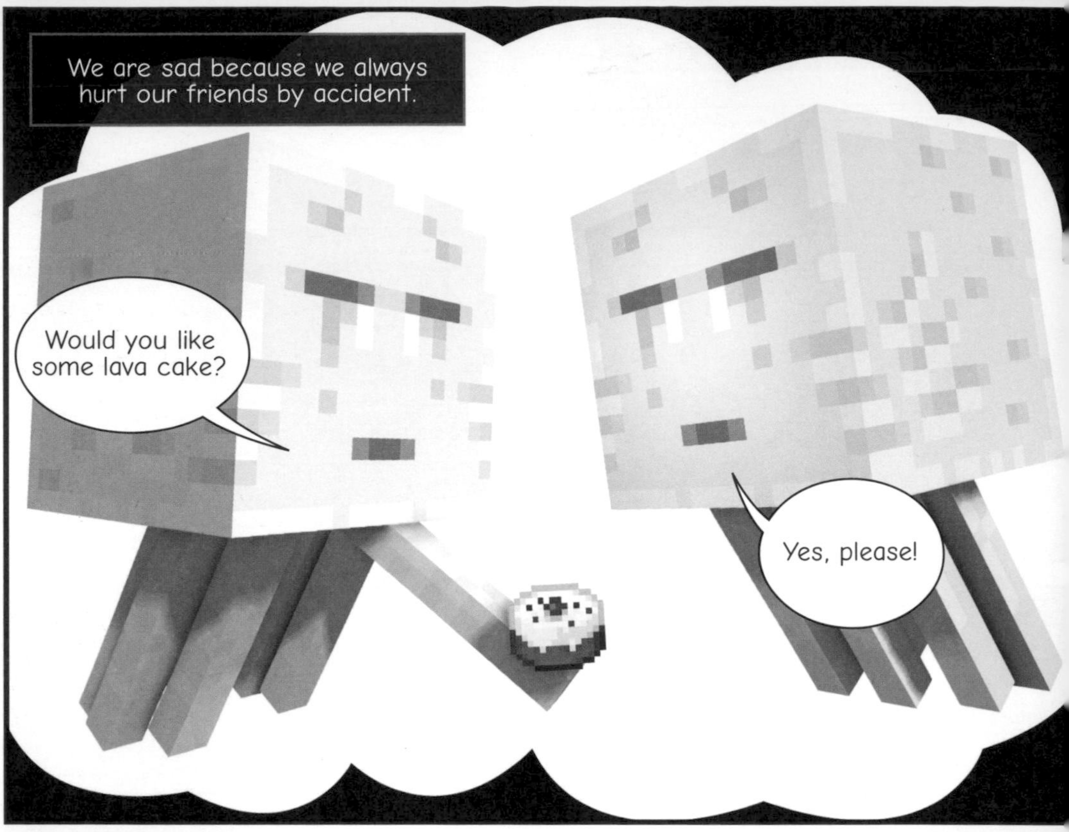
We are sad because we always hurt our friends by accident.
Would you like some lava cake?
Yes, please!

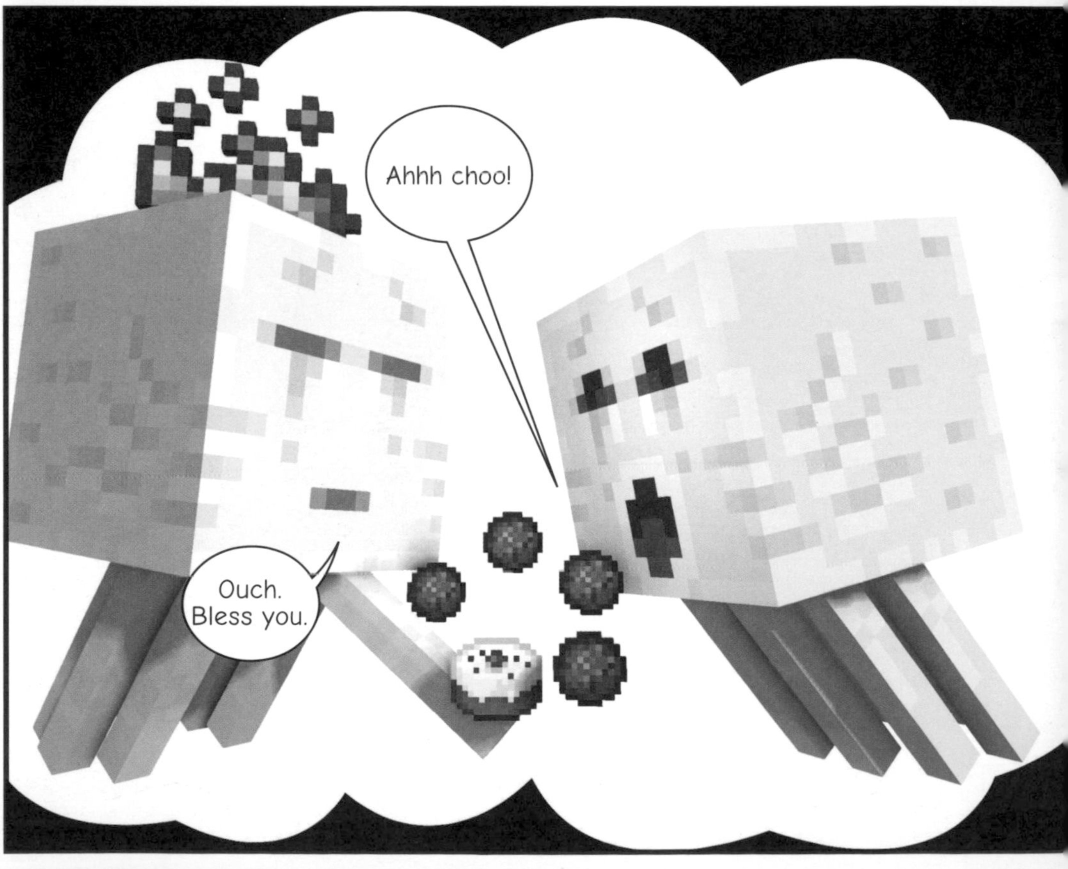
Ahhh choo!
Ouch. Bless you.

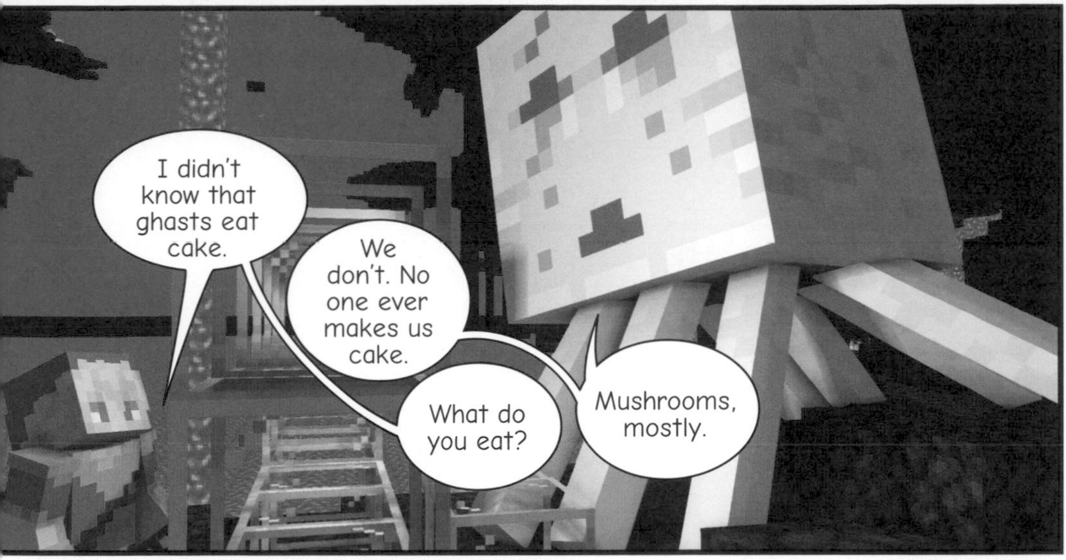

I didn't know that ghasts eat cake.
We don't. No one ever makes us cake.
What do you eat?
Mushrooms, mostly.

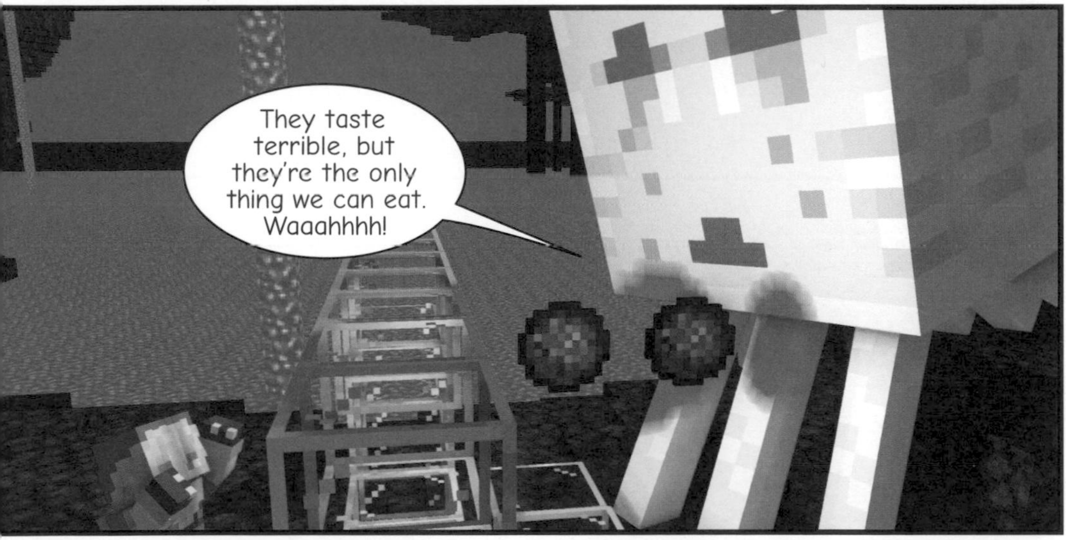

They taste terrible, but they're the only thing we can eat. Waaahhhh!

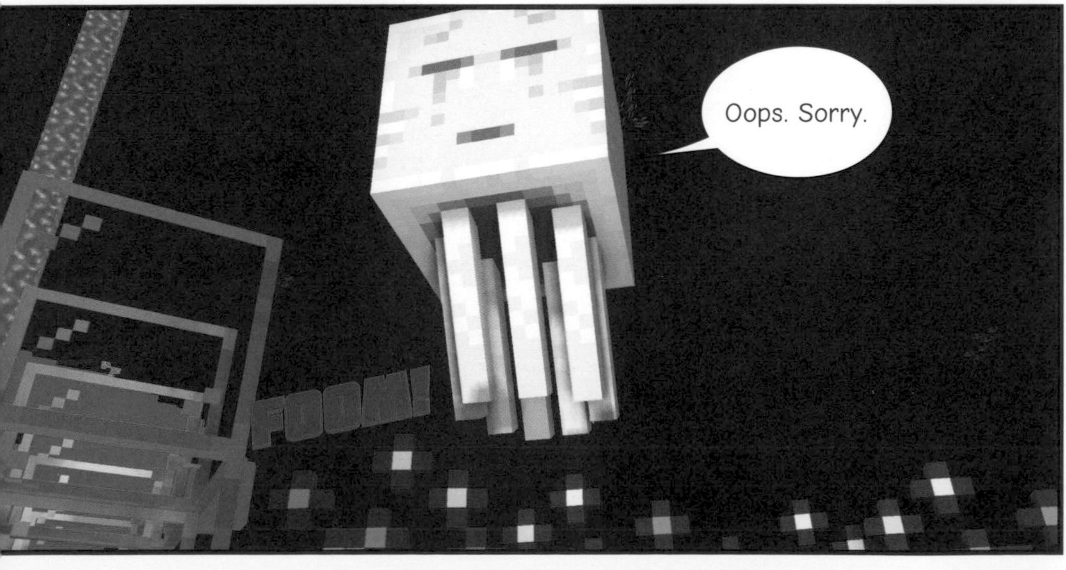

FOOM!
Oops. Sorry.

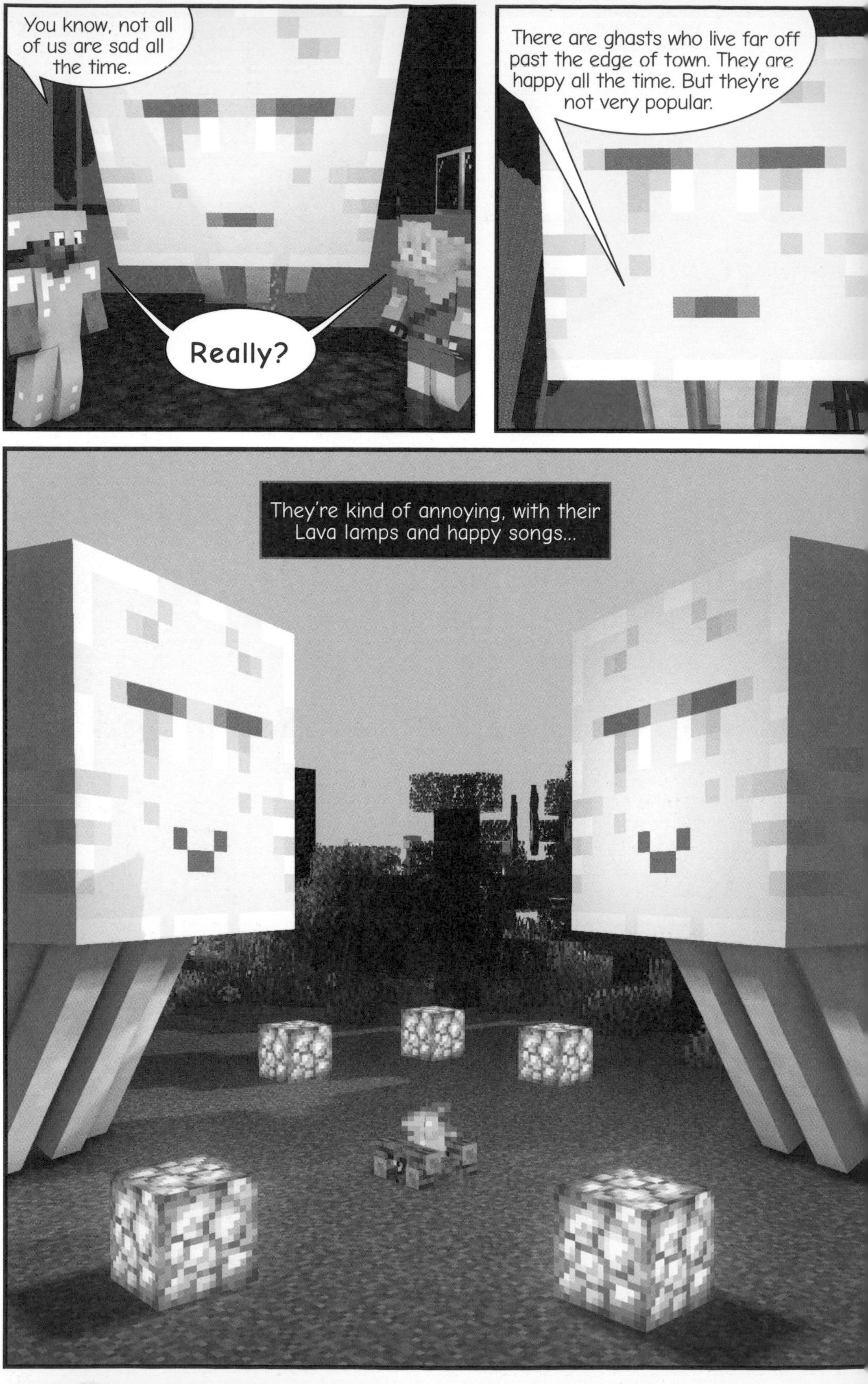
You know, not all of us are sad all the time.
Really?
There are ghasts who live far off past the edge of town. They are happy all the time. But they're not very popular.
They're kind of annoying, with their Lava lamps and happy songs...

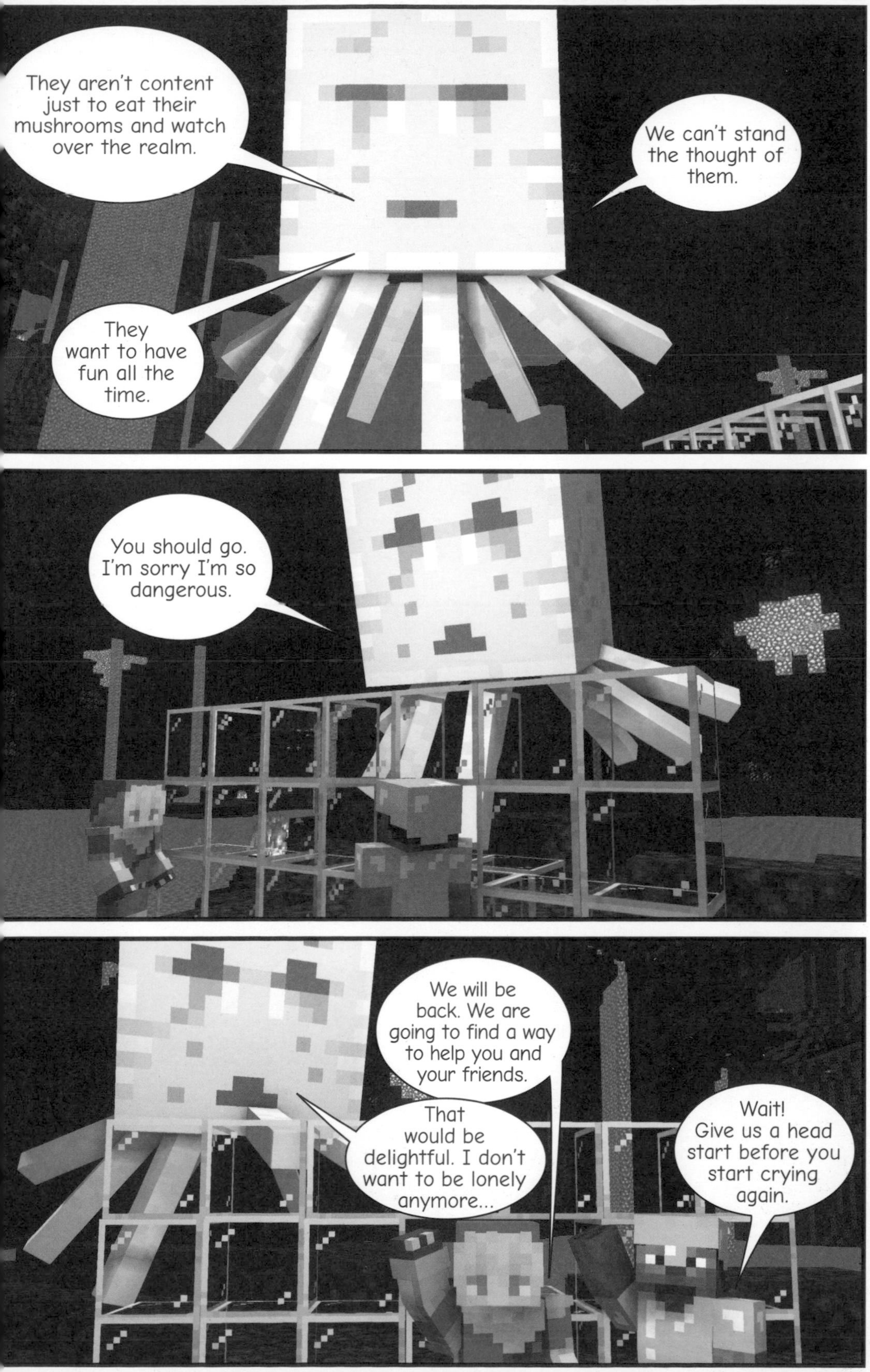
They aren't content just to eat their mushrooms and watch over the realm.
We can't stand the thought of them.
They want to have fun all the time.
You should go. I'm sorry I'm so dangerous.
We will be back. We are going to find a way to help you and your friends.
That would be delightful. I don't want to be lonely anymore...
Wait! Give us a head start before you start crying again.

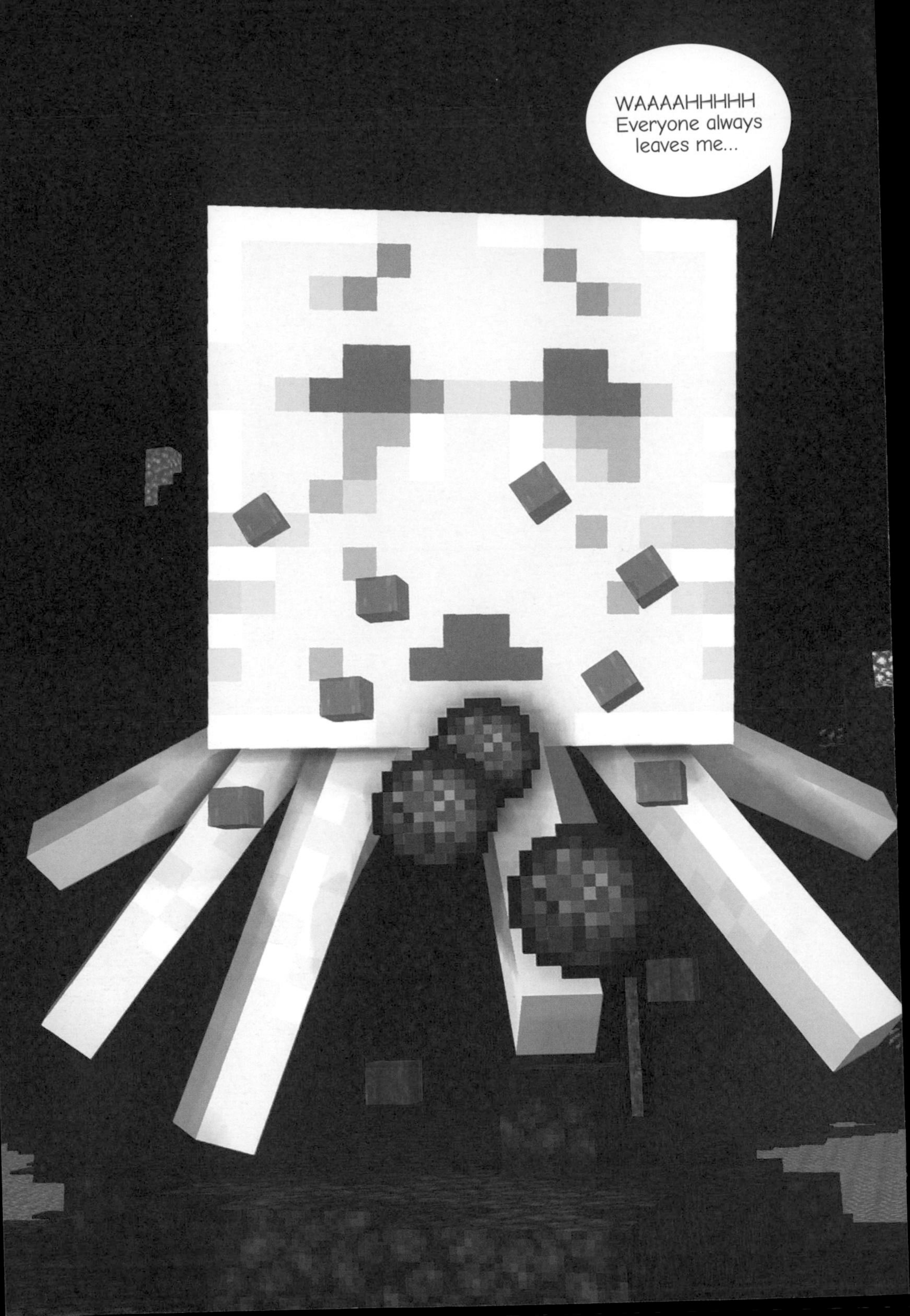
WAAAAHHHHH Everyone always leaves me...

Chapter 4
Happy Campers

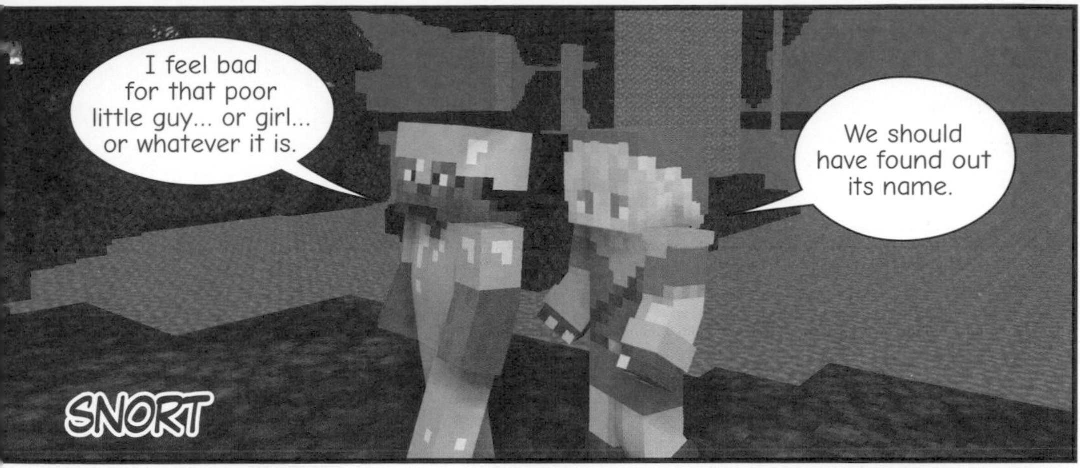
I feel bad for that poor little guy... or girl... or whatever it is.
We should have found out its name.
SNORT

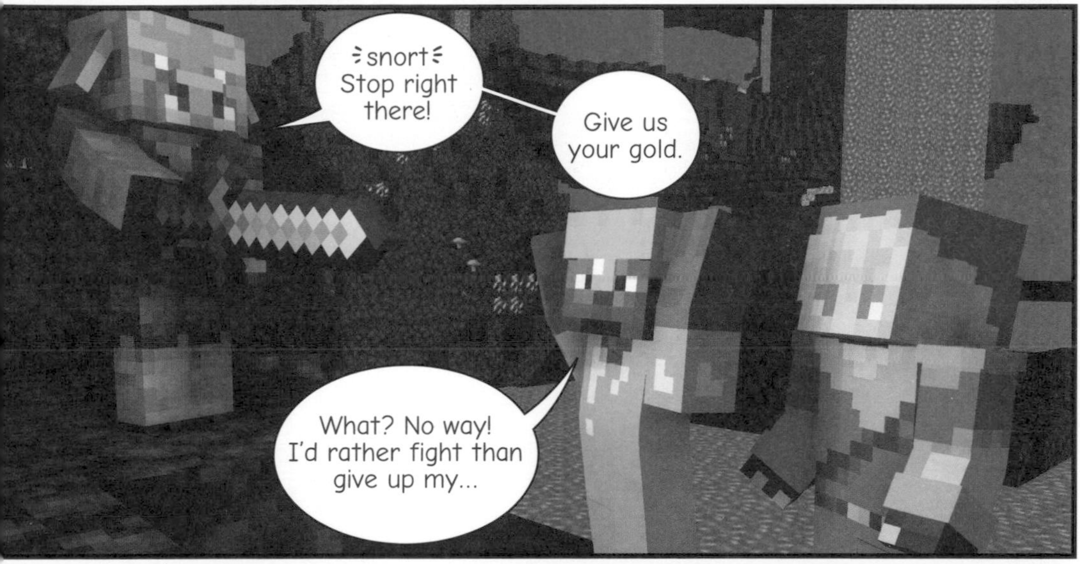
snort Stop right there!
Give us your gold.
What? No way! I'd rather fight than give up my...

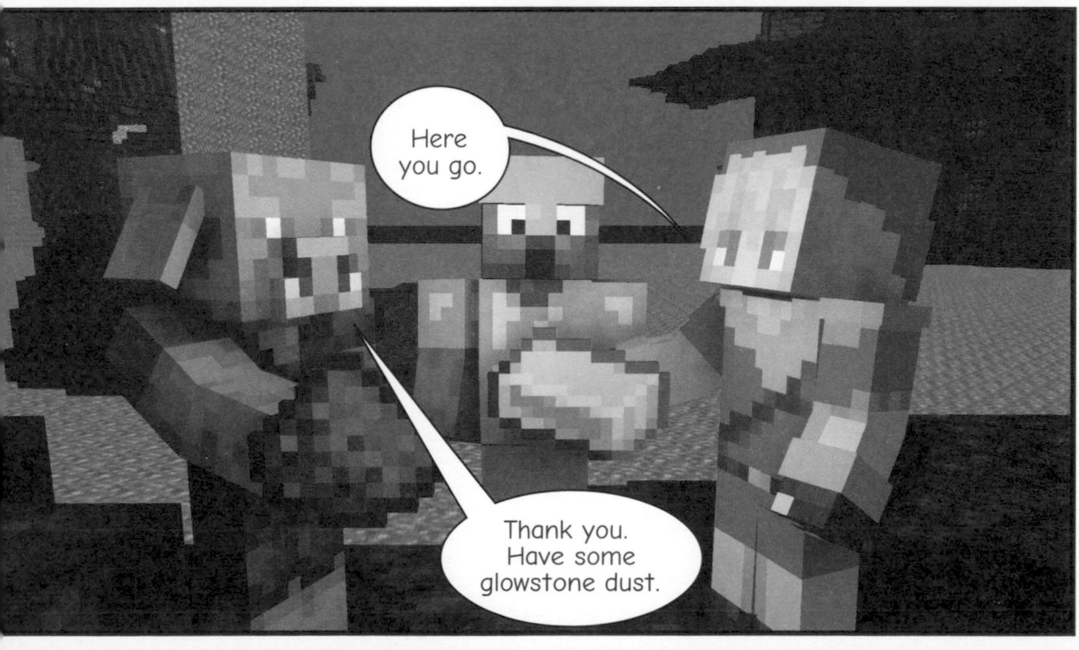
Here you go.
Thank you. Have some glowstone dust.

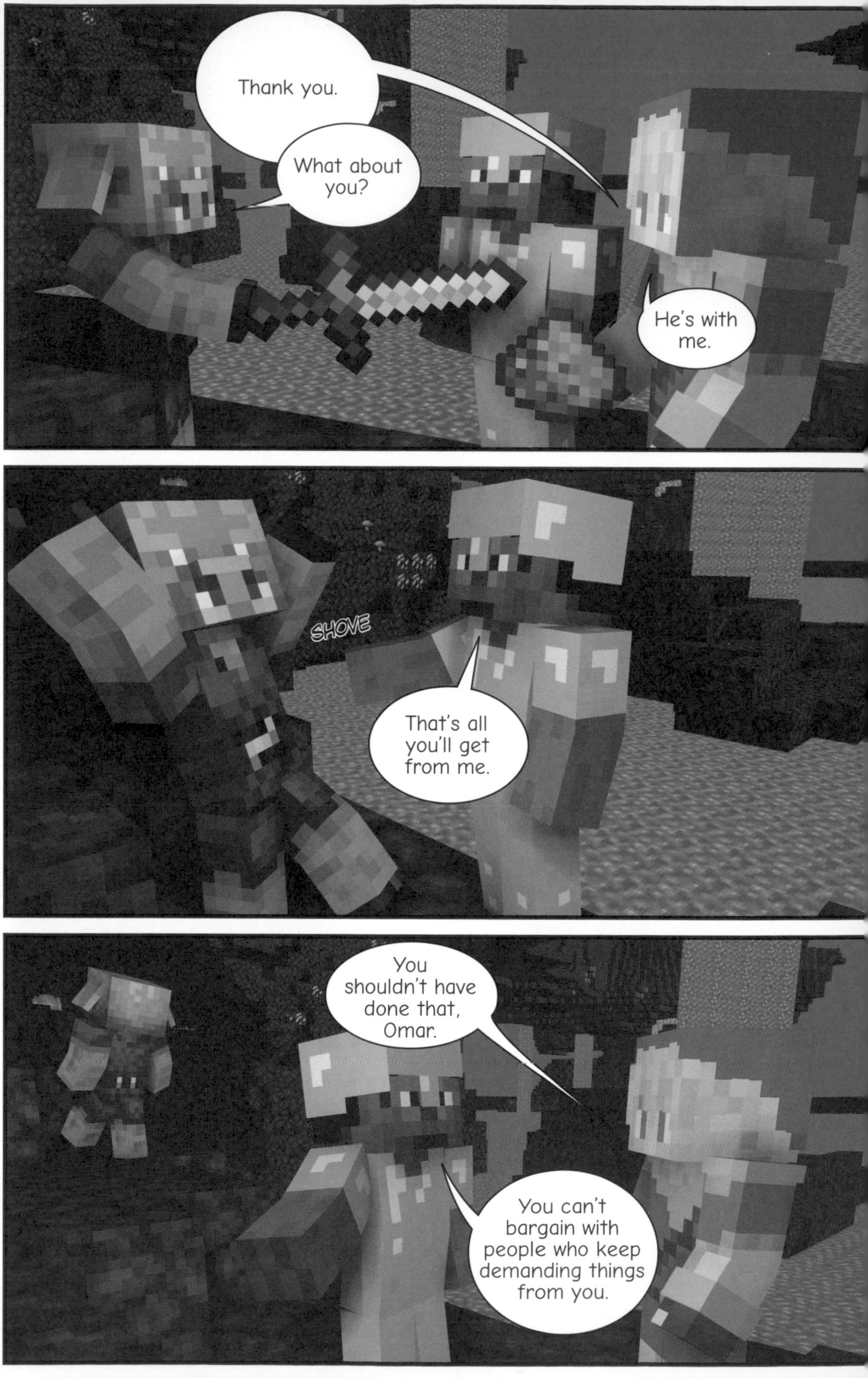
Thank you.
What about you?
He's with me.
SHOVE
That's all you'll get from me.
You shouldn't have done that, Omar.
You can't bargain with people who keep demanding things from you.

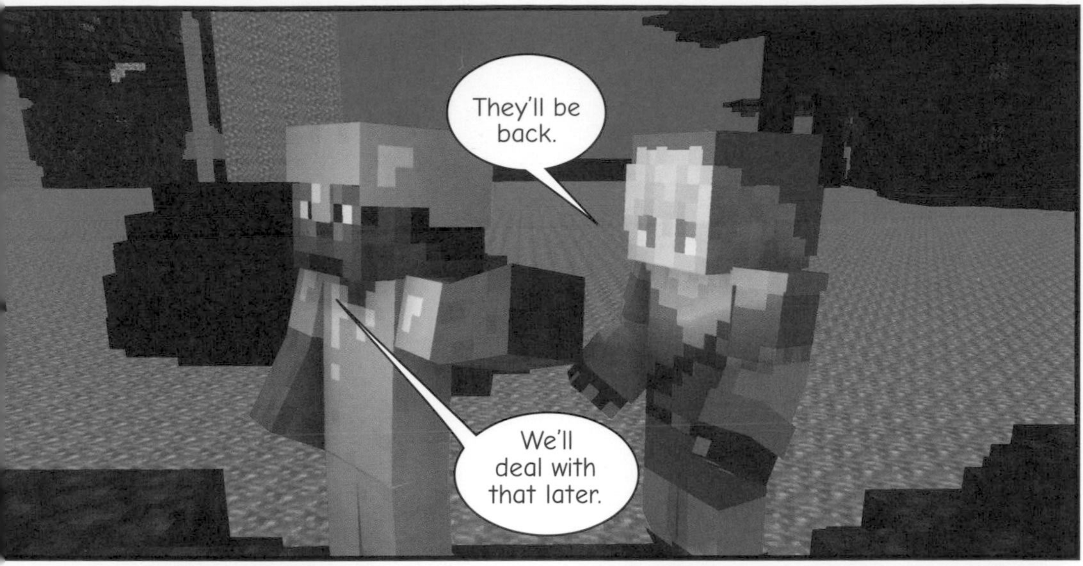
They'll be back.
We'll deal with that later.

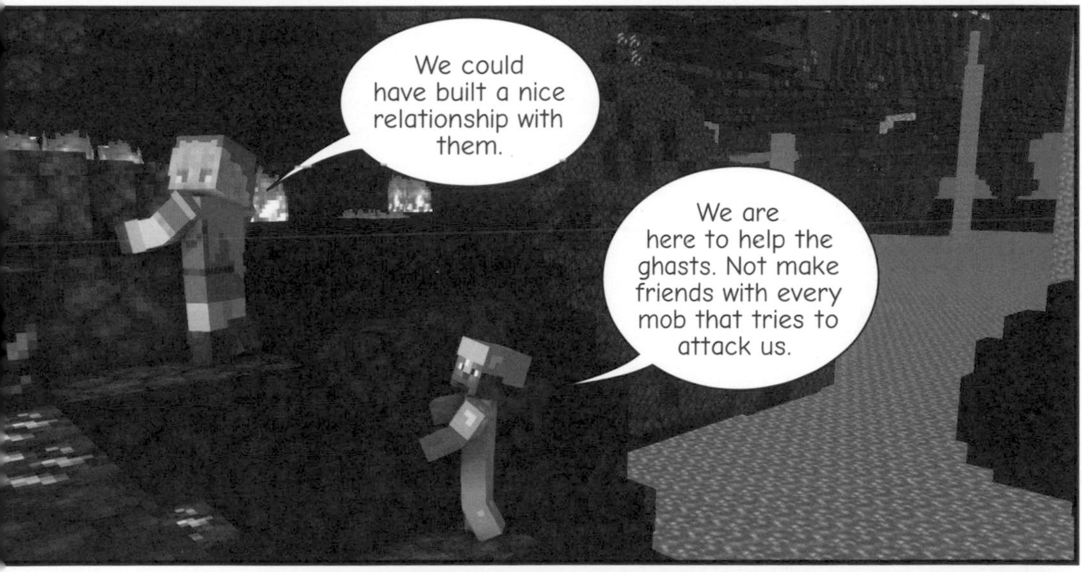
We could have built a nice relationship with them.
We are here to help the ghasts. Not make friends with every mob that tries to attack us.

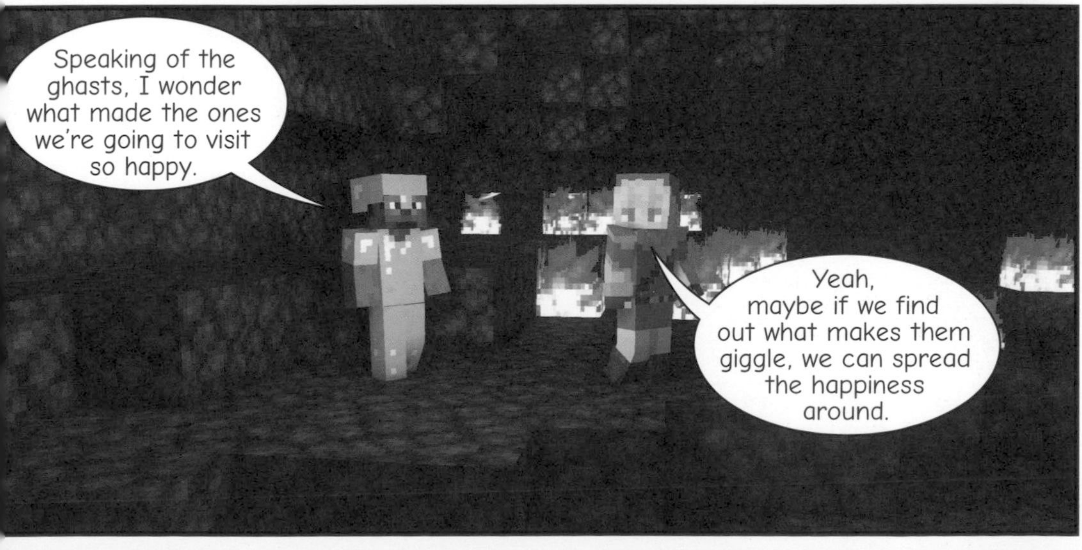
Speaking of the ghasts, I wonder what made the ones we're going to visit so happy.
Yeah, maybe if we find out what makes them giggle, we can spread the happiness around.

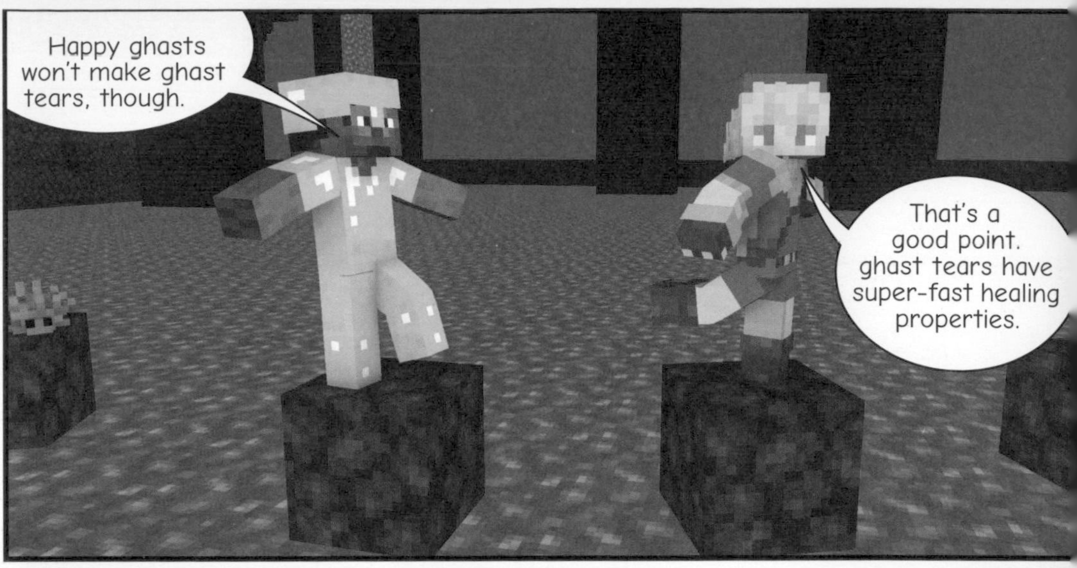
Happy ghasts won't make ghast tears, though.
That's a good point. ghast tears have super-fast healing properties.

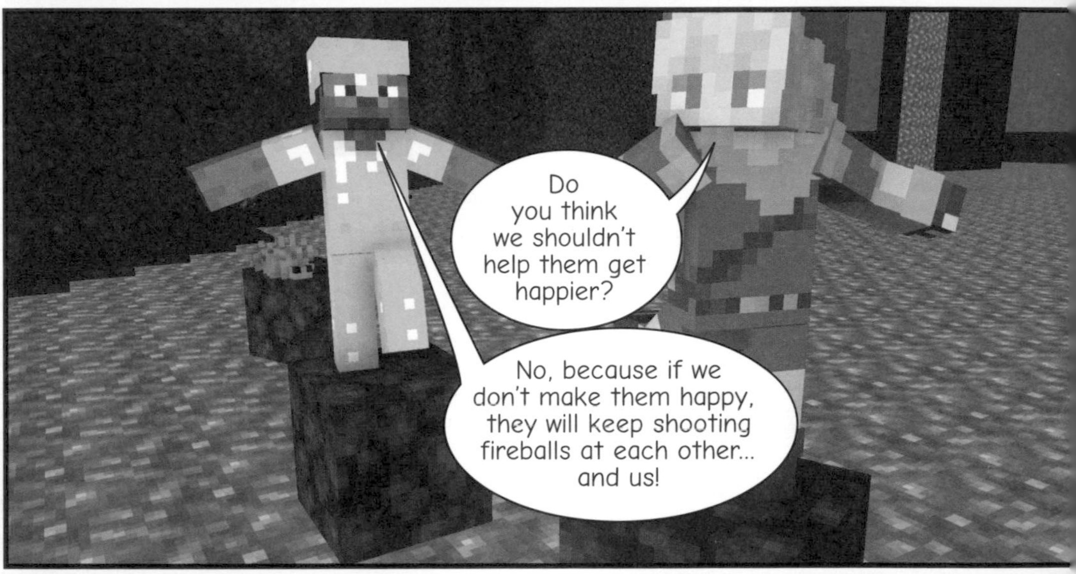
Do you think we shouldn't help them get happier?
No, because if we don't make them happy, they will keep shooting fireballs at each other... and us!

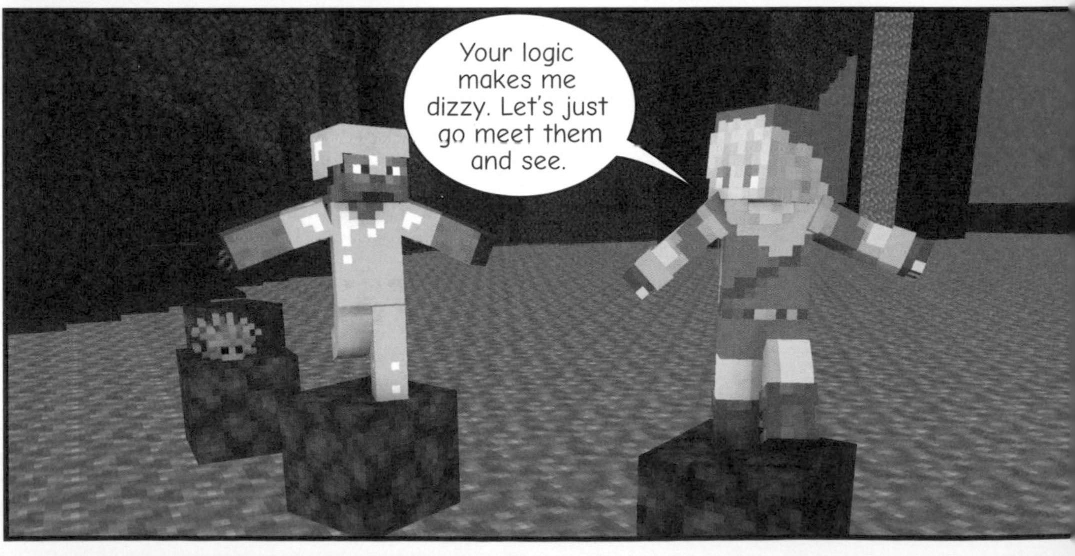
Your logic makes me dizzy. Let's just go meet them and see.

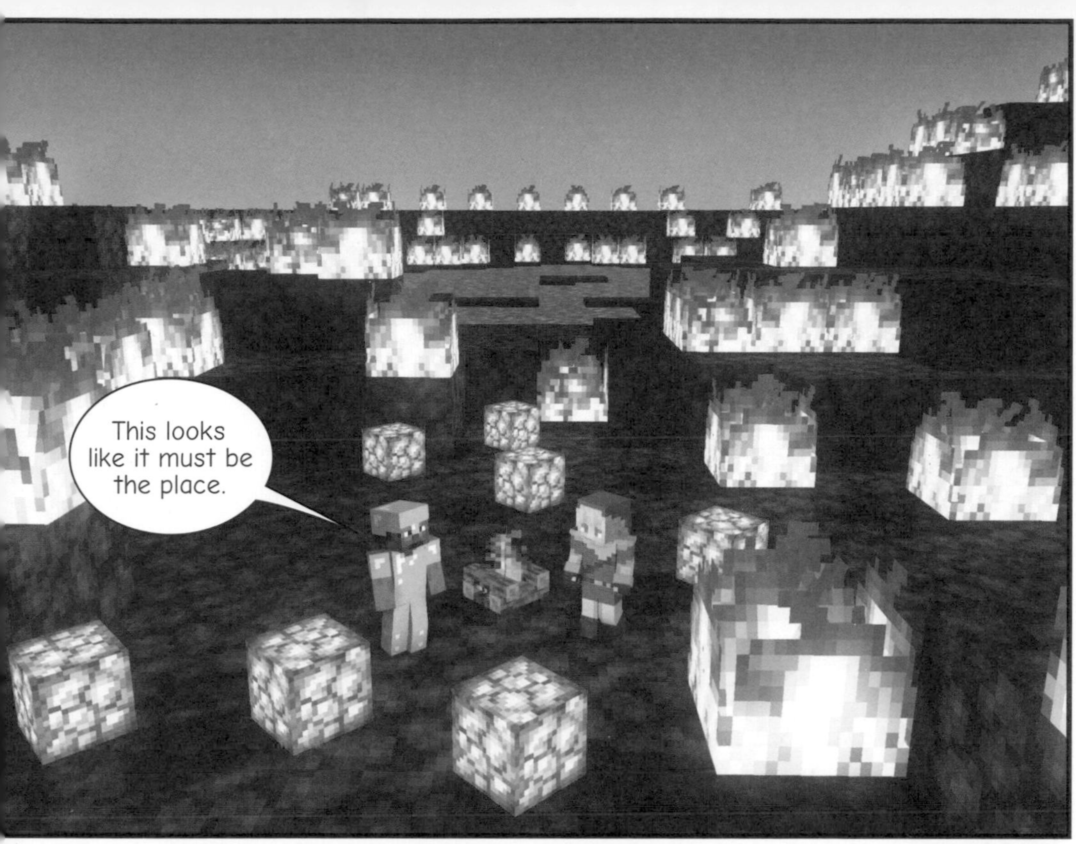
This looks like it must be the place.

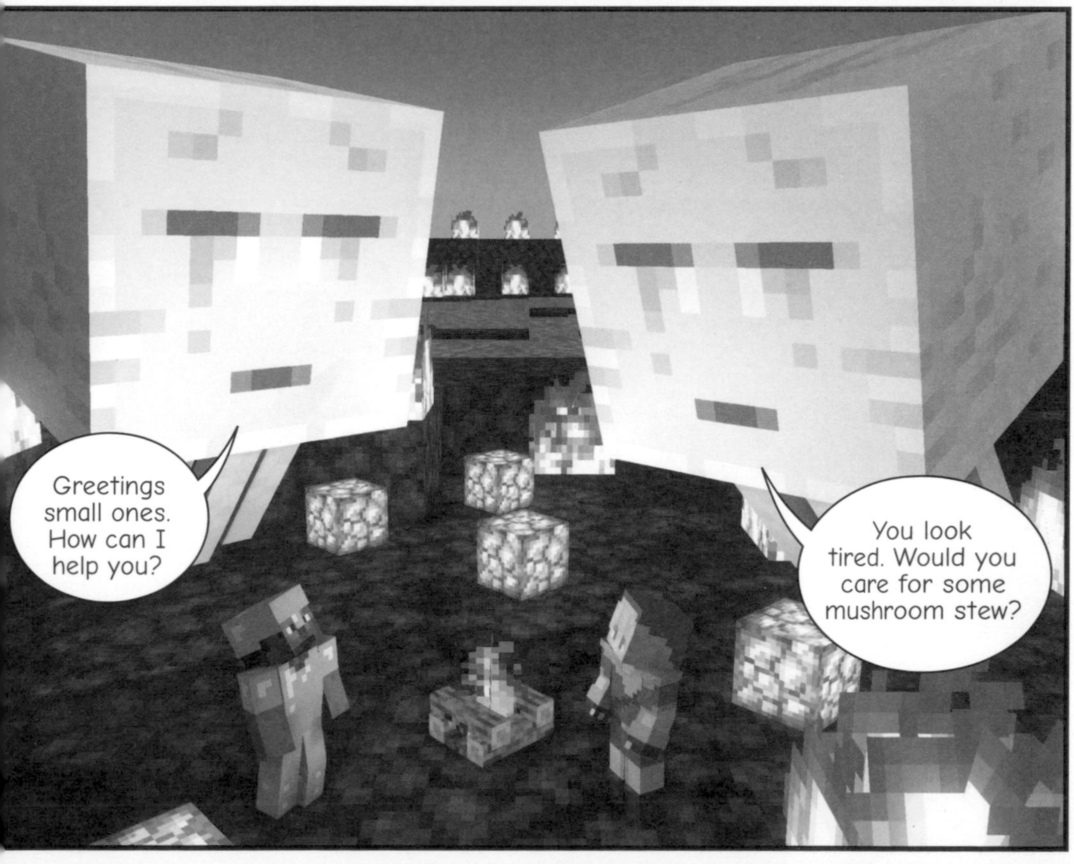
Greetings small ones. How can I help you?
You look tired. Would you care for some mushroom stew?

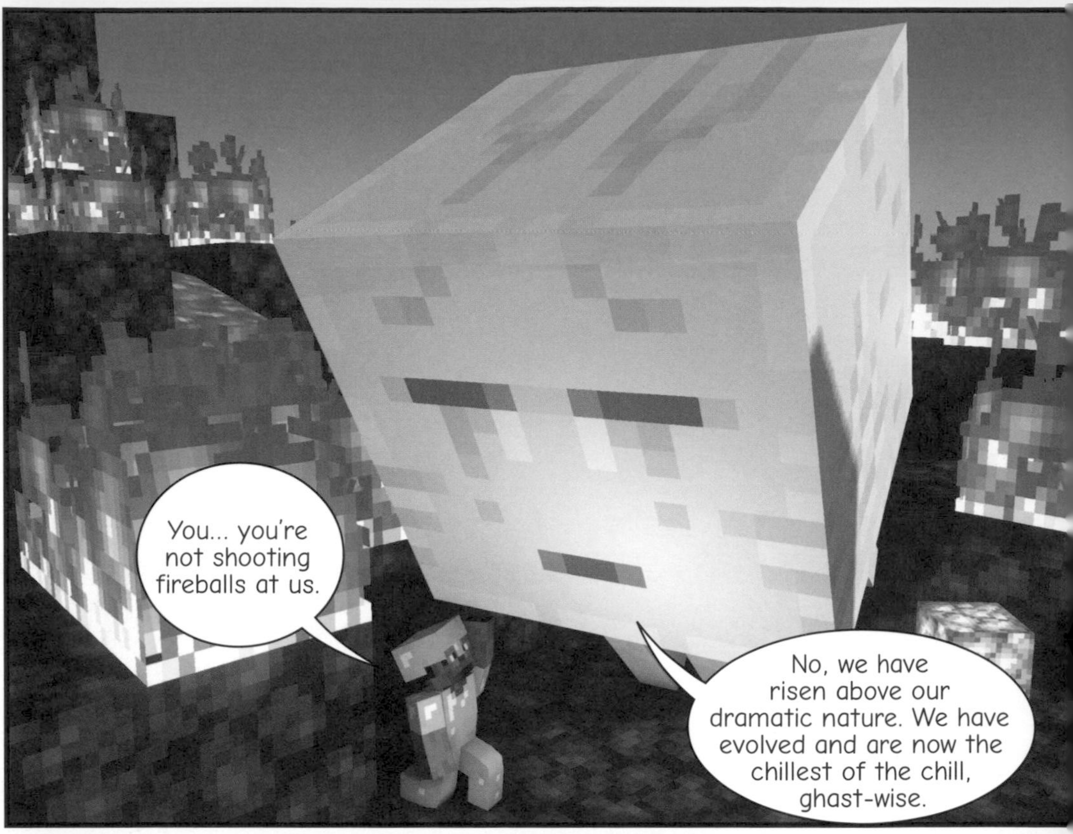
You... you're not shooting fireballs at us.
No, we have risen above our dramatic nature. We have evolved and are now the chillest of the chill, ghast-wise.

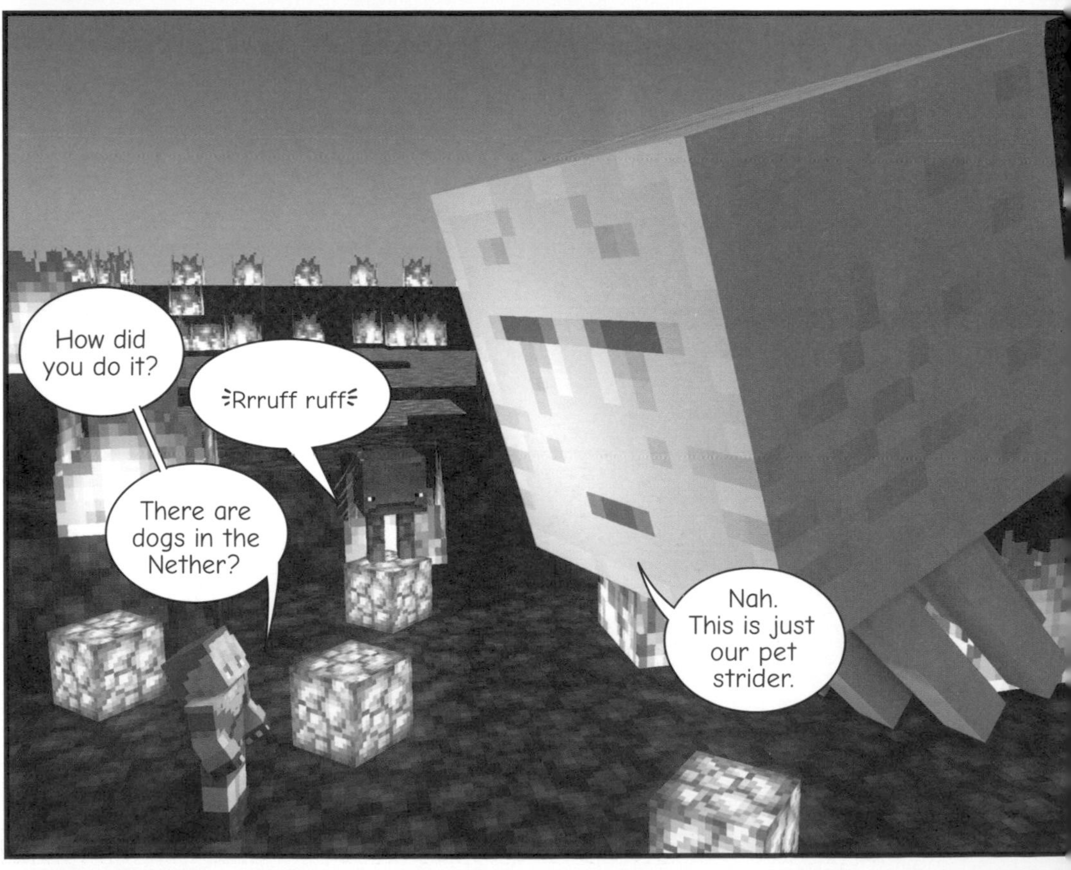
How did you do it?
Rrruff ruff
There are dogs in the Nether?
Nah. This is just our pet strider.

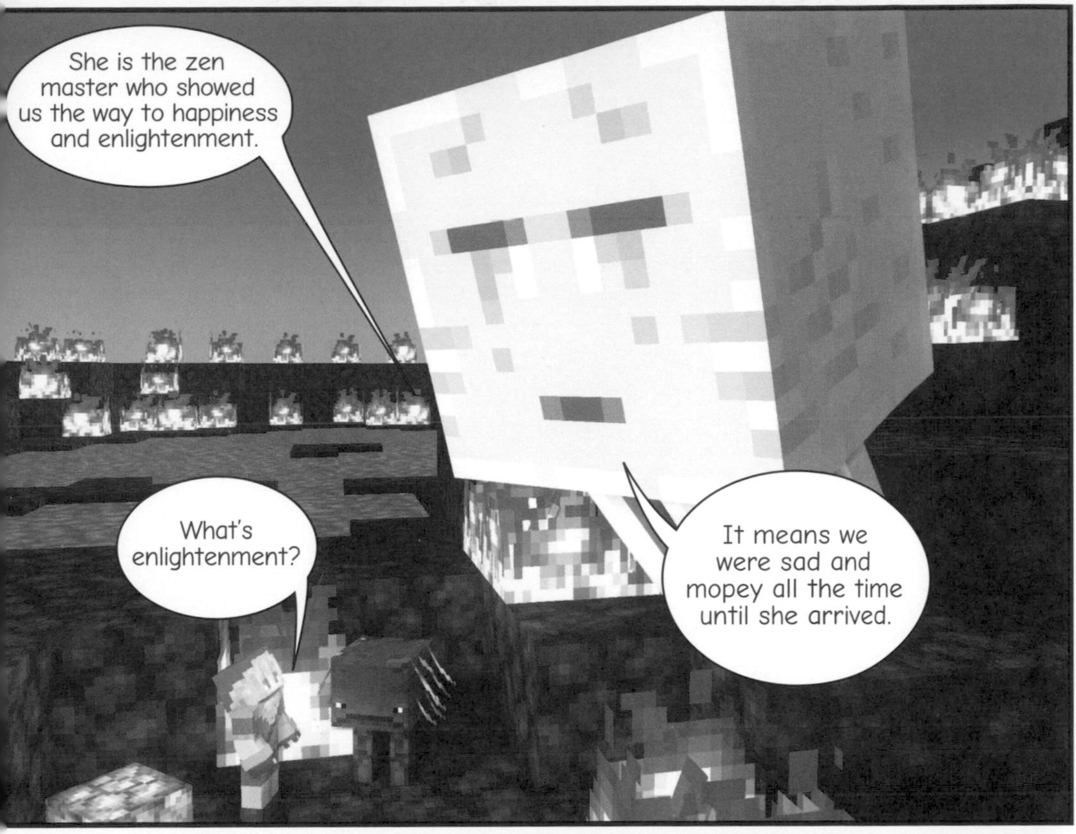
She is the zen master who showed us the way to happiness and enlightenment.
What's enlightenment?
It means we were sad and mopey all the time until she arrived.

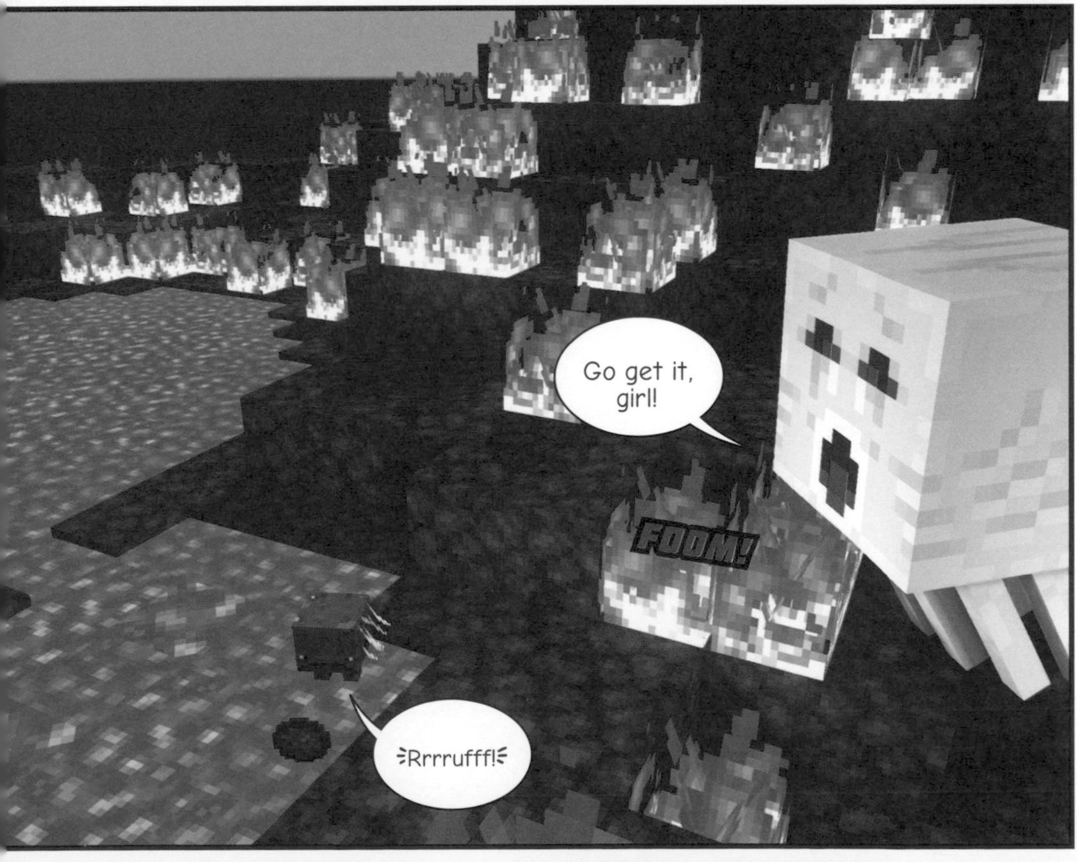
Go get it, girl!
FOOM!
Rrrrufff!

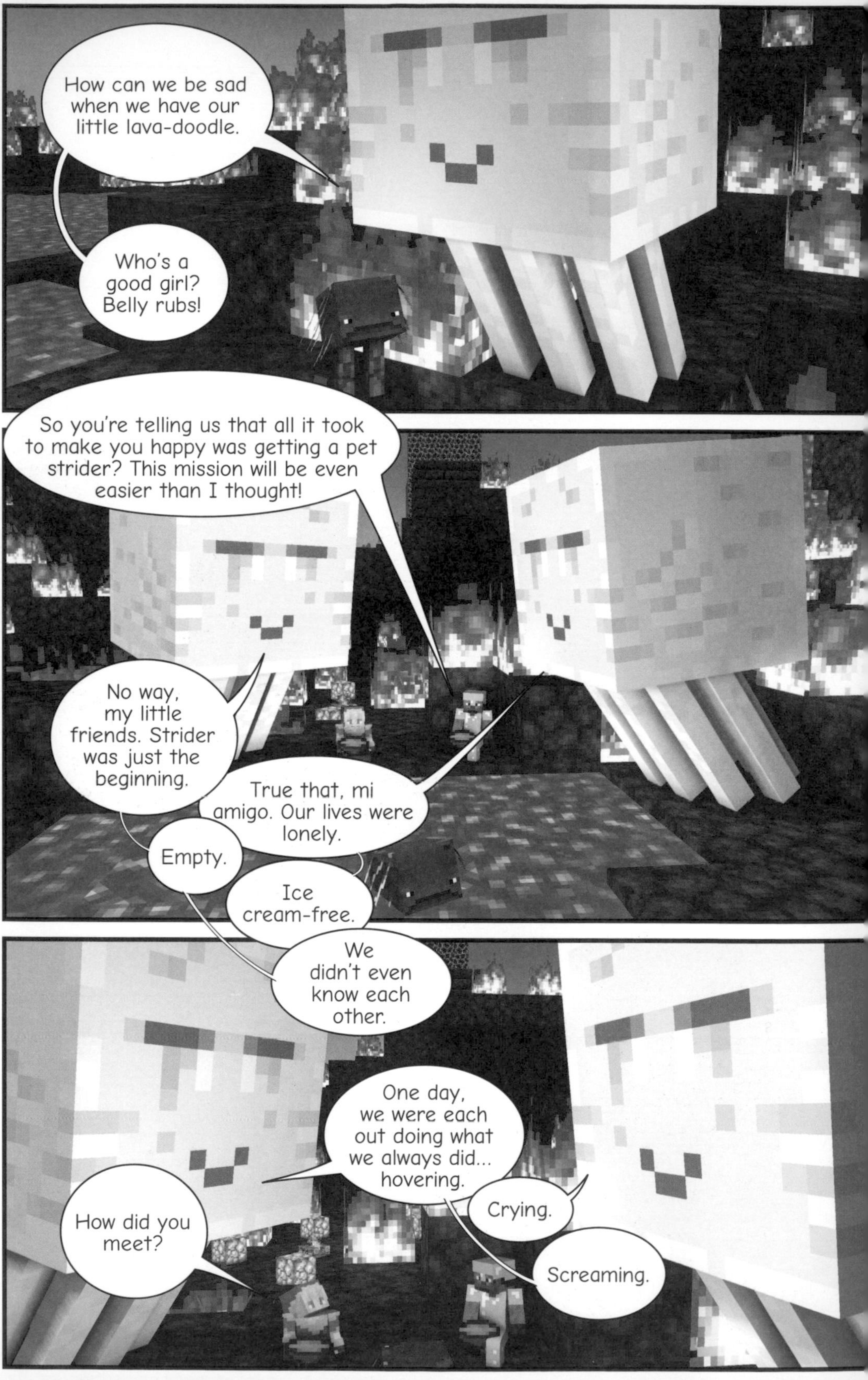
How can we be sad when we have our little lava-doodle.
Who's a good girl? Belly rubs!
So you're telling us that all it took to make you happy was getting a pet strider? This mission will be even easier than I thought!
No way, my little friends. Strider was just the beginning.
True that, mi amigo. Our lives were lonely.
Empty.
Ice cream-free.
We didn't even know each other.
How did you meet?
One day, we were each out doing what we always did... hovering.
Crying.
Screaming.

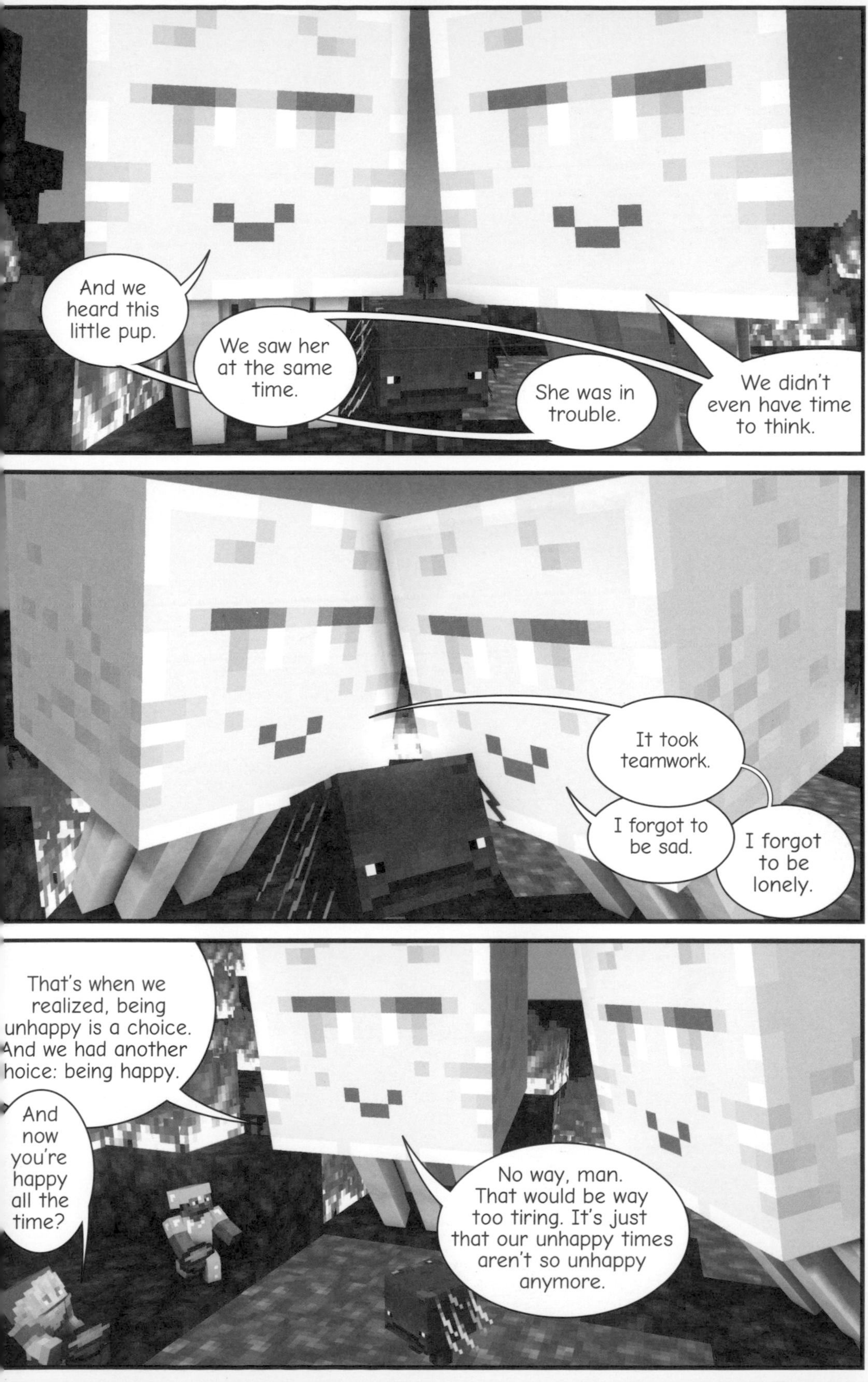
And we heard this little pup.
We saw her at the same time.
She was in trouble.
We didn't even have time to think.
It took teamwork.
I forgot to be sad.
I forgot to be lonely.
That's when we realized, being unhappy is a choice. And we had another hoice: being happy.
And now you're happy all the time?
No way, man. That would be way too tiring. It's just that our unhappy times aren't so unhappy anymore.

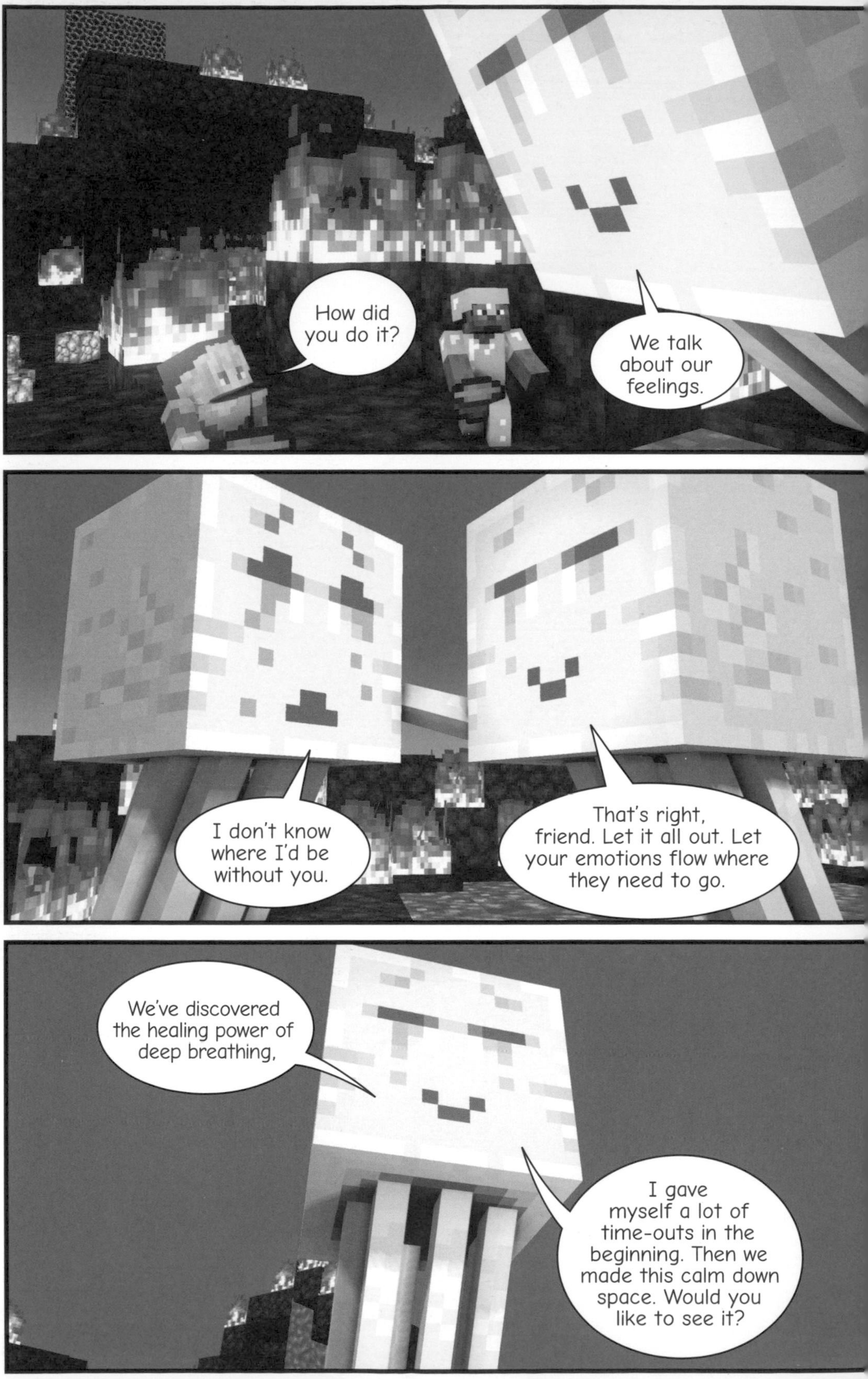
How did you do it?
We talk about our feelings.
I don't know where I'd be without you.
That's right, friend. Let it all out. Let your emotions flow where they need to go.
We've discovered the healing power of deep breathing,
I gave myself a lot of time-outs in the beginning. Then we made this calm down space. Would you like to see it?

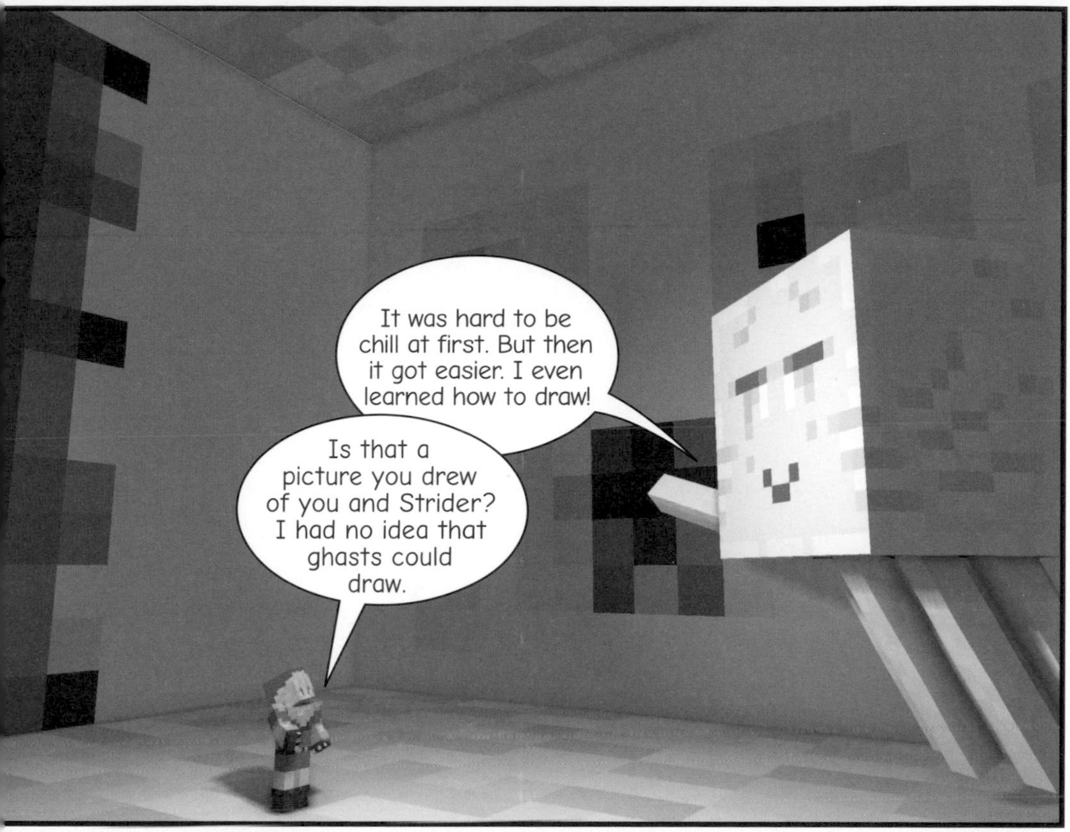
It was hard to be chill at first. But then it got easier. I even learned how to draw!
Is that a picture you drew of you and Strider? I had no idea that ghasts could draw.

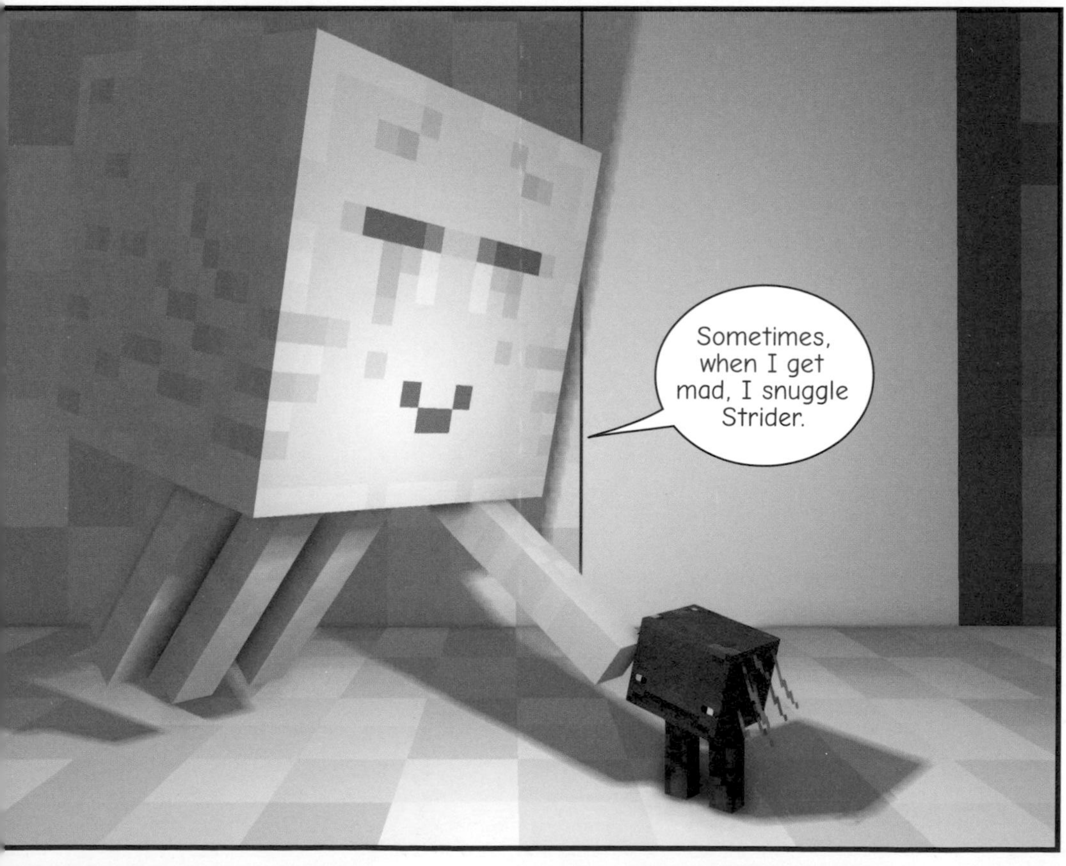
Sometimes, when I get mad, I snuggle Strider.

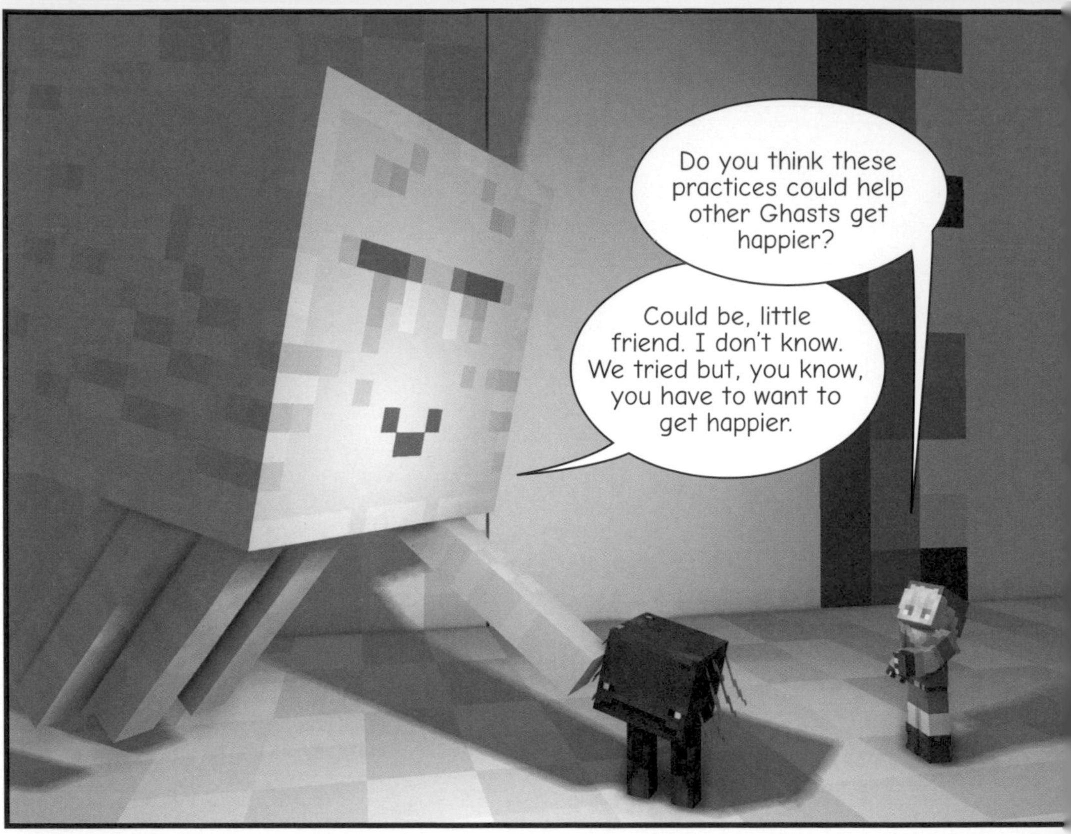
Do you think these practices could help other Ghasts get happier?
Could be, little friend. I don't know. We tried but, you know, you have to want to get happier.

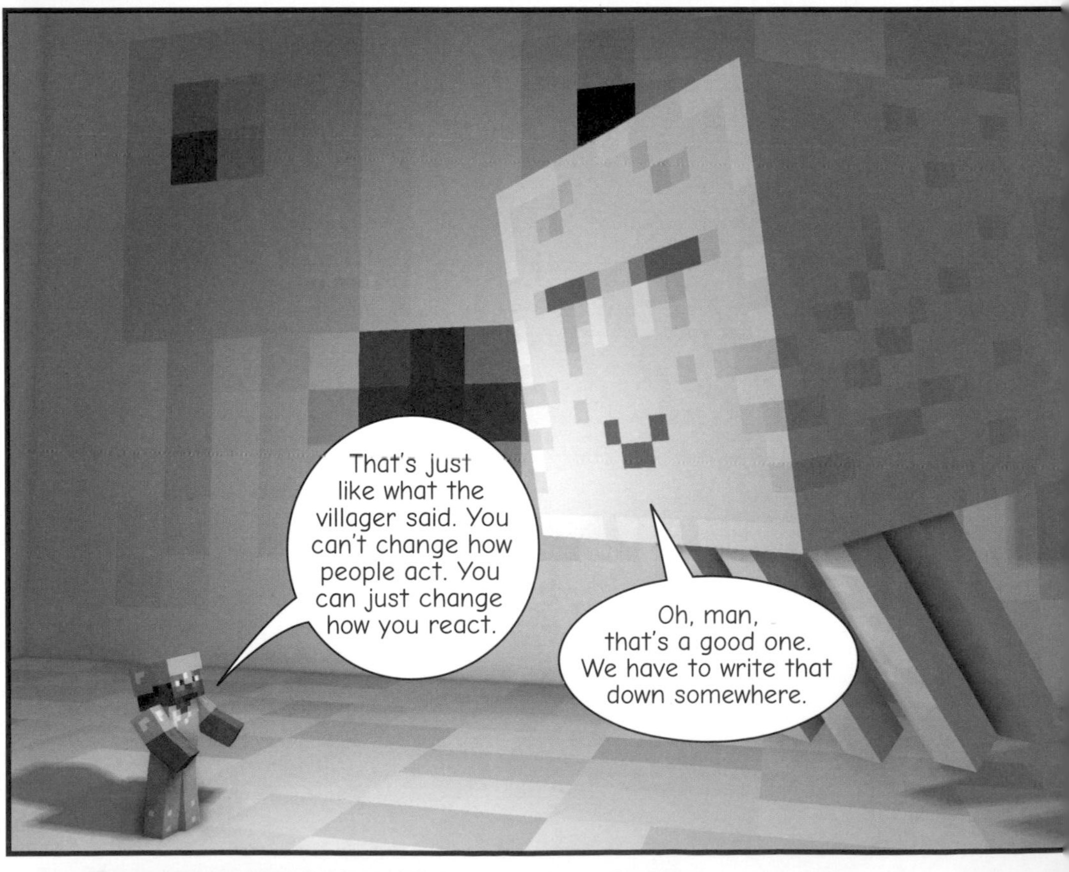
That's just like what the villager said. You can't change how people act. You can just change how you react.
Oh, man, that's a good one. We have to write that down somewhere.

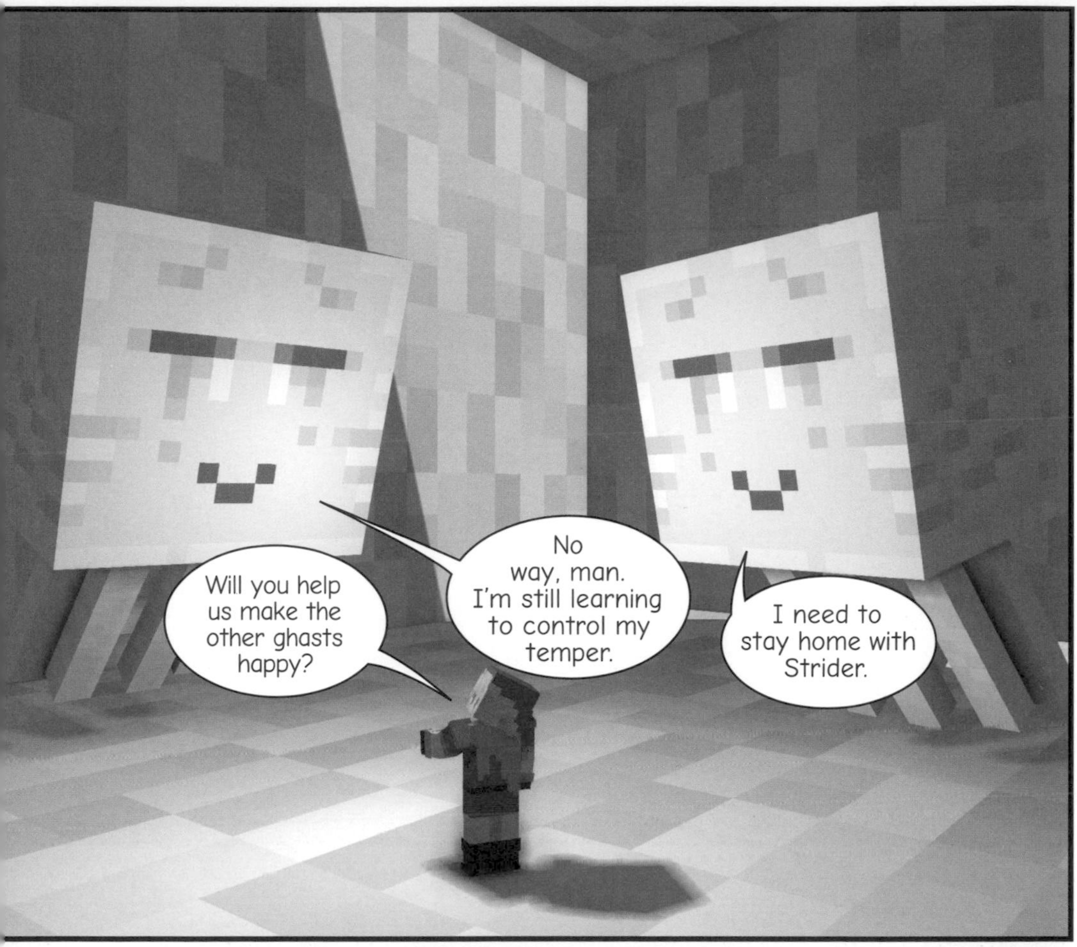
Will you help us make the other ghasts happy?
No way, man. I'm still learning to control my temper.
I need to stay home with Strider.

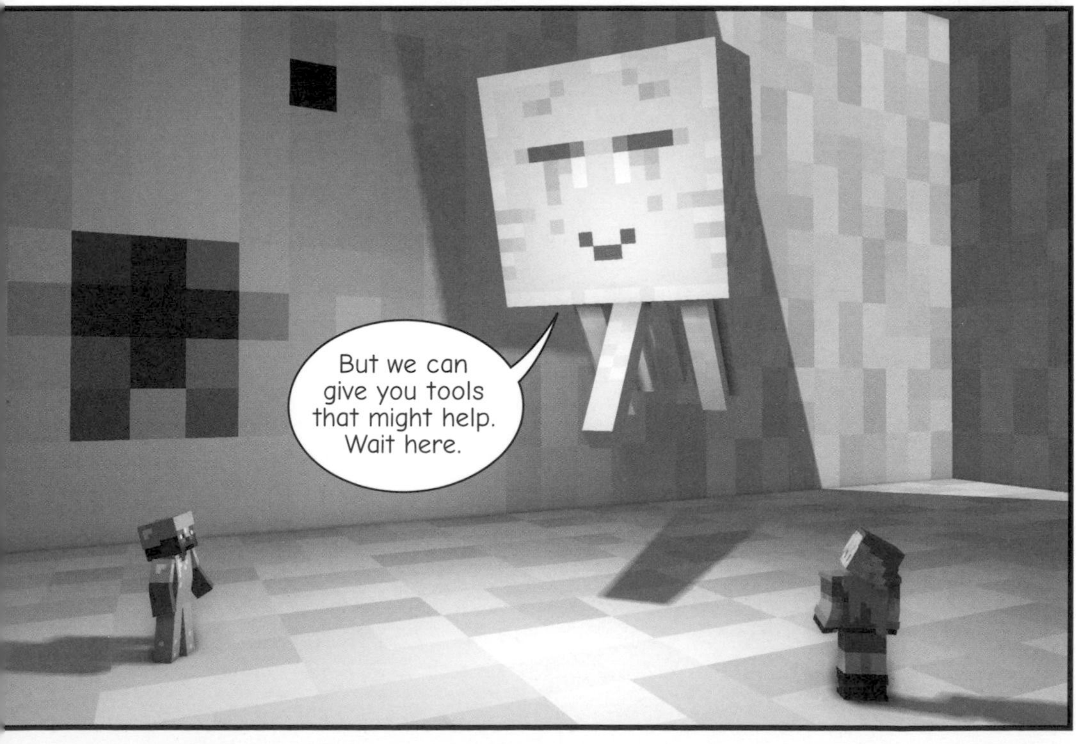
But we can give you tools that might help. Wait here.

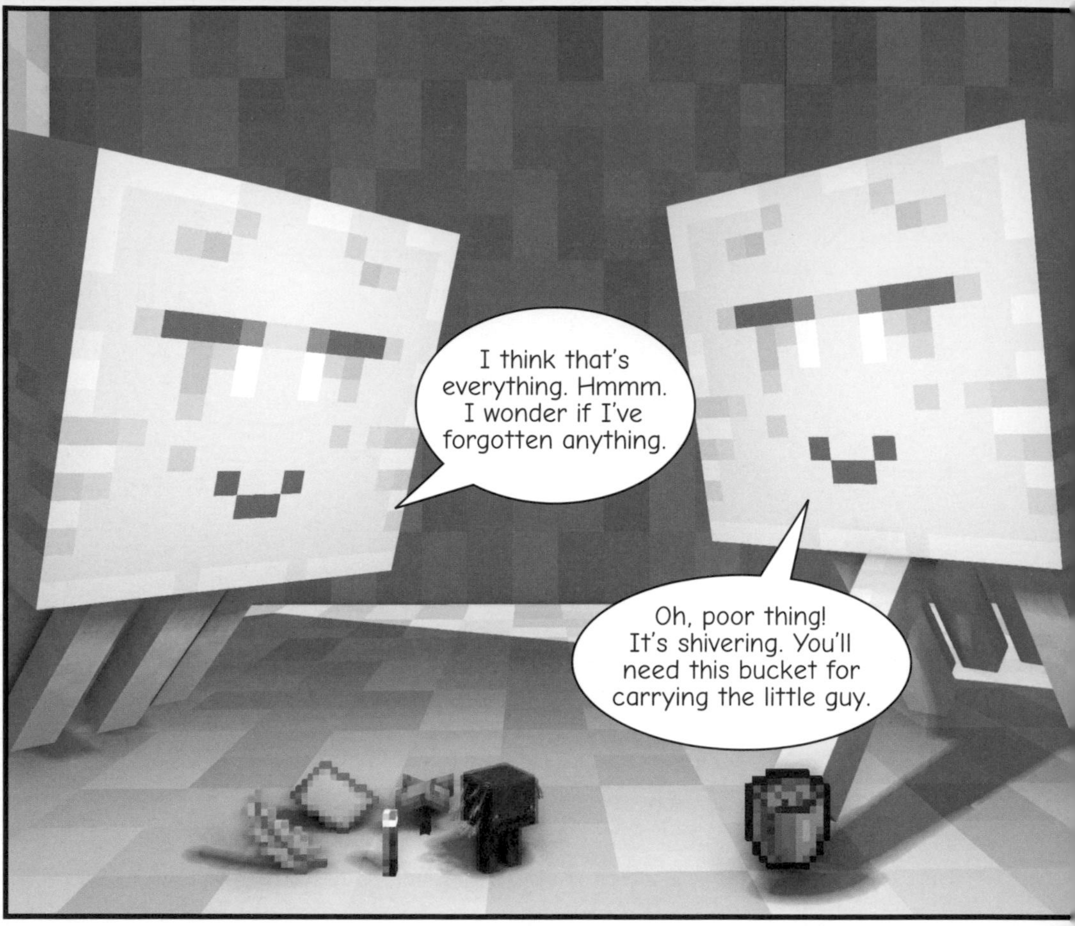
I think that's everything. Hmmm. I wonder if I've forgotten anything.
Oh, poor thing! It's shivering. You'll need this bucket for carrying the little guy.

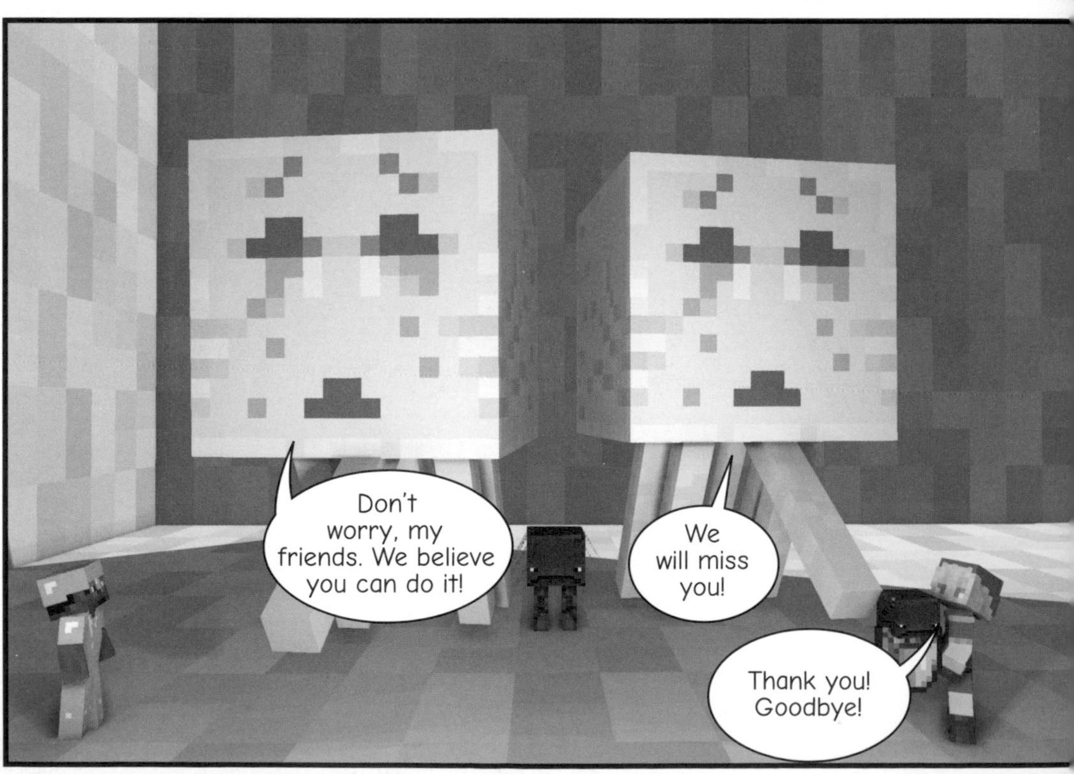
Don't worry, my friends. We believe you can do it!
We will miss you!
Thank you! Goodbye!

Chapter 5
Venting
Feelings

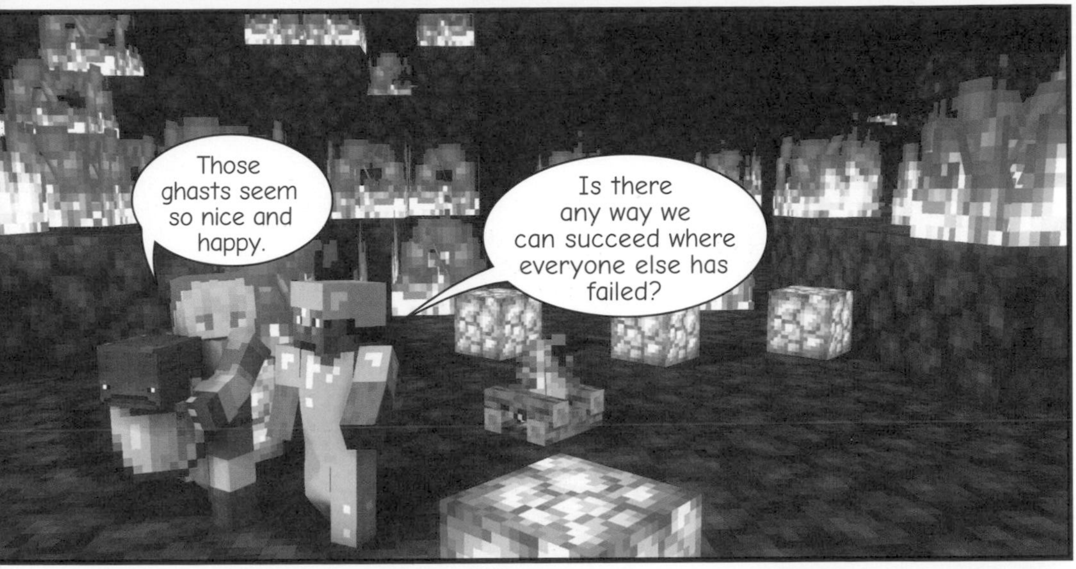
Those ghasts seem so nice and happy.
Is there any way we can succeed where everyone else has failed?

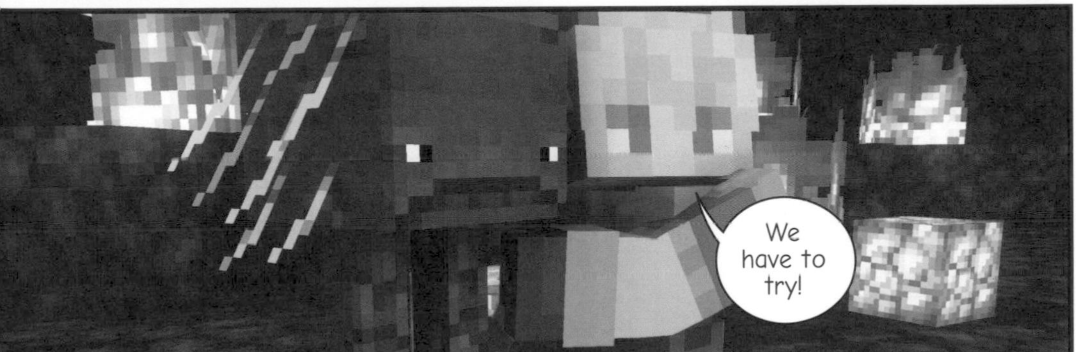
We have to try!

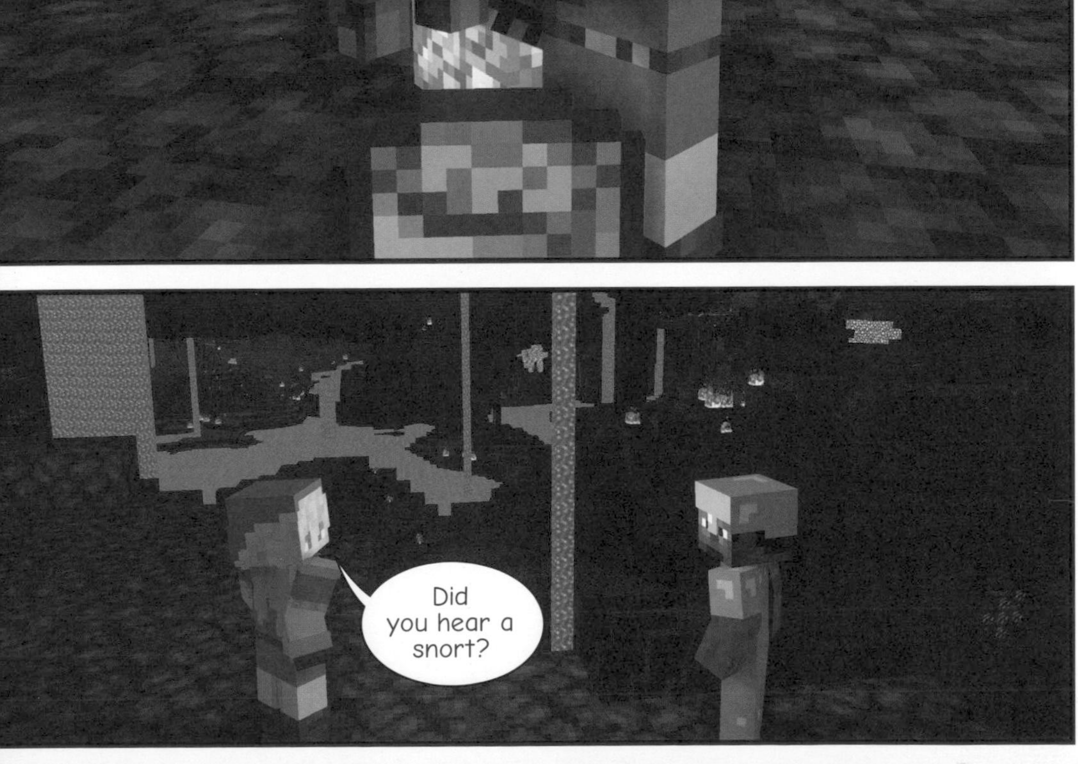
Did you hear a snort?

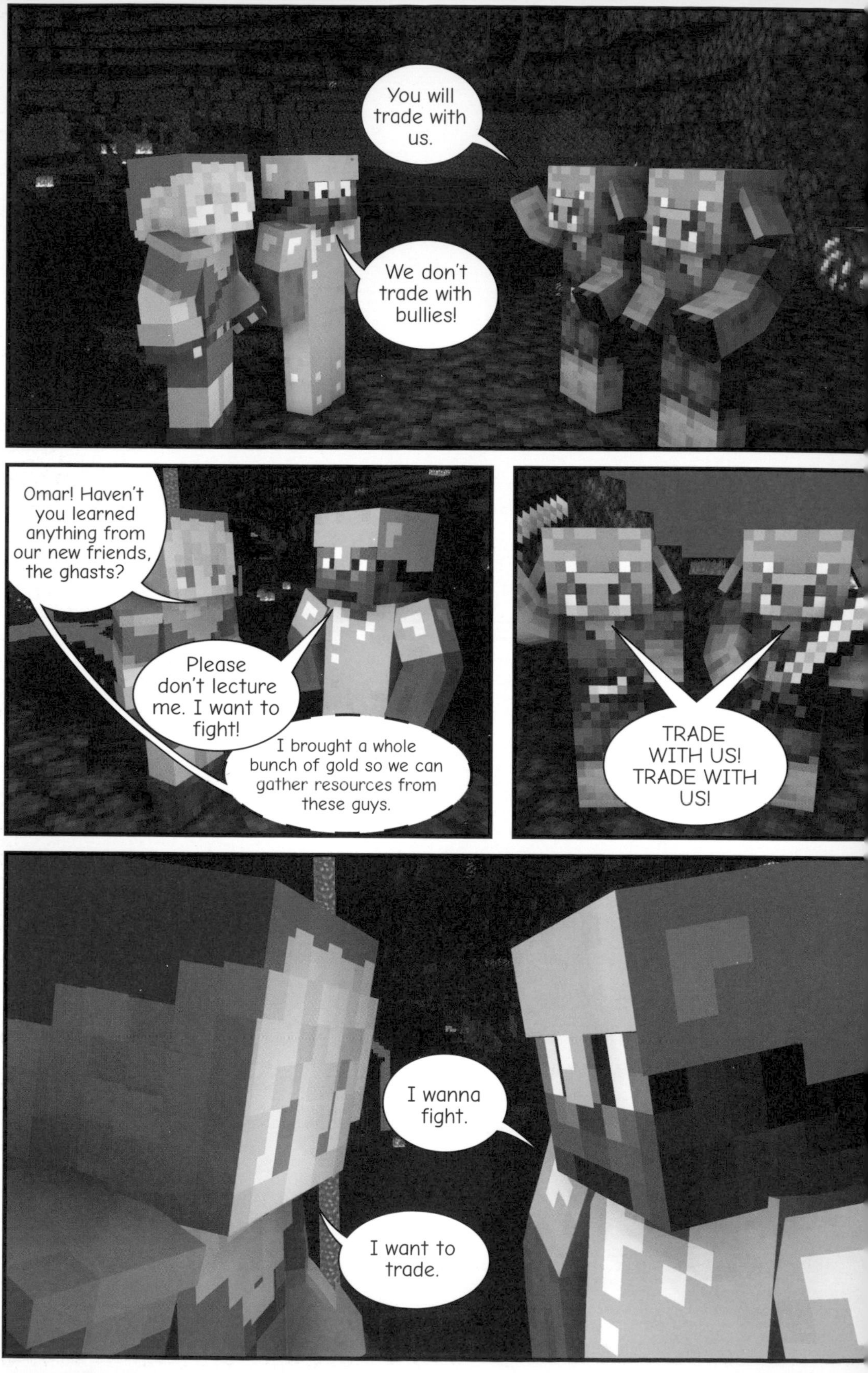
You will trade with us.
We don't trade with bullies!
Omar! Haven't you learned anything from our new friends, the ghasts?
Please don't lecture me. I want to fight!
I brought a whole bunch of gold so we can gather resources from these guys.
TRADE WITH US! TRADE WITH US!
I wanna fight.
I want to trade.

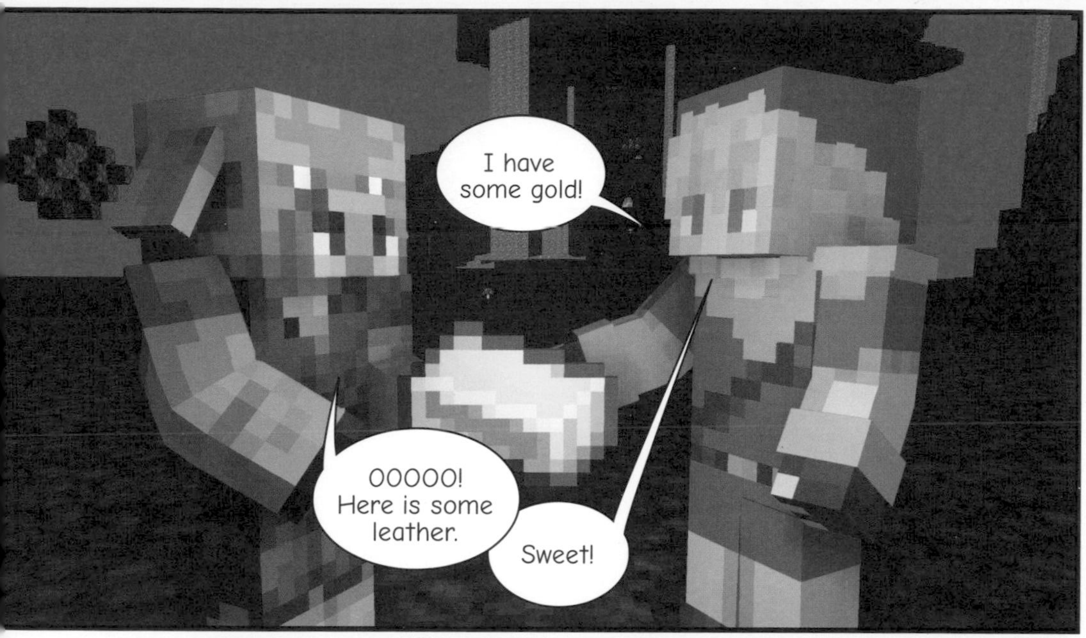
I have some gold!
OOOOO! Here is some leather.
Sweet!
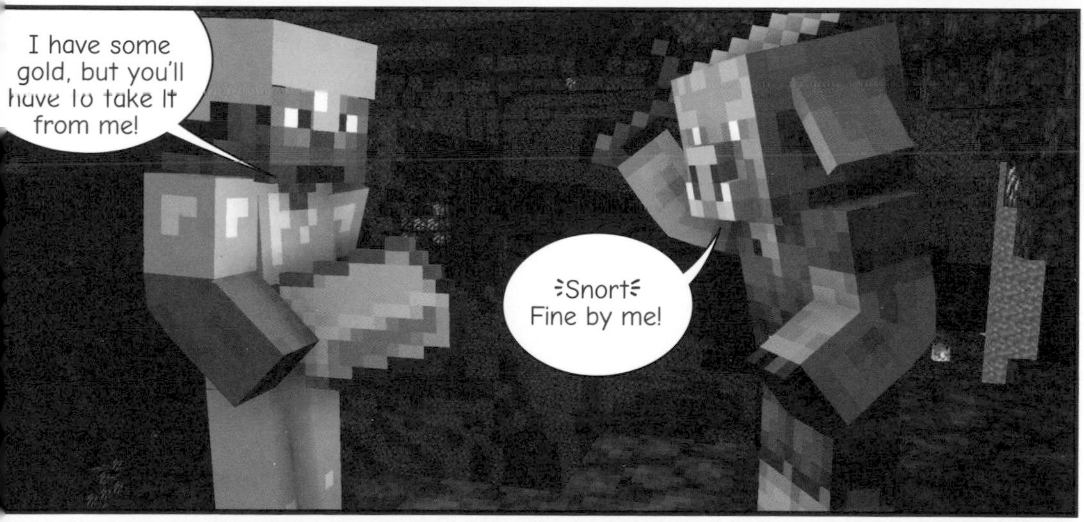
I have some gold, but you'll have to take it from me!
Snort
Fine by me!
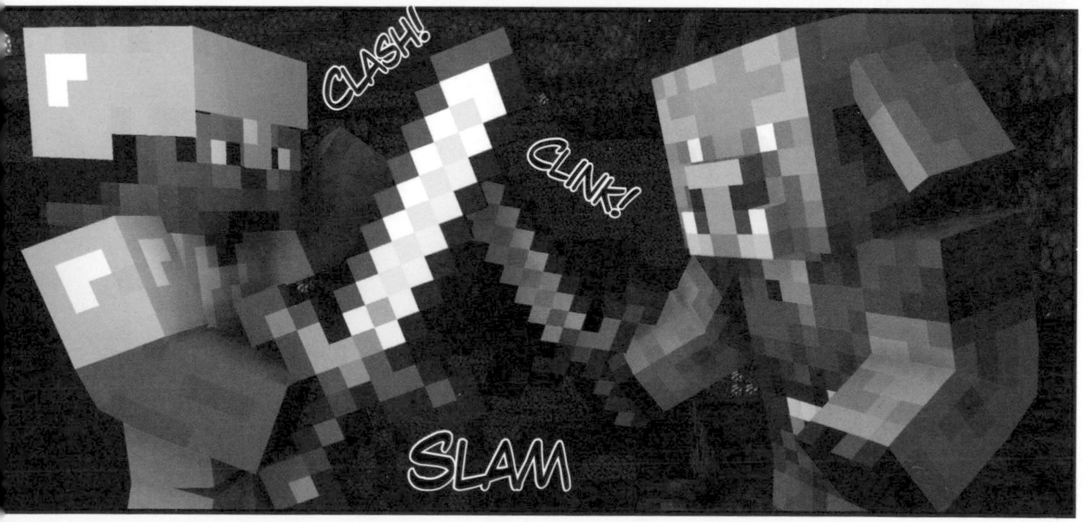
CLASH!
CLINK!
SLAM

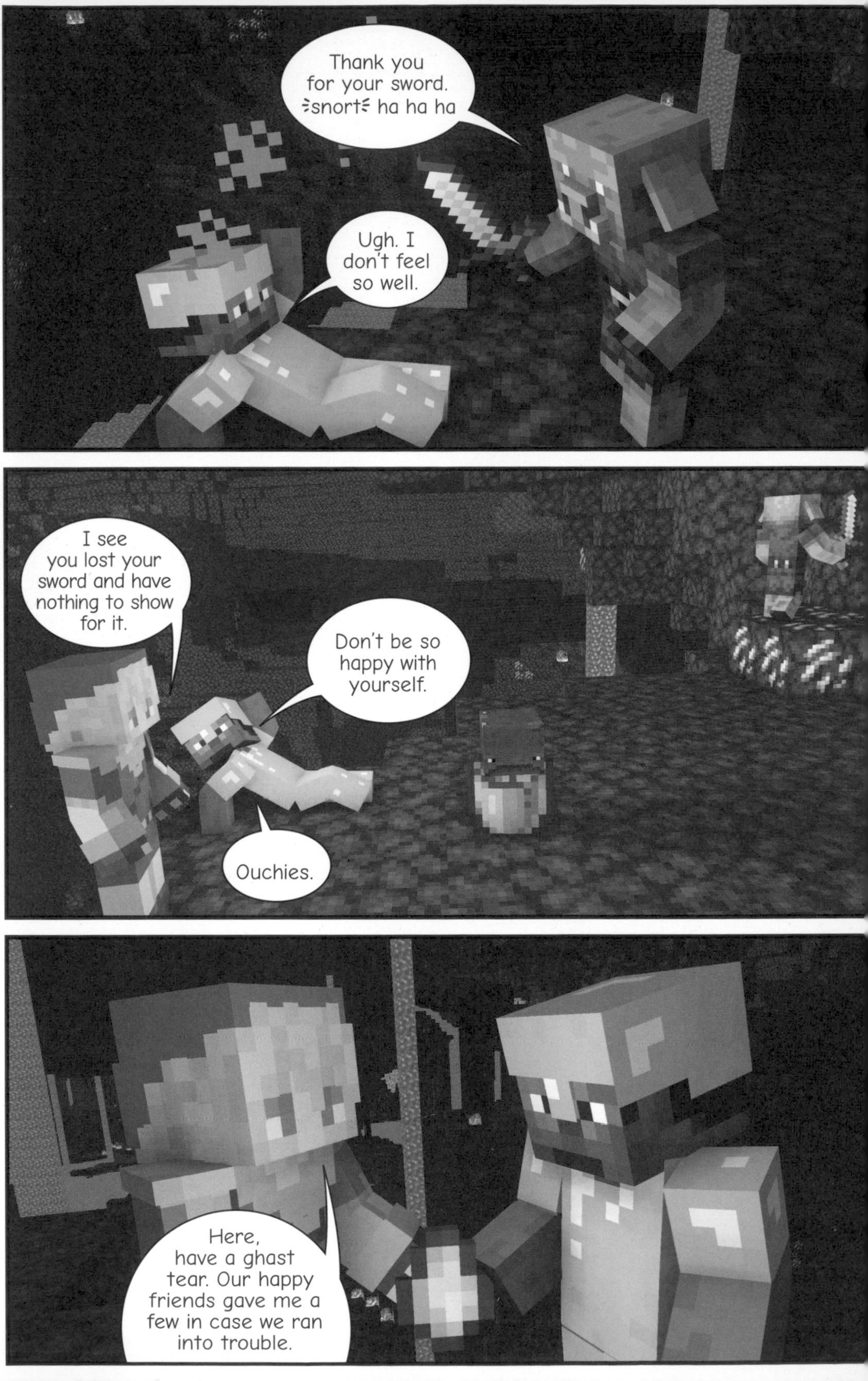
Thank you for your sword. snort ha ha ha
Ugh. I don't feel so well.
I see you lost your sword and have nothing to show for it.
Don't be so happy with yourself.
Ouchies.
Here, have a ghast tear. Our happy friends gave me a few in case we ran into trouble.

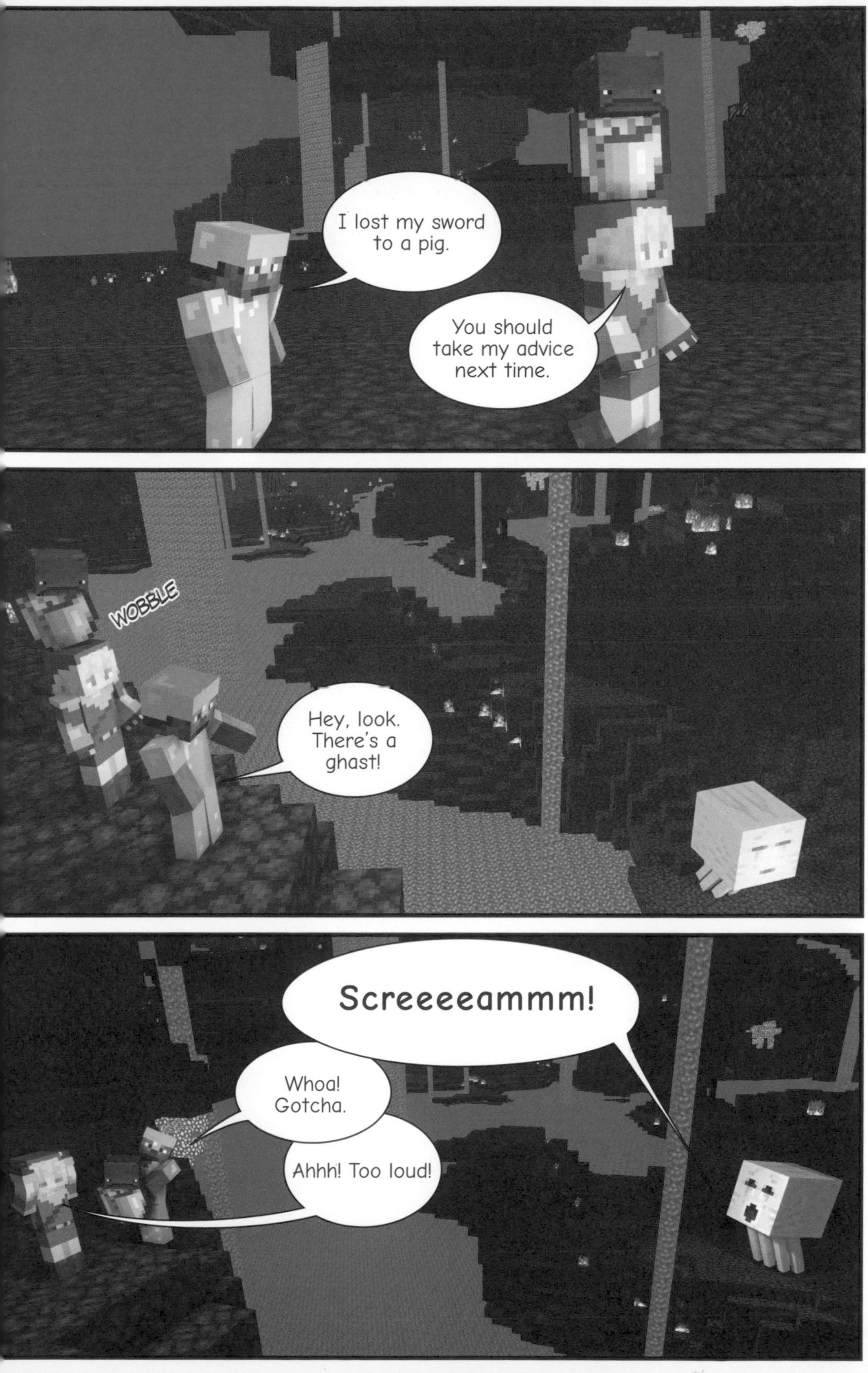
I lost my sword to a pig.
You should take my advice next time.
WOBBLE
Hey, look. There's a ghast!
Screeeeammm!
Whoa! Gotcha.
Ahhh! Too loud!

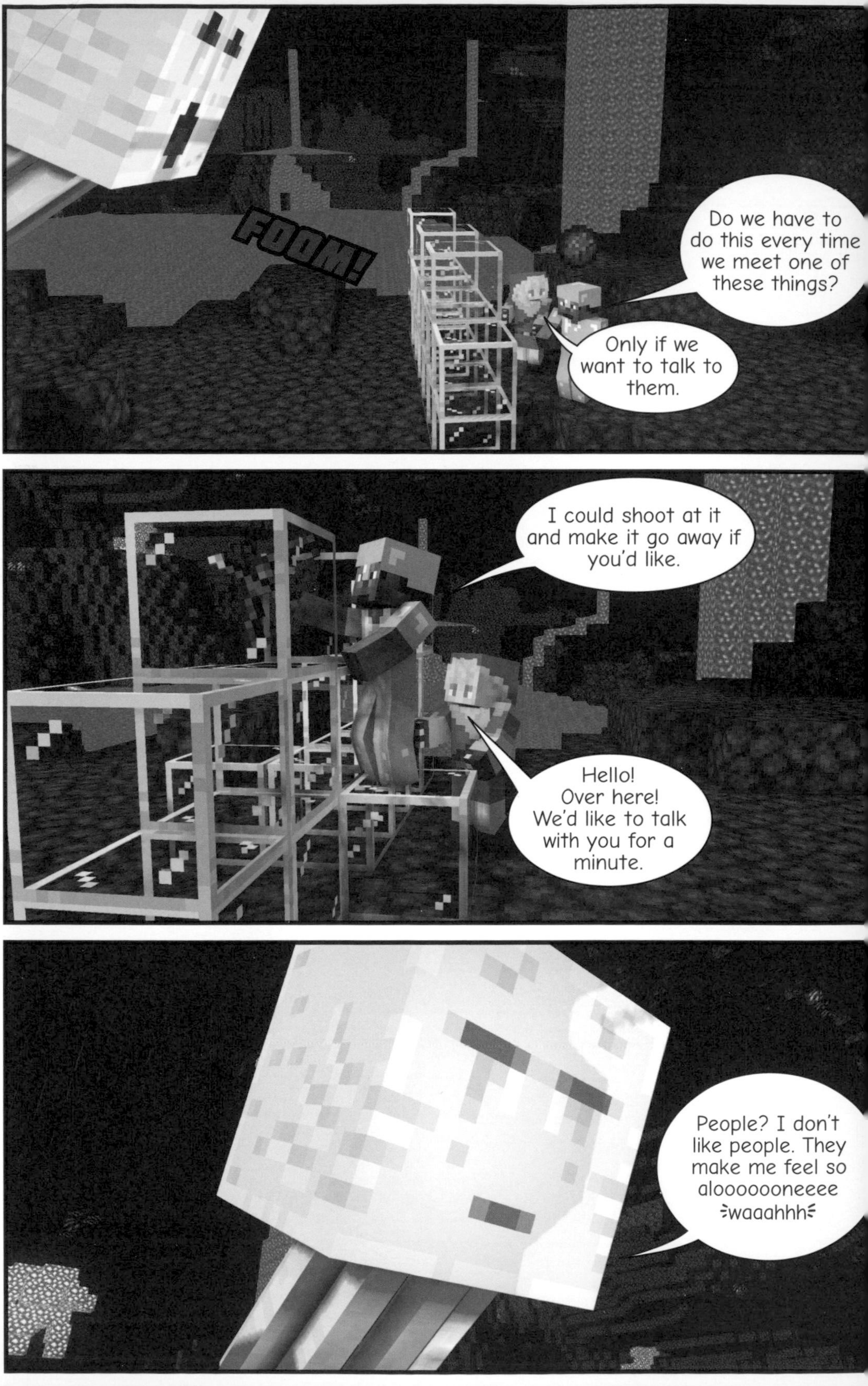
FOOM!
Do we have to do this every time we meet one of these things?
Only if we want to talk to them.
I could shoot at it and make it go away if you'd like.
Hello! Over here! We'd like to talk with you for a minute.
People? I don't like people. They make me feel so aloooooneeee waaahhh

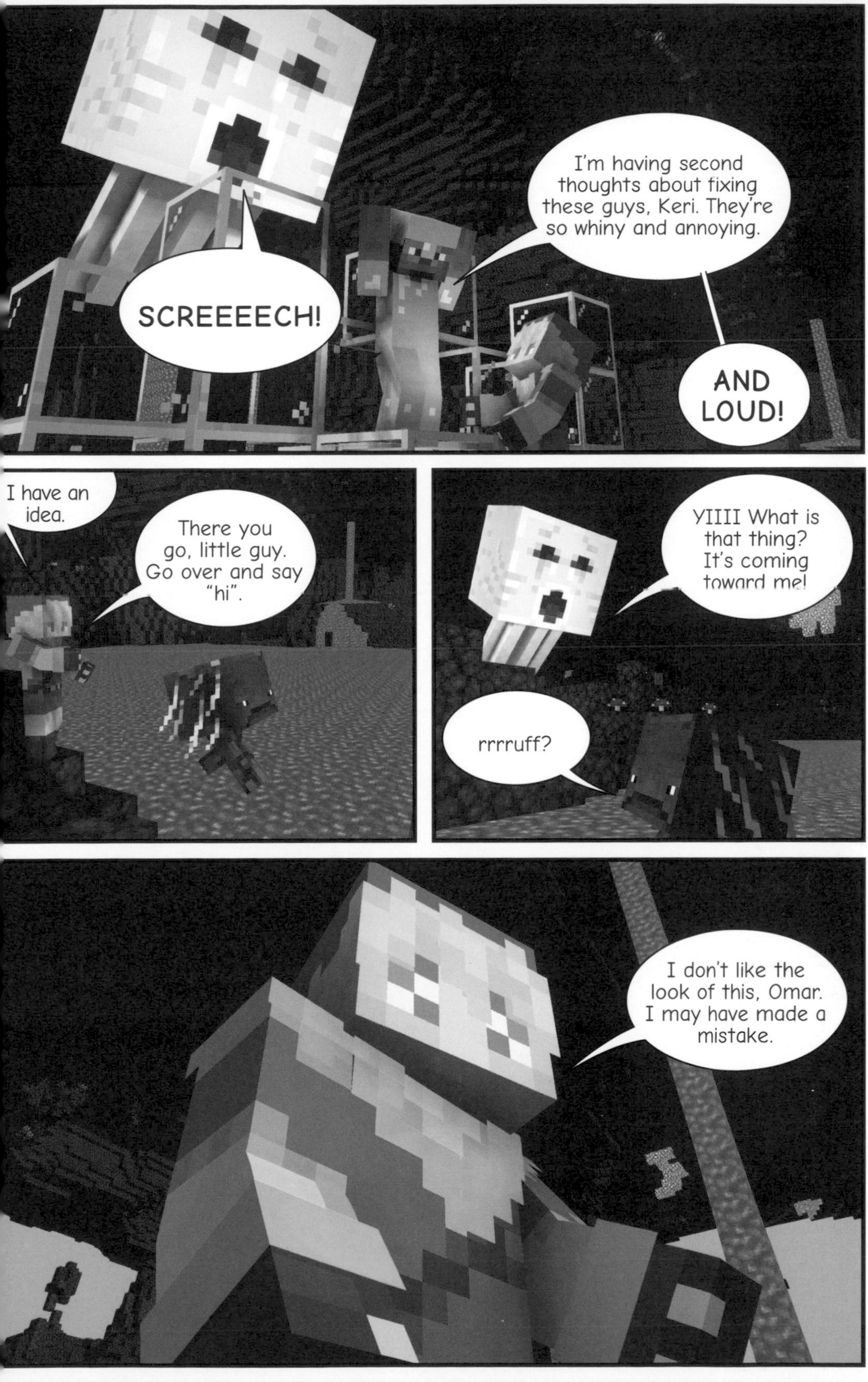
SCREEEECH!
I'm having second thoughts about fixing these guys, Keri. They're so whiny and annoying.
AND LOUD!
I have an idea.
There you go, little guy. Go over and say "hi".
YIIII What is that thing? It's coming toward me!
rrrruff?
I don't like the look of this, Omar. I may have made a mistake.

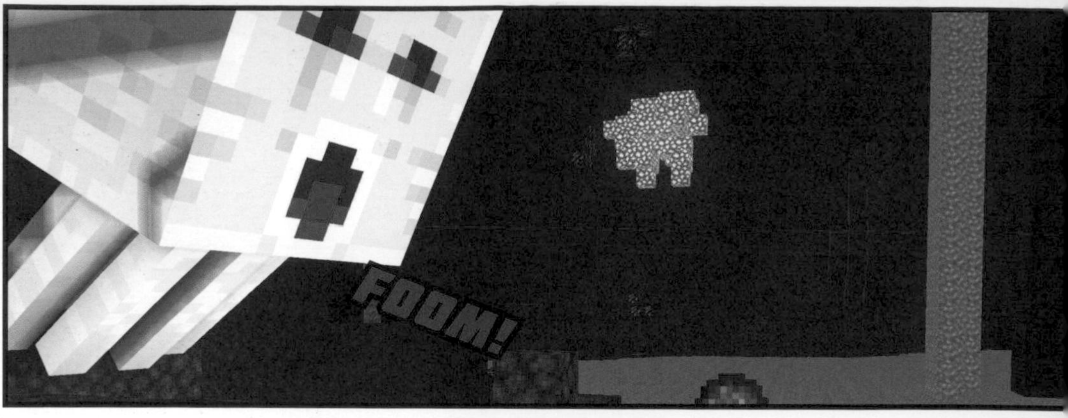
FOOM!

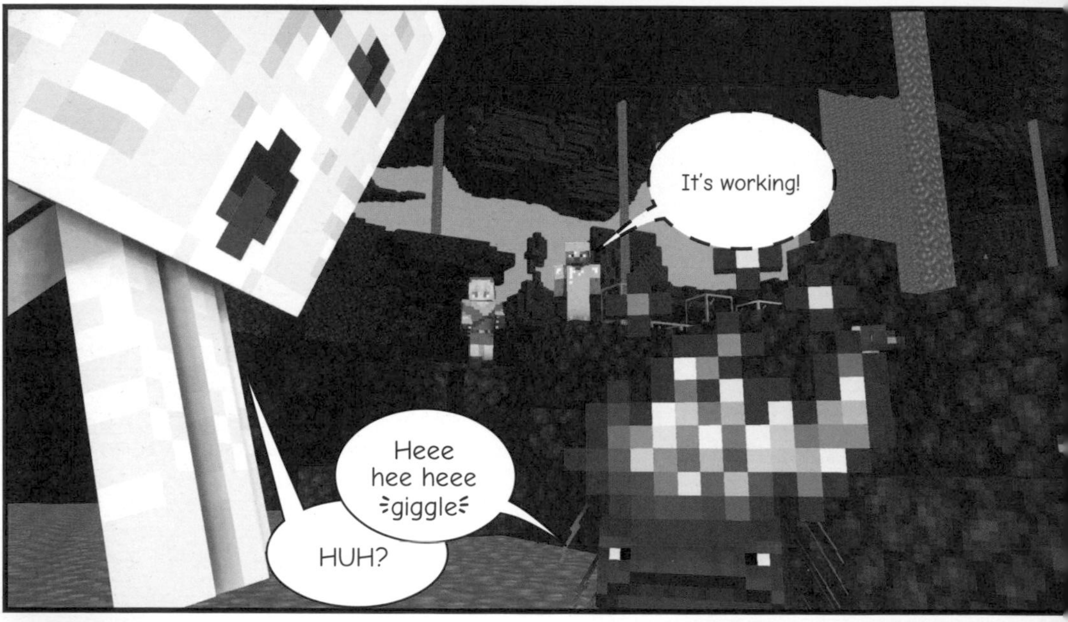
It's working!
Heee hee heee giggle
HUH?

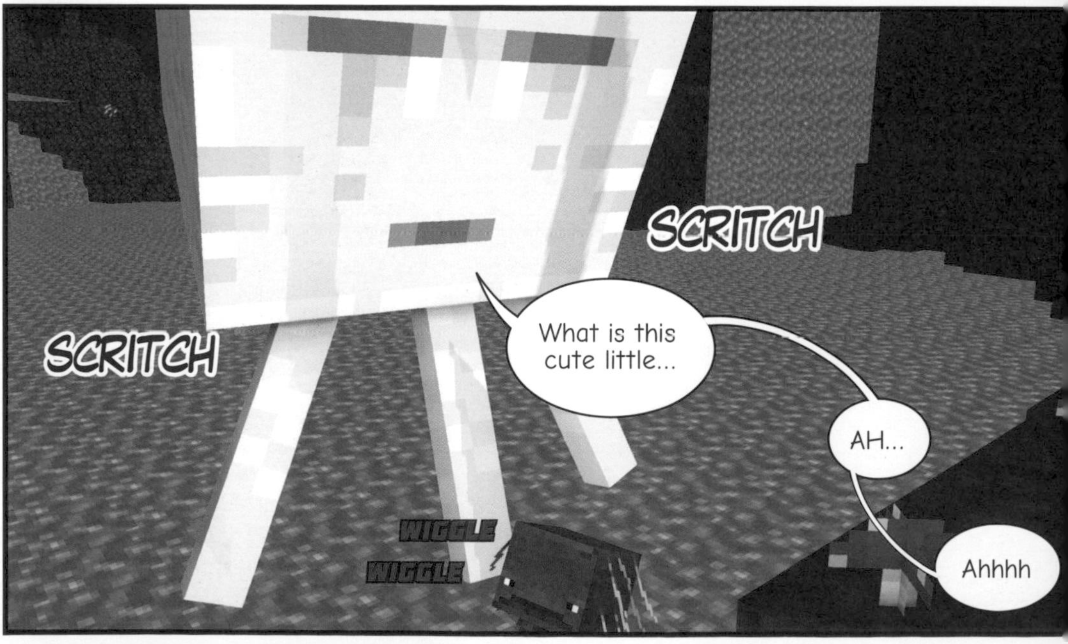
SCRITCH
SCRITCH
What is this cute little...
AH...
Ahhhh
WIGGLE
WIGGLE

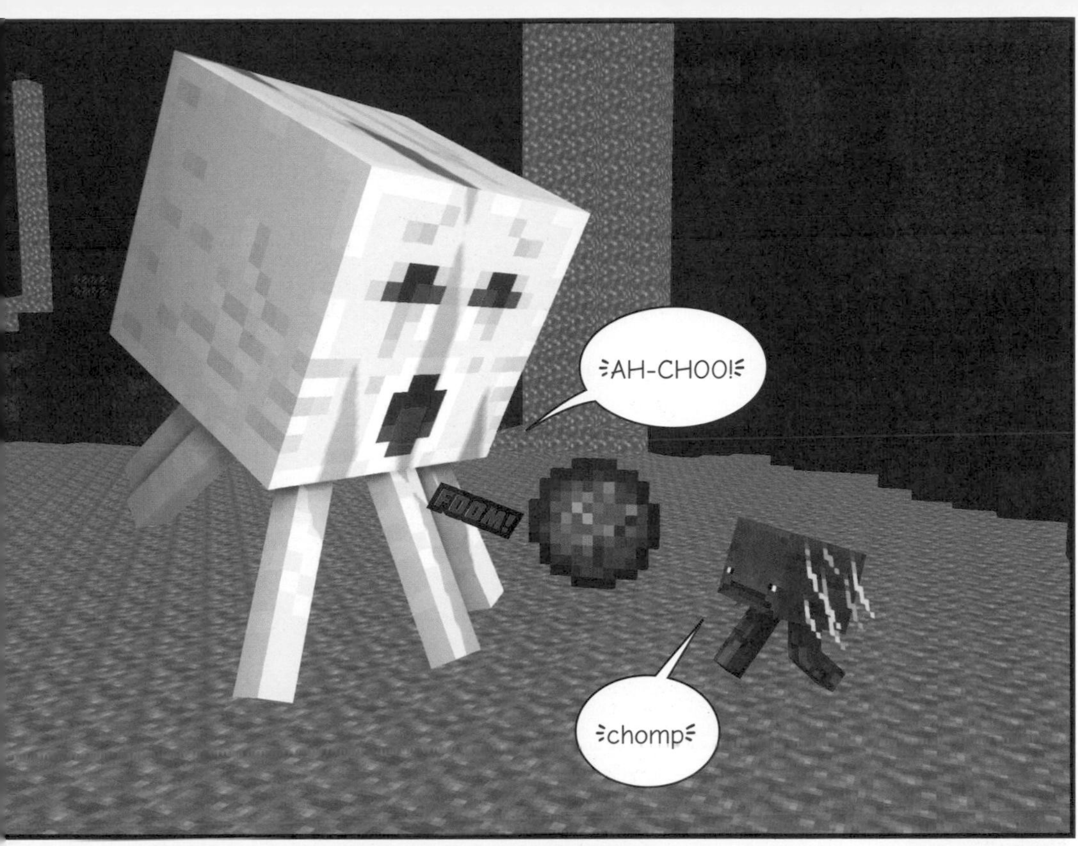
AH-CHOO!
FOOM!
chomp

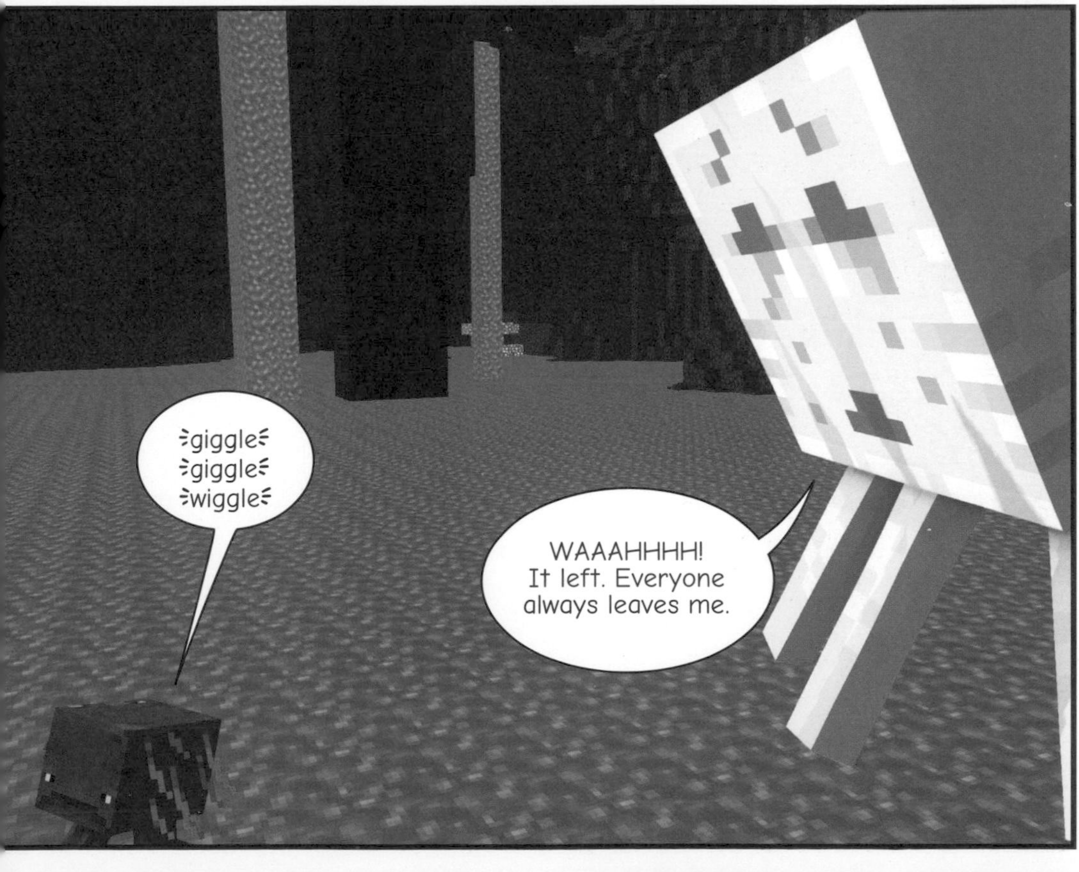
giggle
giggle
wiggle
WAAAHHHH!
It left. Everyone
always leaves me.

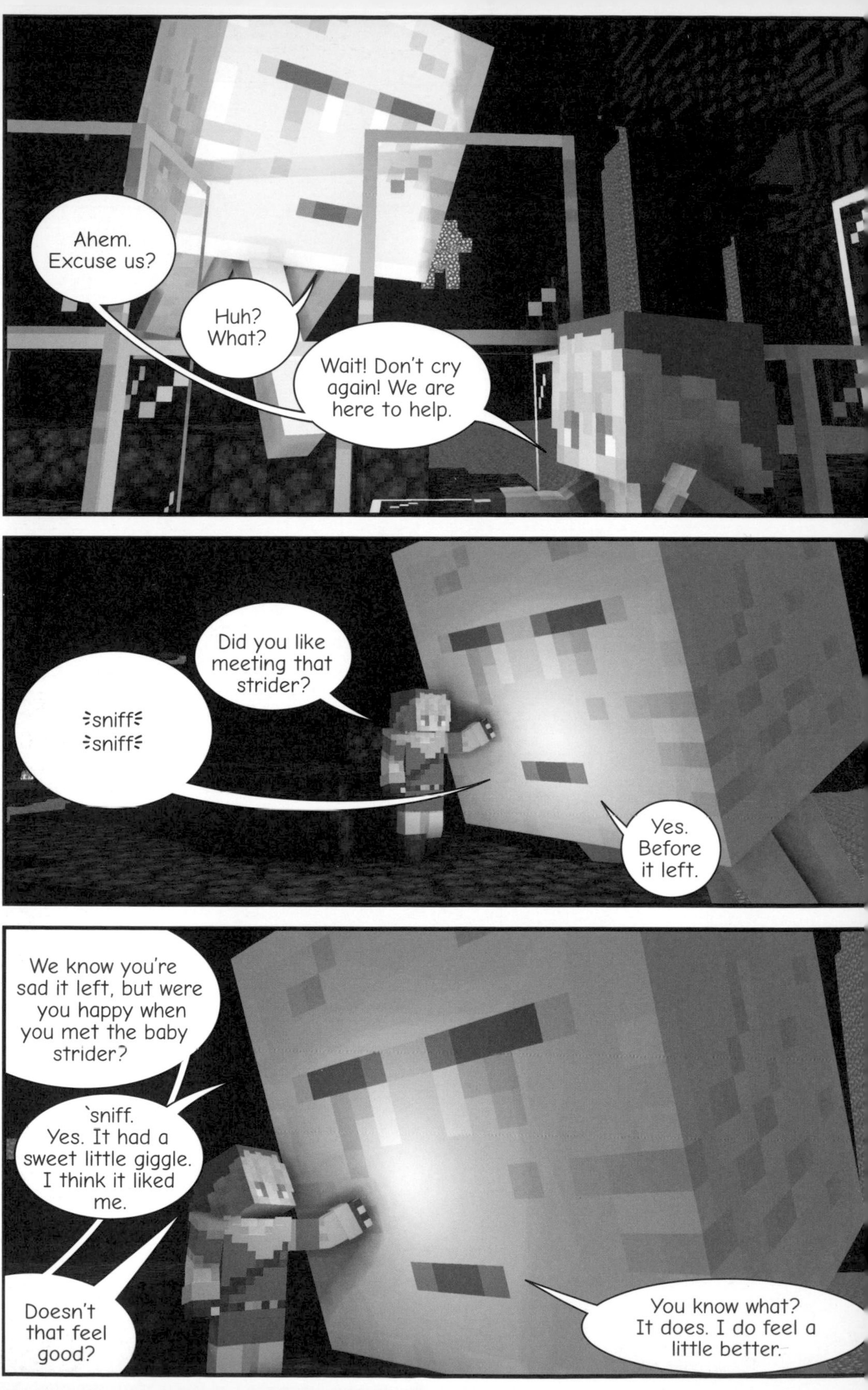
Ahem. Excuse us?
Huh? What?
Wait! Don't cry again! We are here to help.
Did you like meeting that strider?
sniff sniff
Yes. Before it left.
We know you're sad it left, but were you happy when you met the baby strider?
`sniff. Yes. It had a sweet little giggle. I think it liked me.
Doesn't that feel good?
You know what? It does. I do feel a little better.

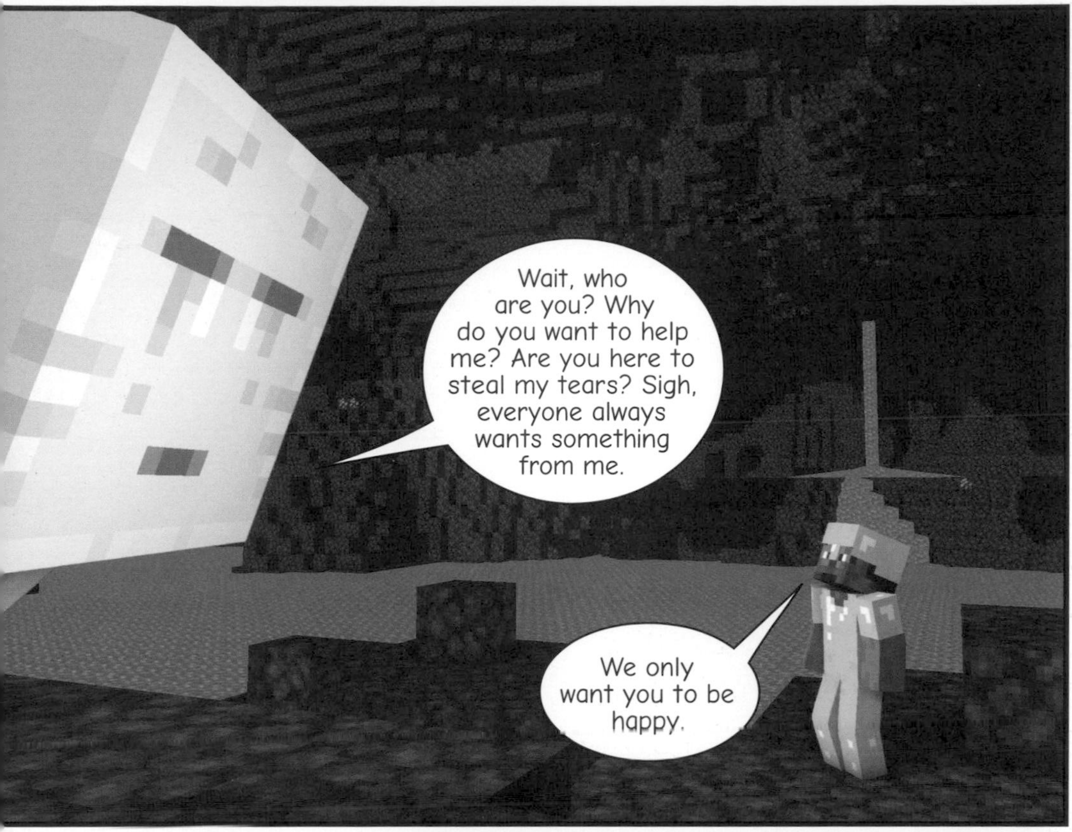
Wait, who are you? Why do you want to help me? Are you here to steal my tears? Sigh, everyone always wants something from me.
We only want you to be happy.

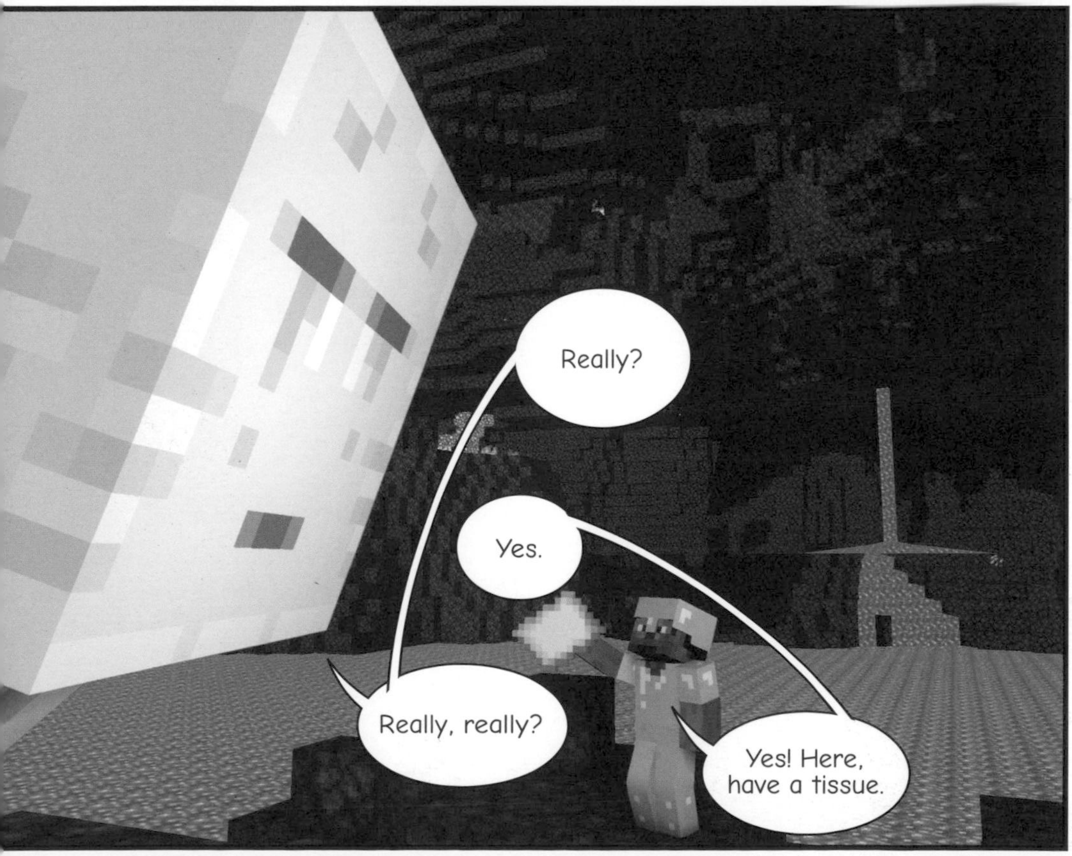
Really?
Yes.
Really, really?
Yes! Here, have a tissue.

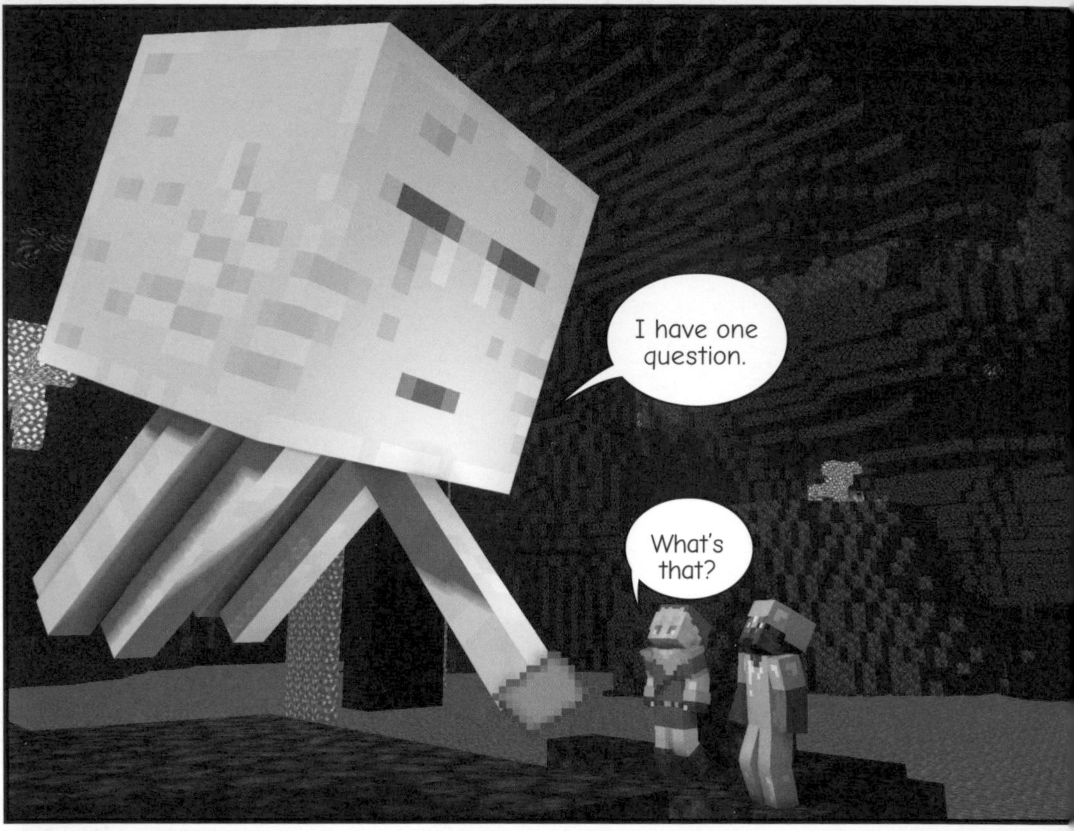
I have one question.
What's that?

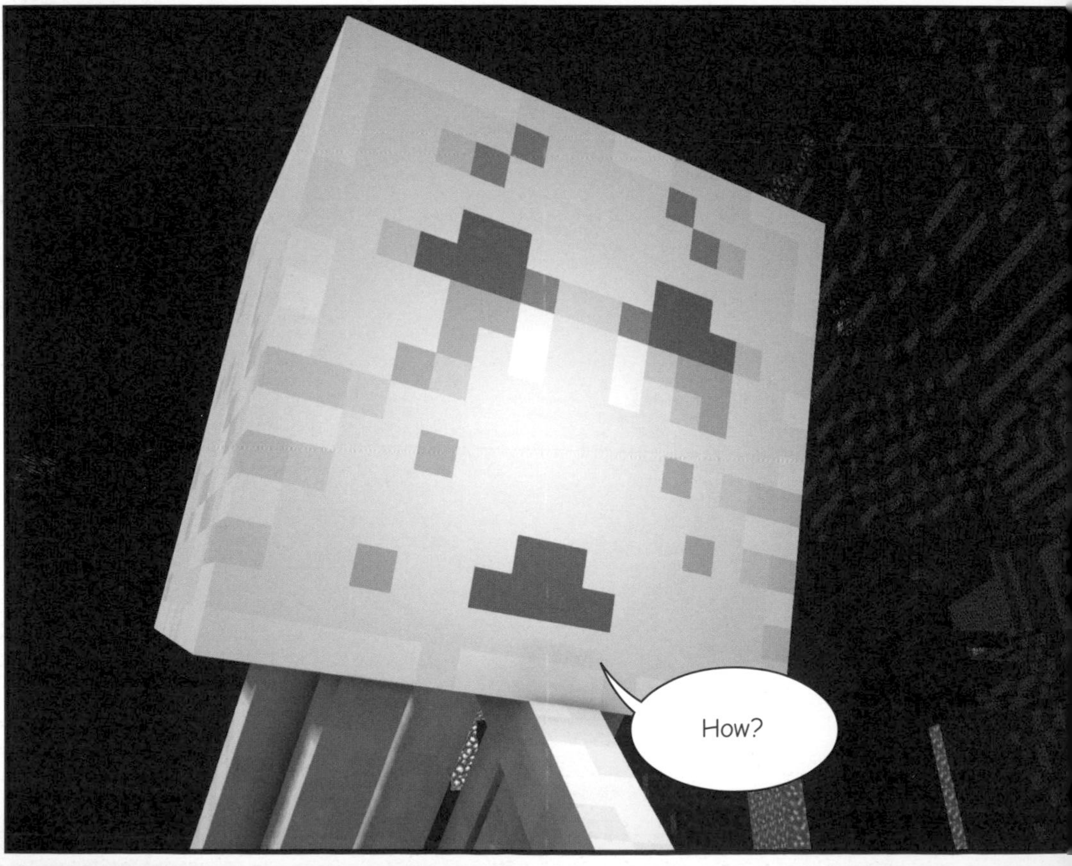
How?

Chapter 6
Spreading Happiness

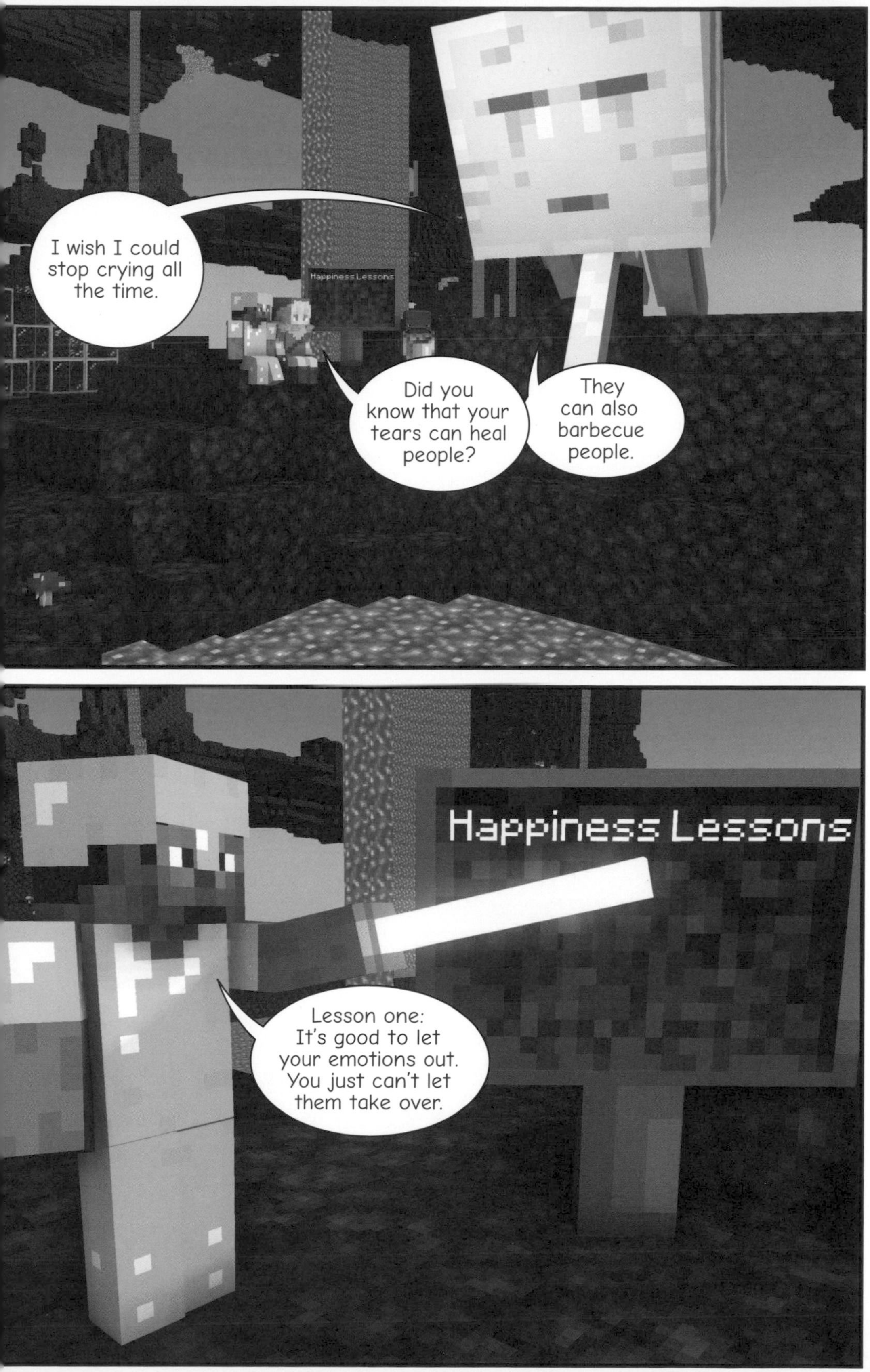
I wish I could stop crying all the time.
Happiness Lessons
Did you know that your tears can heal people?
They can also barbecue people.
Happiness Lessons
Lesson one: It's good to let your emotions out. You just can't let them take over.

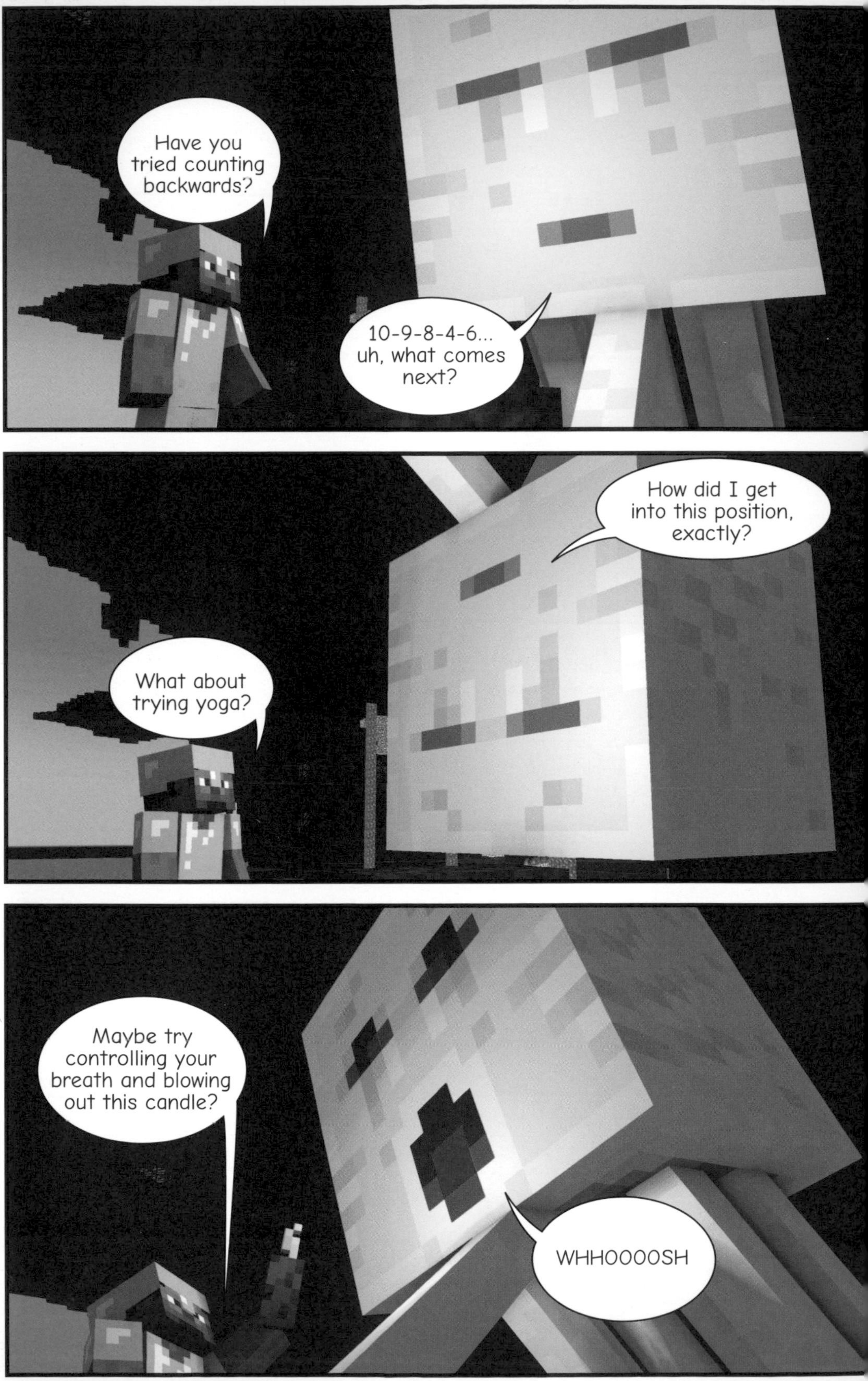
Have you tried counting backwards?
10-9-8-4-6... uh, what comes next?
How did I get into this position, exactly?
What about trying yoga?
Maybe try controlling your breath and blowing out this candle?
WHHOOOOSH

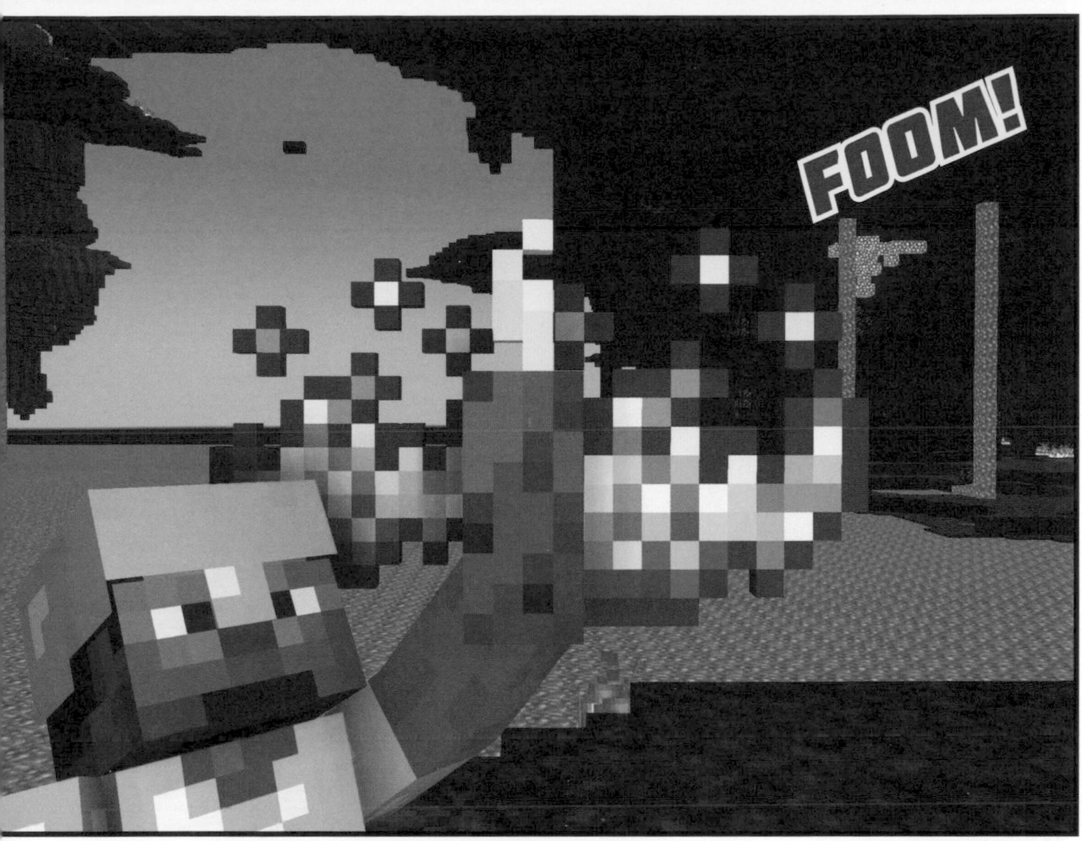
FOOM!

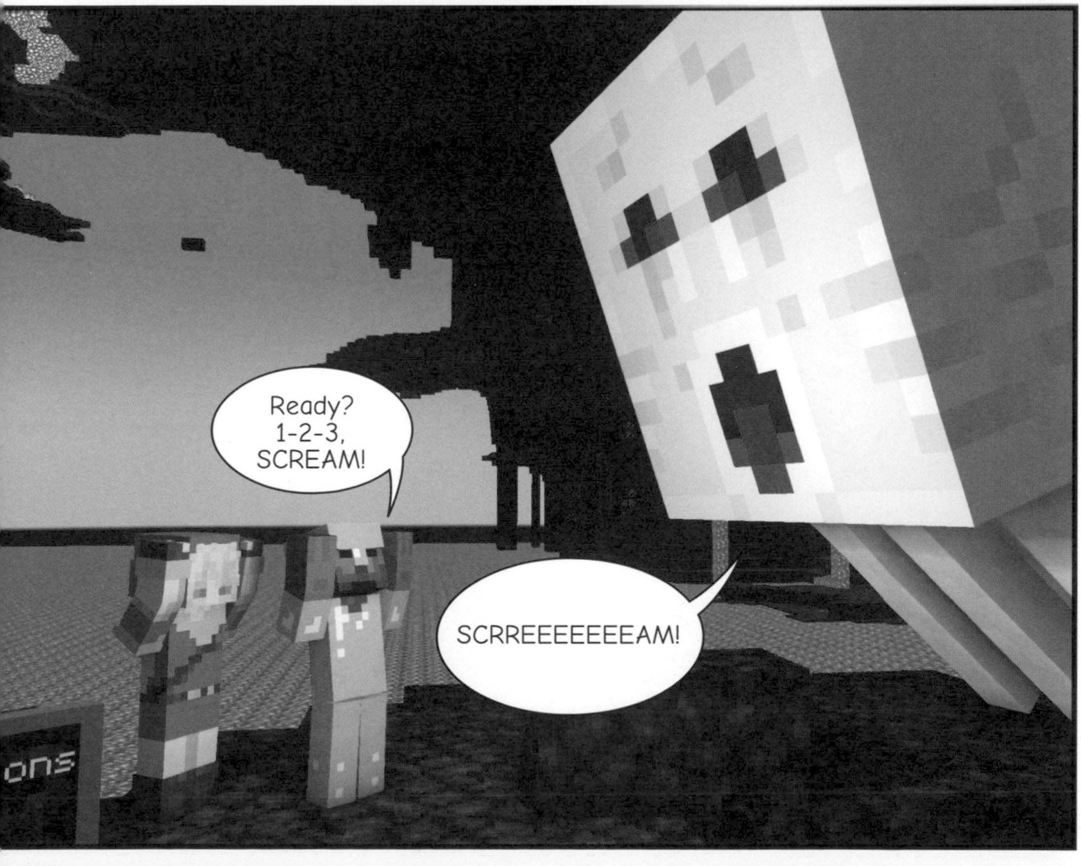
Ready? 1-2-3, SCREAM!
SCRREEEEEEEAM!

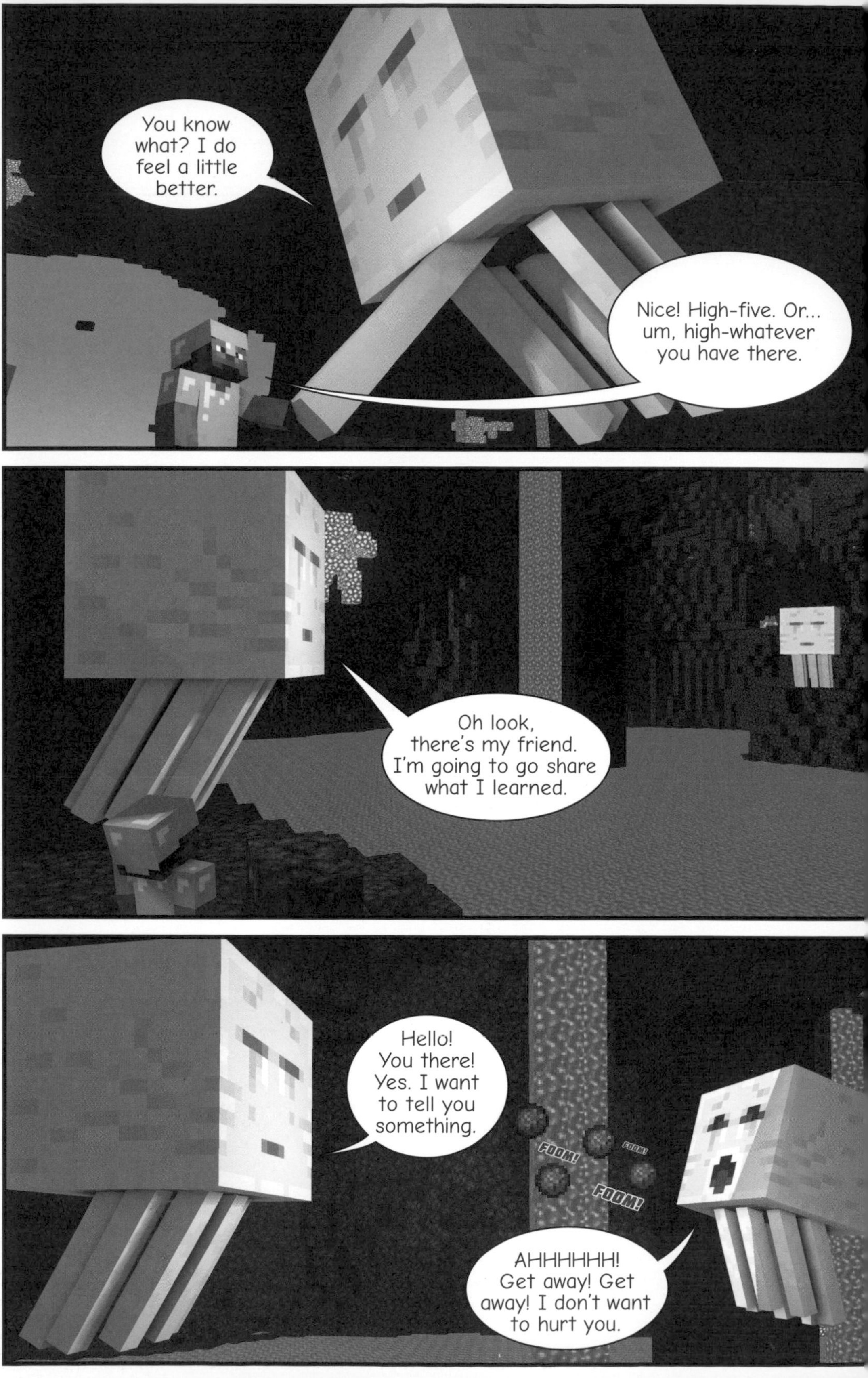
You know what? I do feel a little better.
Nice! High-five. Or... um, high-whatever you have there.
Oh look, there's my friend. I'm going to go share what I learned.
Hello! You there! Yes. I want to tell you something.
FOOM!
FOOM!
FOOM!
AHHHHHH! Get away! Get away! I don't want to hurt you.

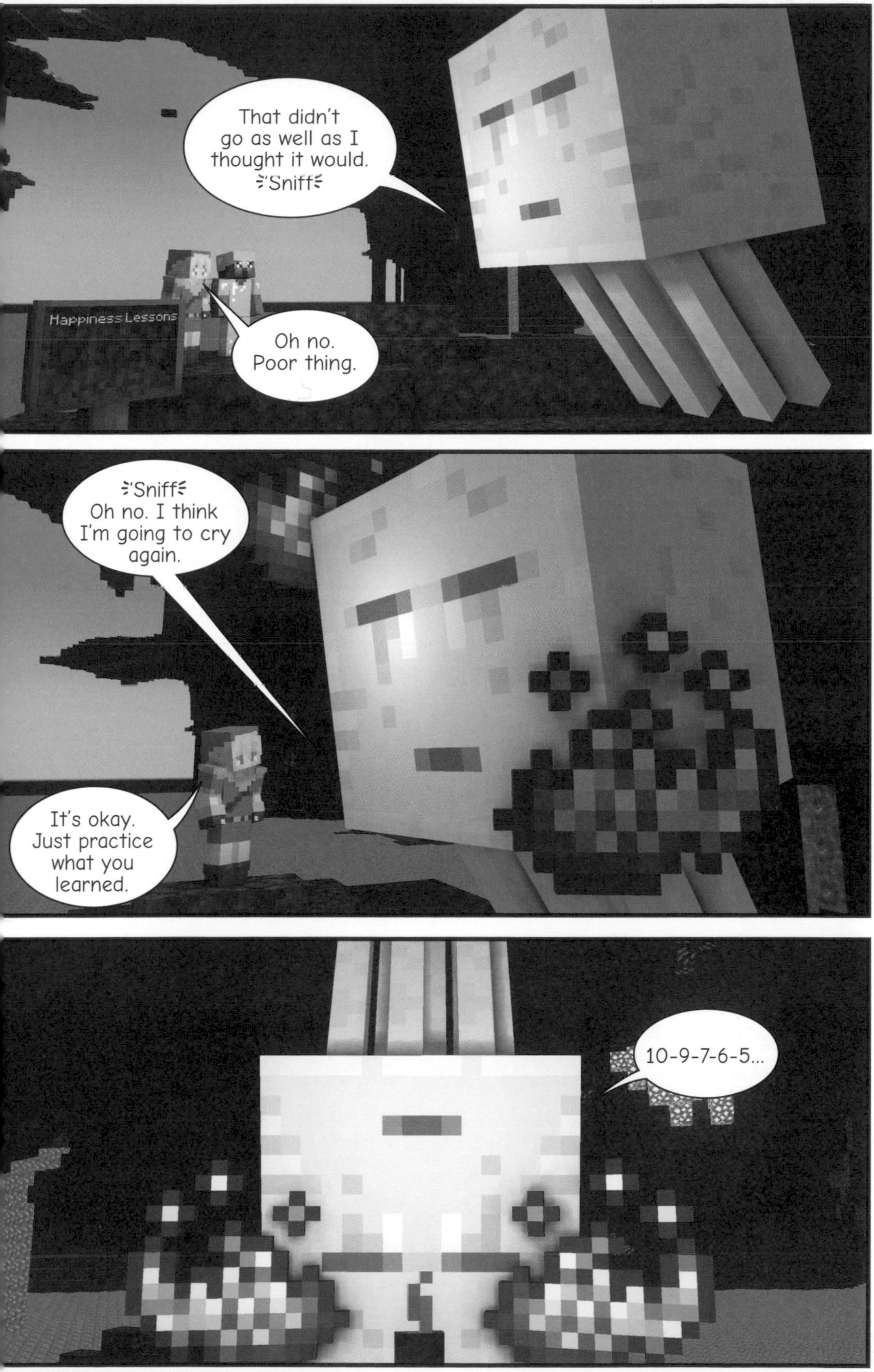
That didn't go as well as I thought it would. *Sniff*
Happiness Lessons
Oh no. Poor thing.
Sniff Oh no. I think I'm going to cry again.
It's okay. Just practice what you learned.
10-9-7-6-5...

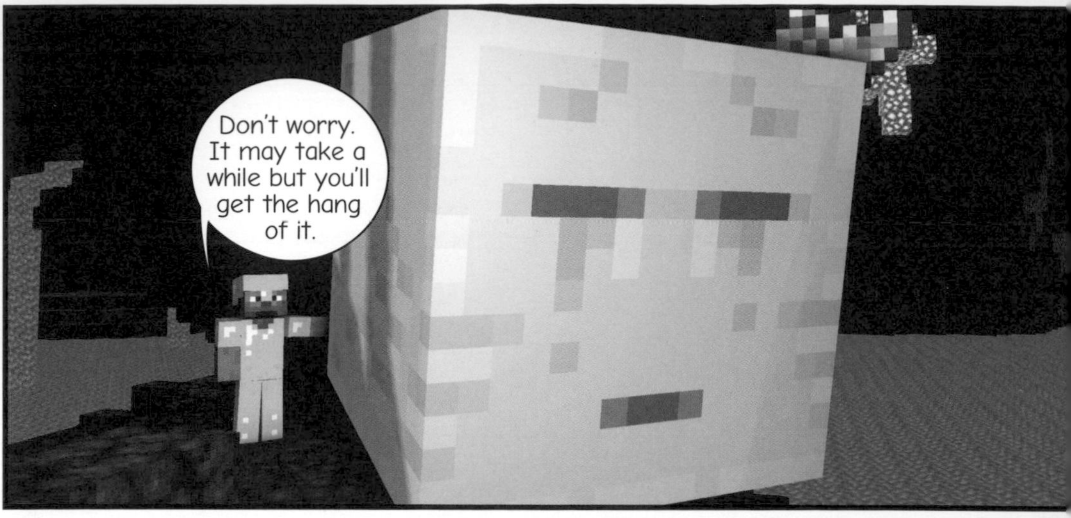
Don't worry. It may take a while but you'll get the hang of it.

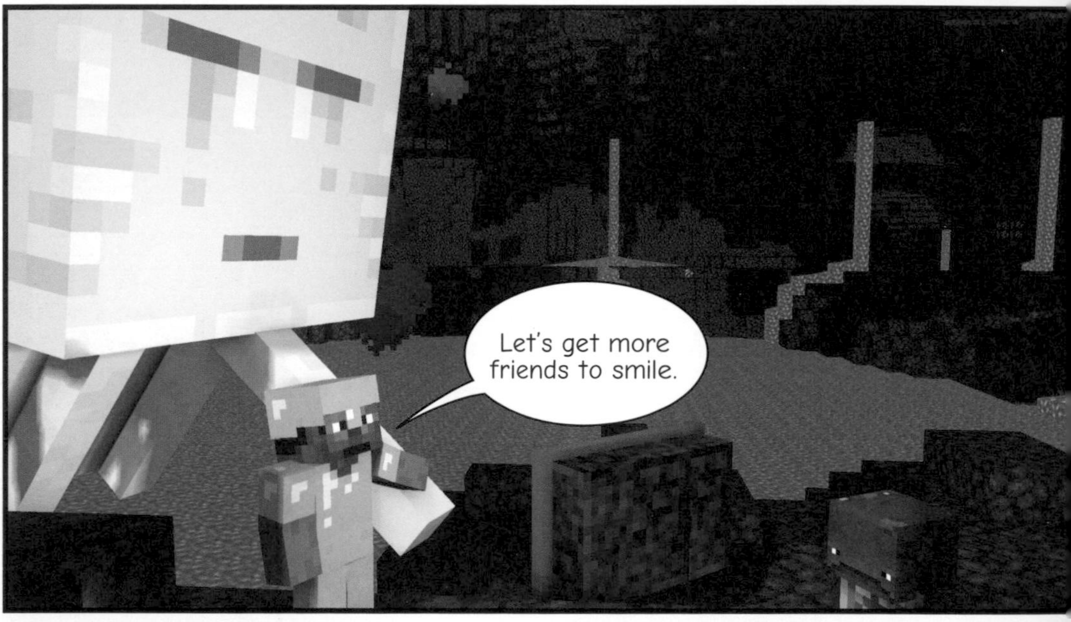
Let's get more friends to smile.

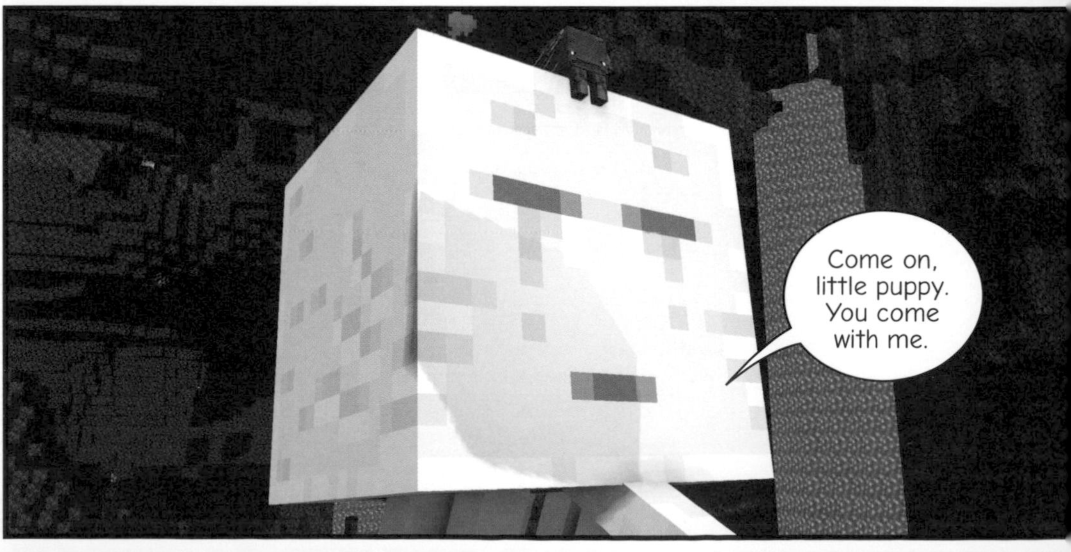
Come on, little puppy. You come with me.

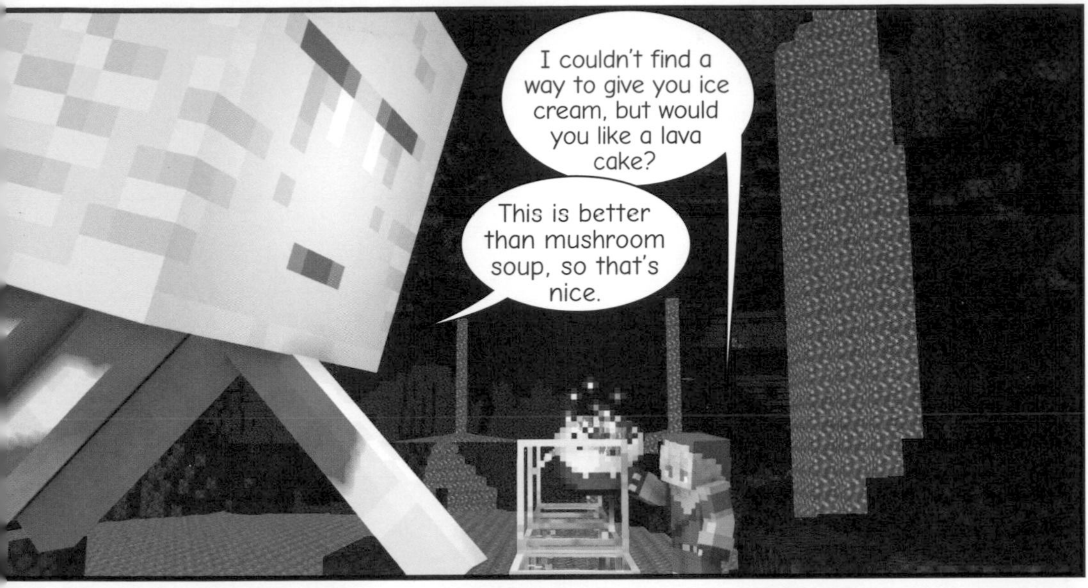
I couldn't find a way to give you ice cream, but would you like a lava cake?
This is better than mushroom soup, so that's nice.

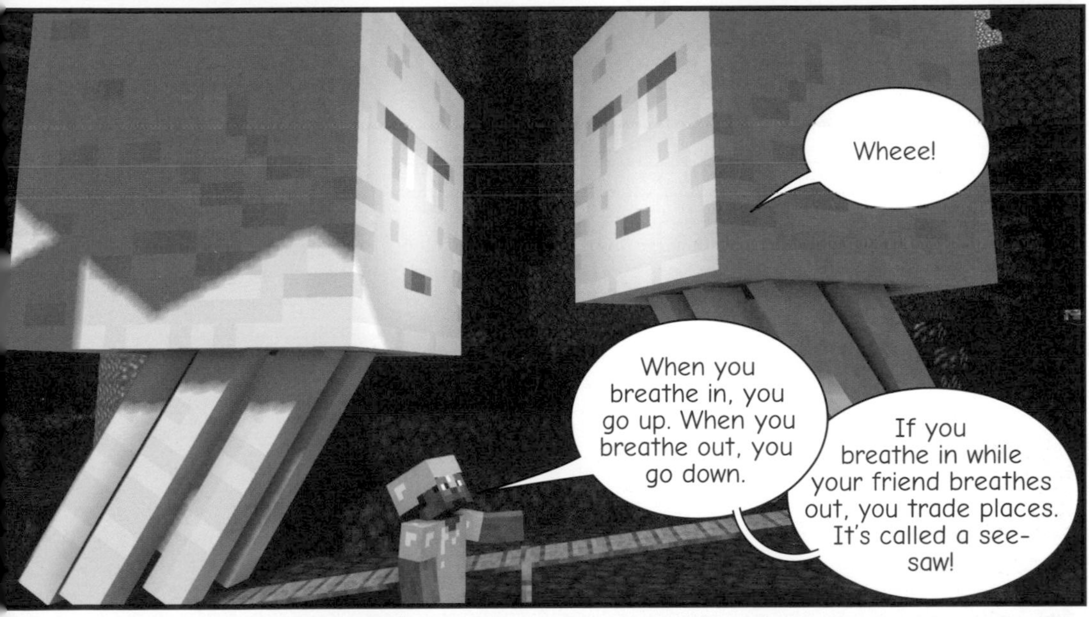
Wheee!
When you breathe in, you go up. When you breathe out, you go down.
If you breathe in while your friend breathes out, you trade places. It's called a see-saw!

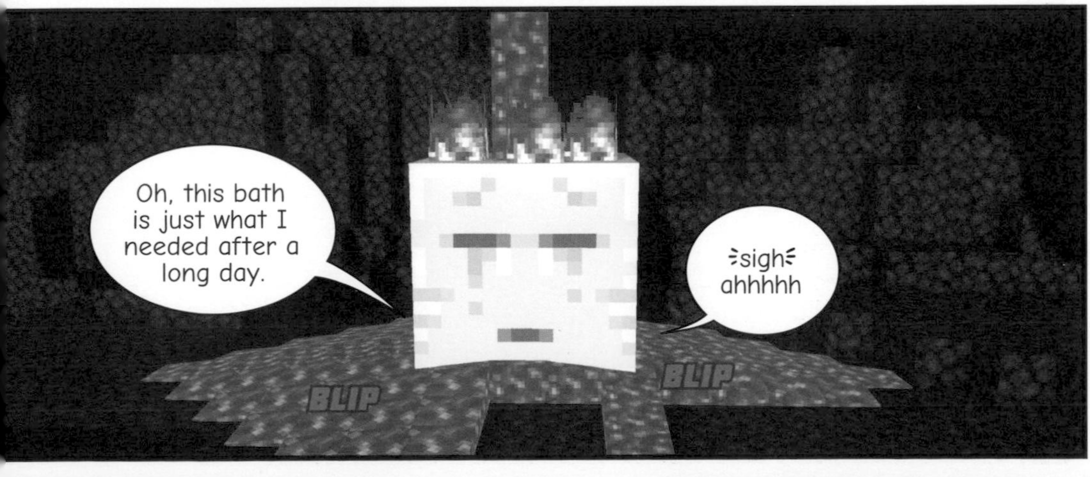
Oh, this bath is just what I needed after a long day.
sigh ahhhhh
BLIP
BLIP

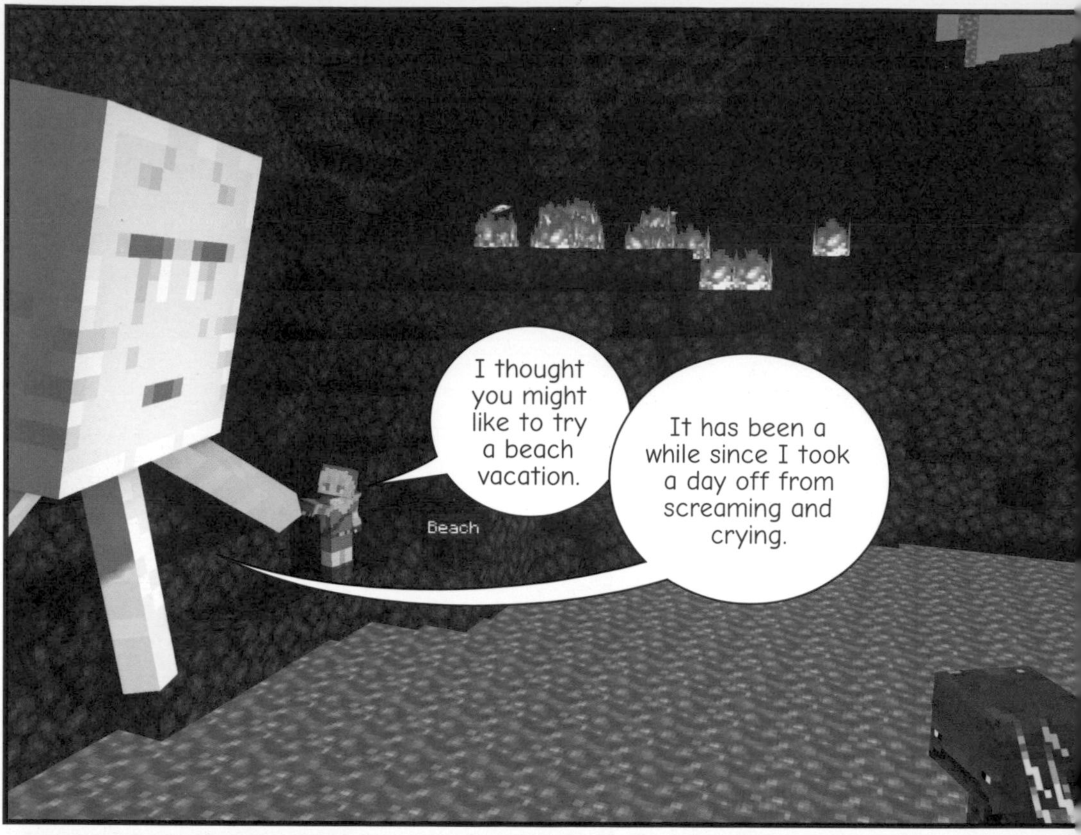
I thought you might like to try a beach vacation.
Beach
It has been a while since I took a day off from screaming and crying.

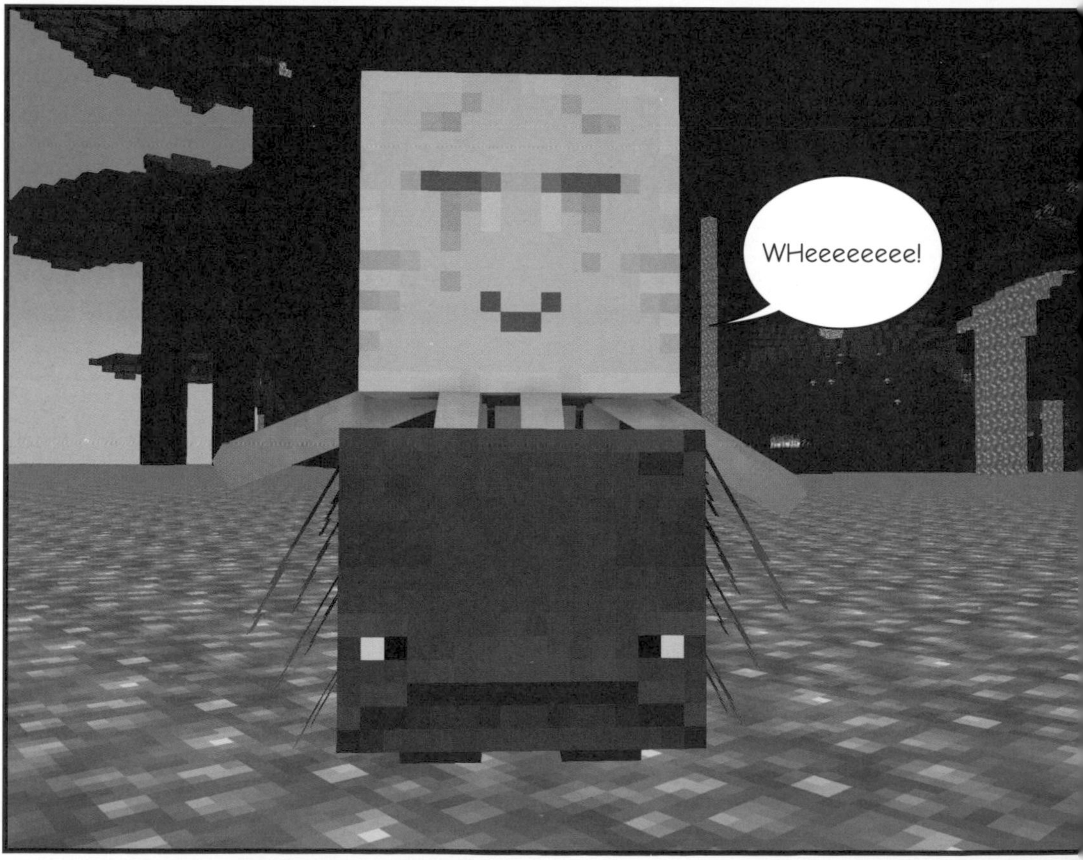
WHeeeeeeee!

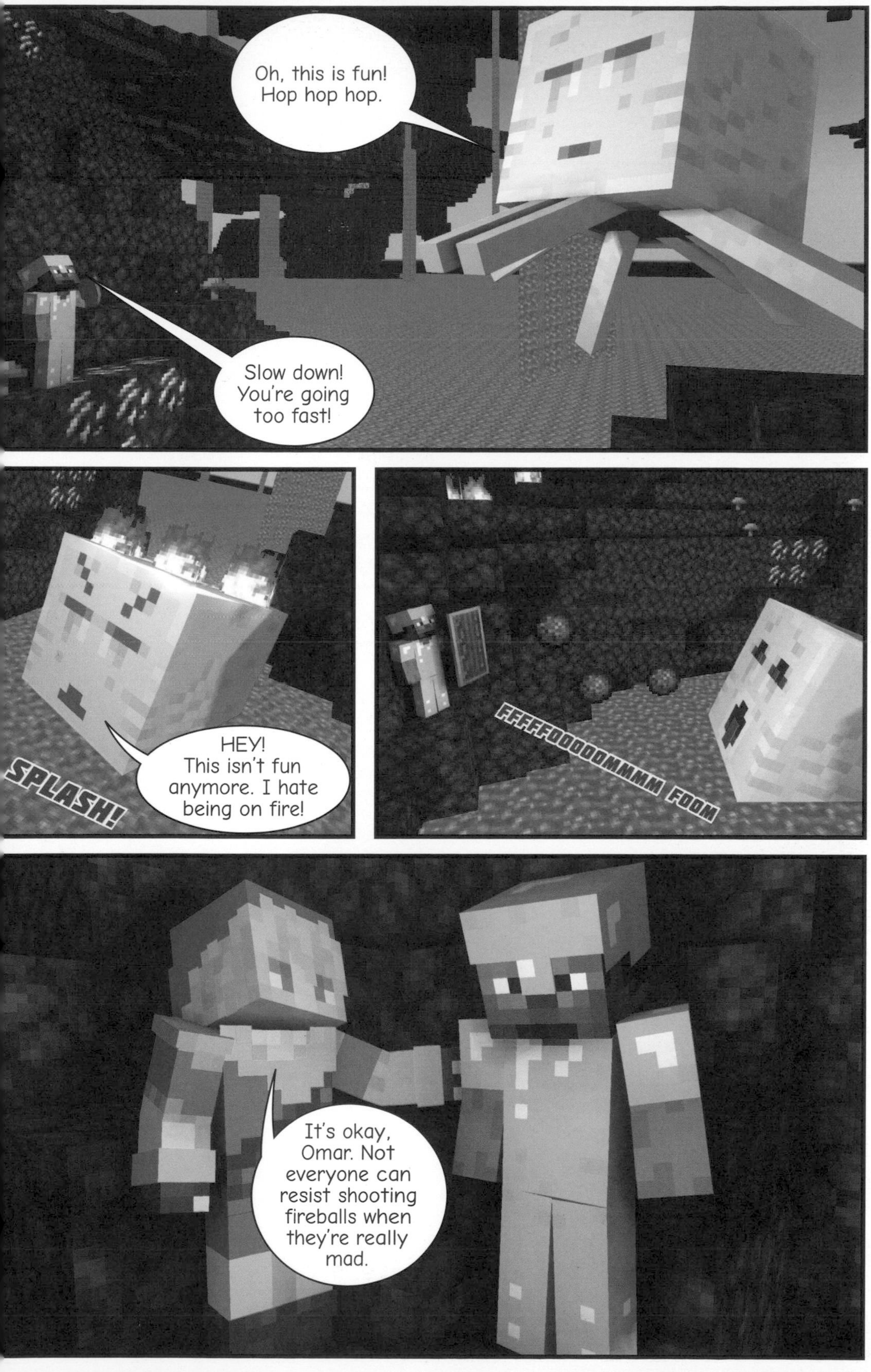
Oh, this is fun! Hop hop hop.
Slow down! You're going too fast!
SPLASH!
HEY! This isn't fun anymore. I hate being on fire!
FFFFFOOOOOOMMMM FOOM
It's okay, Omar. Not everyone can resist shooting fireballs when they're really mad.

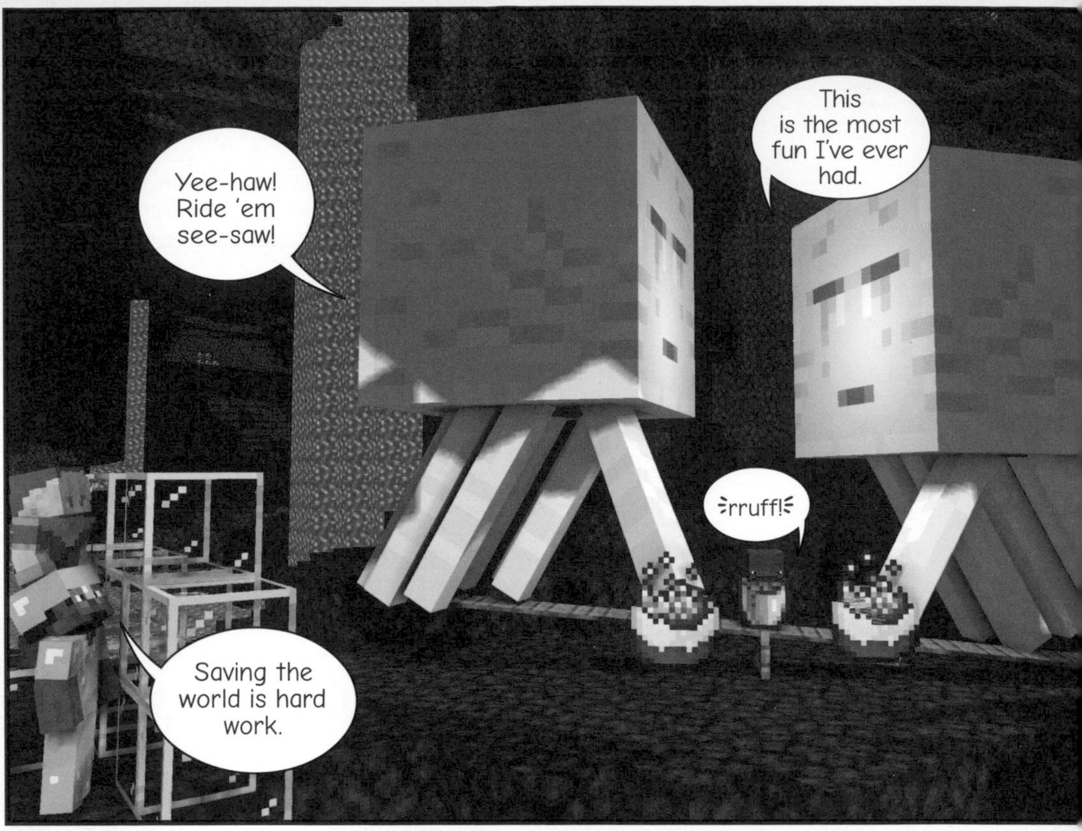
Yee-haw! Ride 'em see-saw!
This is the most fun I've ever had.
rruff!
Saving the world is hard work.

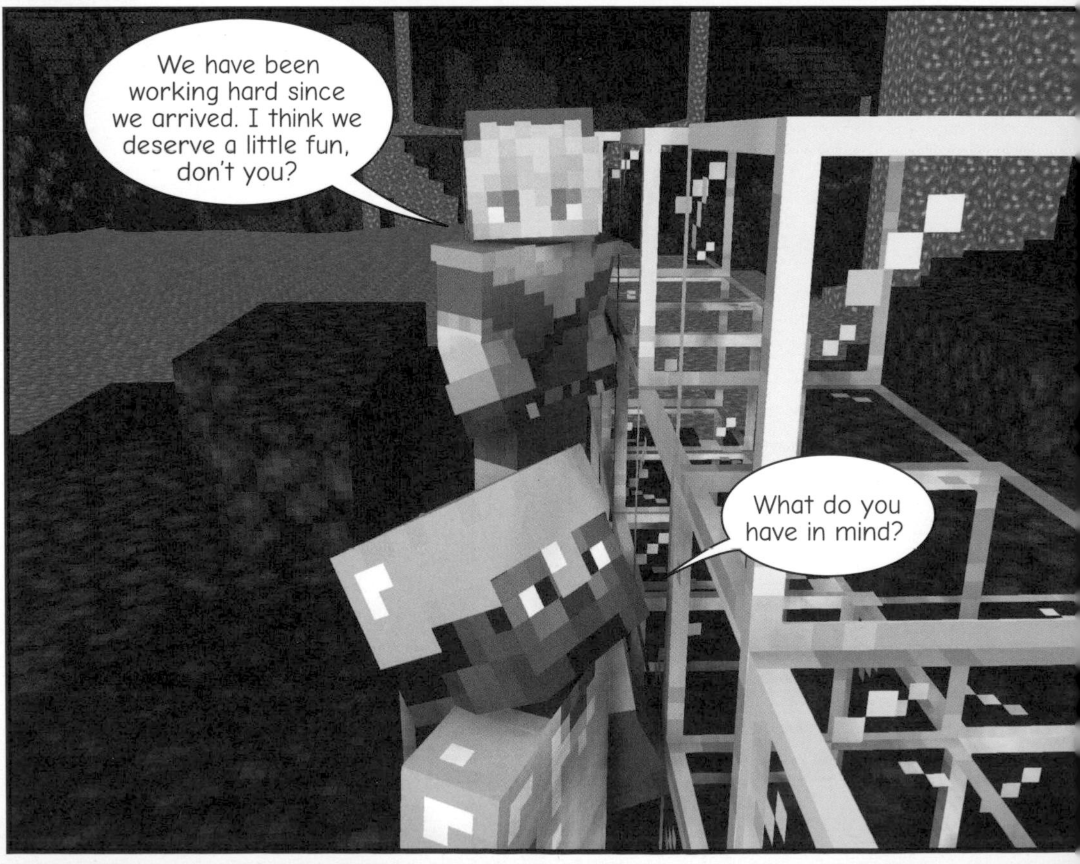
We have been working hard since we arrived. I think we deserve a little fun, don't you?
What do you have in mind?

Chapter 7
Despair

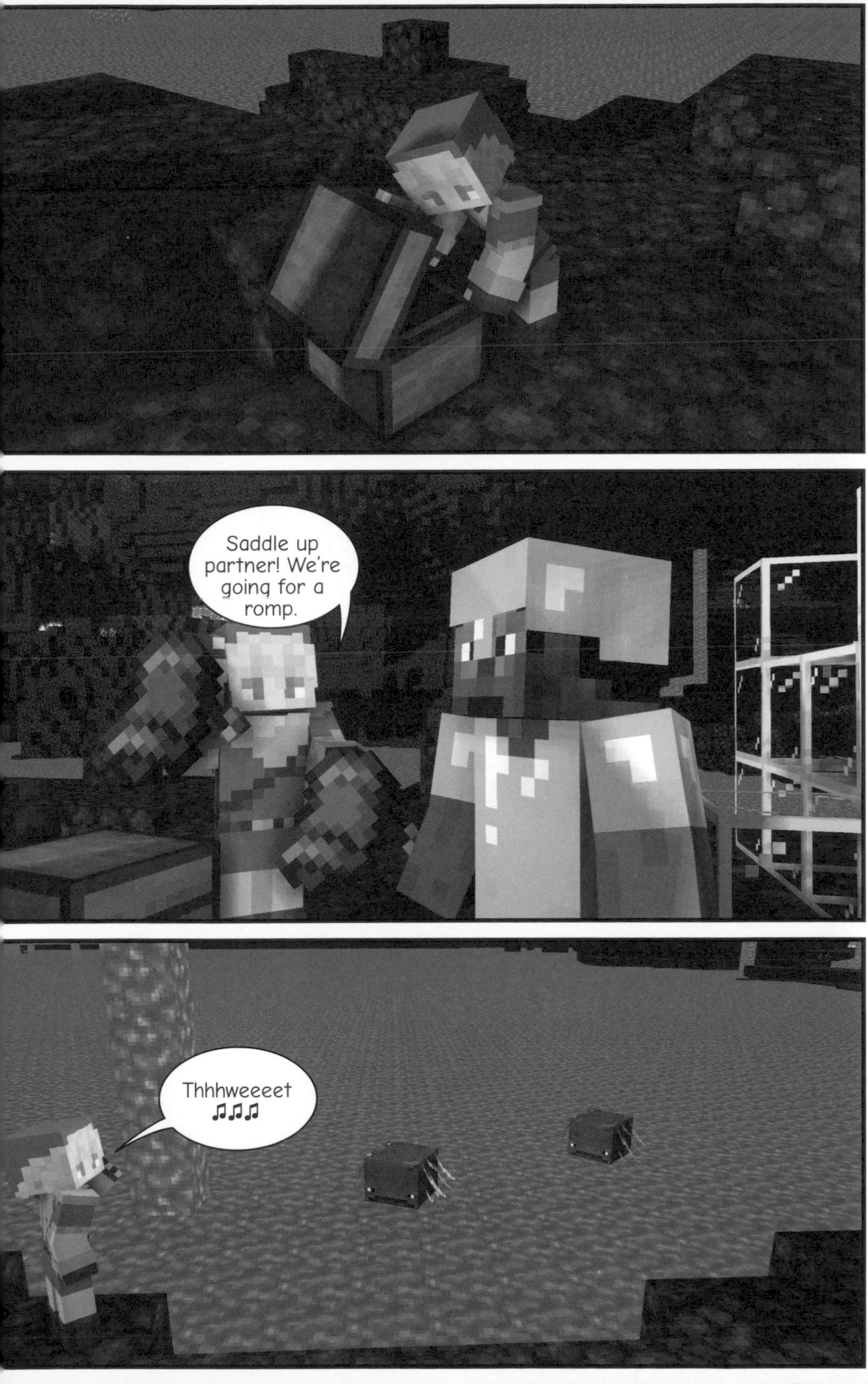
Saddle up partner! We're going for a romp.
Thhhweeeet ♫♫♫

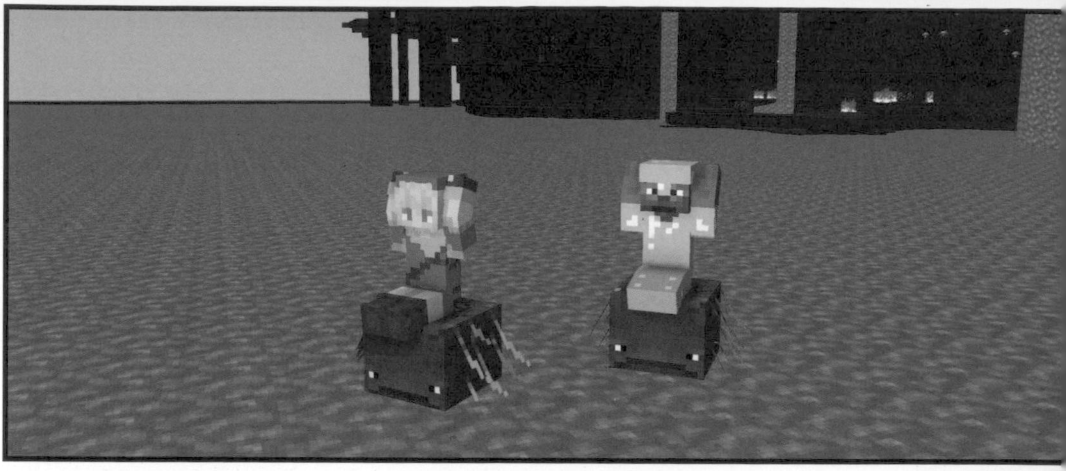

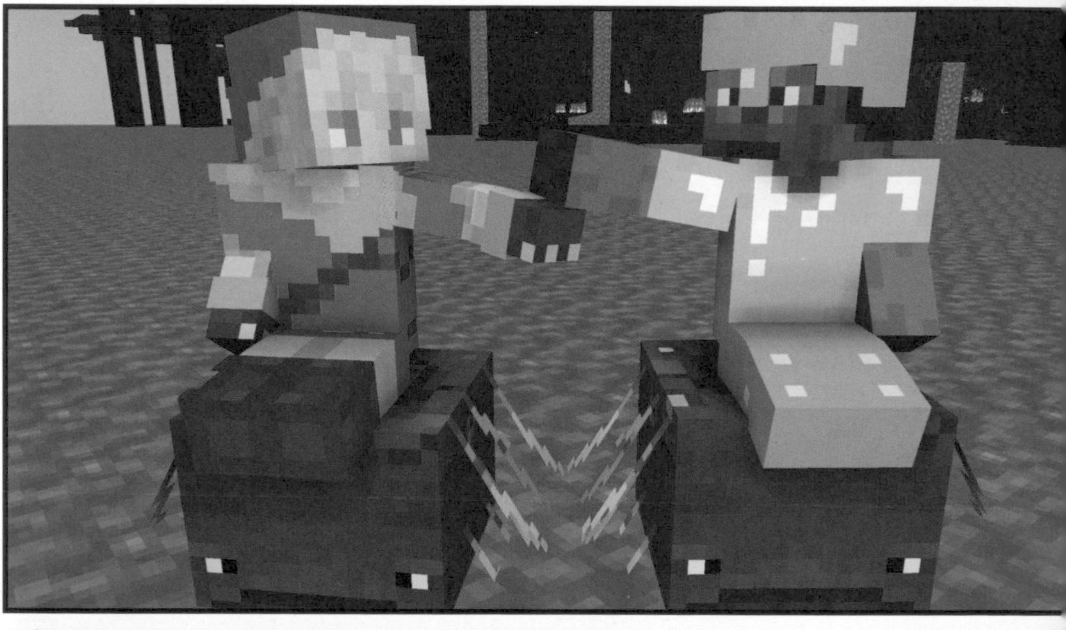

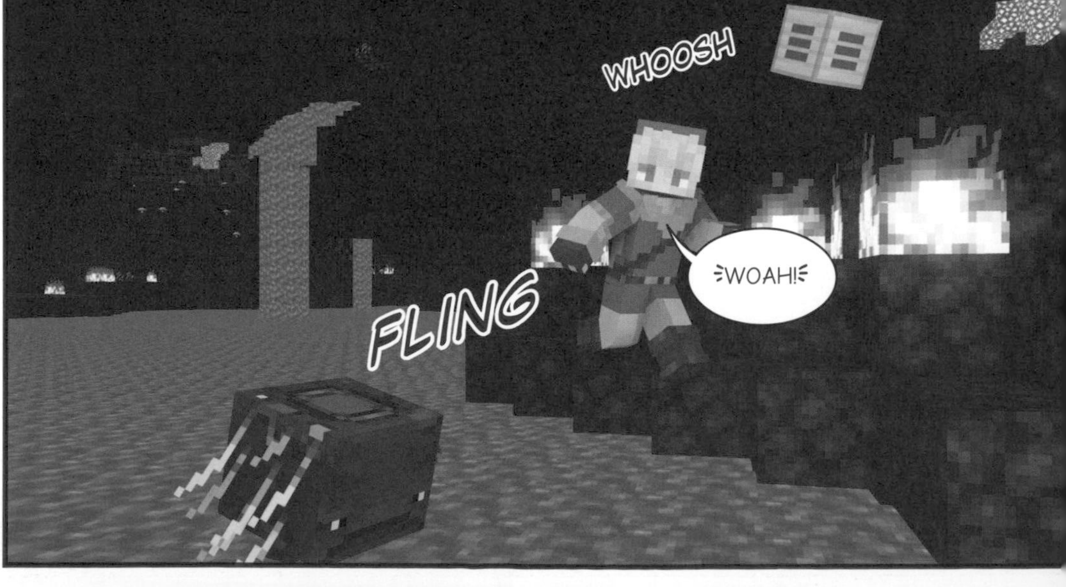
WHOOSH
WOAH!
FLING

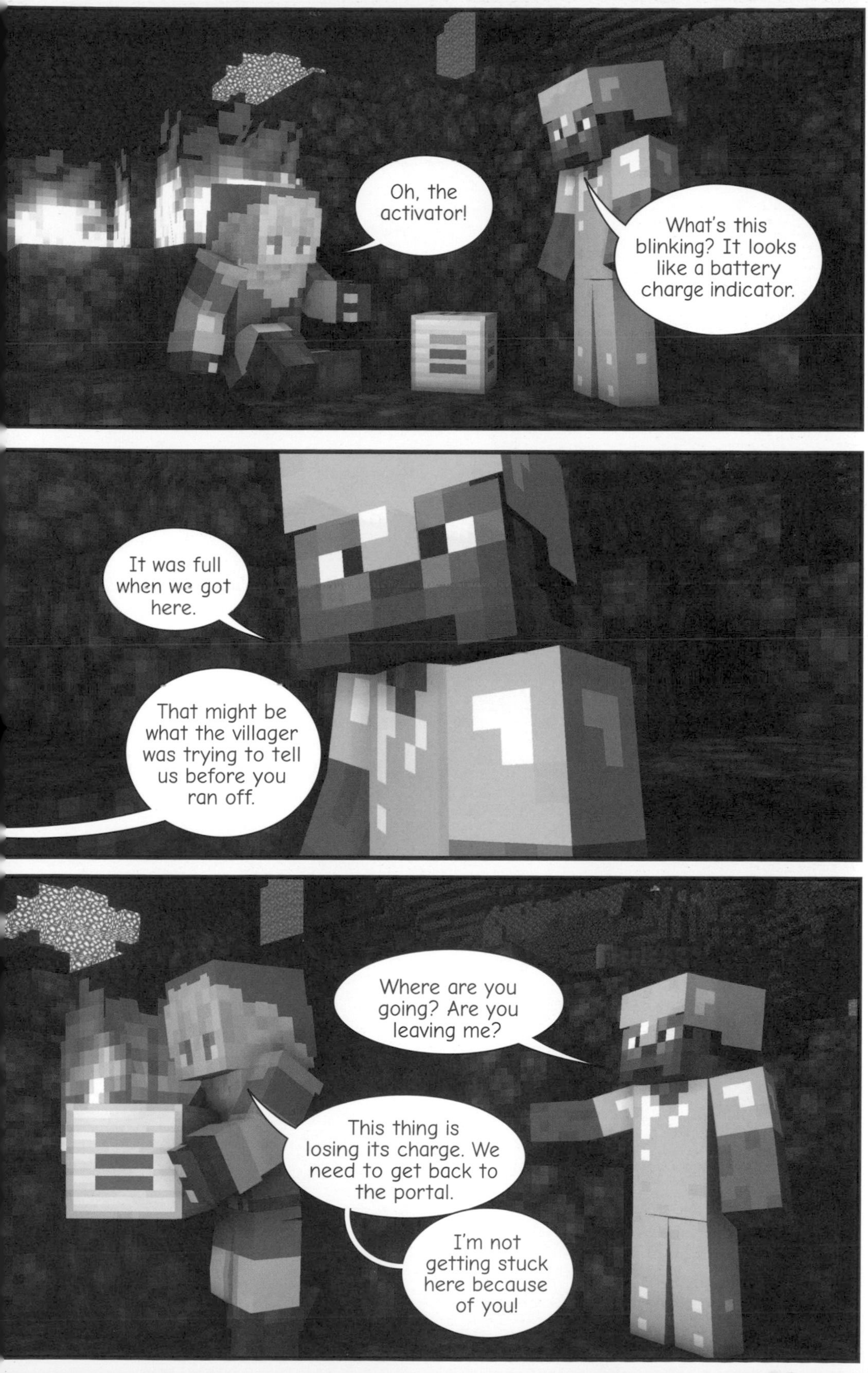

What's this blinking? It looks like a battery charge indicator.
Oh, the activator!
It was full when we got here.
That might be what the villager was trying to tell us before you ran off.
Where are you going? Are you leaving me?
This thing is losing its charge. We need to get back to the portal.
I'm not getting stuck here because of you!

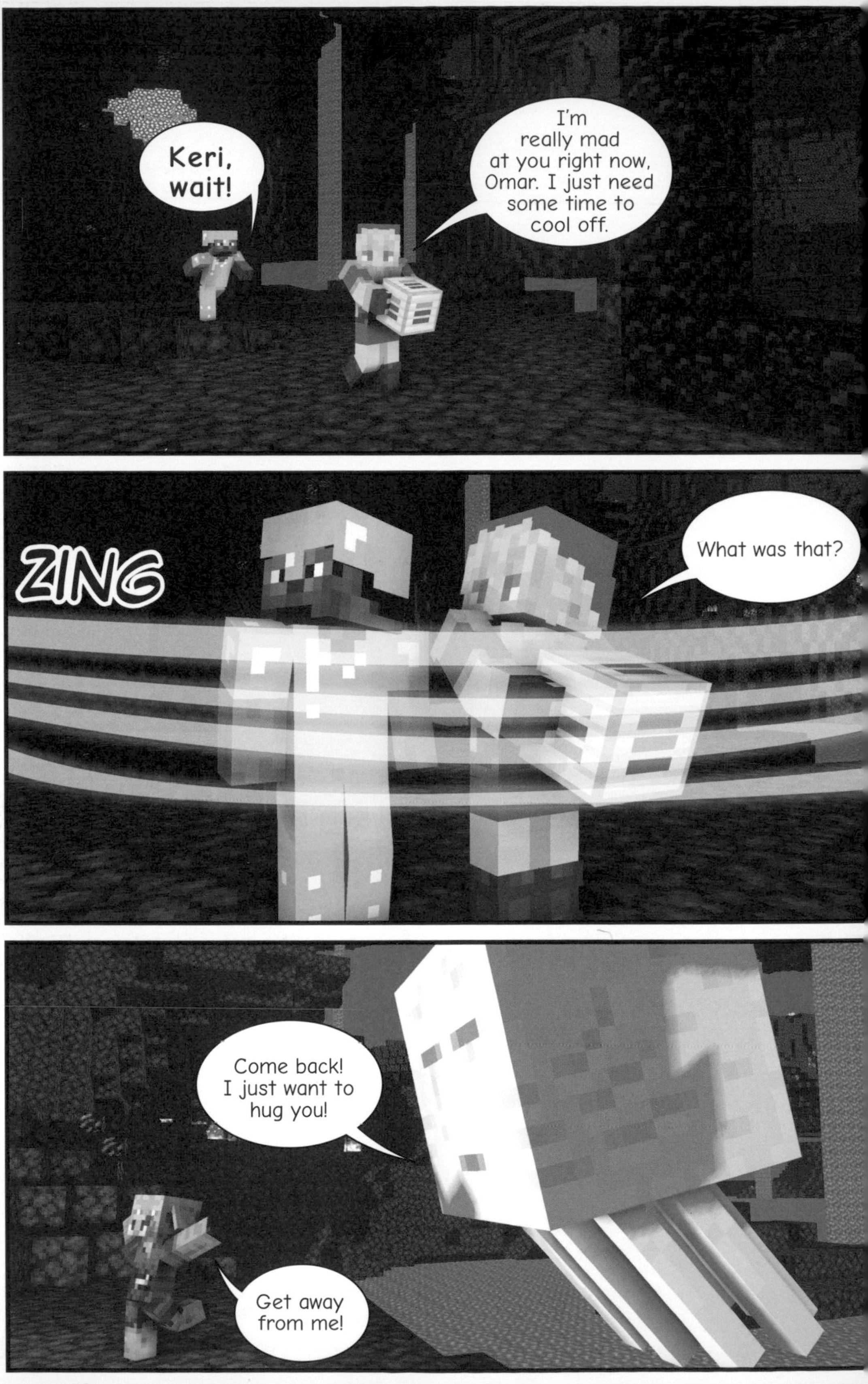
Keri, wait!
I'm really mad at you right now, Omar. I just need some time to cool off.
ZING
What was that?
Come back! I just want to hug you!
Get away from me!

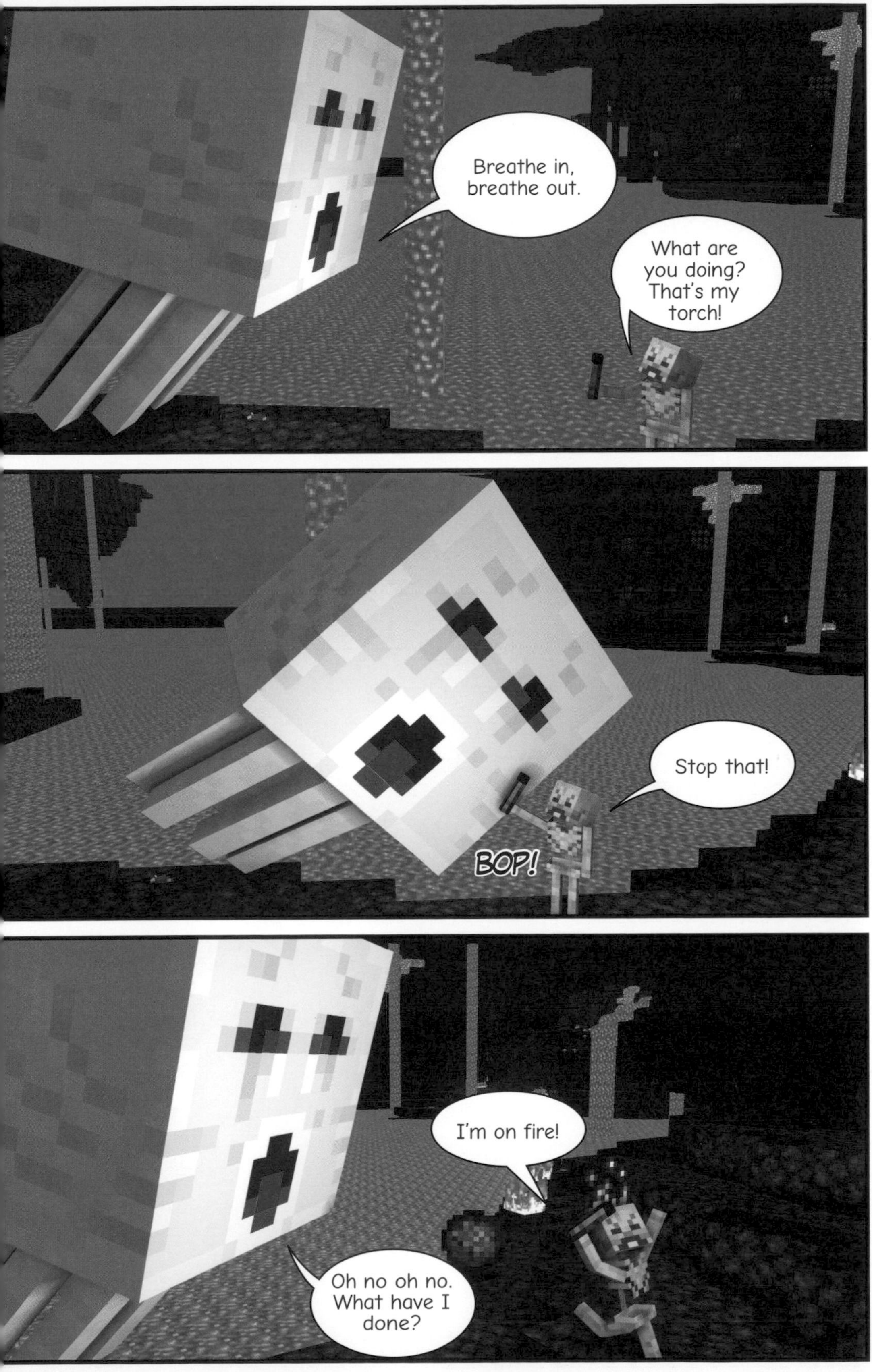
Breathe in, breathe out.
What are you doing? That's my torch!
Stop that!
BOP!
I'm on fire!
Oh no oh no. What have I done?

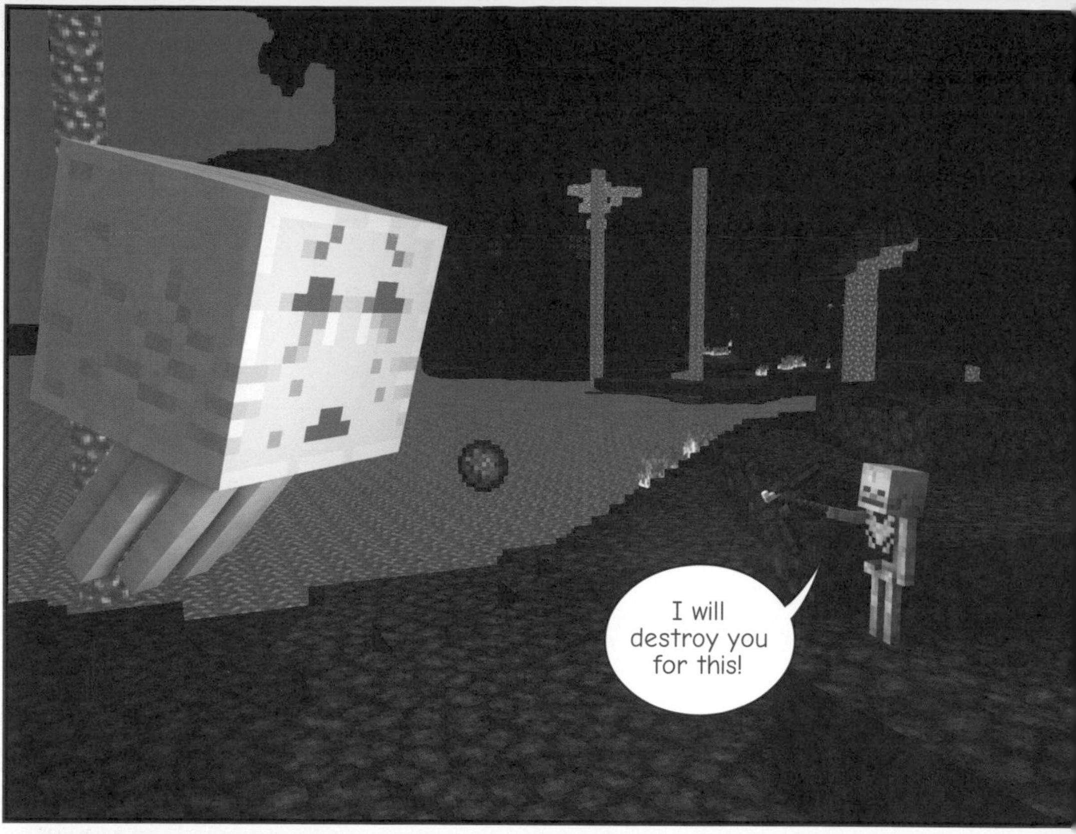
I will destroy you for this!

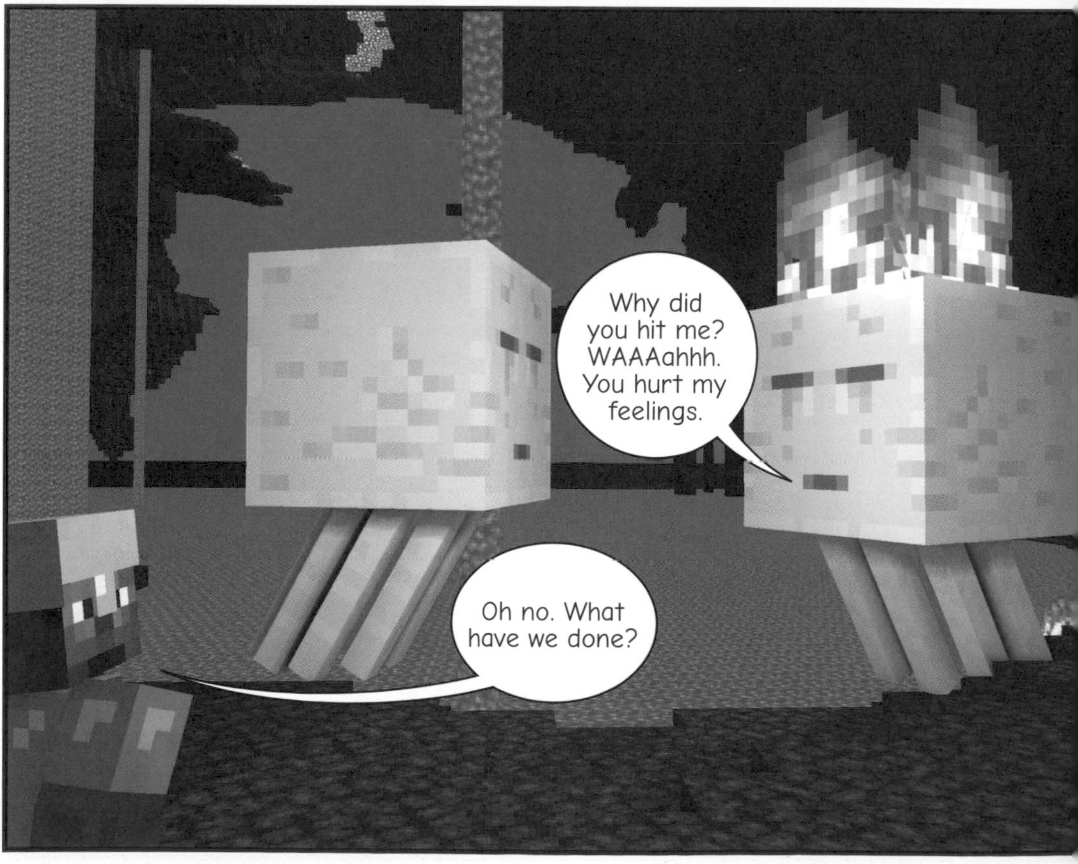
Why did you hit me? WAAAahhh. You hurt my feelings.
Oh no. What have we done?

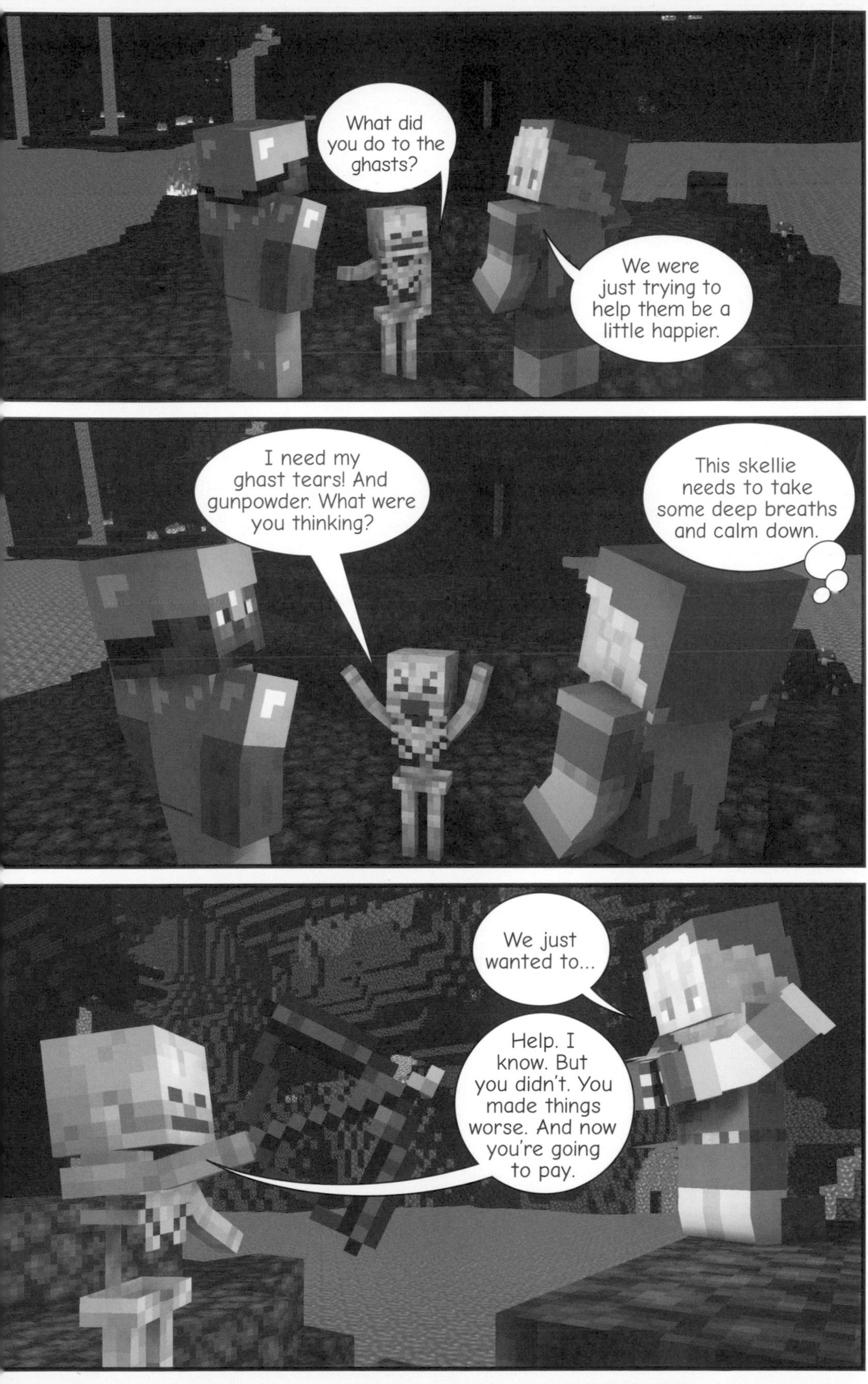
What did you do to the ghasts?
We were just trying to help them be a little happier.
I need my ghast tears! And gunpowder. What were you thinking?
This skellie needs to take some deep breaths and calm down.
We just wanted to...
Help. I know. But you didn't. You made things worse. And now you're going to pay.

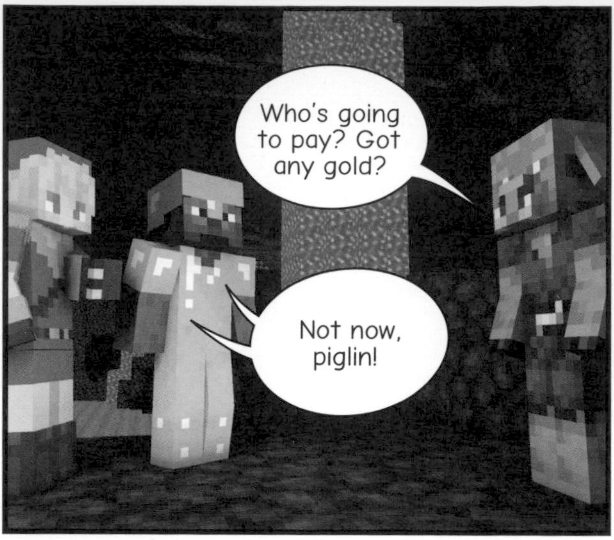
Who's going to pay? Got any gold?
Not now, piglin!

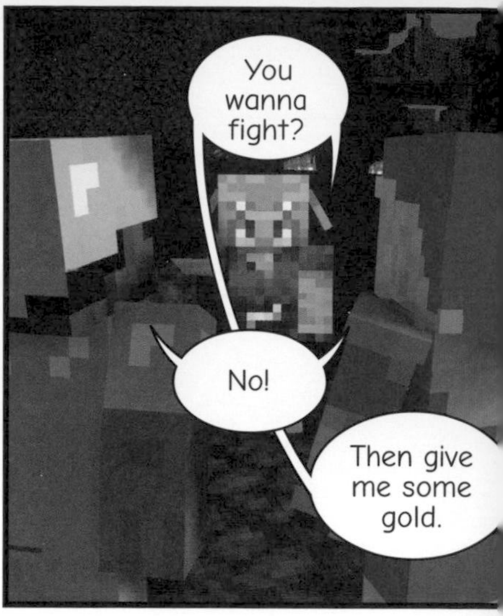
You wanna fight?
No!
Then give me some gold.

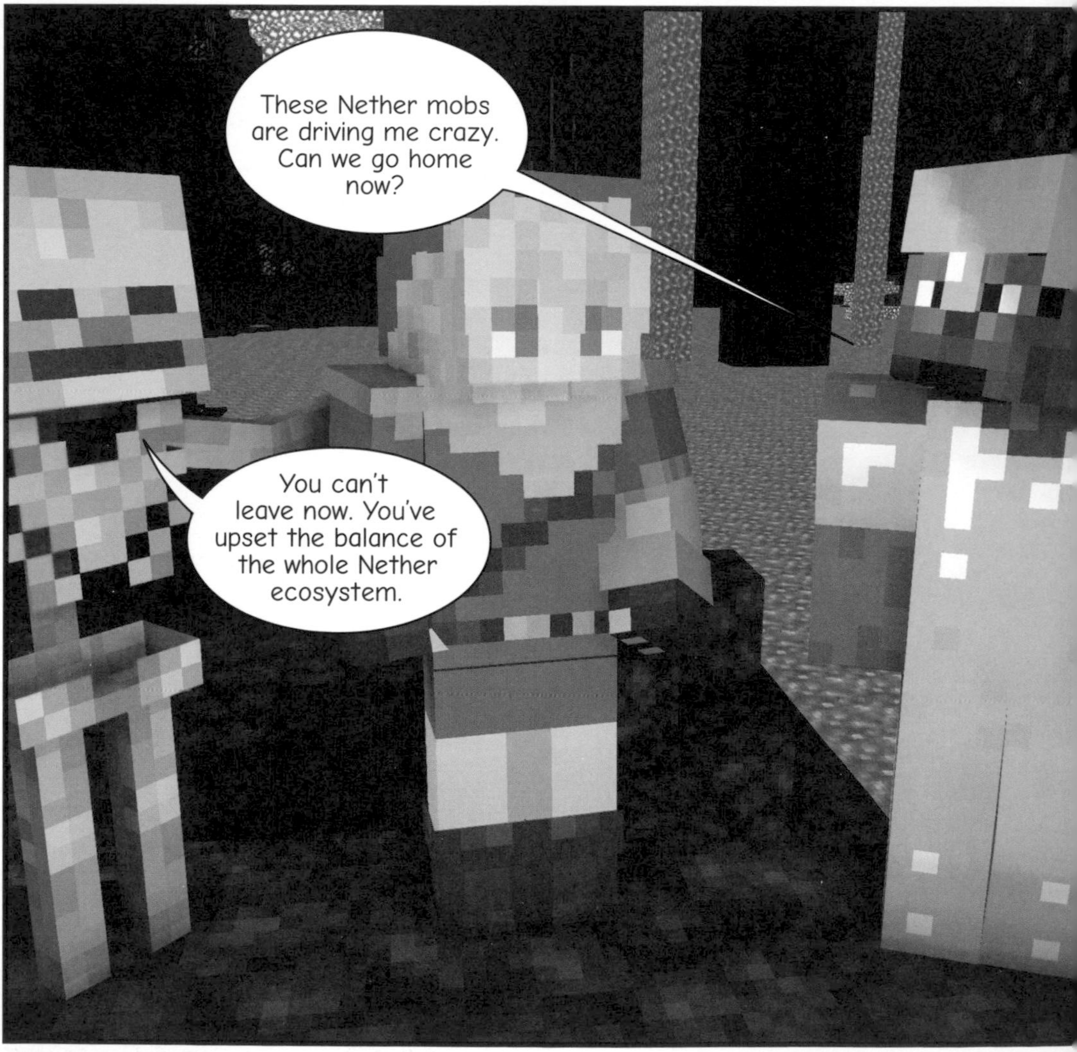
These Nether mobs are driving me crazy. Can we go home now?
You can't leave now. You've upset the balance of the whole Nether ecosystem.

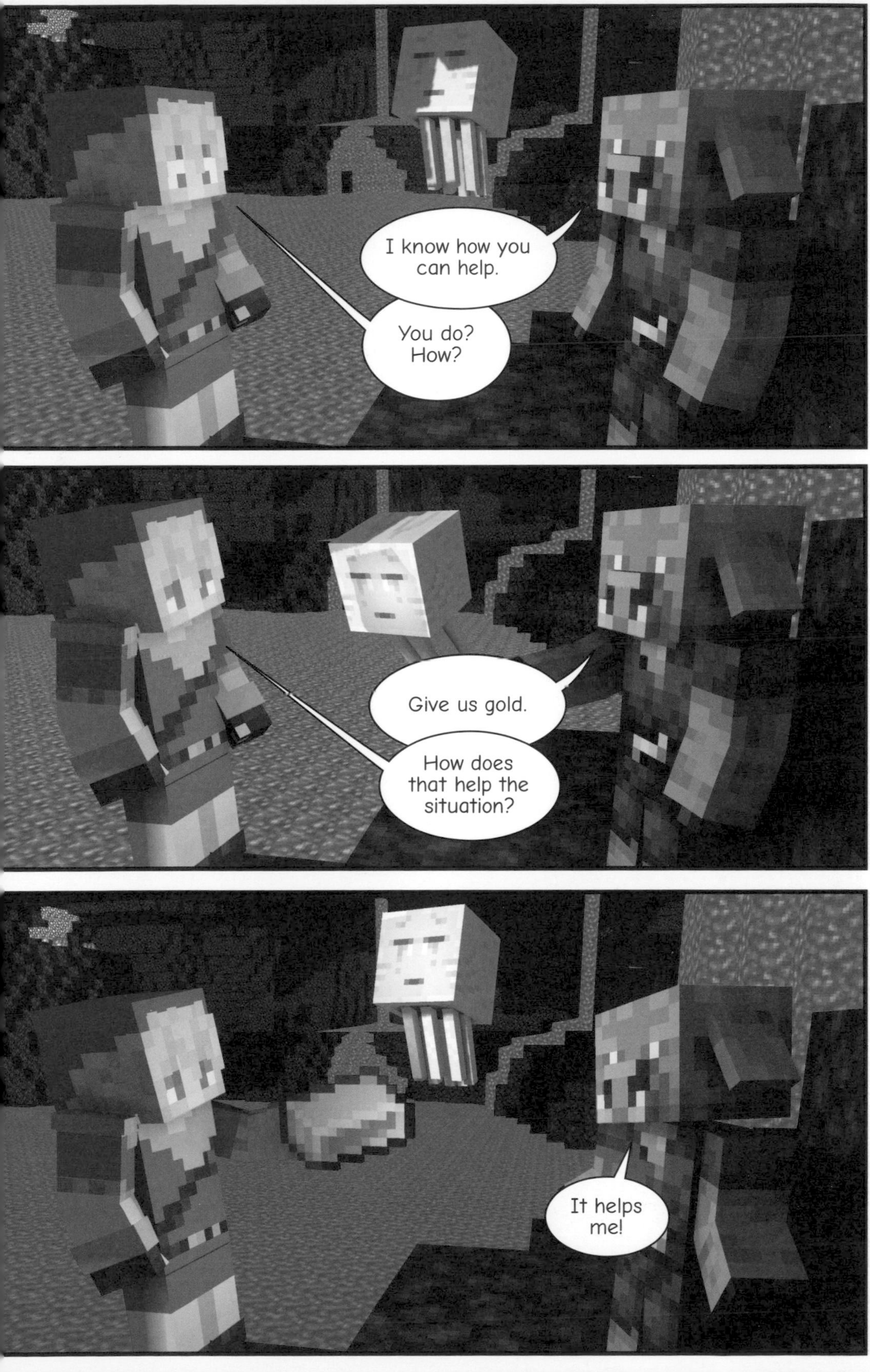
I know how you can help.
You do? How?
Give us gold.
How does that help the situation?
It helps me!

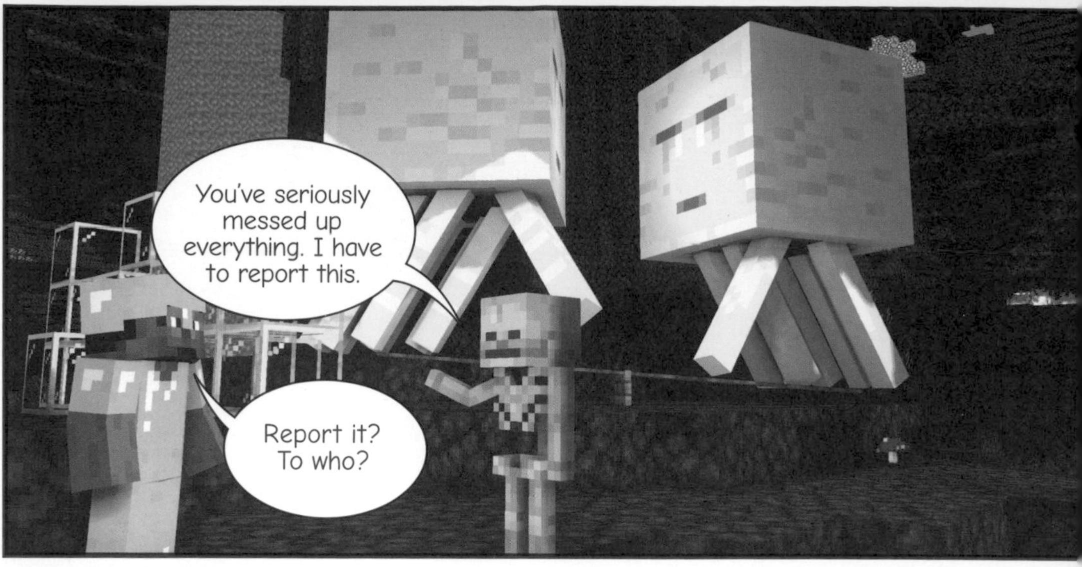
You've seriously messed up everything. I have to report this.
Report it? To who?

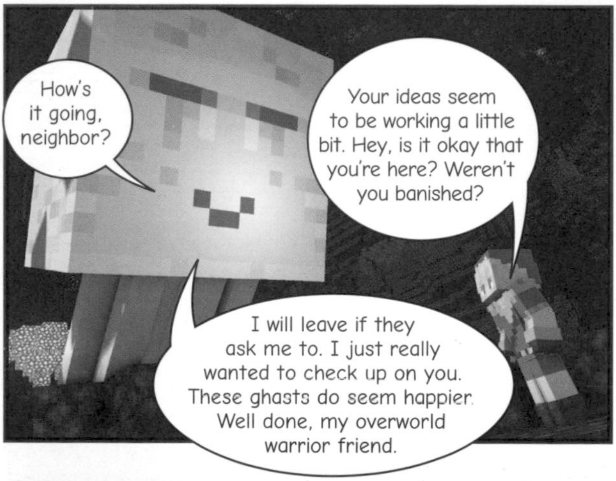
How's it going, neighbor?
Your ideas seem to be working a little bit. Hey, is it okay that you're here? Weren't you banished?
I will leave if they ask me to. I just really wanted to check up on you. These ghasts do seem happier. Well done, my overworld warrior friend.

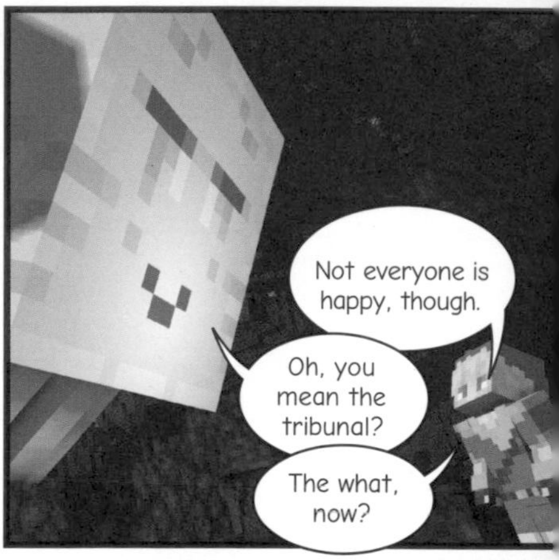
Not everyone is happy, though.
Oh, you mean the tribunal?
The what, now?

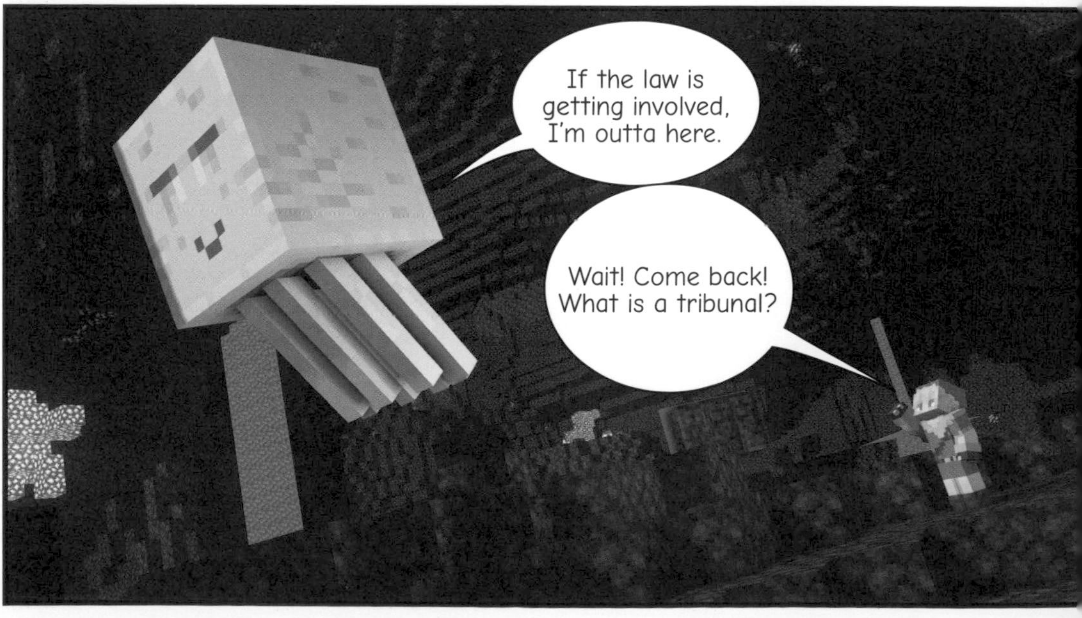
If the law is getting involved, I'm outta here.
Wait! Come back! What is a tribunal?

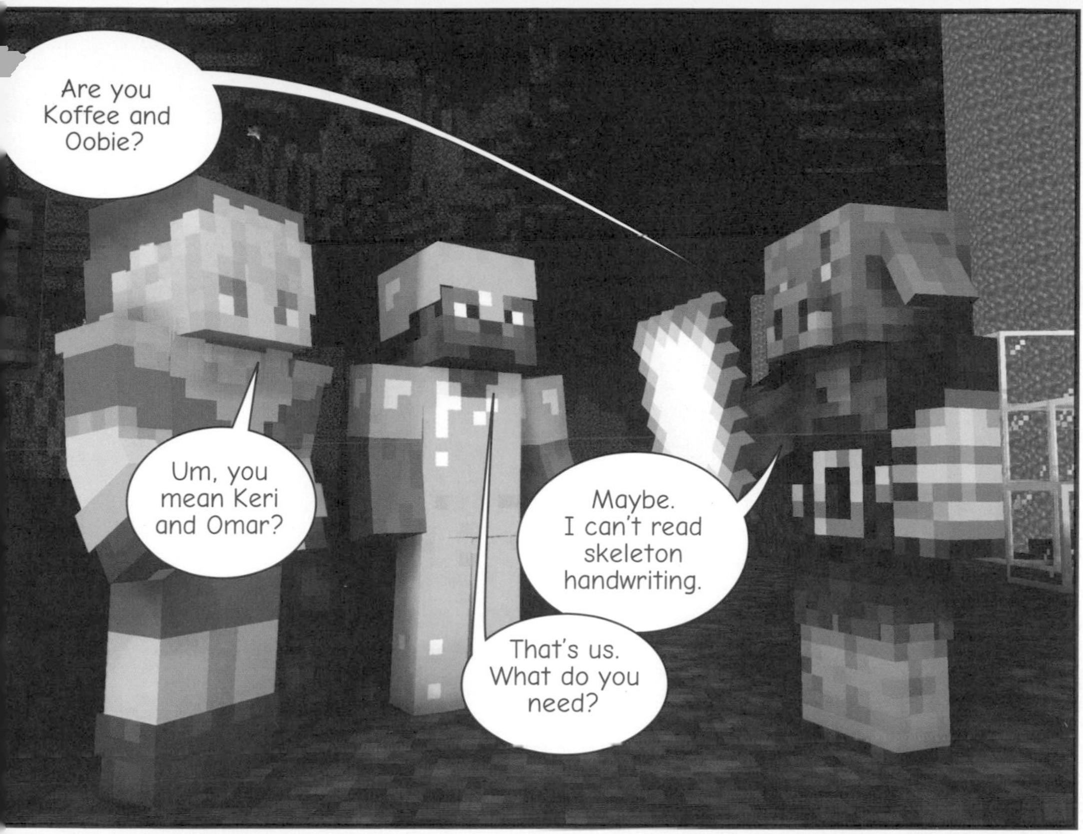
Are you Koffee and Oobie?
Um, you mean Keri and Omar?
Maybe. I can't read skeleton handwriting.
That's us. What do you need?

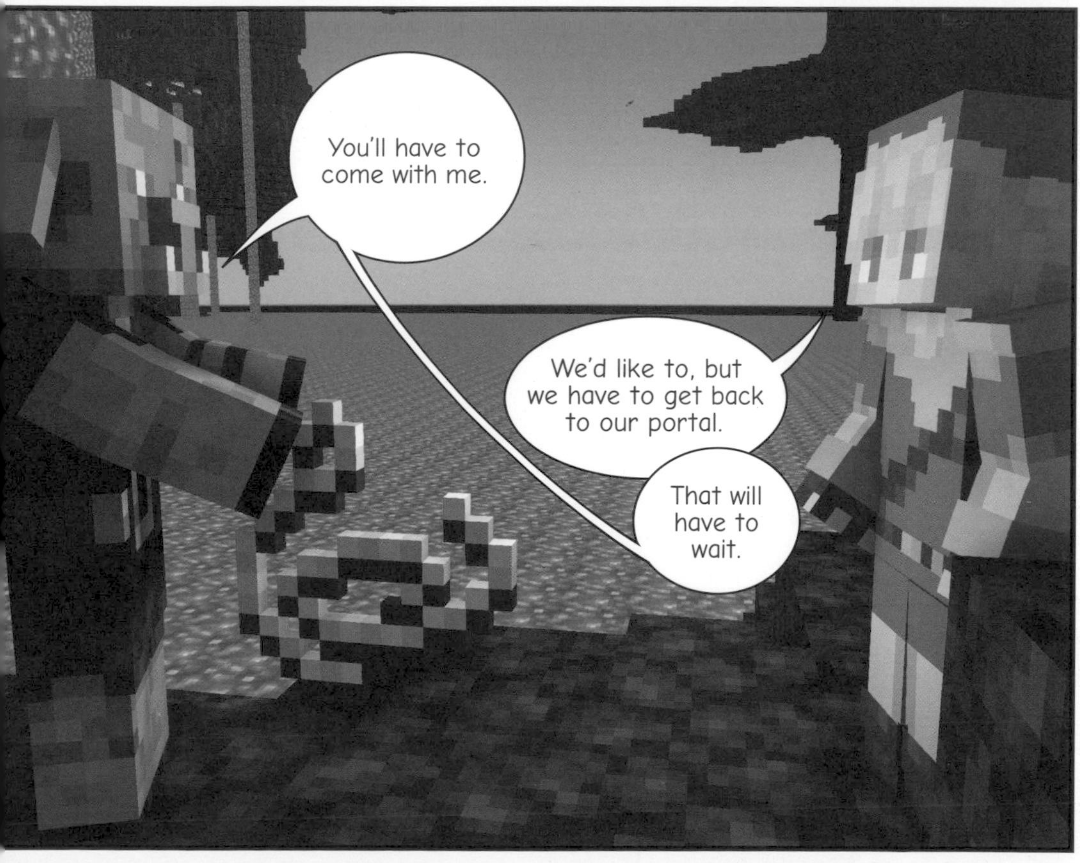
You'll have to come with me.
We'd like to, but we have to get back to our portal.
That will have to wait.

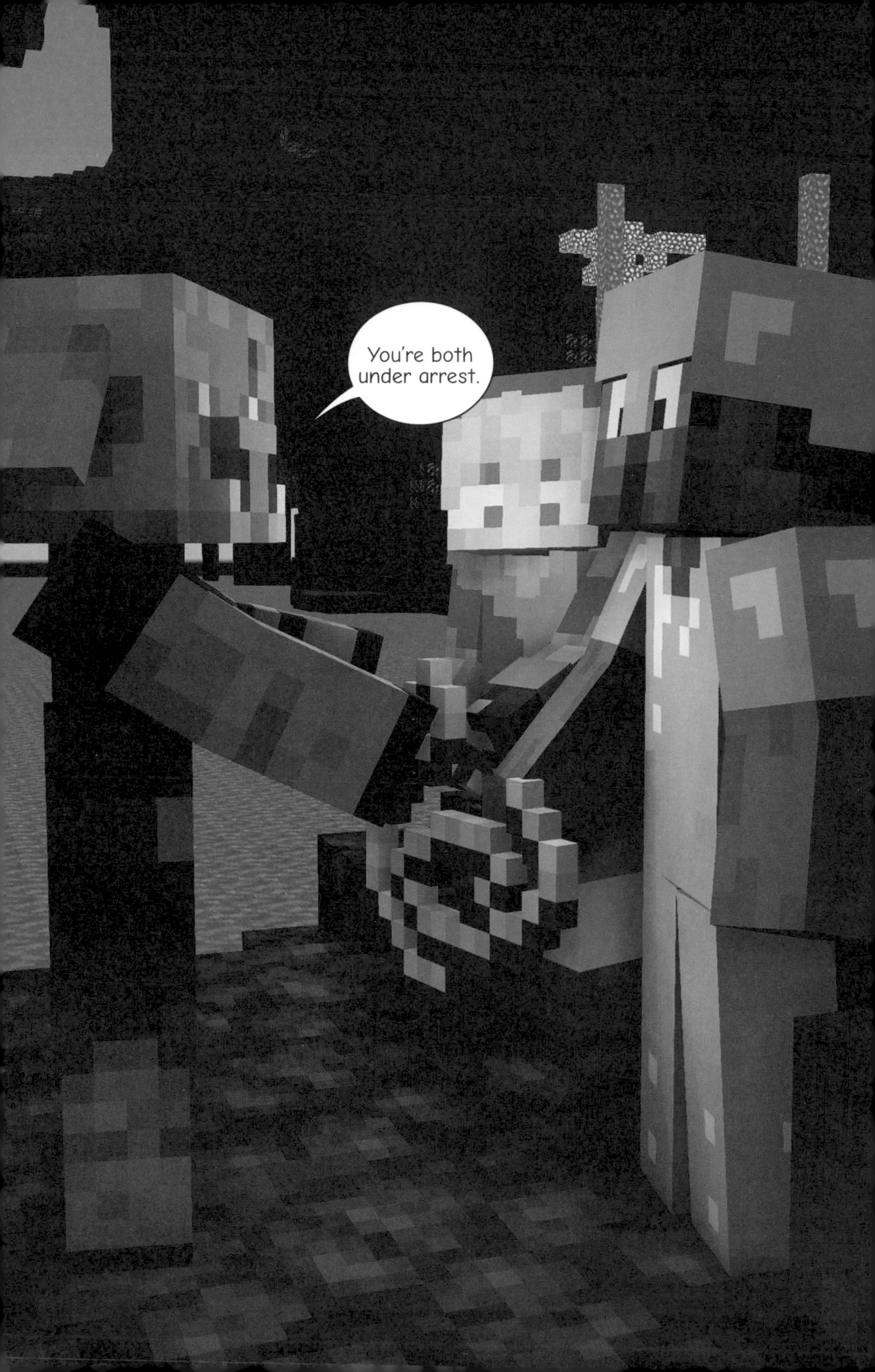
You're both under arrest.

Chapter 8
The Trial

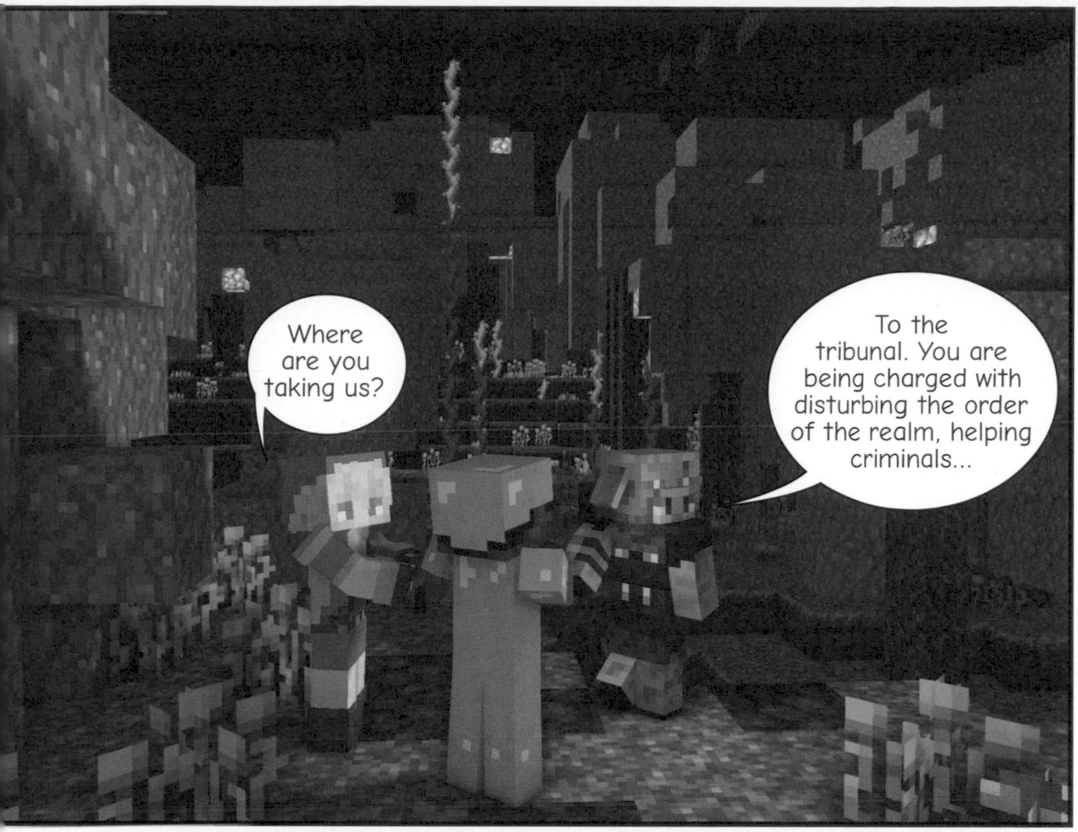
Where are you taking us?
To the tribunal. You are being charged with disturbing the order of the realm, helping criminals...

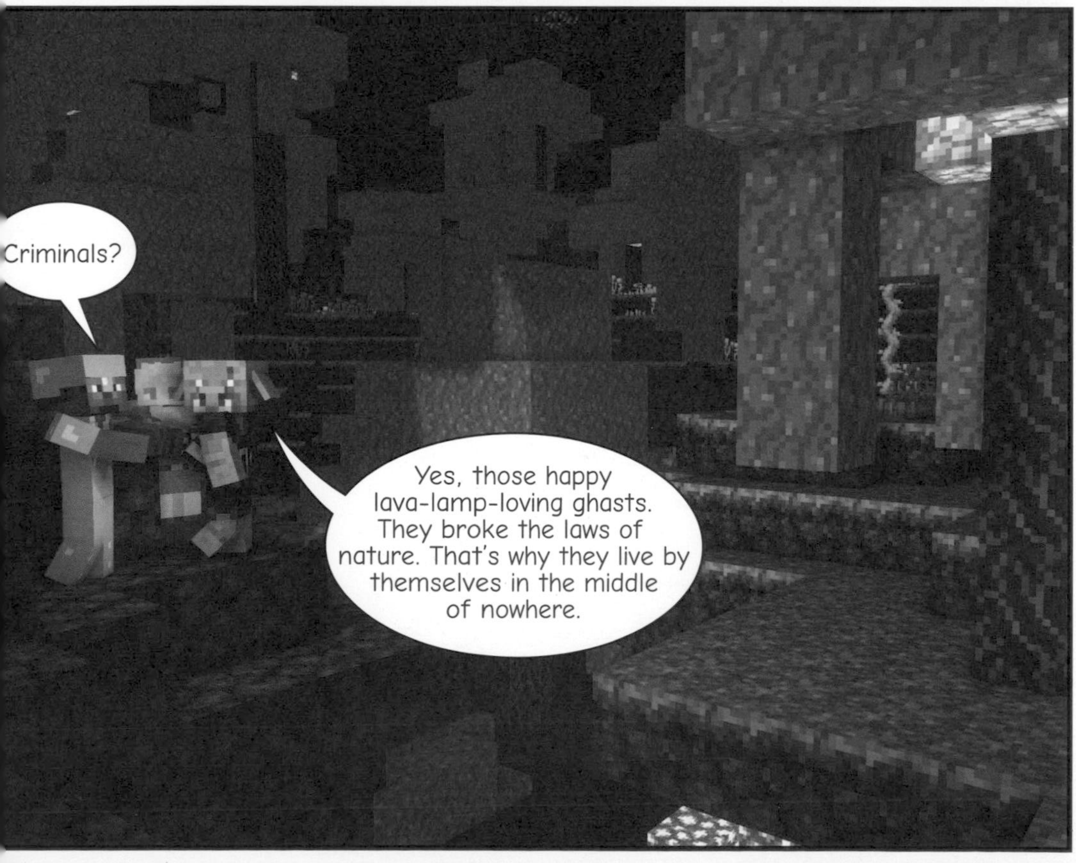
Criminals?
Yes, those happy lava-lamp-loving ghasts. They broke the laws of nature. That's why they live by themselves in the middle of nowhere.

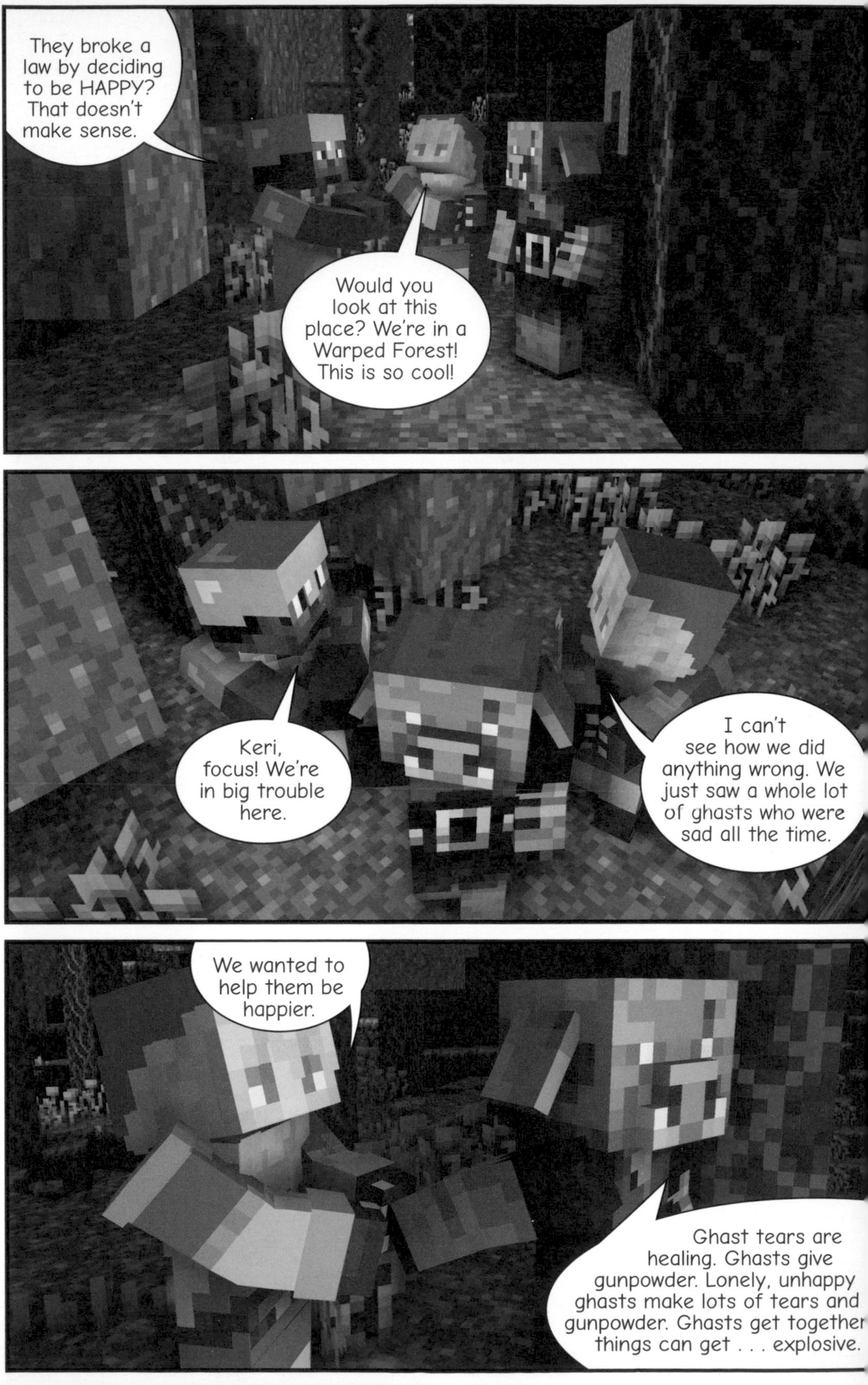
They broke a law by deciding to be HAPPY? That doesn't make sense.
Would you look at this place? We're in a Warped Forest! This is so cool!
Keri, focus! We're in big trouble here.
I can't see how we did anything wrong. We just saw a whole lot of ghasts who were sad all the time.
We wanted to help them be happier.
Ghast tears are healing. Ghasts give gunpowder. Lonely, unhappy ghasts make lots of tears and gunpowder. Ghasts get together things can get . . . explosive.

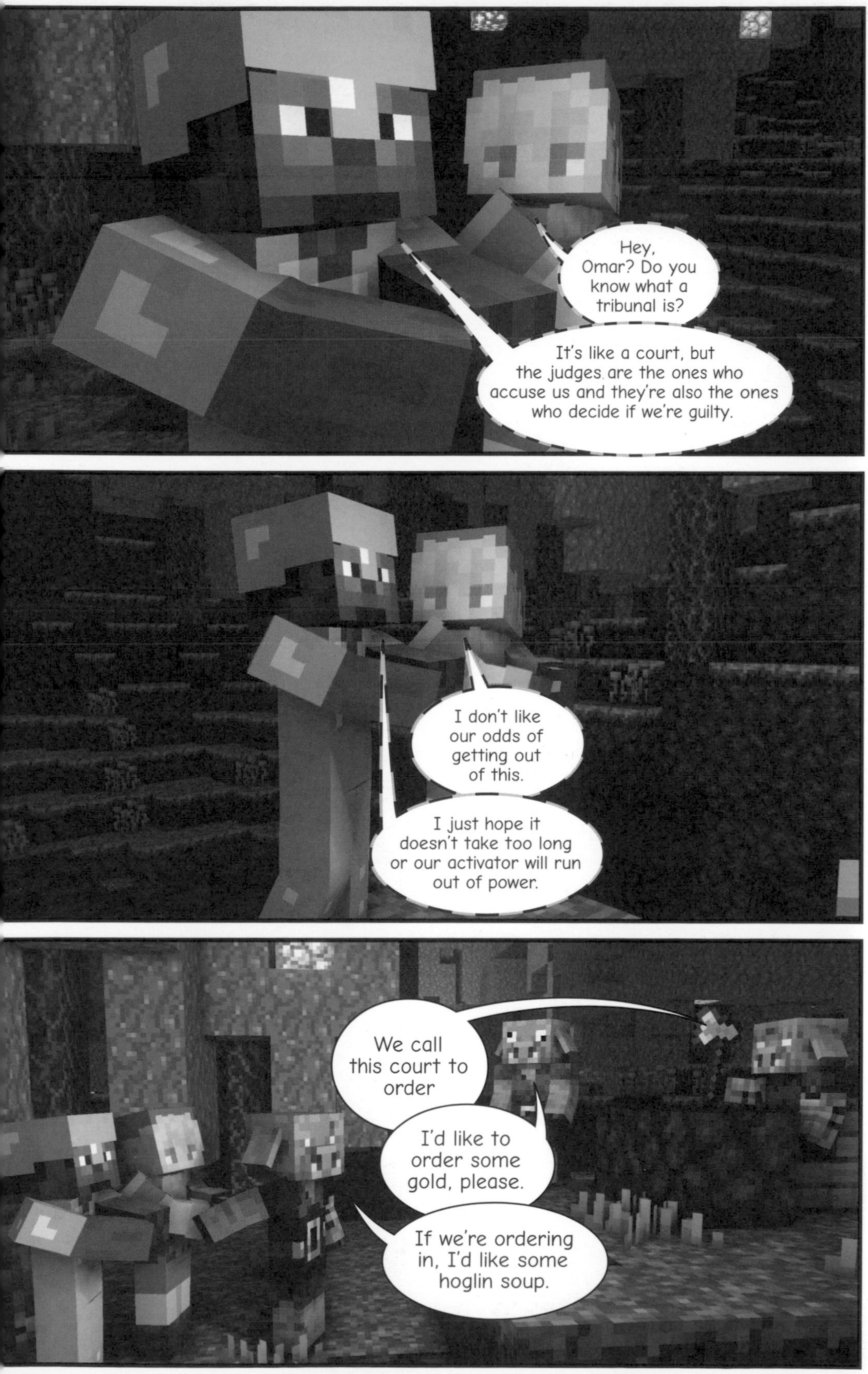
Hey, Omar? Do you know what a tribunal is?
It's like a court, but the judges are the ones who accuse us and they're also the ones who decide if we're guilty.
I don't like our odds of getting out of this.
I just hope it doesn't take too long or our activator will run out of power.
We call this court to order
I'd like to order some gold, please.
If we're ordering in, I'd like some hoglin soup.

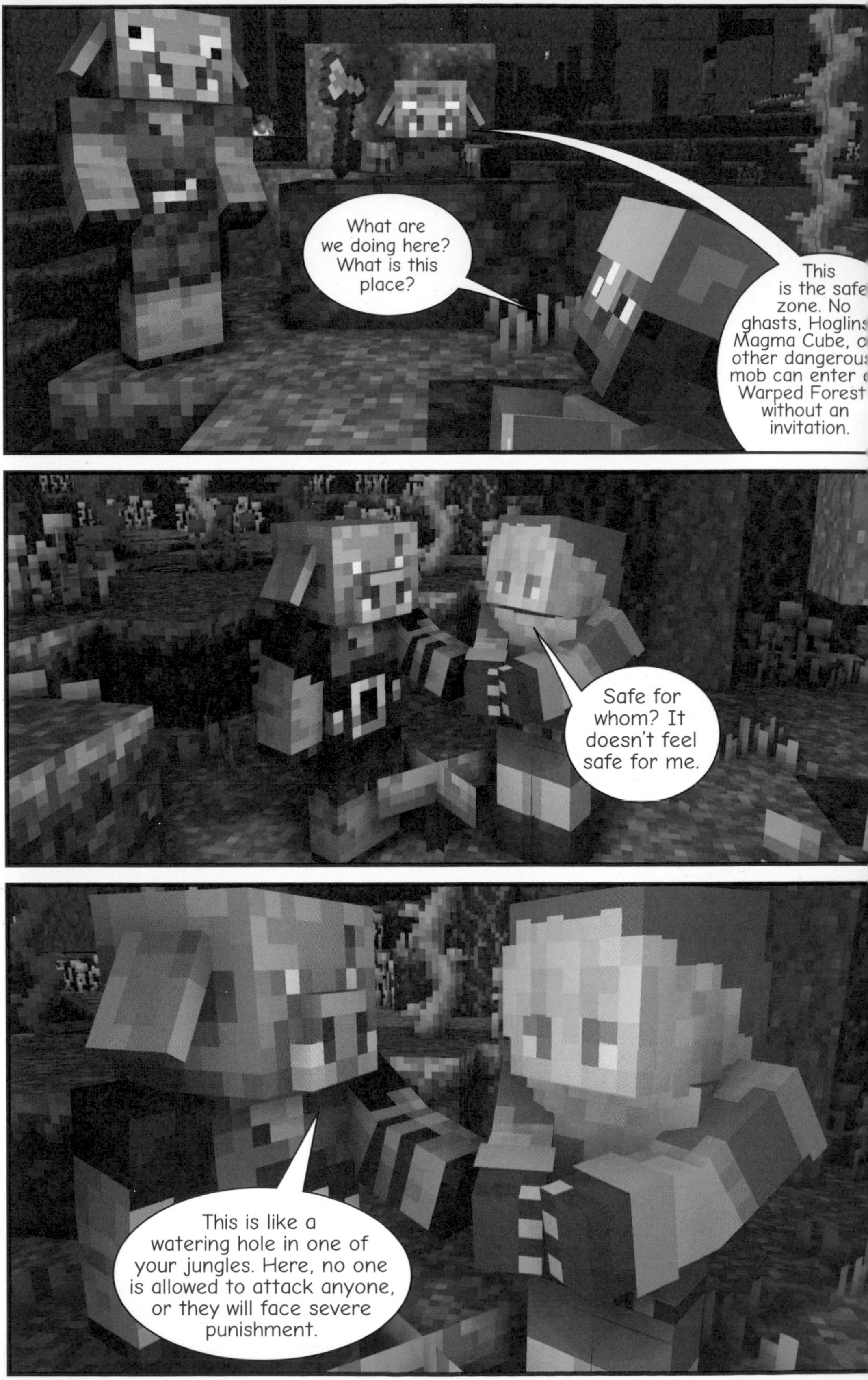
What are we doing here? What is this place?
This is the safe zone. No ghasts, Hoglins Magma Cube, o other dangerous mob can enter Warped Forest without an invitation.
Safe for whom? It doesn't feel safe for me.
This is like a watering hole in one of your jungles. Here, no one is allowed to attack anyone, or they will face severe punishment.

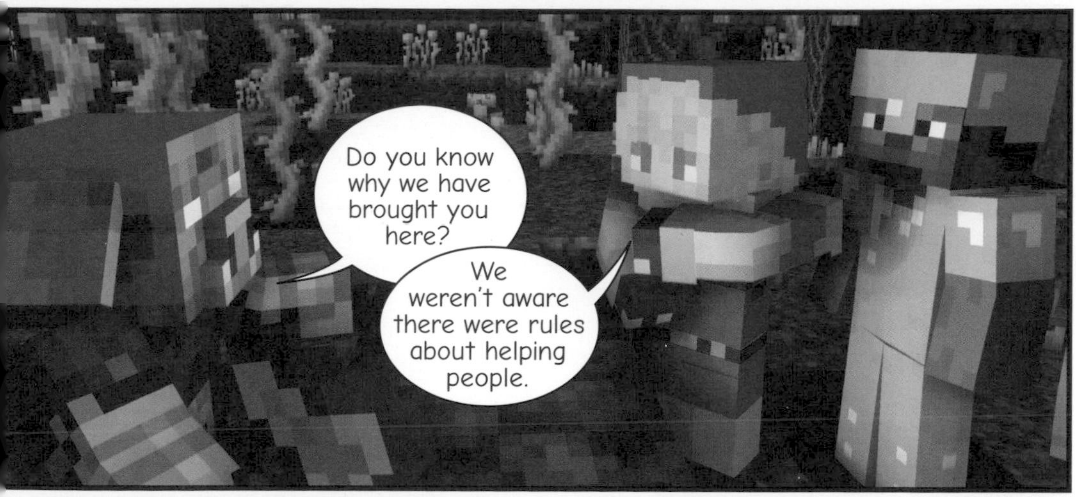
Do you know why we have brought you here?
We weren't aware there were rules about helping people.

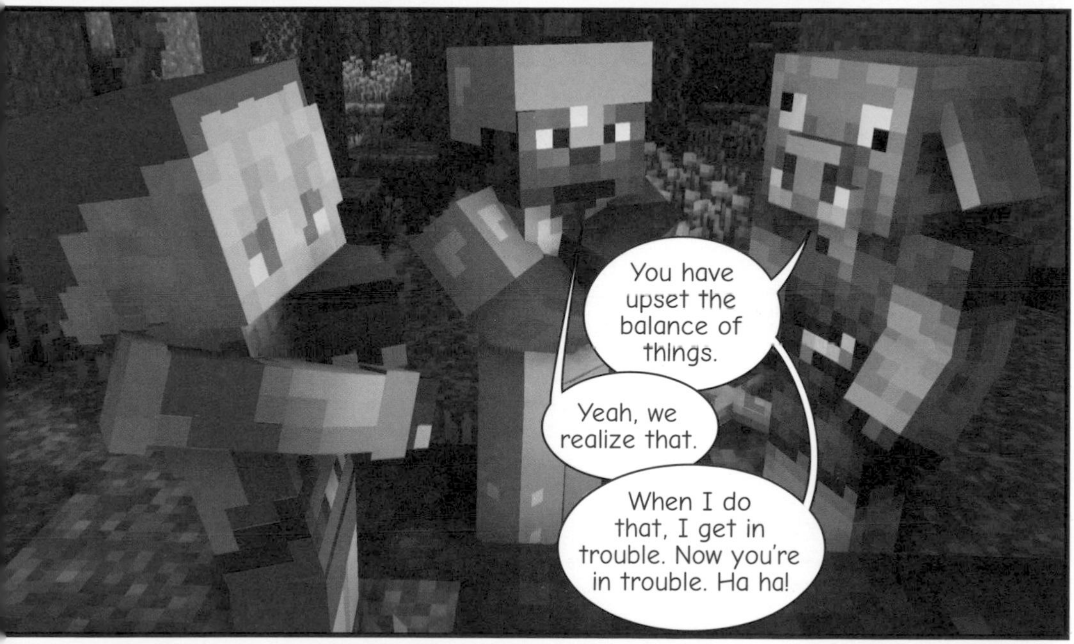
You have upset the balance of things.
Yeah, we realize that.
When I do that, I get in trouble. Now you're in trouble. Ha ha!

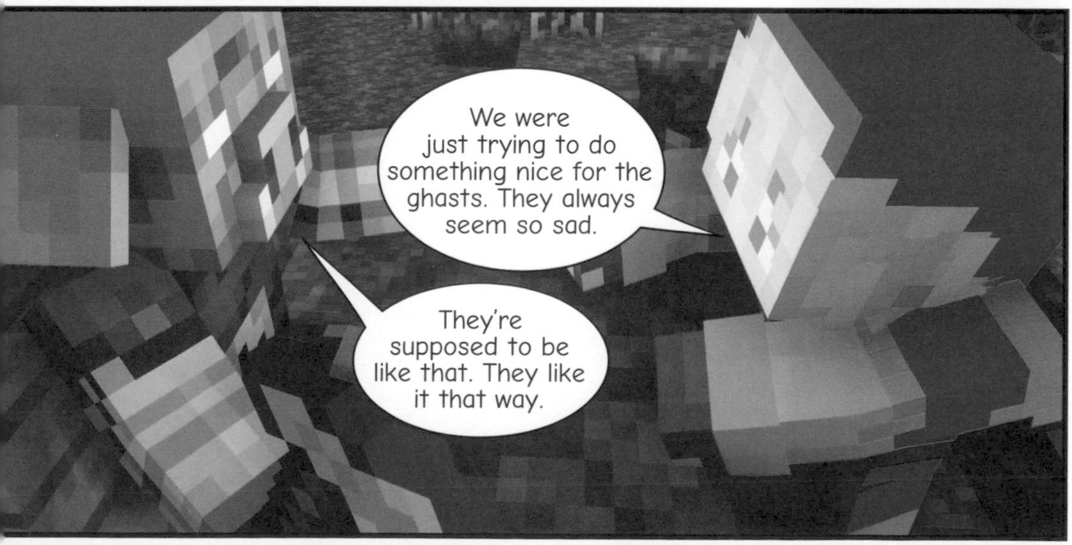
We were just trying to do something nice for the ghasts. They always seem so sad.
They're supposed to be like that. They like it that way.

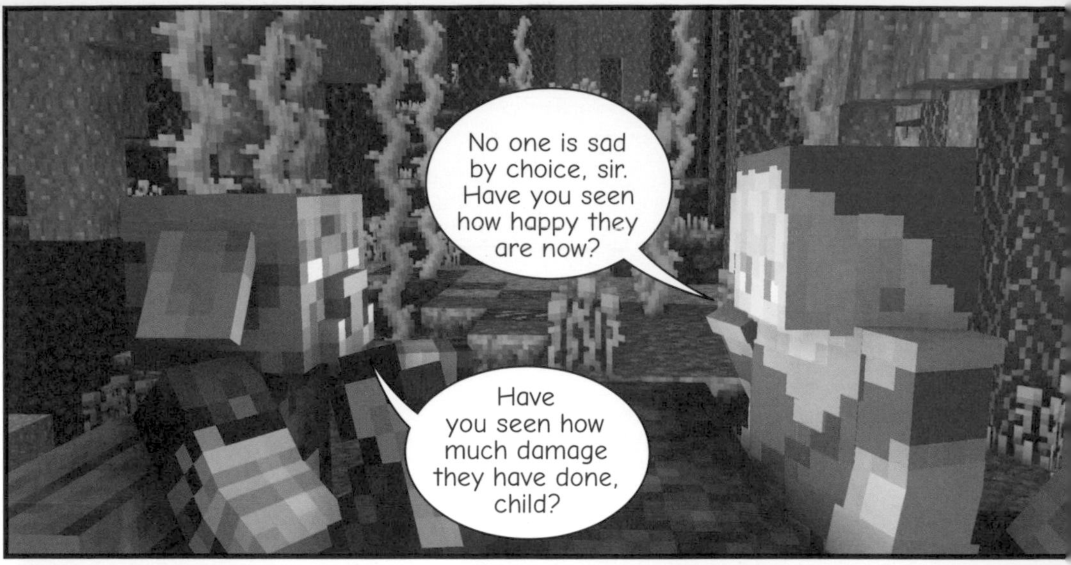
No one is sad by choice, sir. Have you seen how happy they are now?
Have you seen how much damage they have done, child?

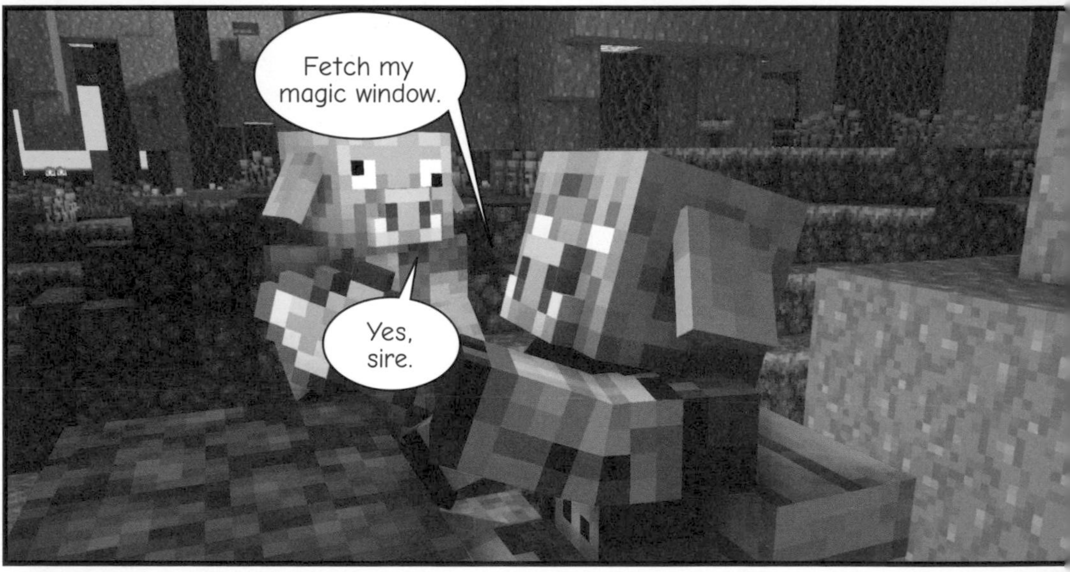
Fetch my magic window.
Yes, sire.

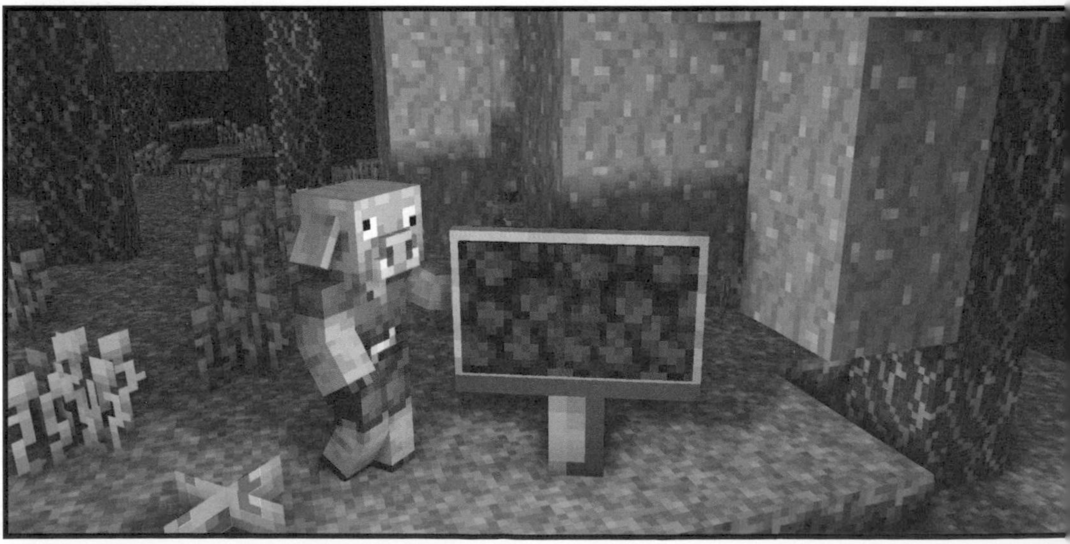

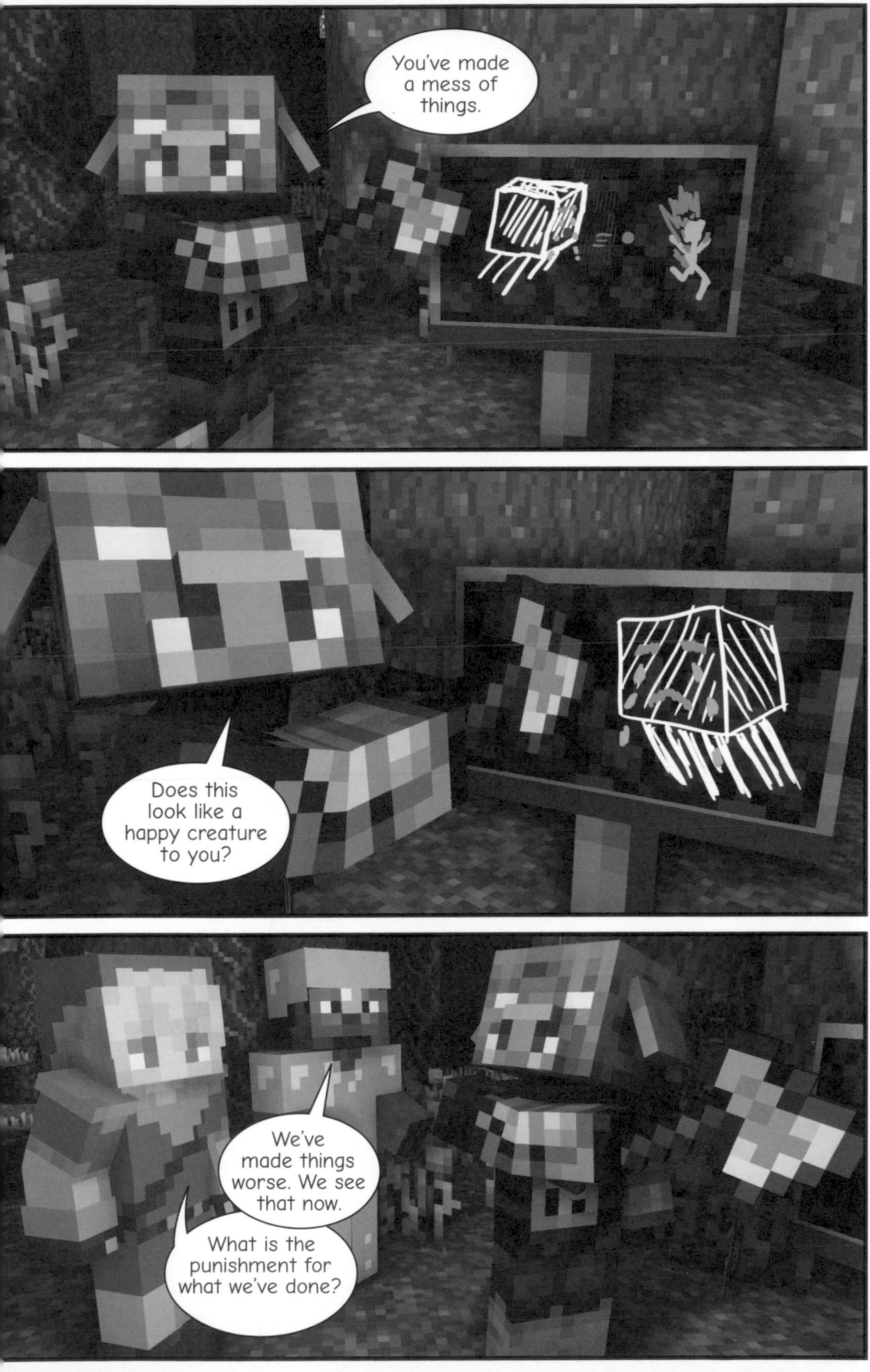
You've made a mess of things.
Does this look like a happy creature to you?
We've made things worse. We see that now.
What is the punishment for what we've done?

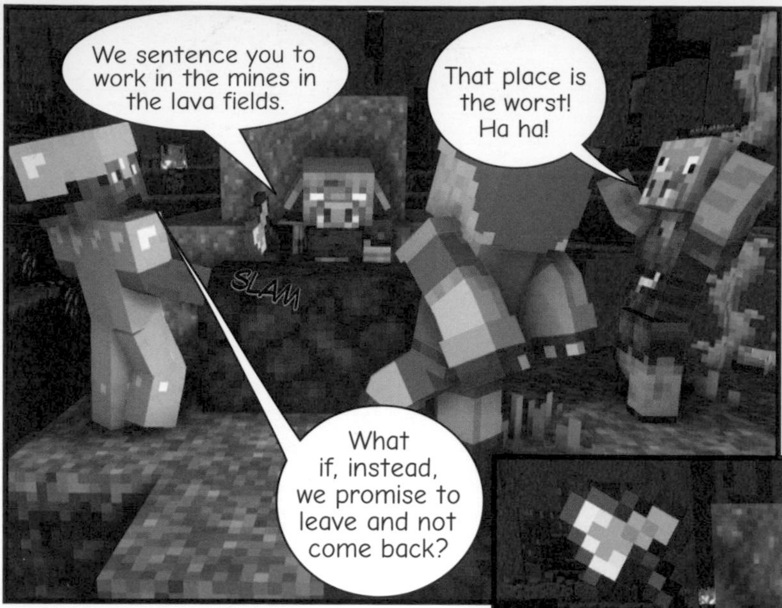
We sentence you to work in the mines in the lava fields.
That place is the worst! Ha ha!
SLAM
What if, instead, we promise to leave and not come back?

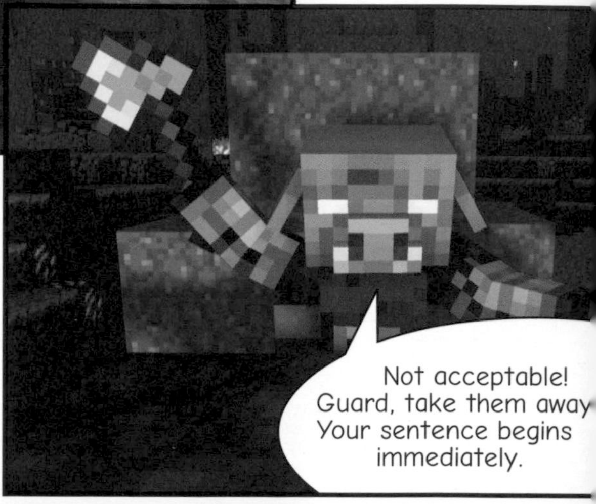
Not acceptable! Guard, take them away
Your sentence begins immediately.

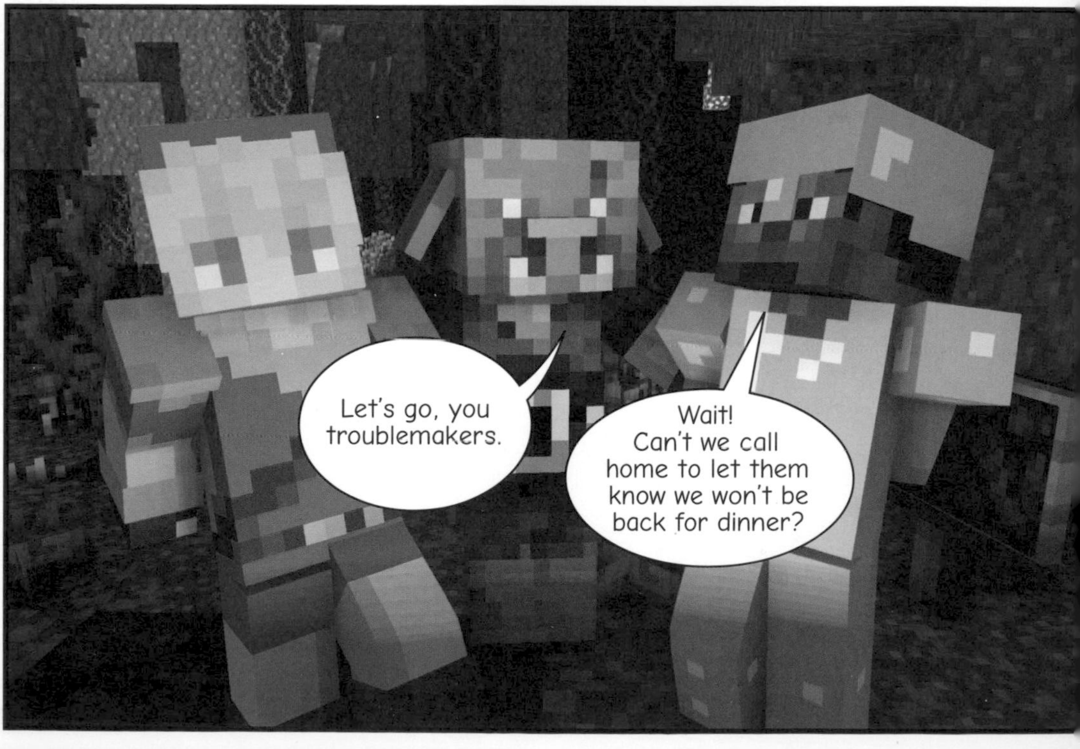
Let's go, you troublemakers.
Wait! Can't we call home to let them know we won't be back for dinner?

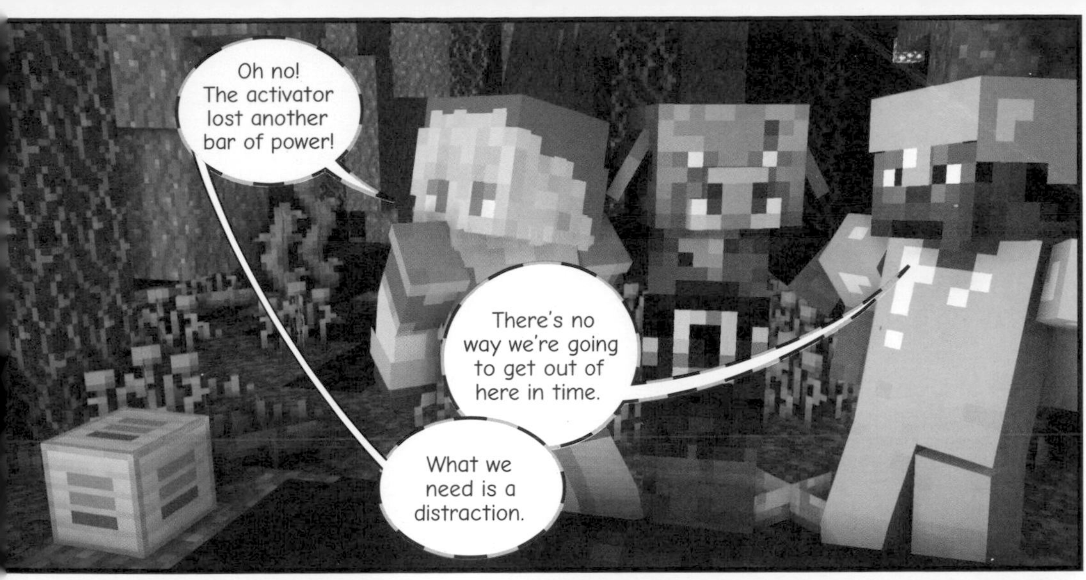
Oh no! The activator lost another bar of power!
There's no way we're going to get out of here in time.
What we need is a distraction.

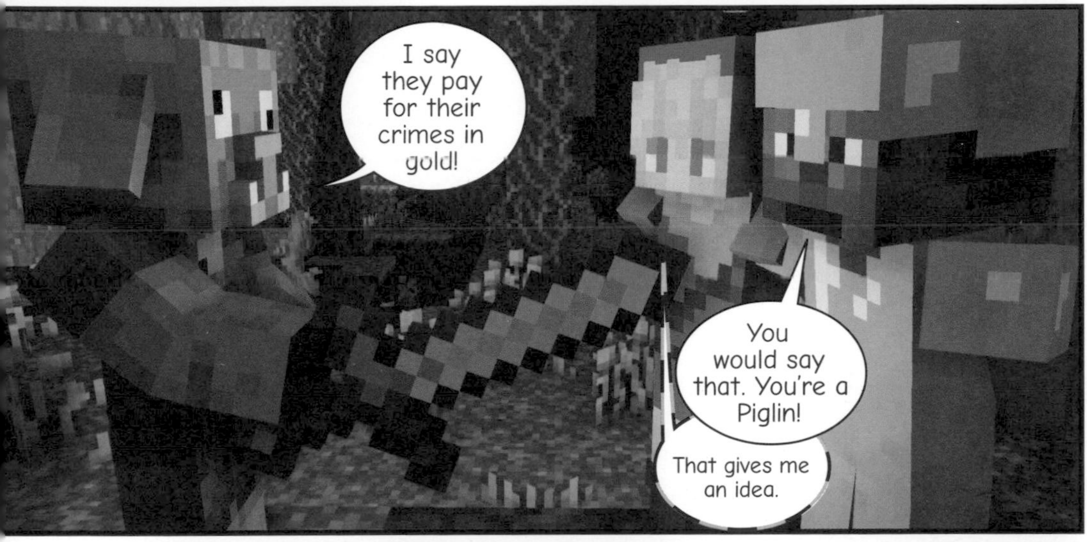
I say they pay for their crimes in gold!
You would say that. You're a Piglin!
That gives me an idea.

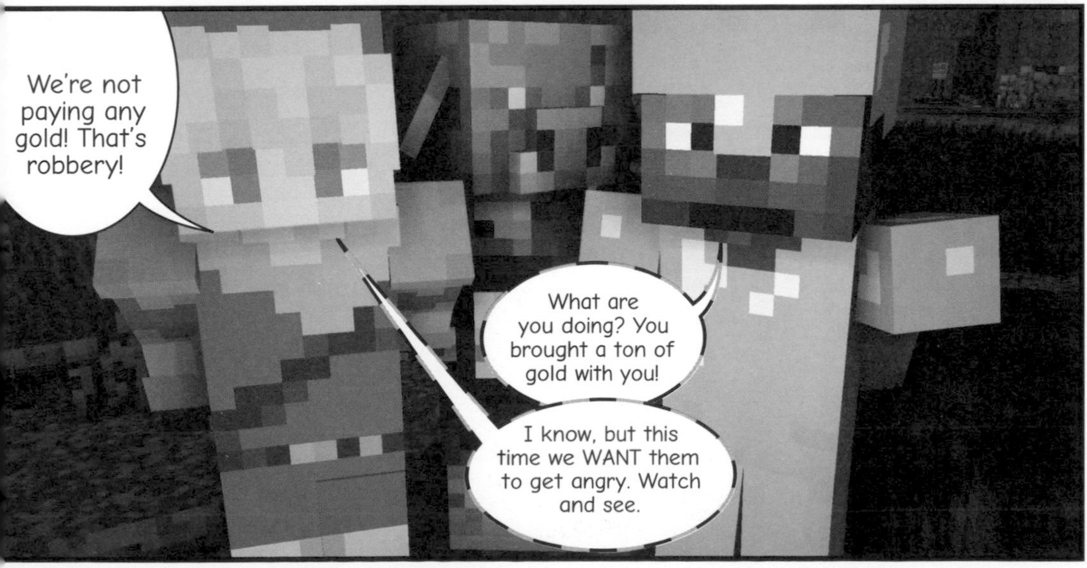
We're not paying any gold! That's robbery!
What are you doing? You brought a ton of gold with you!
I know, but this time we WANT them to get angry. Watch and see.

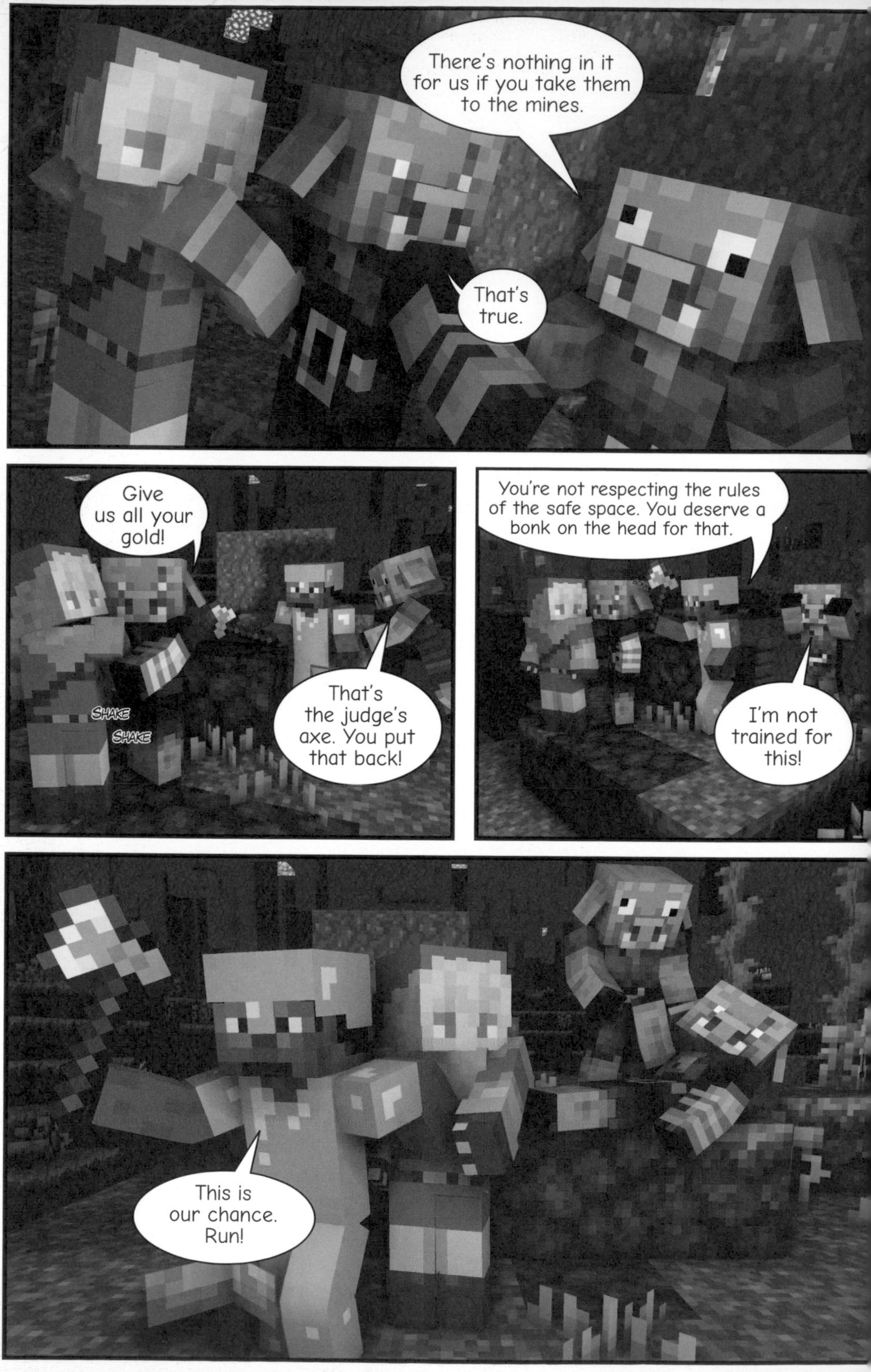
There's nothing in it for us if you take them to the mines.
That's true.
Give us all your gold!
SHAKE
SHAKE
That's the judge's axe. You put that back!
You're not respecting the rules of the safe space. You deserve a bonk on the head for that.
I'm not trained for this!
This is our chance. Run!

Chapter 9
Attack

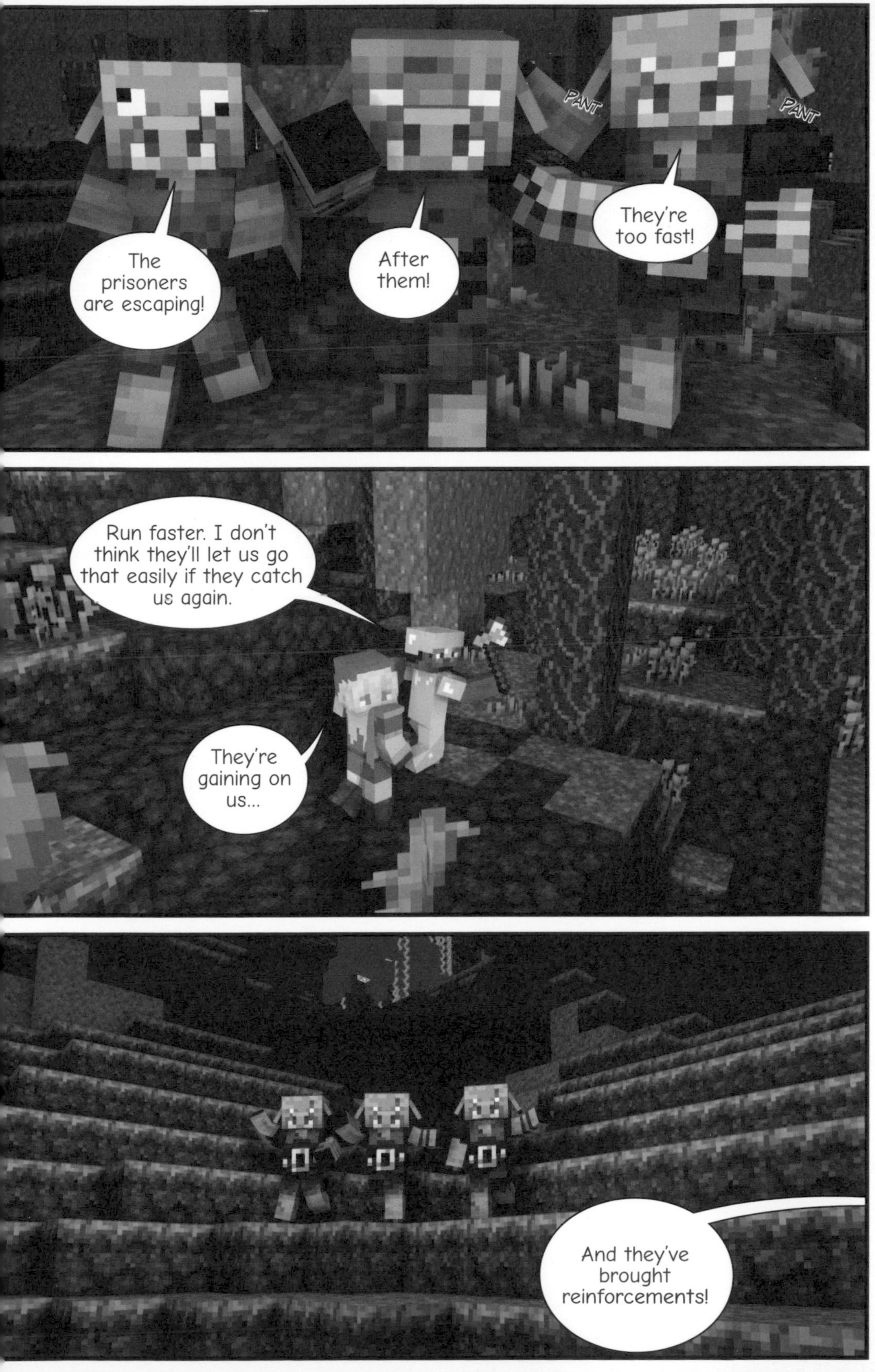
The prisoners are escaping!
After them!
PANT
PANT
They're too fast!
Run faster. I don't think they'll let us go that easily if they catch us again.
They're gaining on us...
And they've brought reinforcements!

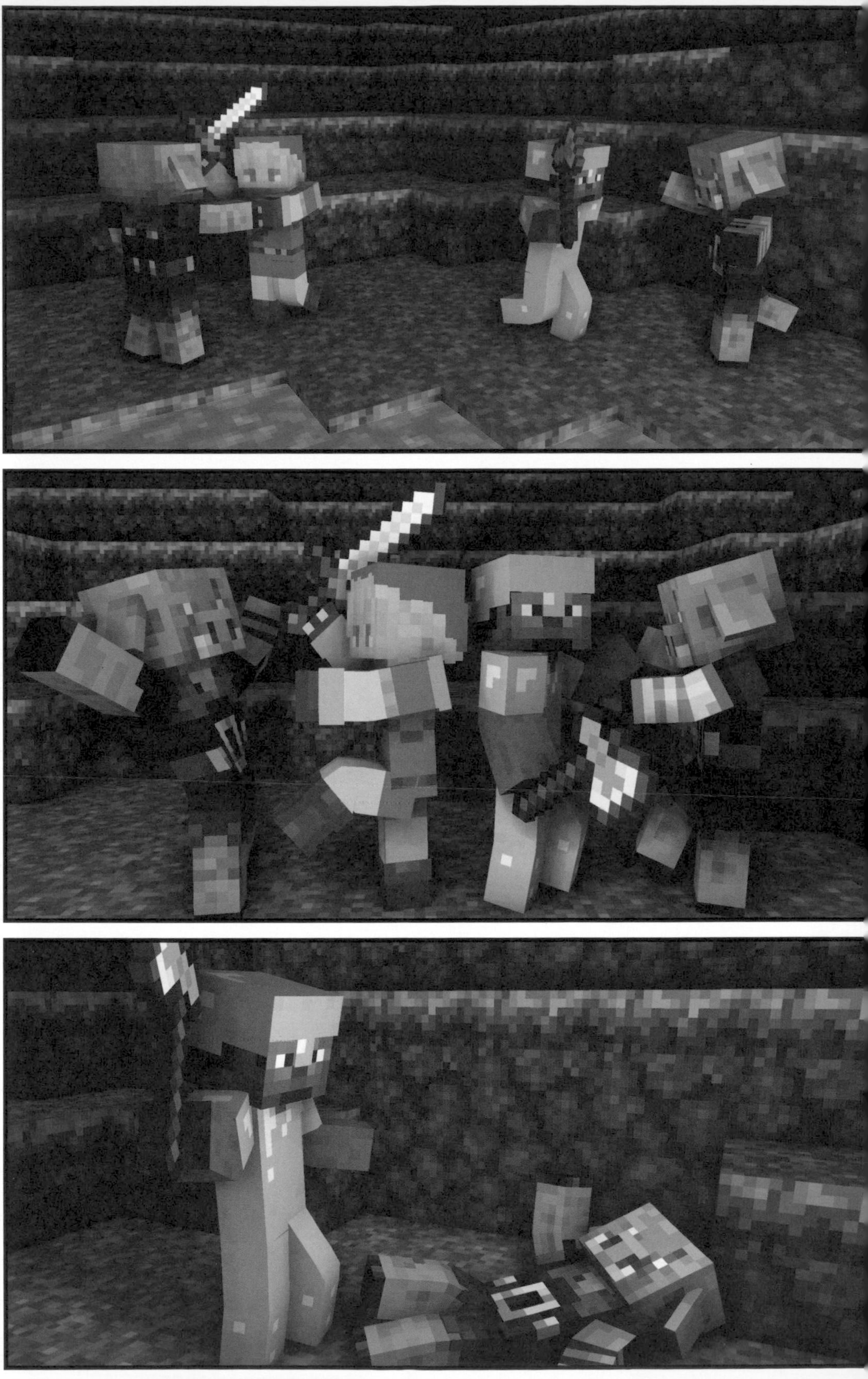

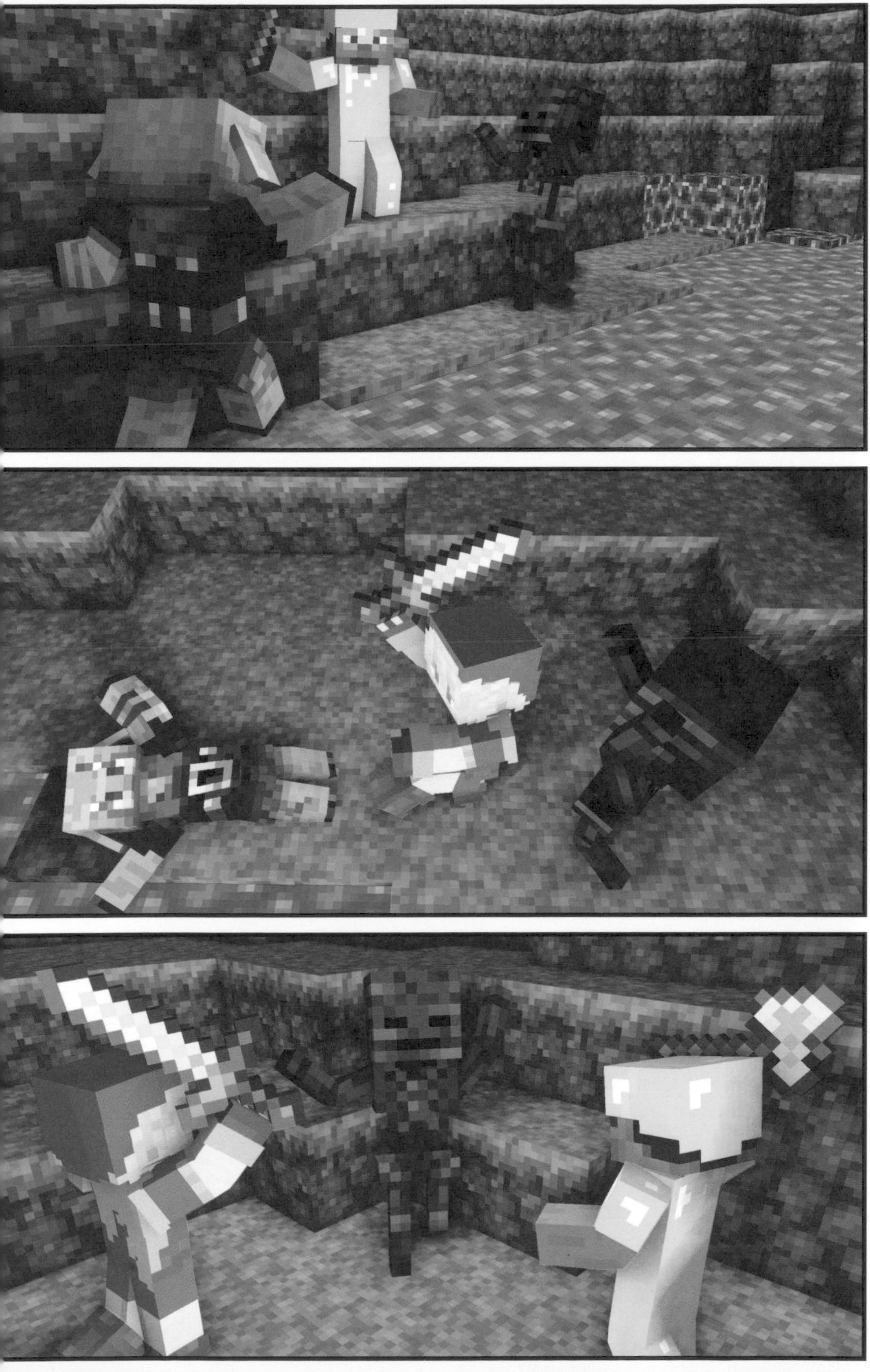

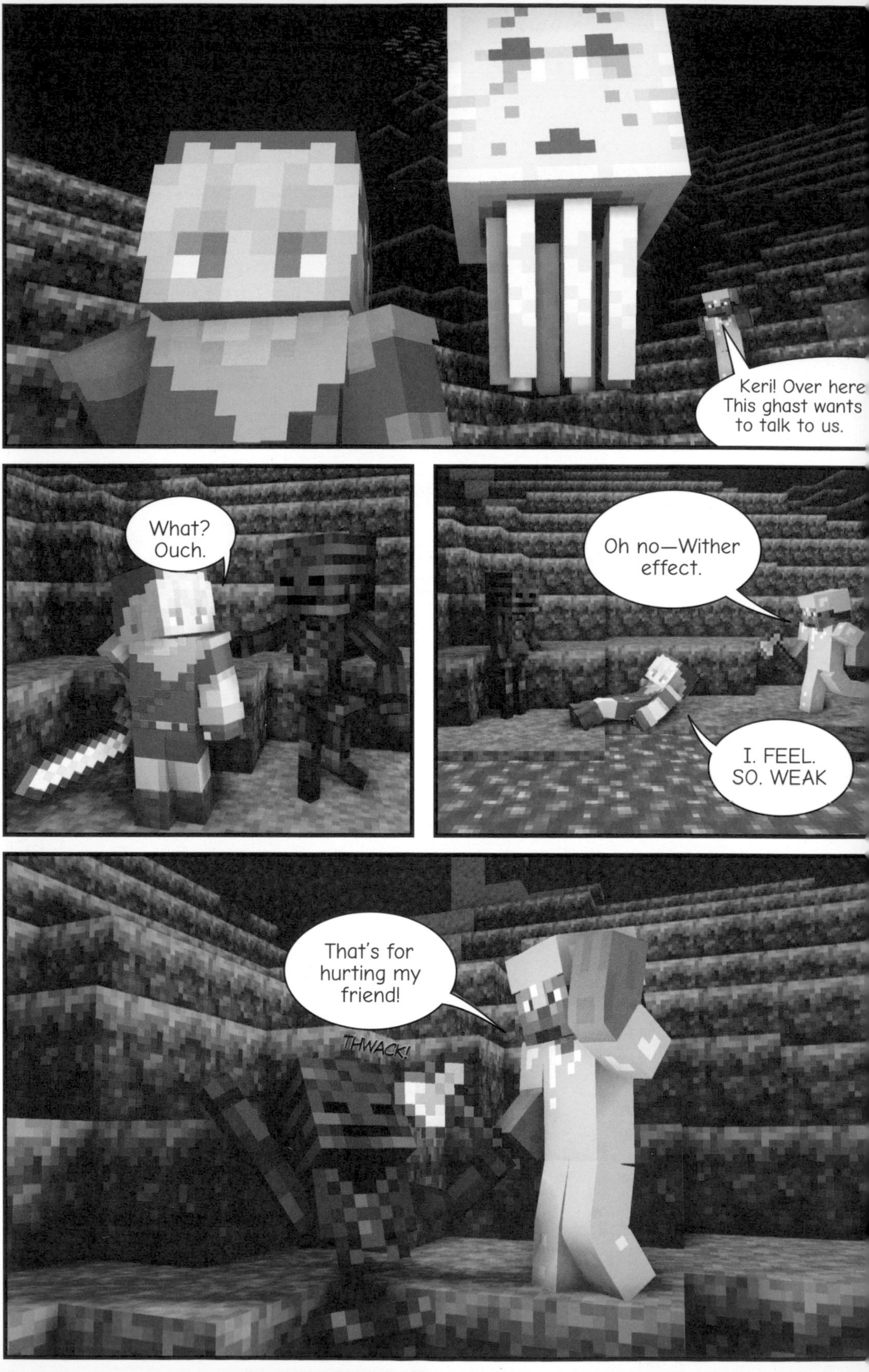
Keri! Over here
This ghast wants
to talk to us.
What?
Ouch.
Oh no—Wither
effect.
I. FEEL.
SO. WEAK
That's for
hurting my
friend!
THWACK!

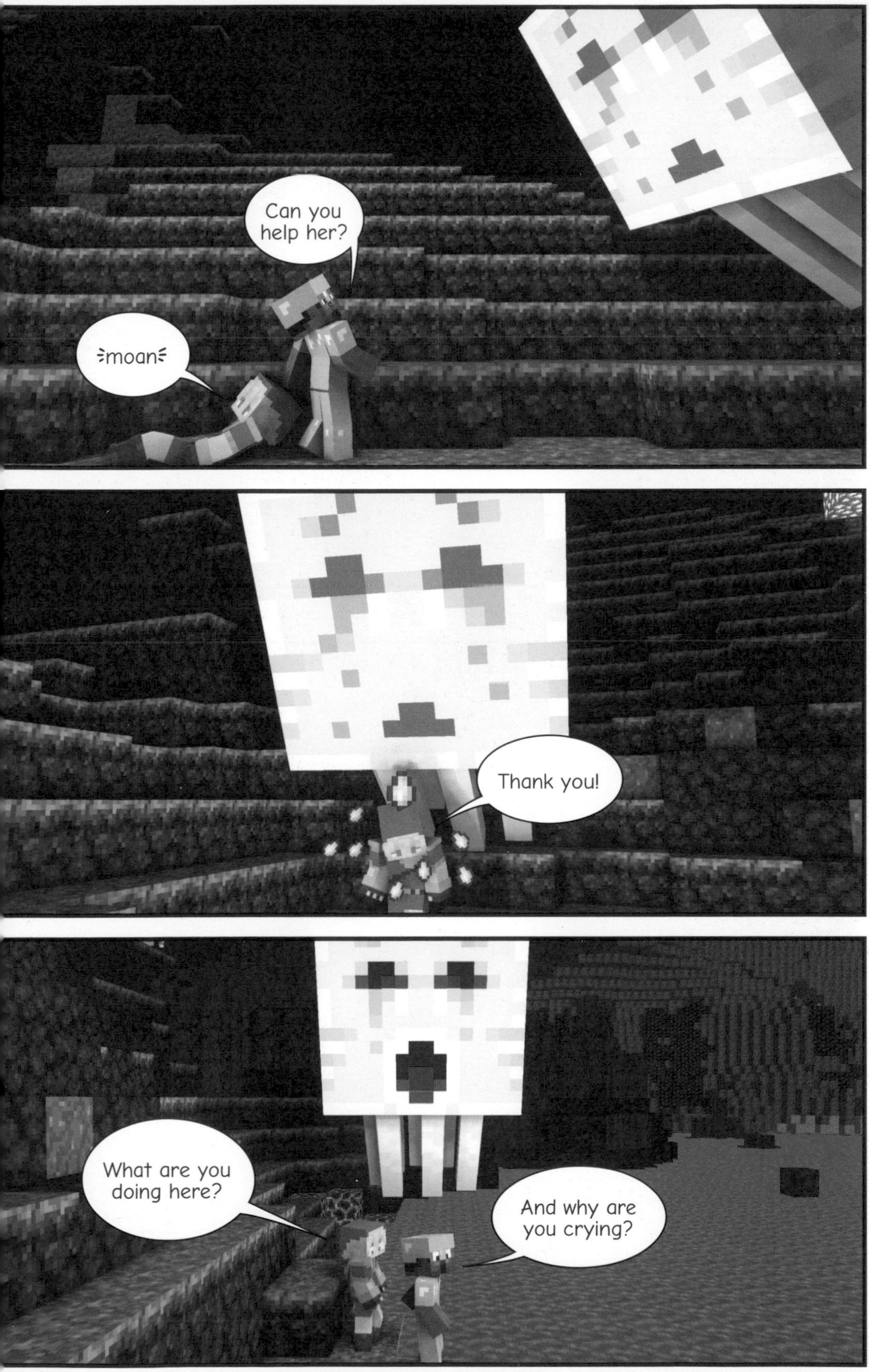
Can you help her?
moan
Thank you!
What are you doing here?
And why are you crying?

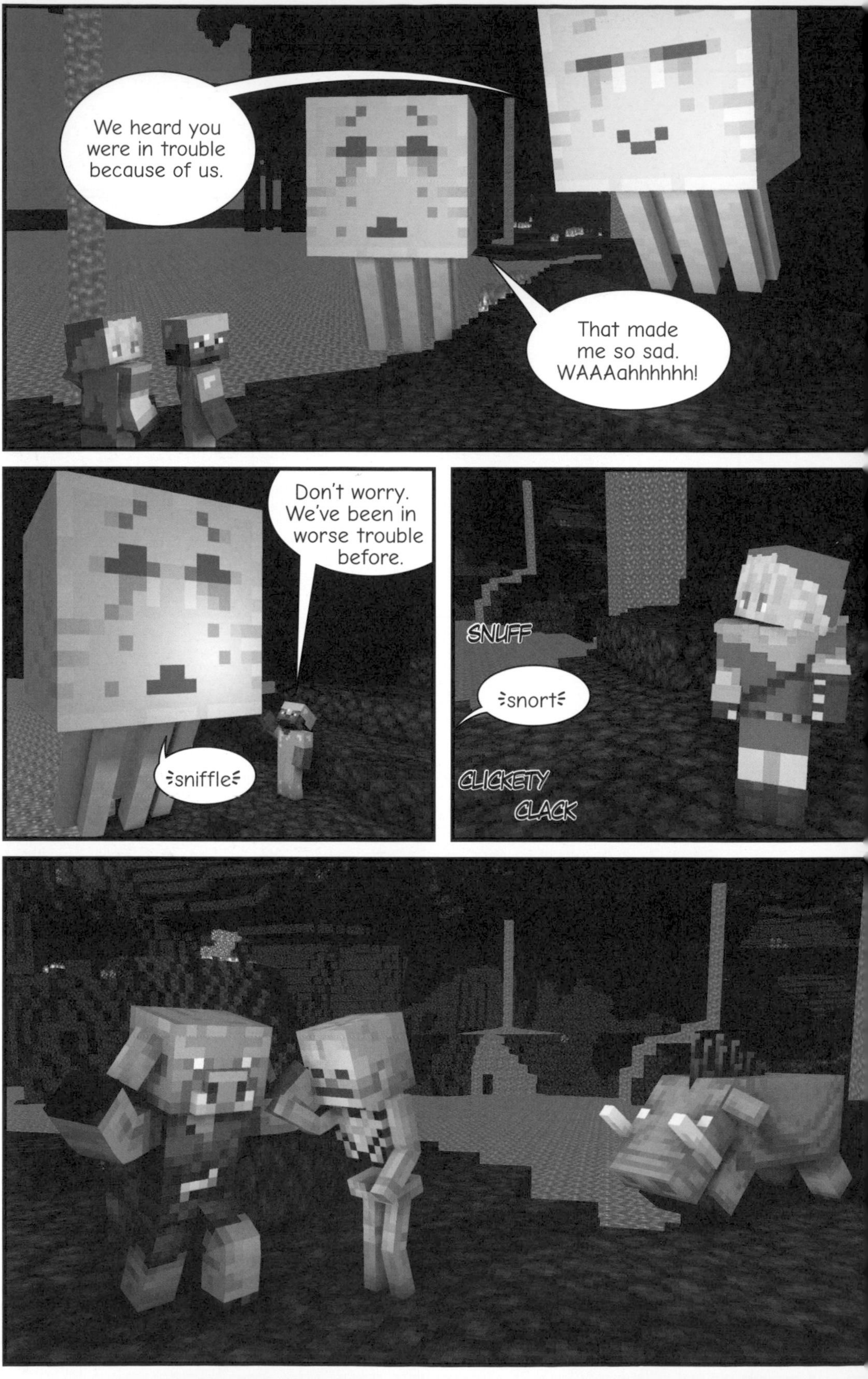
We heard you were in trouble because of us.
That made me so sad. WAAAahhhhhh!
Don't worry. We've been in worse trouble before.
sniffle
SNUFF
snort
CLICKETY
CLACK

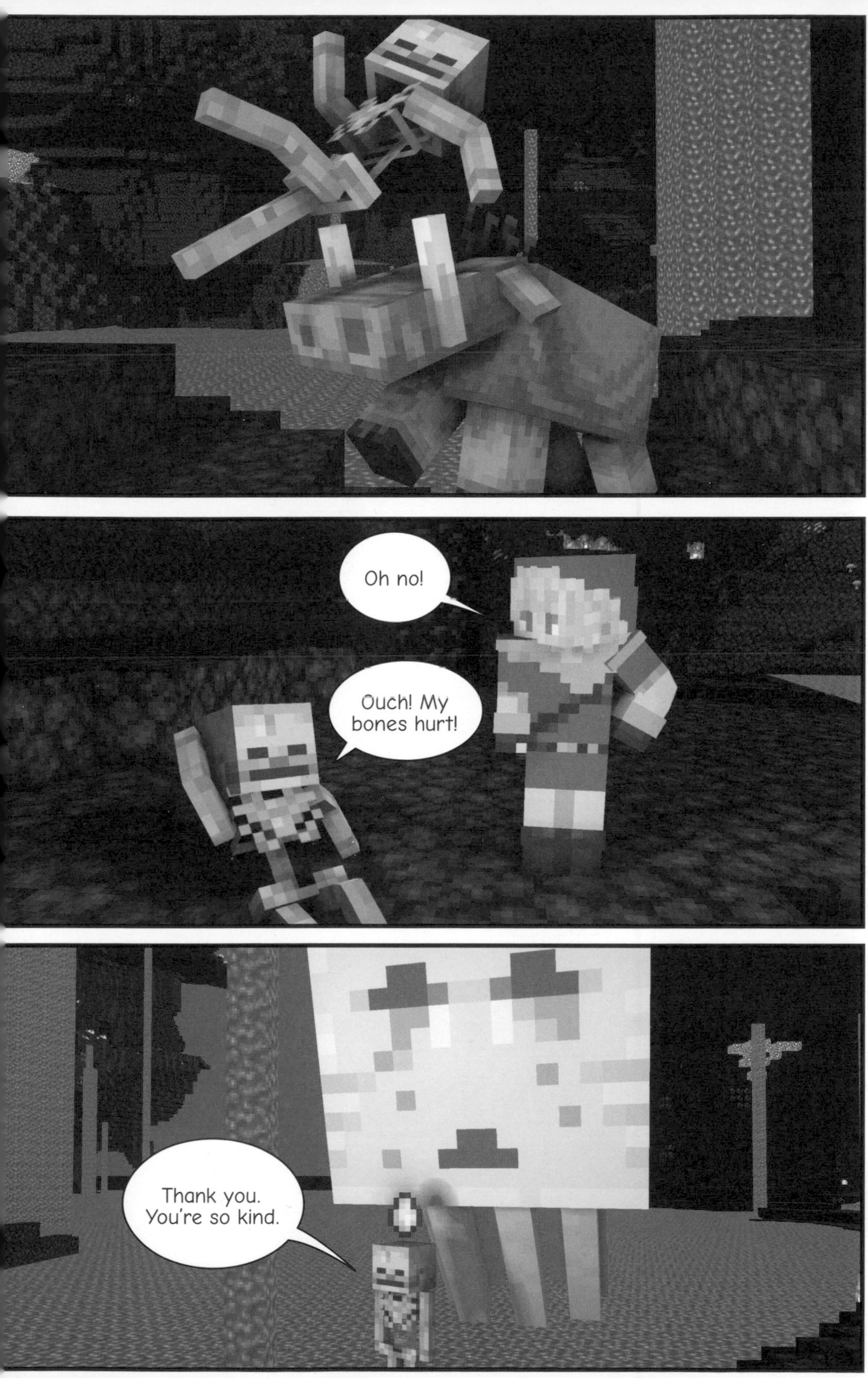

Oh no!
Ouch! My bones hurt!
Thank you. You're so kind.

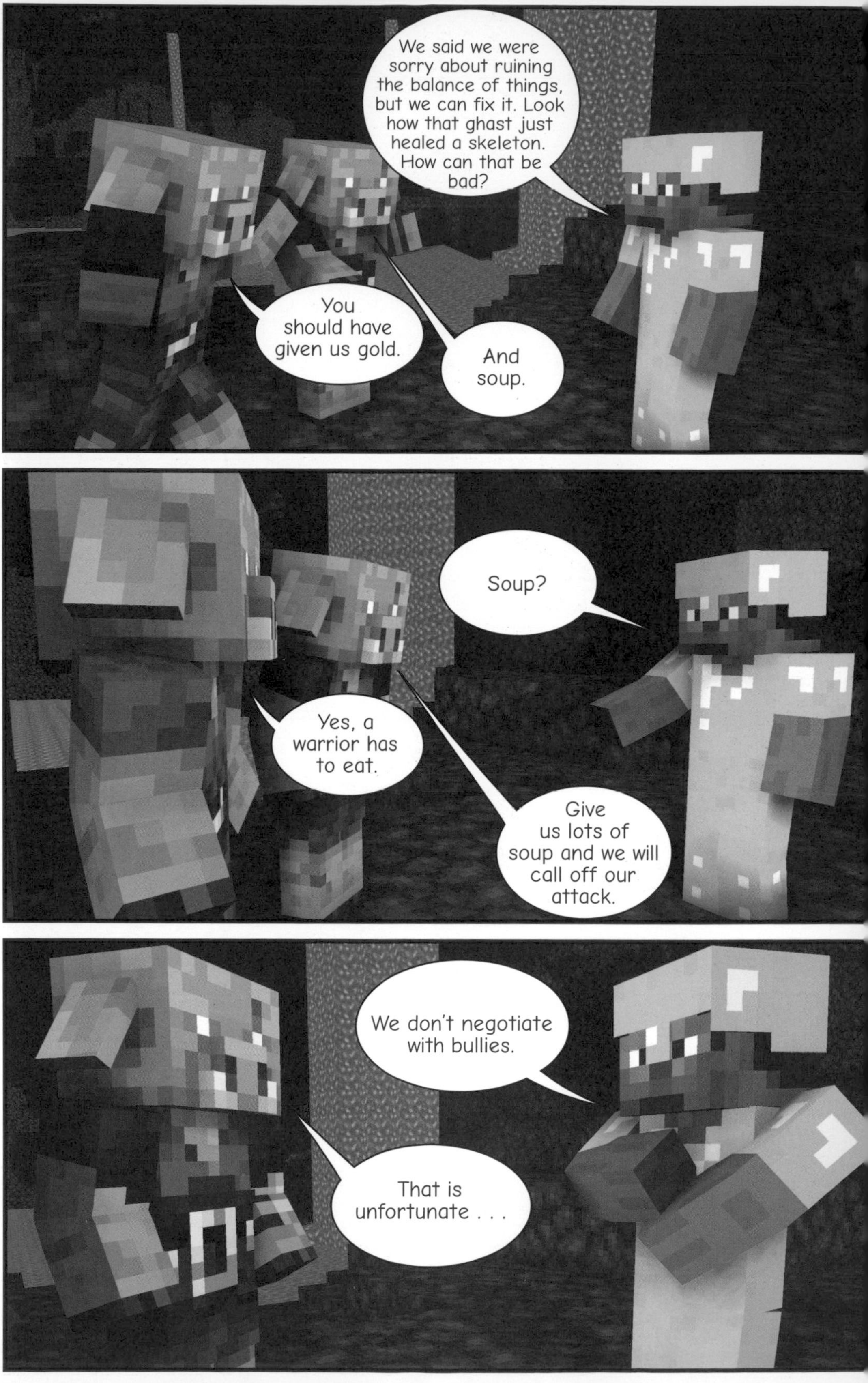
We said we were sorry about ruining the balance of things, but we can fix it. Look how that ghast just healed a skeleton. How can that be bad?
You should have given us gold.
And soup.
Soup?
Yes, a warrior has to eat.
Give us lots of soup and we will call off our attack.
We don't negotiate with bullies.
That is unfortunate . . .

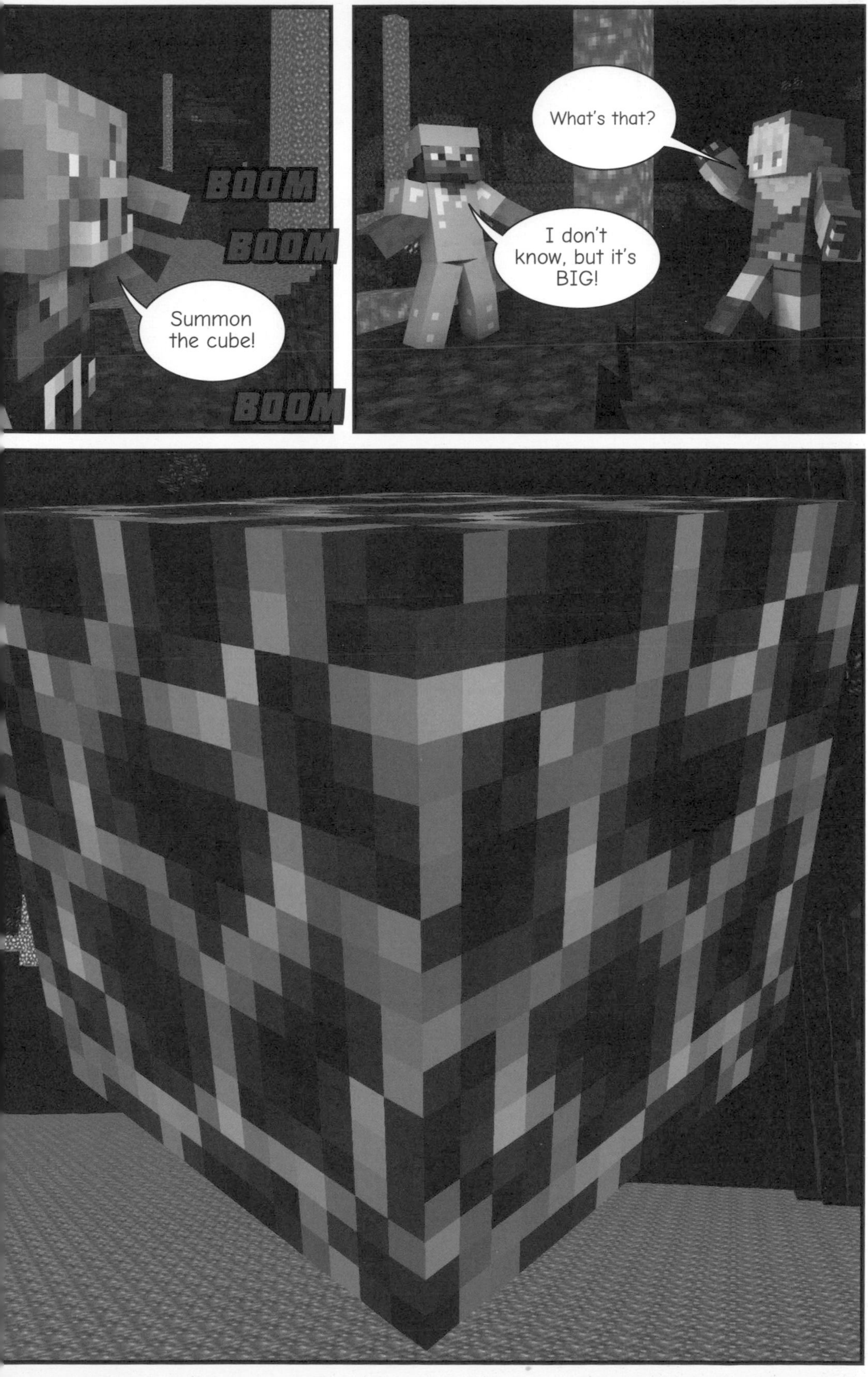
BOOM
BOOM
Summon the cube!
BOOM
What's that?
I don't know, but it's BIG!

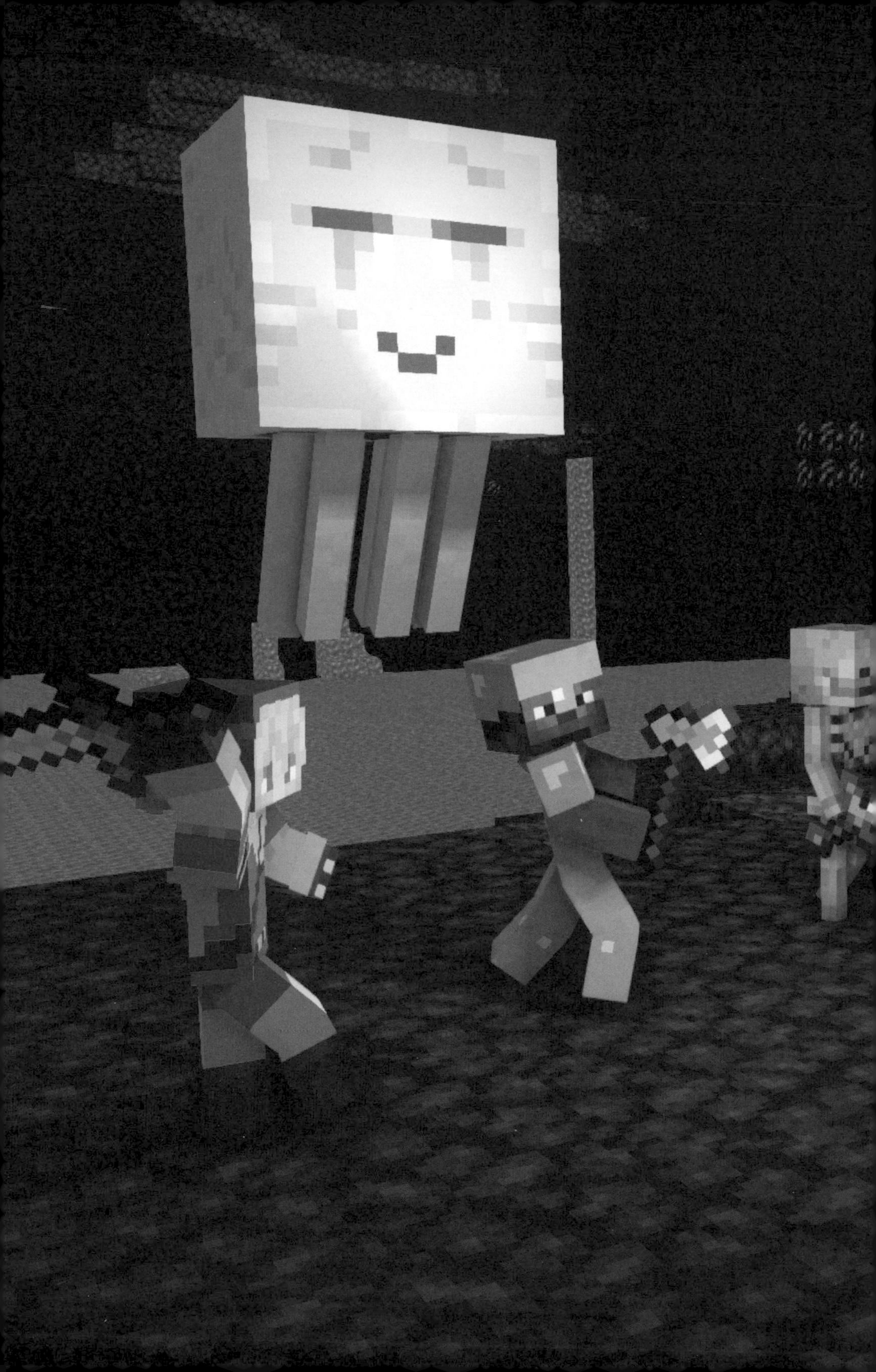

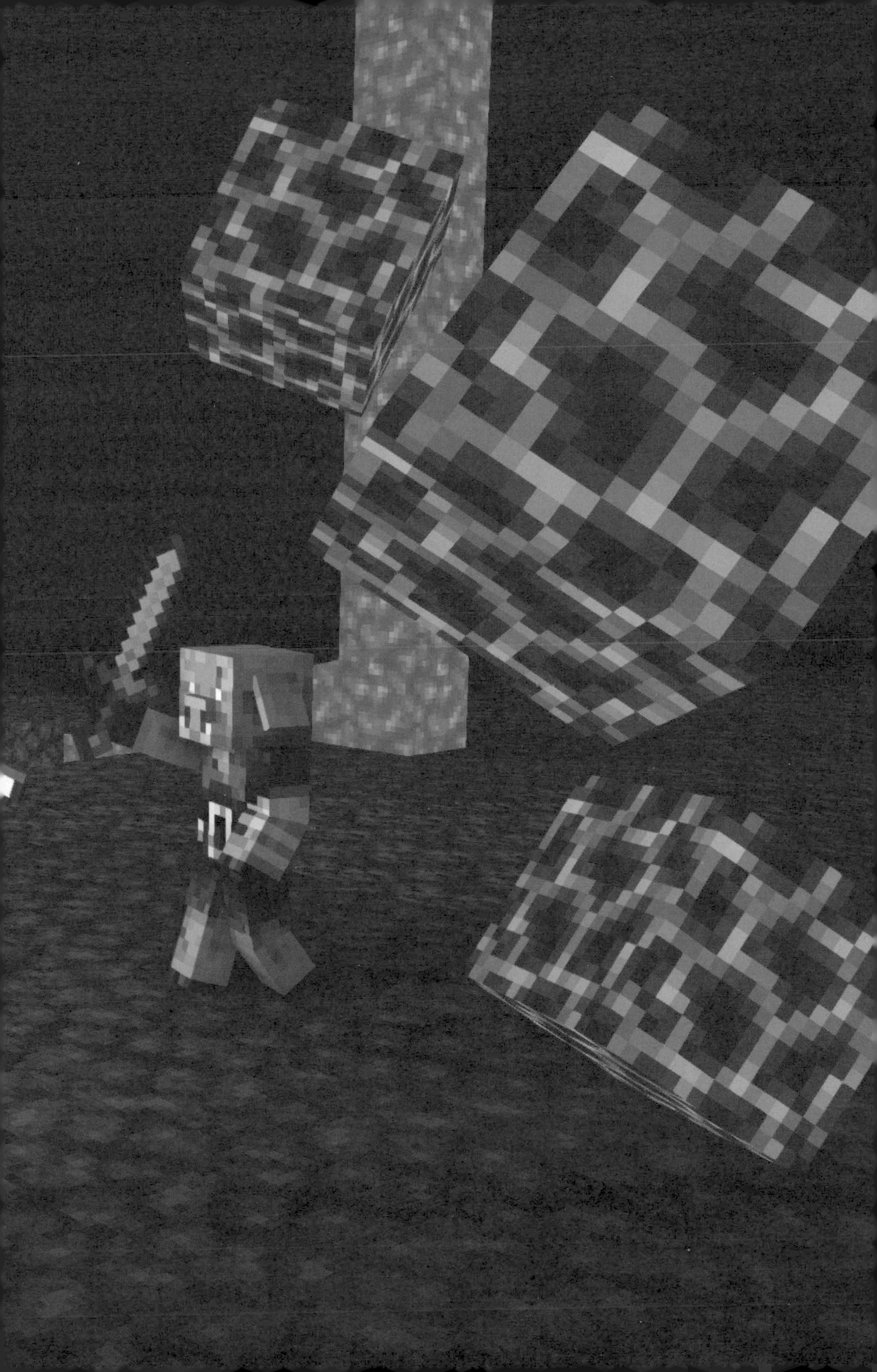

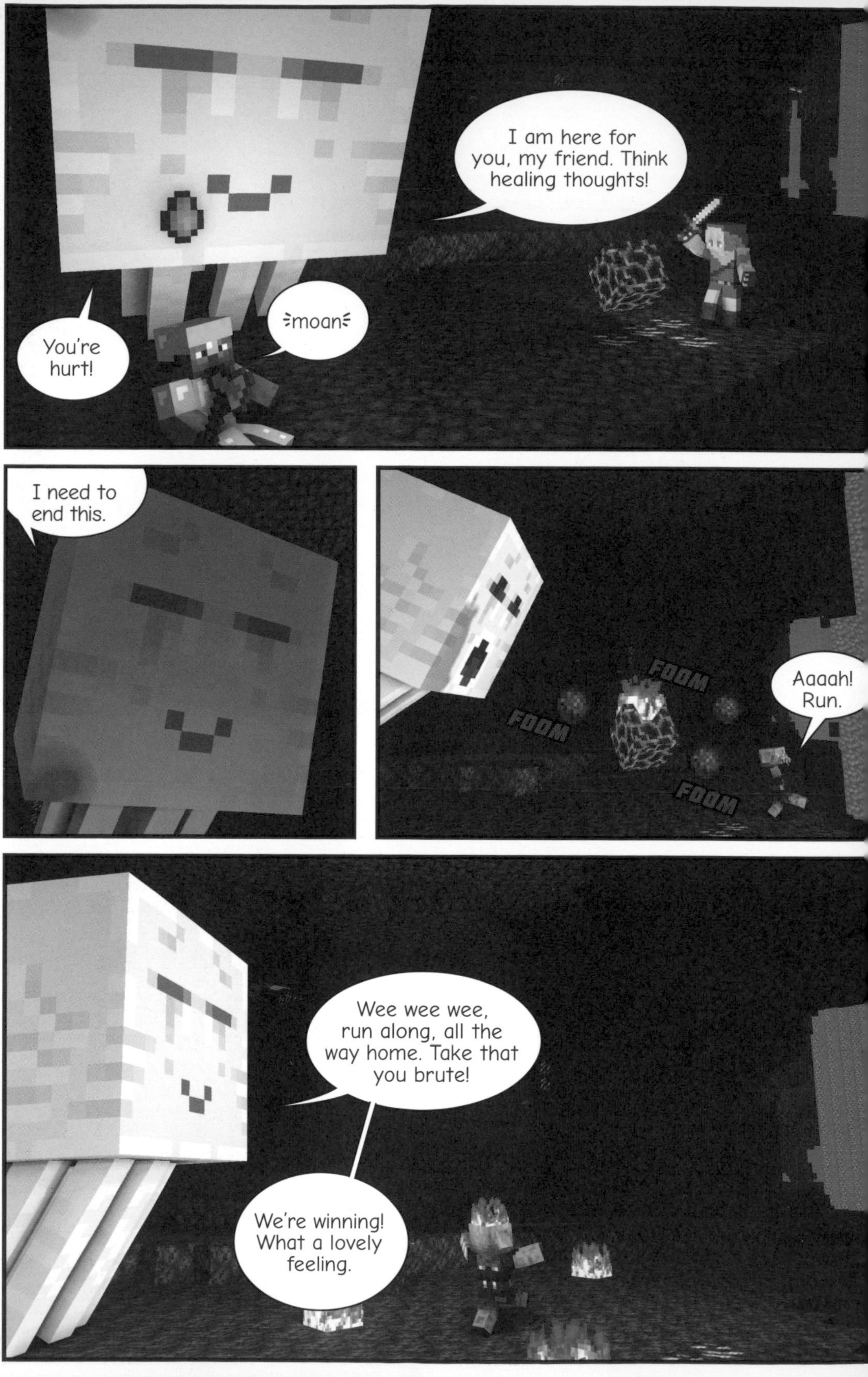
I am here for you, my friend. Think healing thoughts!
You're hurt!
moan
I need to end this.
FOOM
FOOM
FOOM
Aaaah! Run.
Wee wee wee, run along, all the way home. Take that you brute!
We're winning! What a lovely feeling.

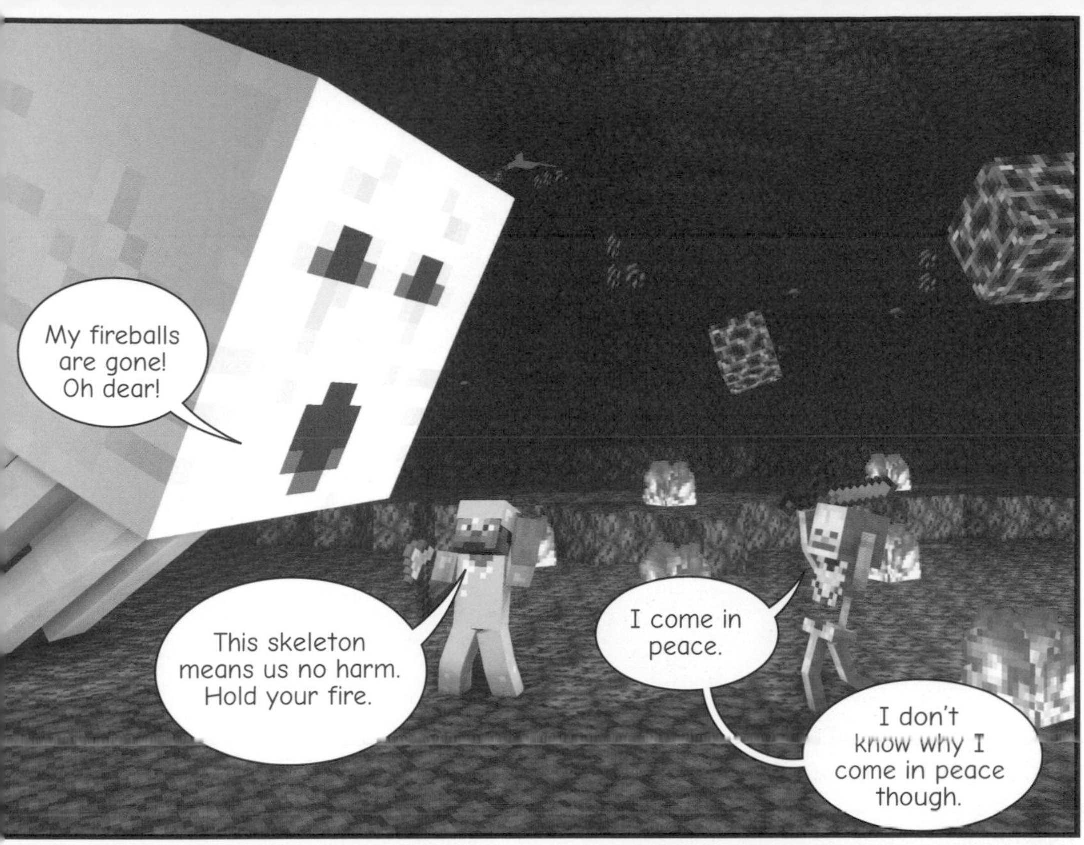
My fireballs are gone! Oh dear!
This skeleton means us no harm. Hold your fire.
I come in peace.
I don't know why I come in peace though.

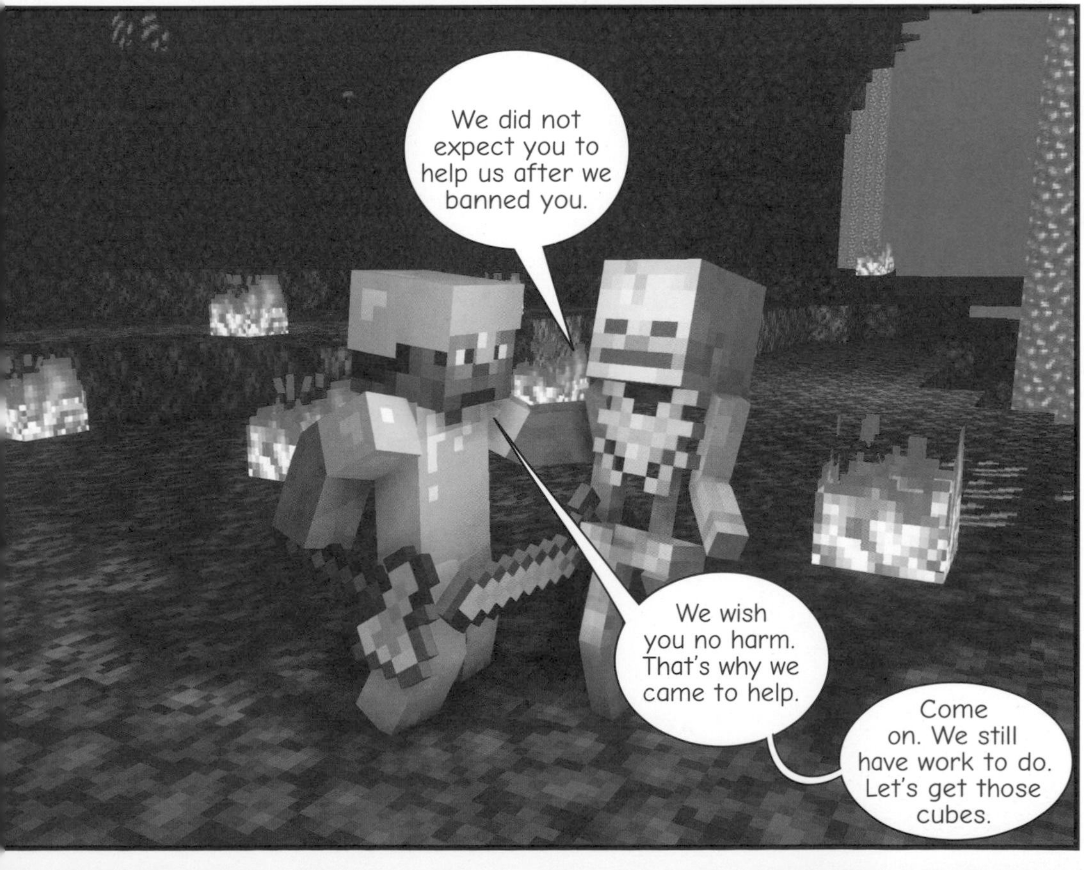
We did not expect you to help us after we banned you.
We wish you no harm. That's why we came to help.
Come on. We still have work to do. Let's get those cubes.

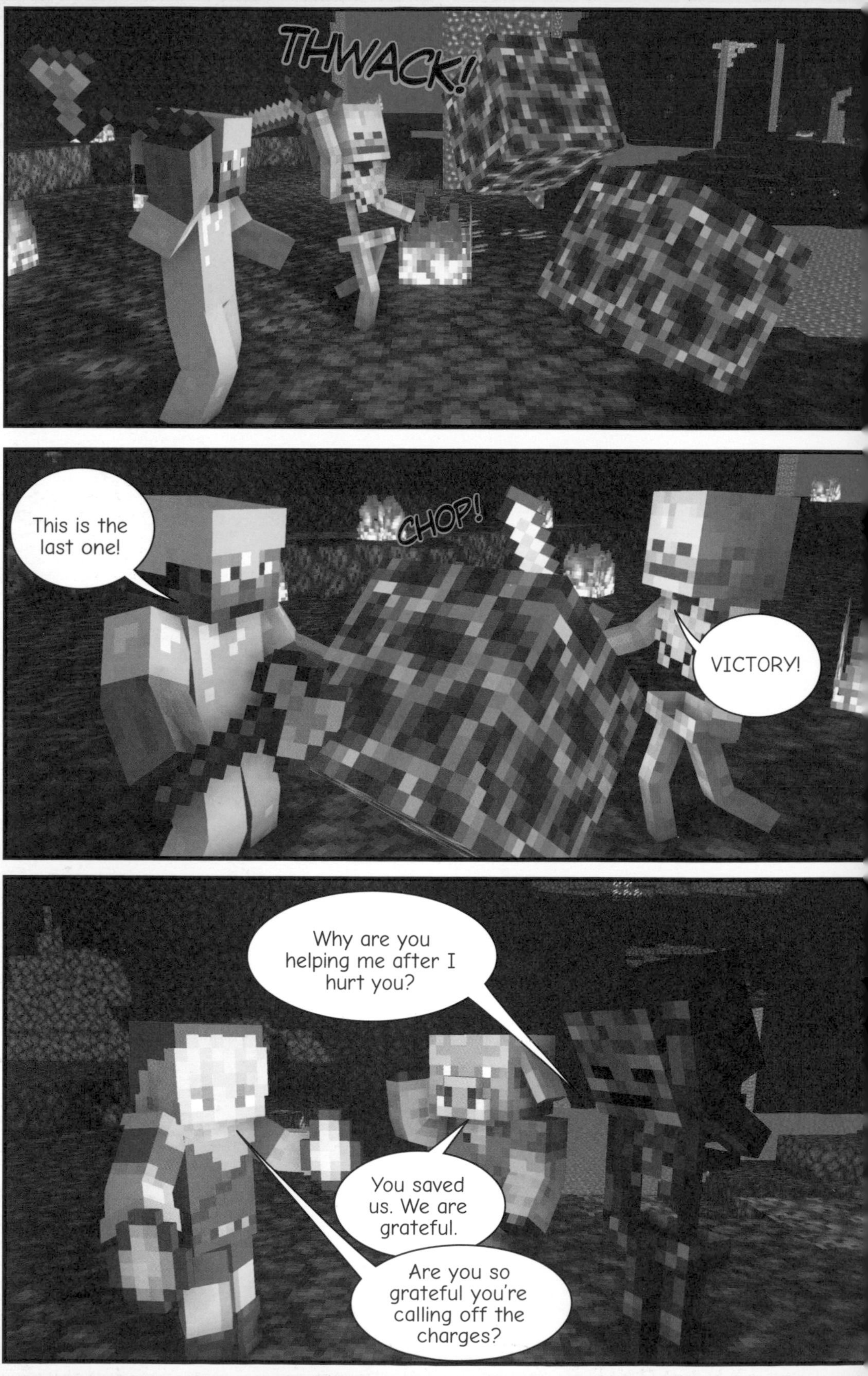
THWACK!
This is the last one!
CHOP!
VICTORY!
Why are you helping me after I hurt you?
You saved us. We are grateful.
Are you so grateful you're calling off the charges?

Chapter 10
A Win and a Loss

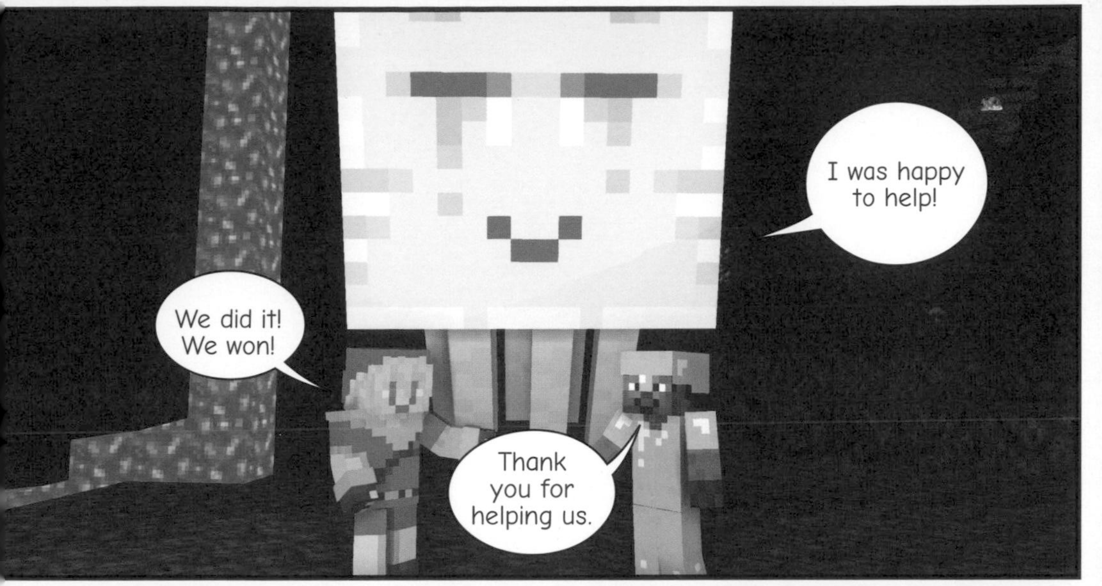
I was happy to help!
We did it! We won!
Thank you for helping us.

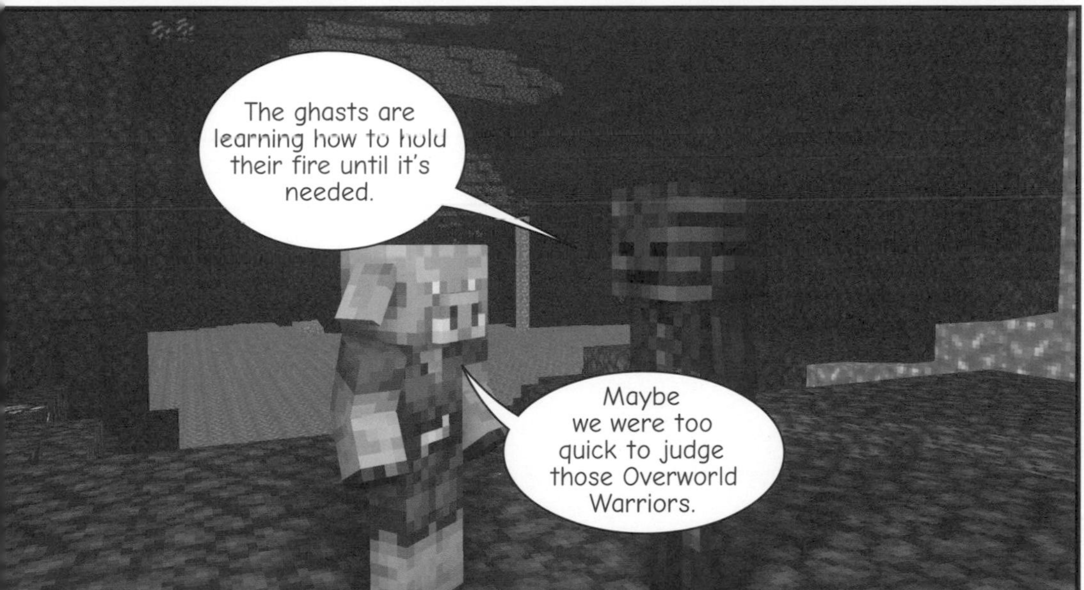
The ghasts are learning how to hold their fire until it's needed.
Maybe we were too quick to judge those Overworld Warriors.

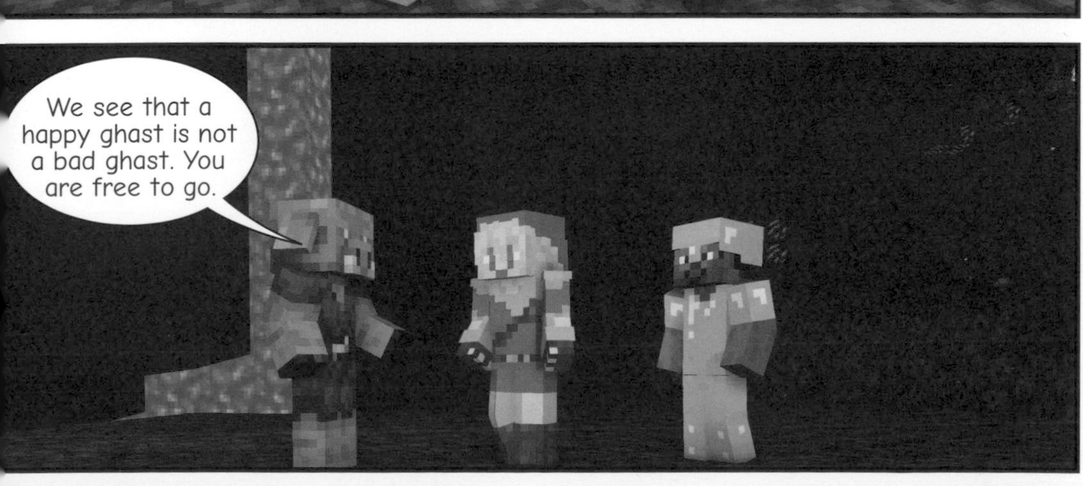
We see that a happy ghast is not a bad ghast. You are free to go.

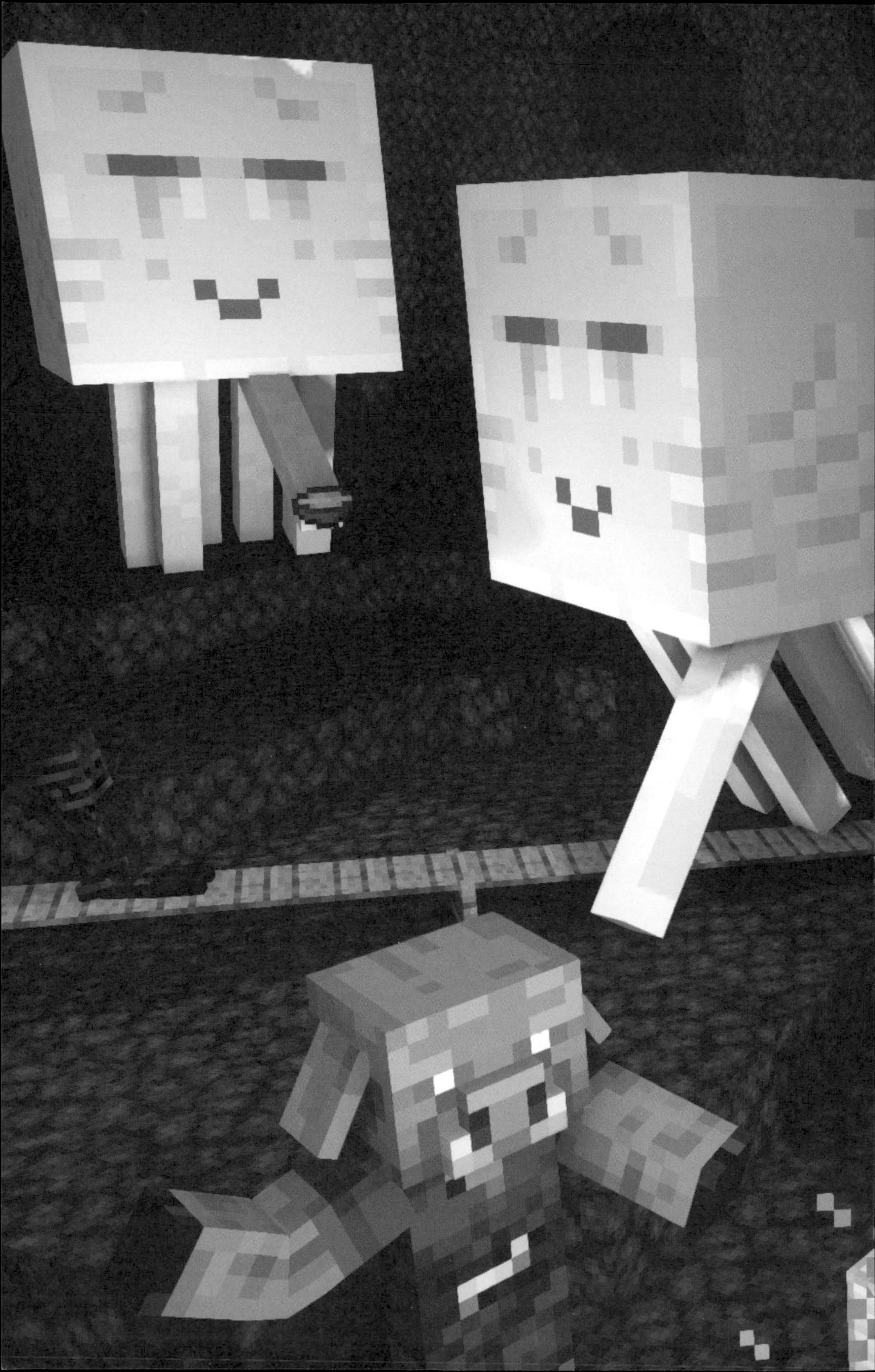

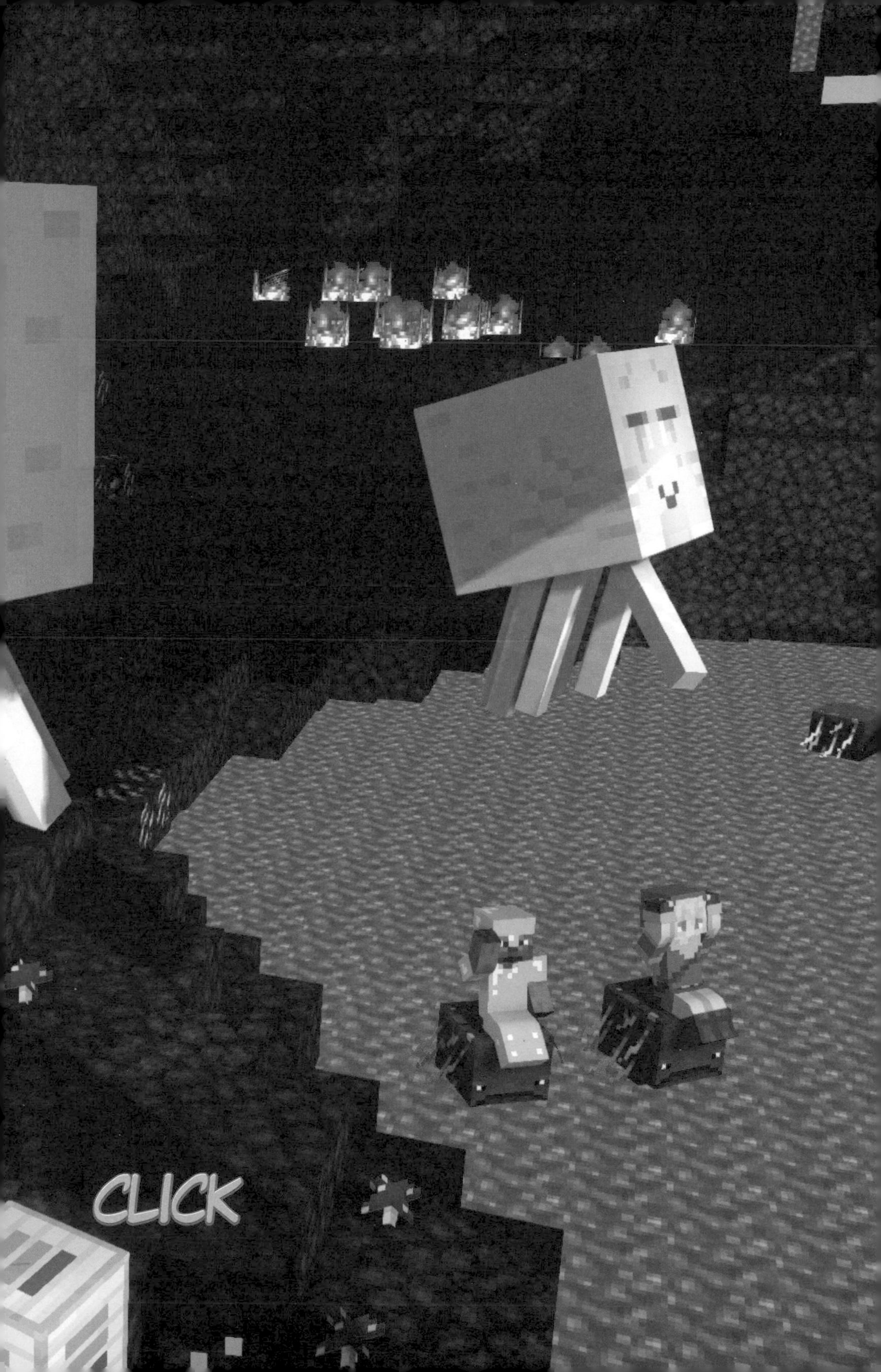
CLICK

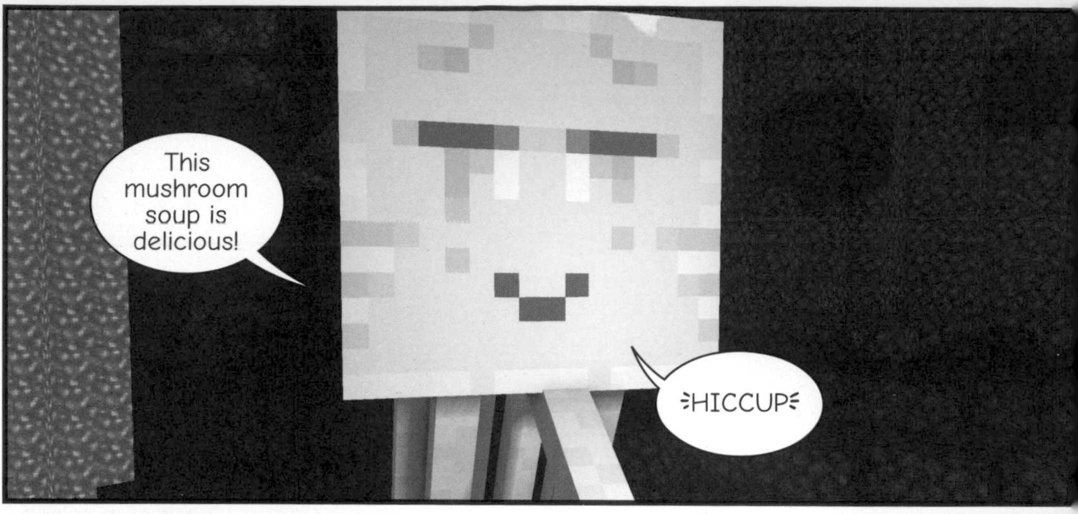
This mushroom soup is delicious!
≡HICCUP≡

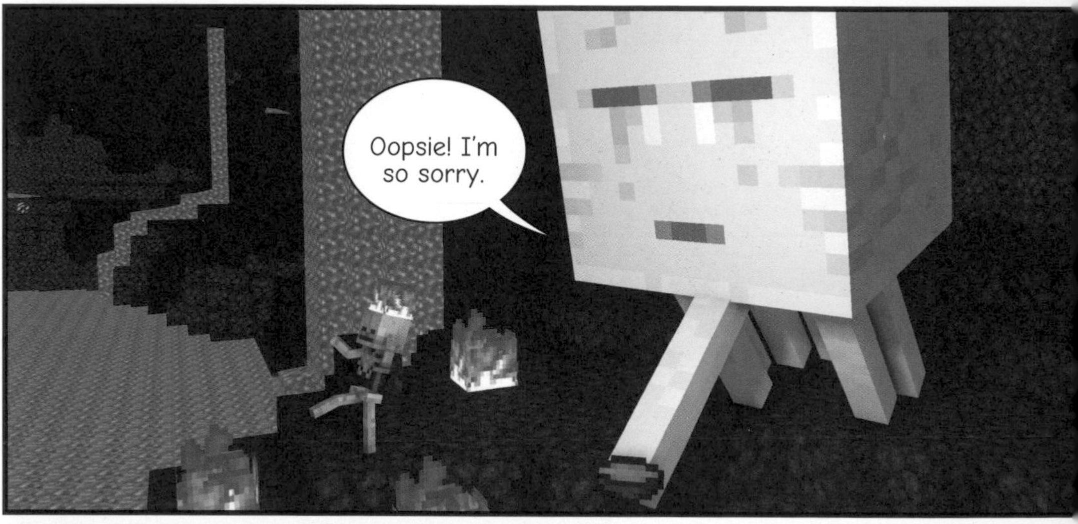
Oopsie! I'm so sorry.

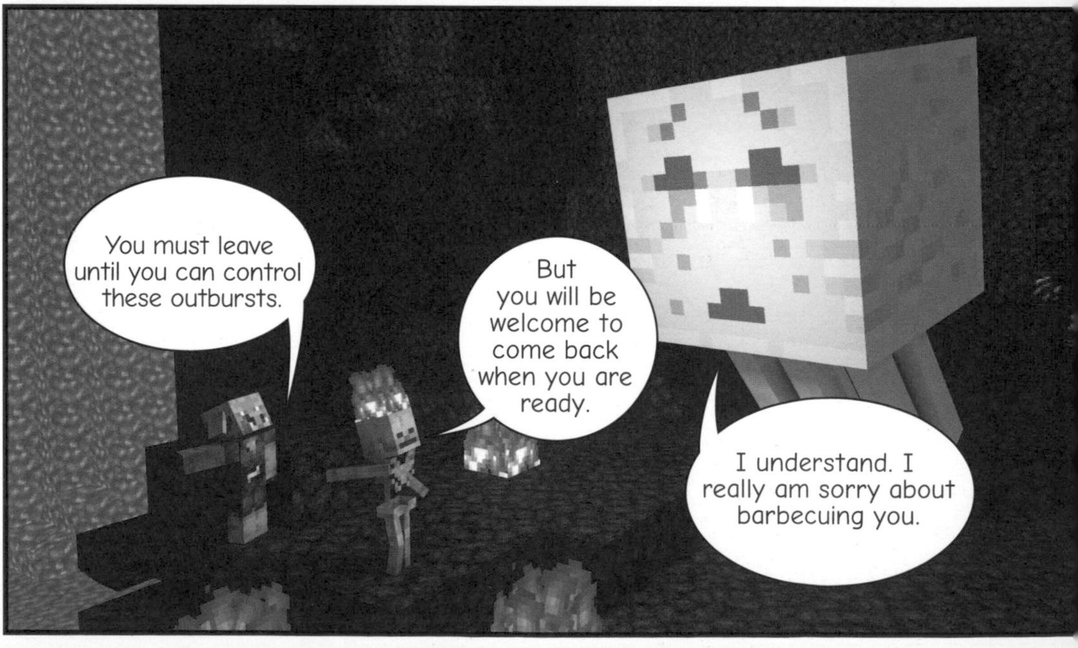
You must leave until you can control these outbursts.
But you will be welcome to come back when you are ready.
I understand. I really am sorry about barbecuing you.

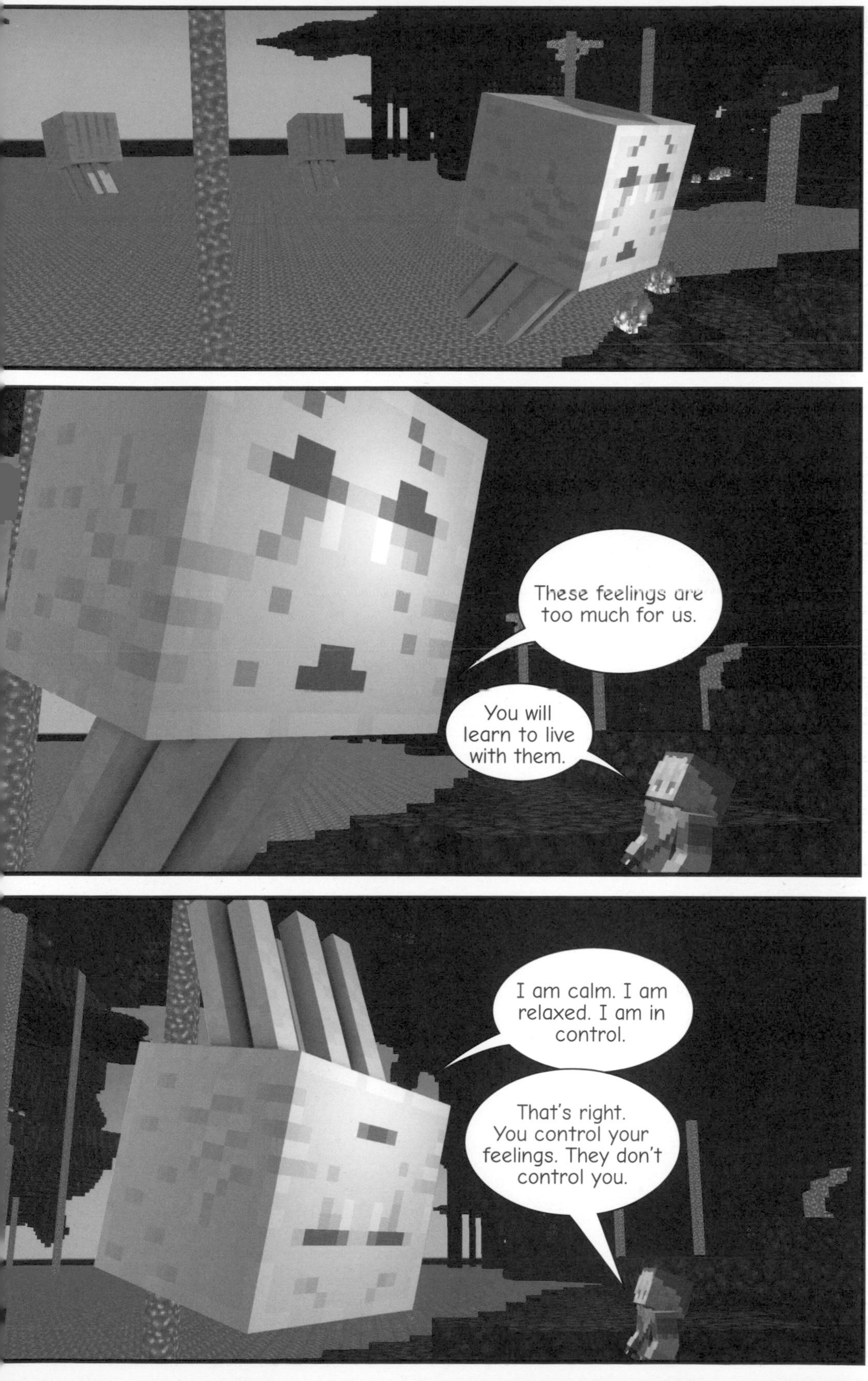
These feelings are too much for us.
You will learn to live with them.
I am calm. I am relaxed. I am in control.
That's right. You control your feelings. They don't control you.

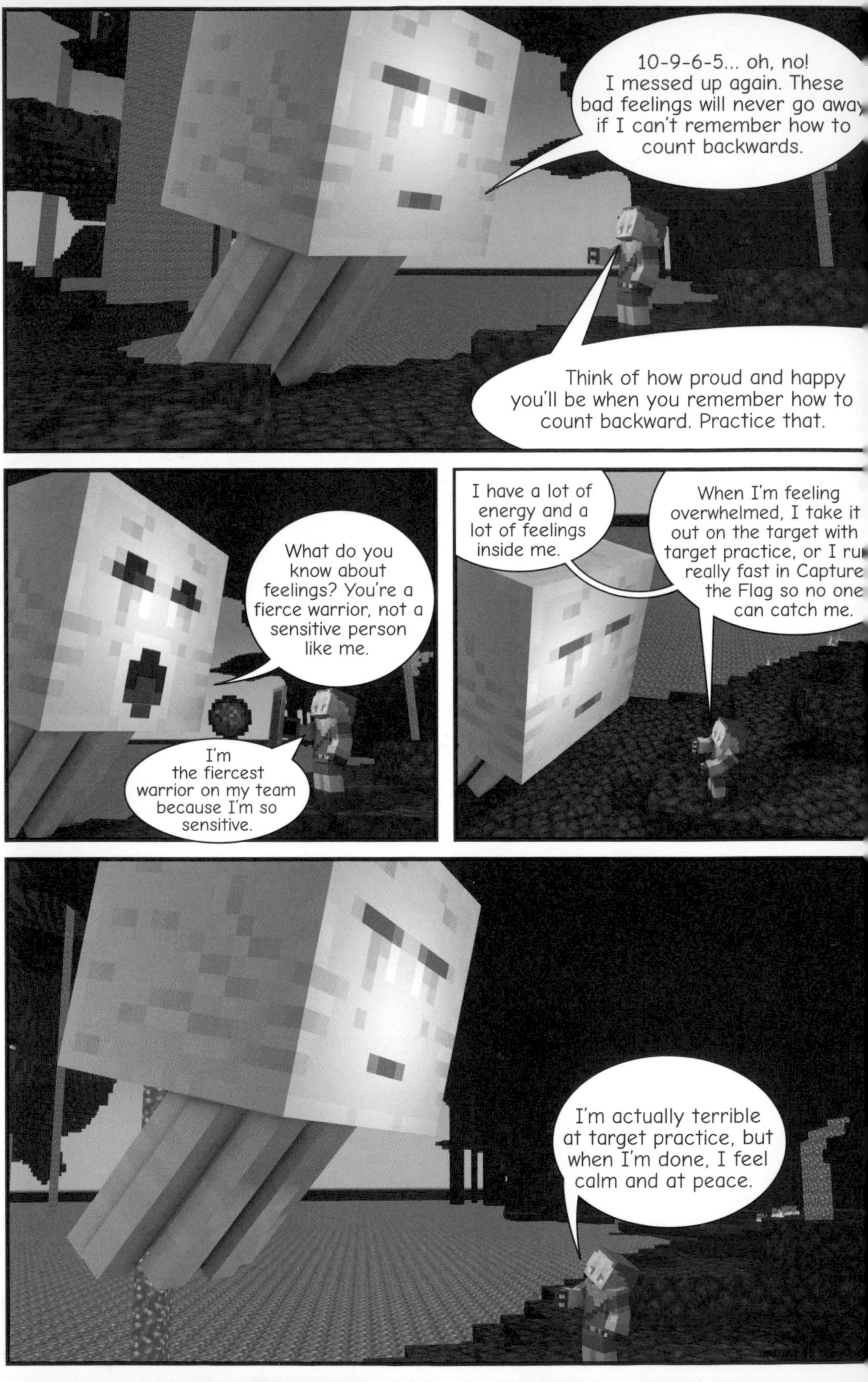
10-9-6-5... oh, no! I messed up again. These bad feelings will never go awa if I can't remember how to count backwards.
Think of how proud and happy you'll be when you remember how to count backward. Practice that.
What do you know about feelings? You're a fierce warrior, not a sensitive person like me.
I'm the fiercest warrior on my team because I'm so sensitive.
I have a lot of energy and a lot of feelings inside me.
When I'm feeling overwhelmed, I take it out on the target with target practice, or I ru really fast in Capture the Flag so no one can catch me.
I'm actually terrible at target practice, but when I'm done, I feel calm and at peace.

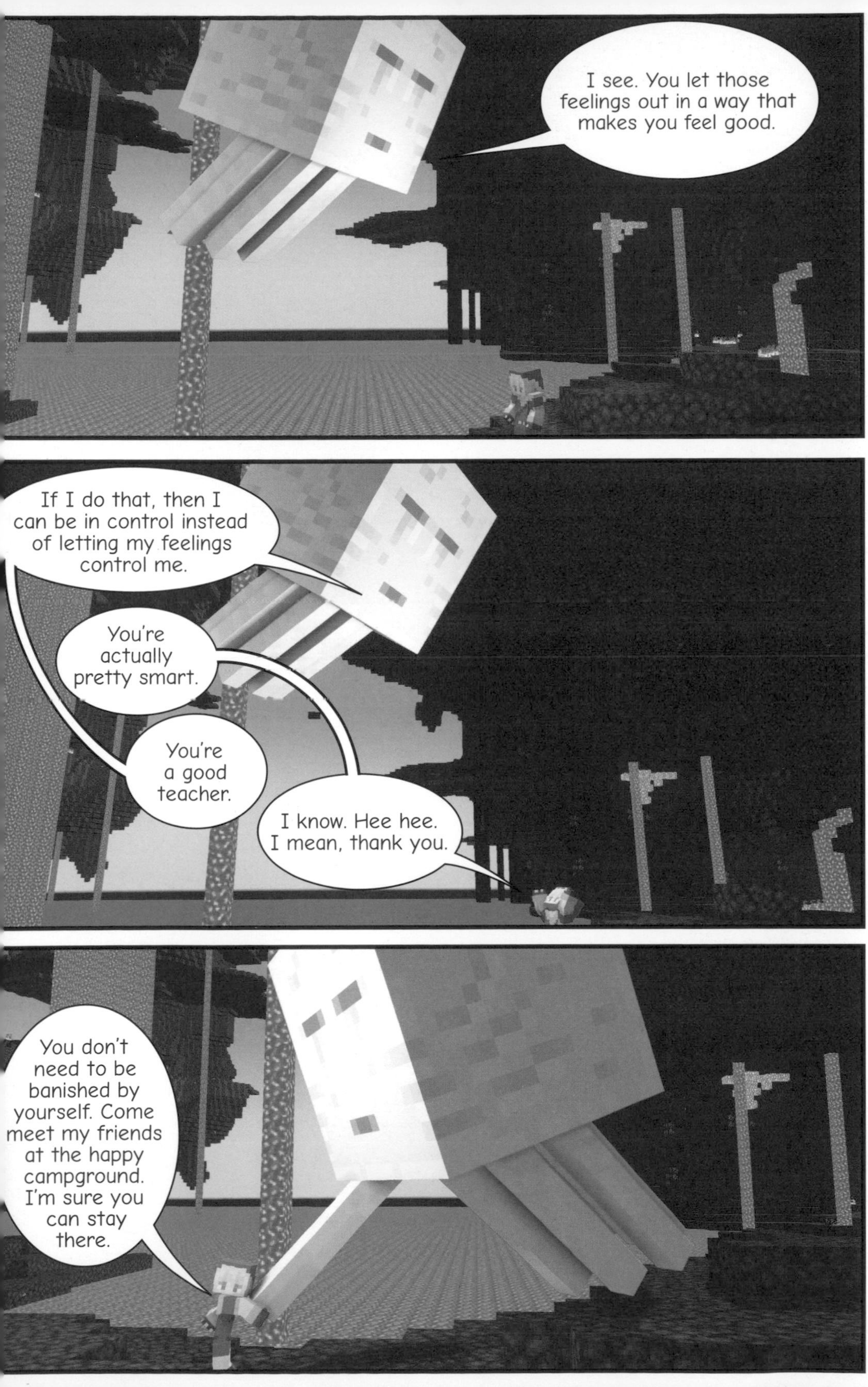
I see. You let those feelings out in a way that makes you feel good.
If I do that, then I can be in control instead of letting my feelings control me.
You're actually pretty smart.
You're a good teacher.
I know. Hee hee. I mean, thank you.
You don't need to be banished by yourself. Come meet my friends at the happy campground. I'm sure you can stay there.

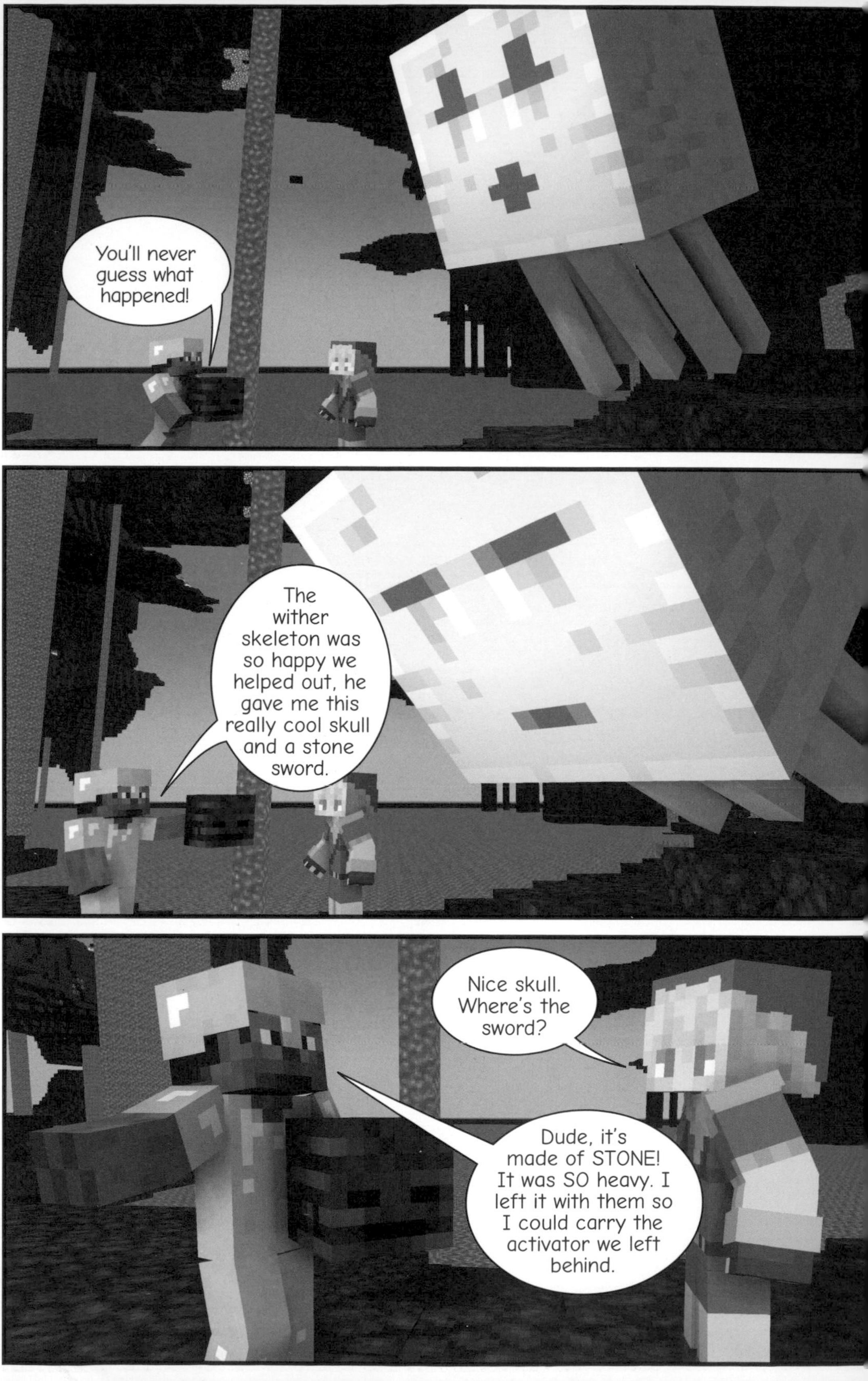
You'll never guess what happened!
The wither skeleton was so happy we helped out, he gave me this really cool skull and a stone sword.
Nice skull. Where's the sword?
Dude, it's made of STONE! It was SO heavy. I left it with them so I could carry the activator we left behind.

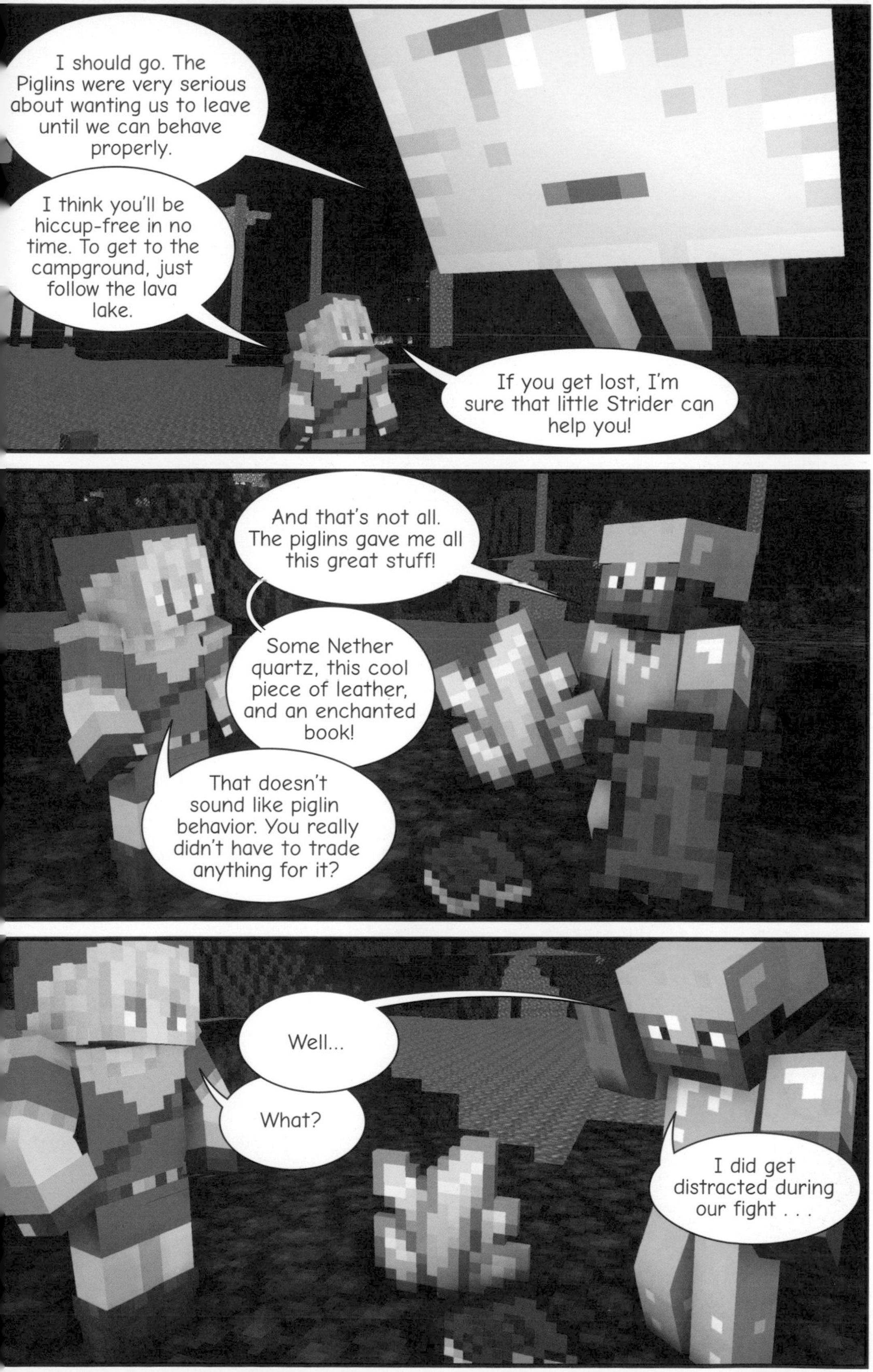
I should go. The Piglins were very serious about wanting us to leave until we can behave properly.
I think you'll be hiccup-free in no time. To get to the campground, just follow the lava lake.
If you get lost, I'm sure that little Strider can help you!
And that's not all. The piglins gave me all this great stuff!
Some Nether quartz, this cool piece of leather, and an enchanted book!
That doesn't sound like piglin behavior. You really didn't have to trade anything for it?
Well...
What?
I did get distracted during our fight . . .

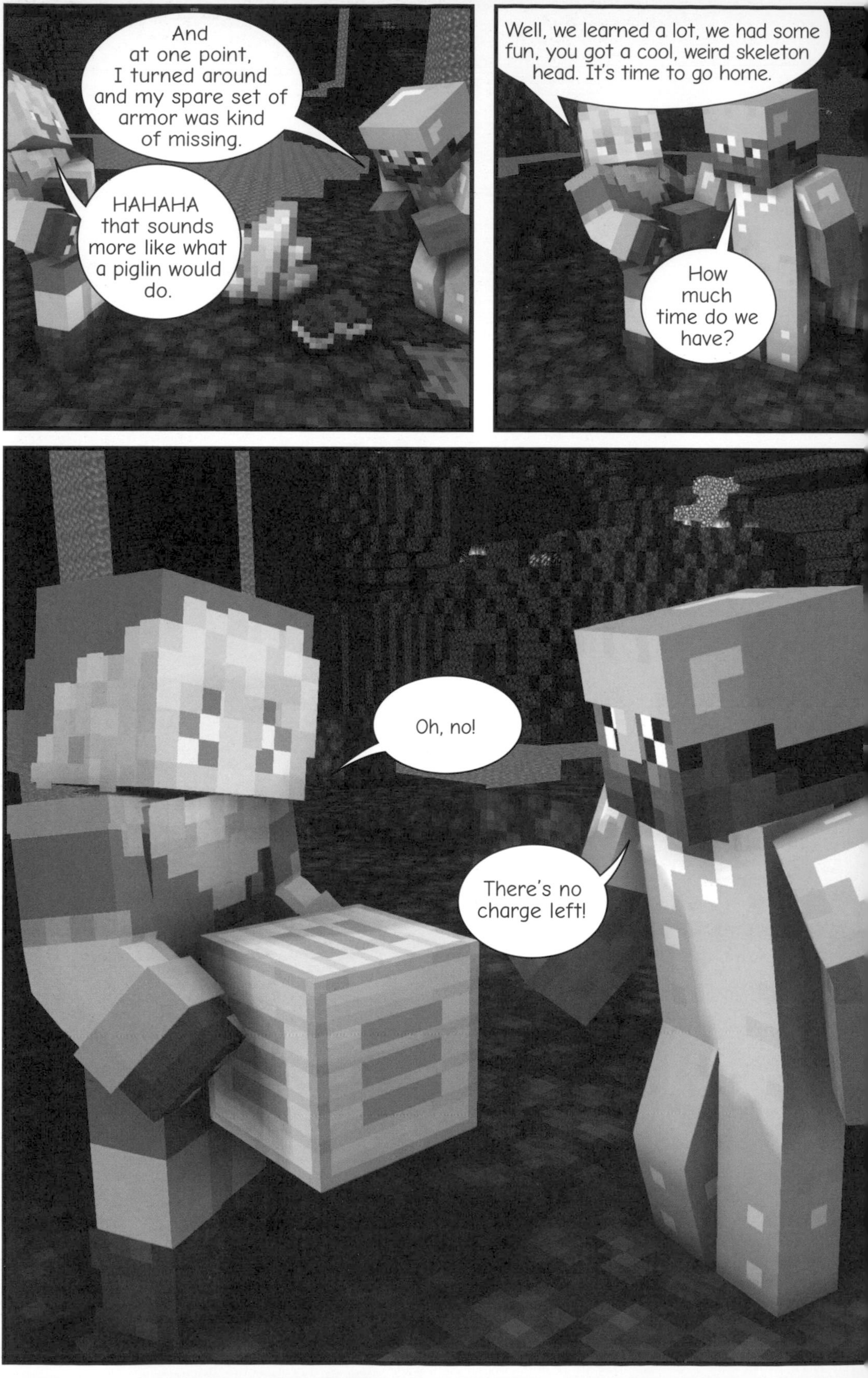
And at one point, I turned around and my spare set of armor was kind of missing.
HAHAHA that sounds more like what a piglin would do.
Well, we learned a lot, we had some fun, you got a cool, weird skeleton head. It's time to go home.
How much time do we have?
Oh, no!
There's no charge left!

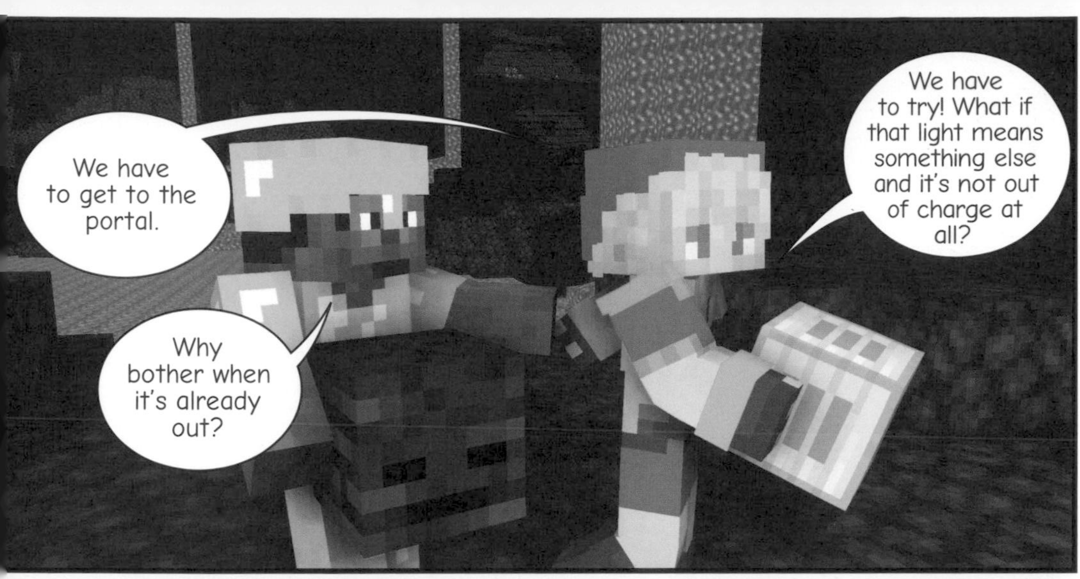
We have to get to the portal.
Why bother when it's already out?
We have to try! What if that light means something else and it's not out of charge at all?

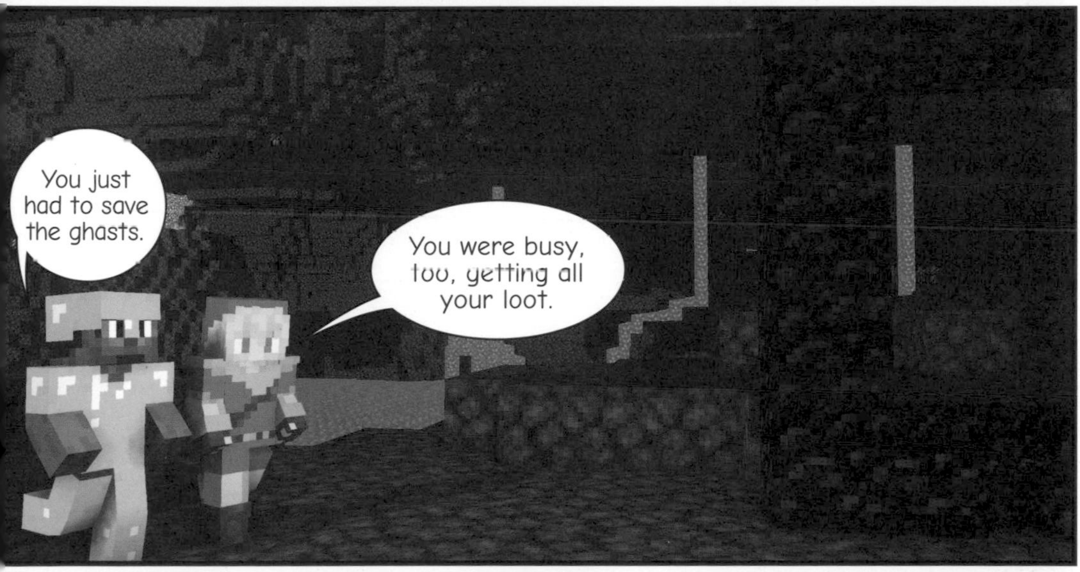
You just had to save the ghasts.
You were busy, too, getting all your loot.

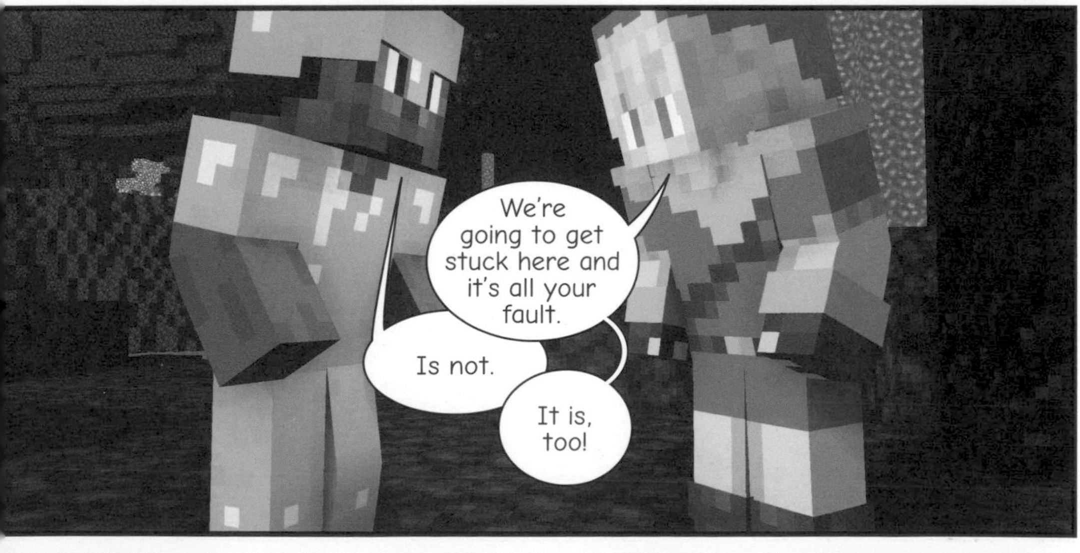
We're going to get stuck here and it's all your fault.
Is not.
It is, too!

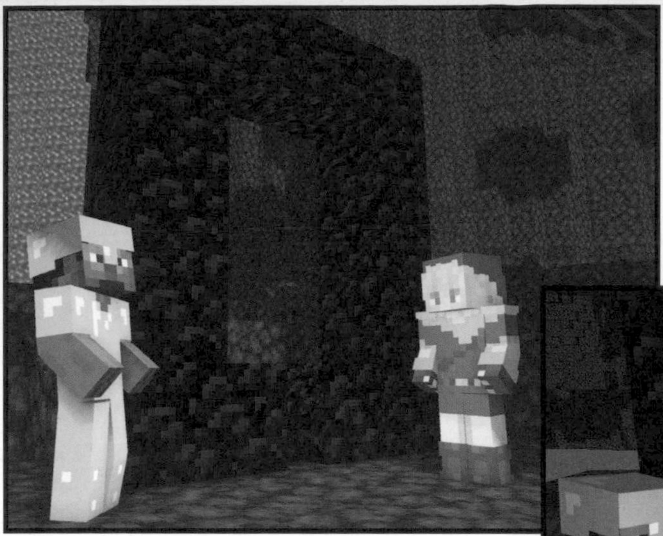

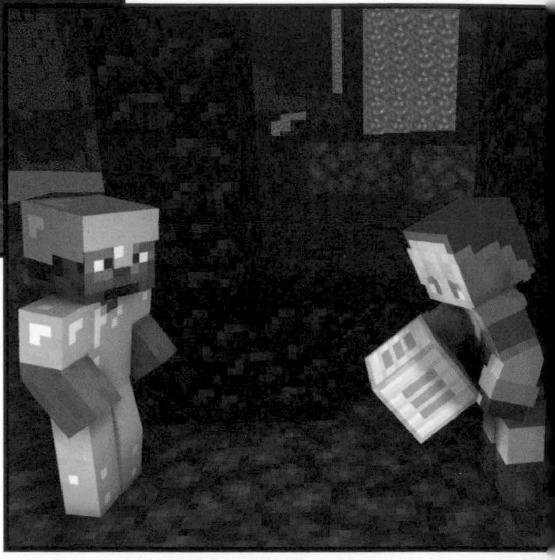

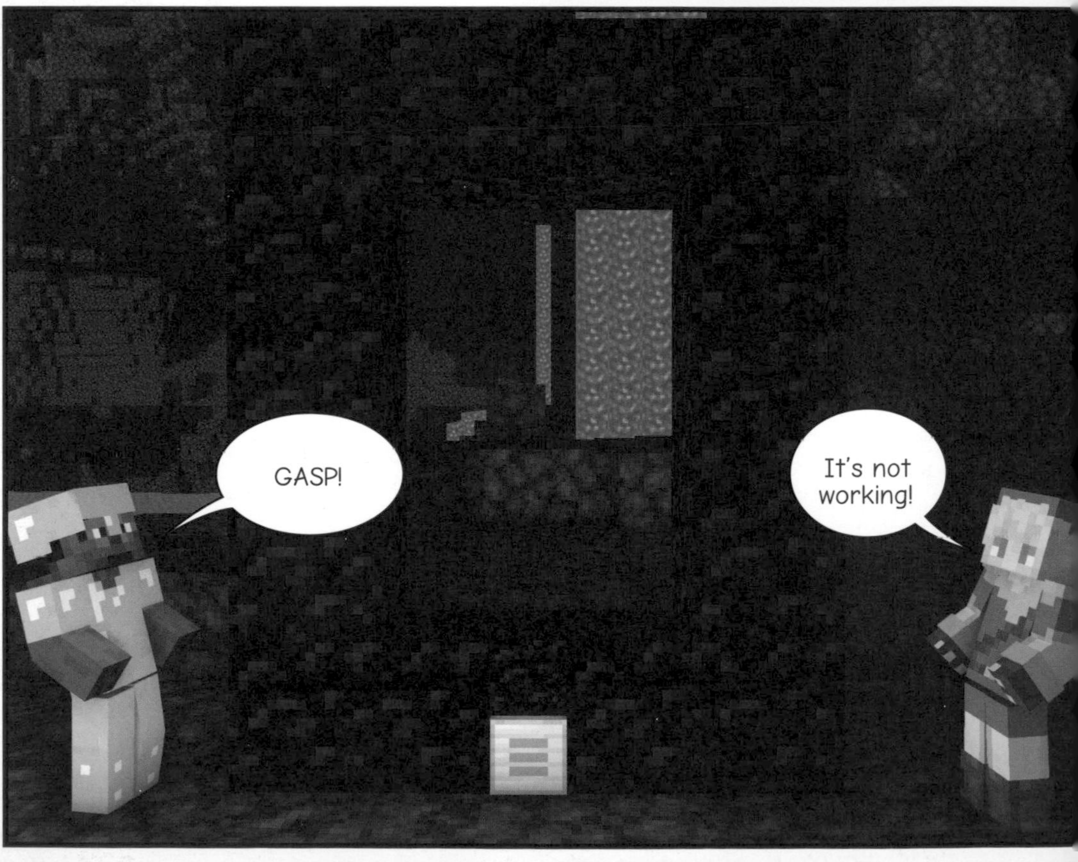
GASP!
It's not working!

Chapter 11
Saved by
a Ghast

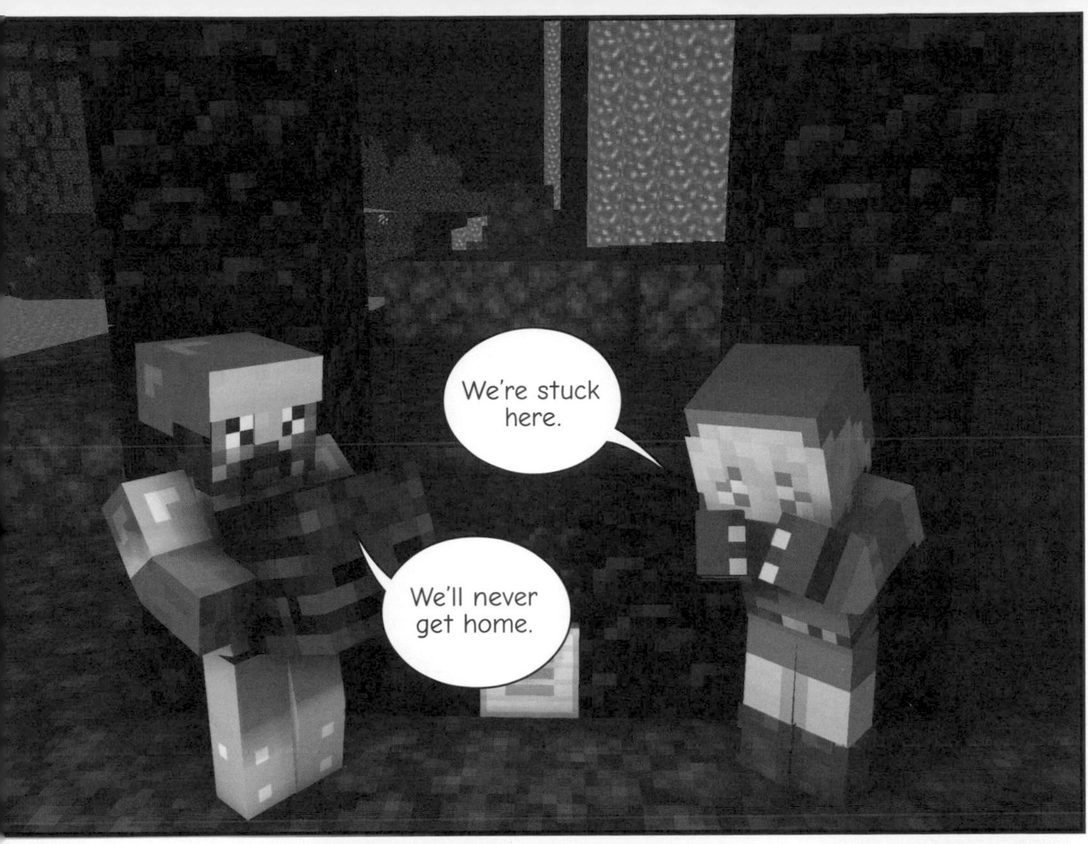
We're stuck here.
We'll never get home.

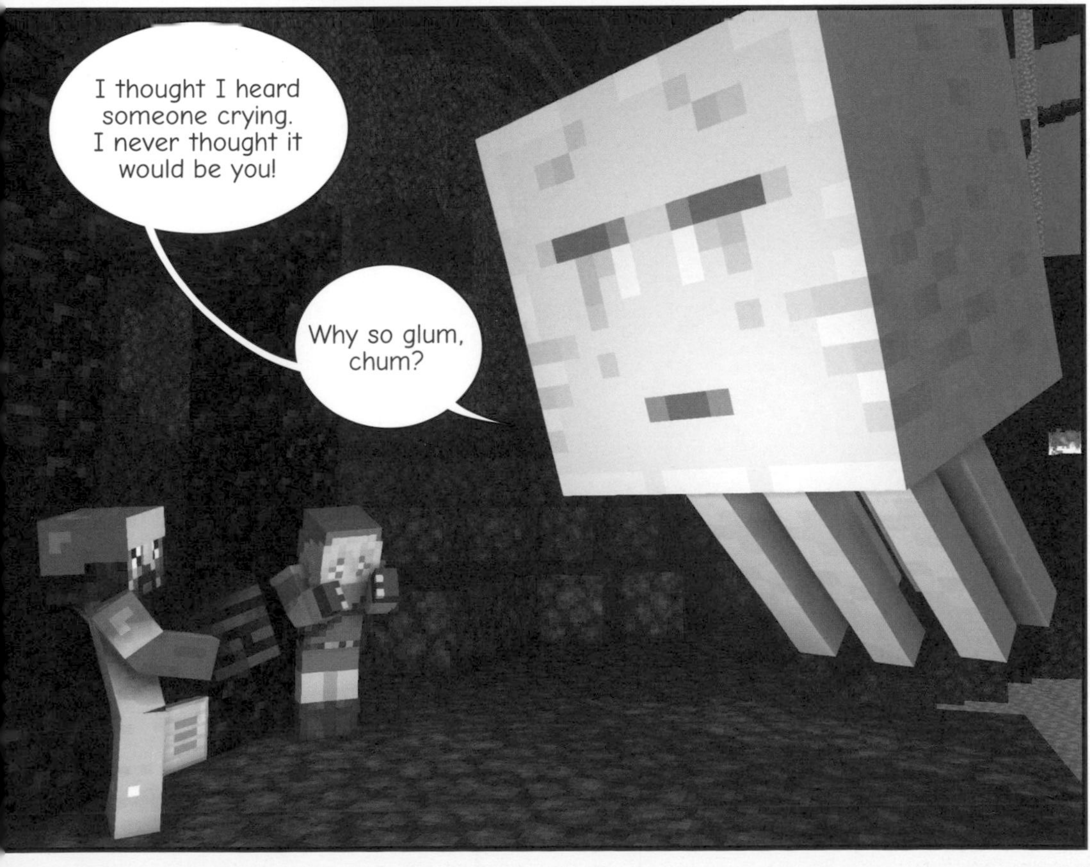
I thought I heard someone crying. I never thought it would be you!
Why so glum, chum?

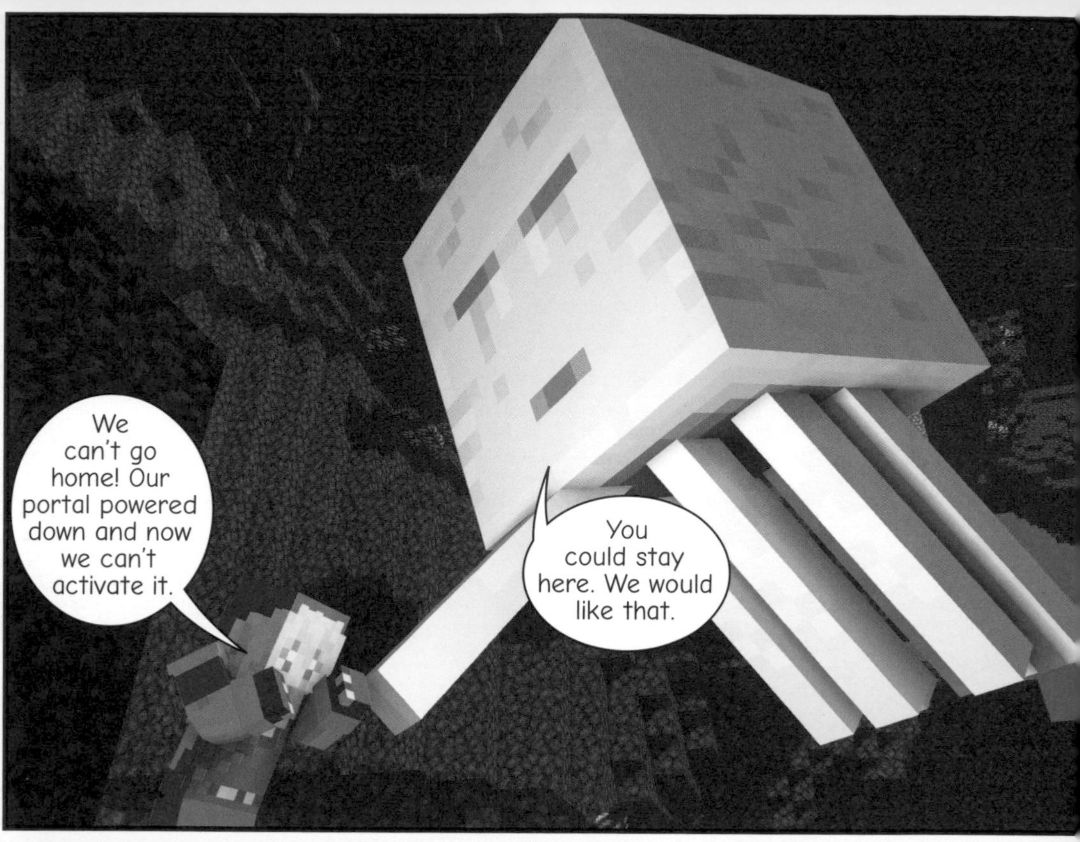
We can't go home! Our portal powered down and now we can't activate it.
You could stay here. We would like that.

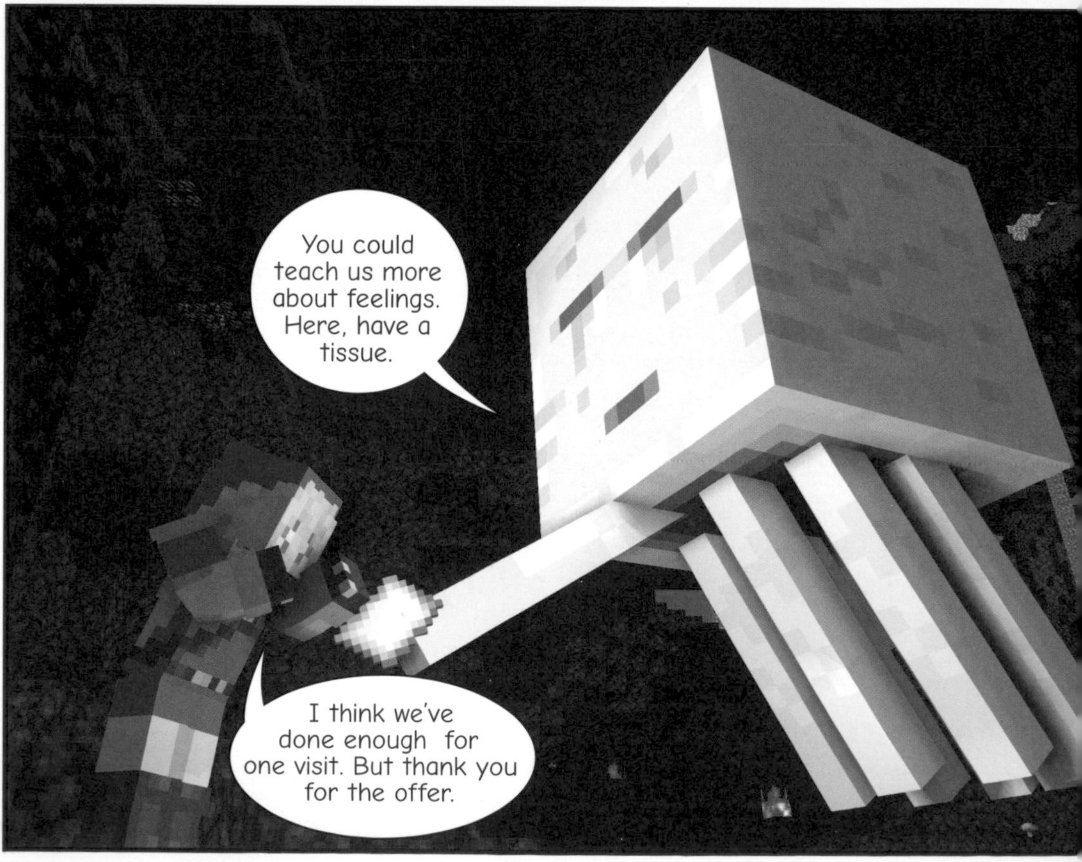
You could teach us more about feelings. Here, have a tissue.
I think we've done enough for one visit. But thank you for the offer.

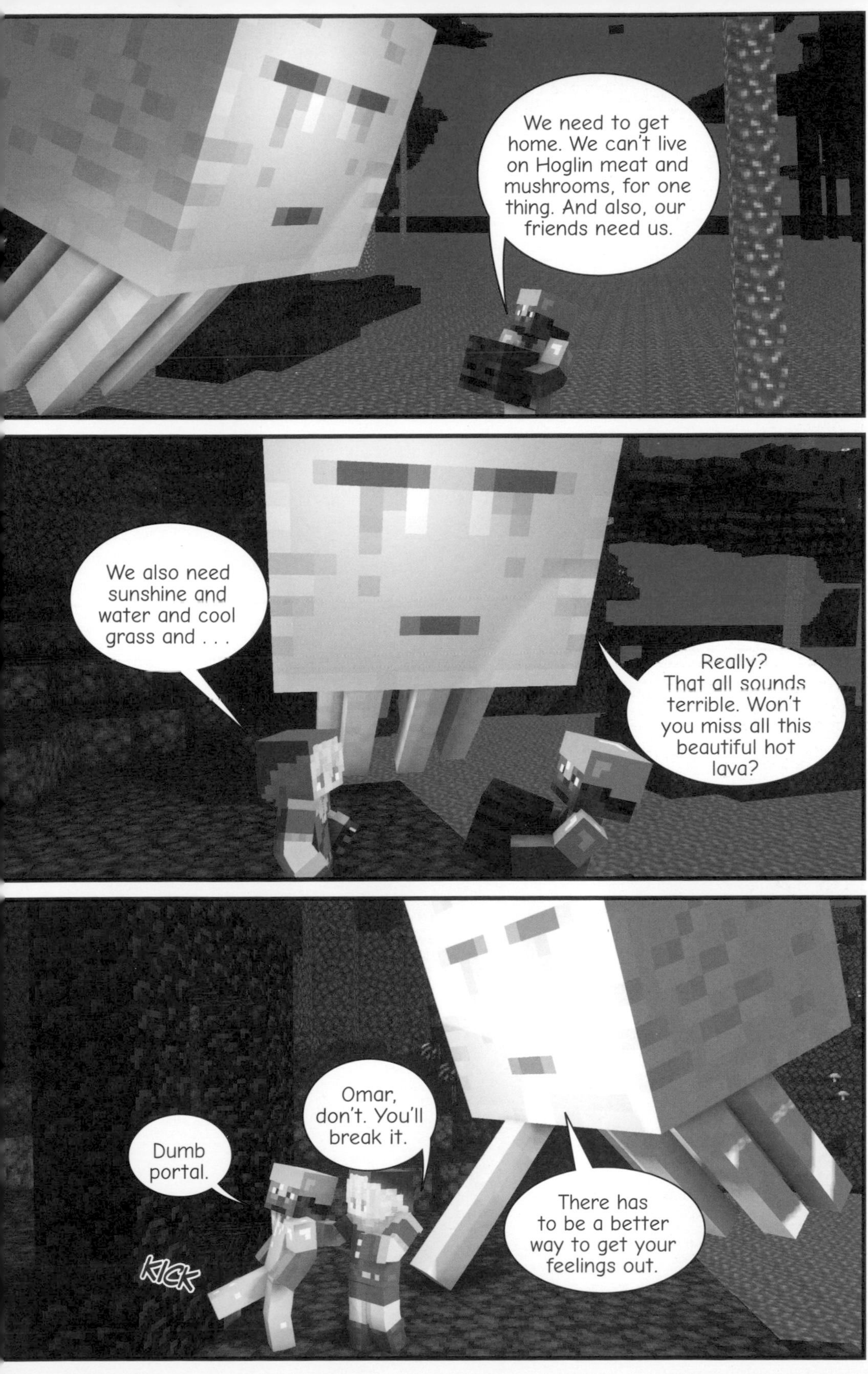

We need to get home. We can't live on Hoglin meat and mushrooms, for one thing. And also, our friends need us.
We also need sunshine and water and cool grass and . . .
Really? That all sounds terrible. Won't you miss all this beautiful hot lava?
Dumb portal.
Omar, don't. You'll break it.
KICK
There has to be a better way to get your feelings out.

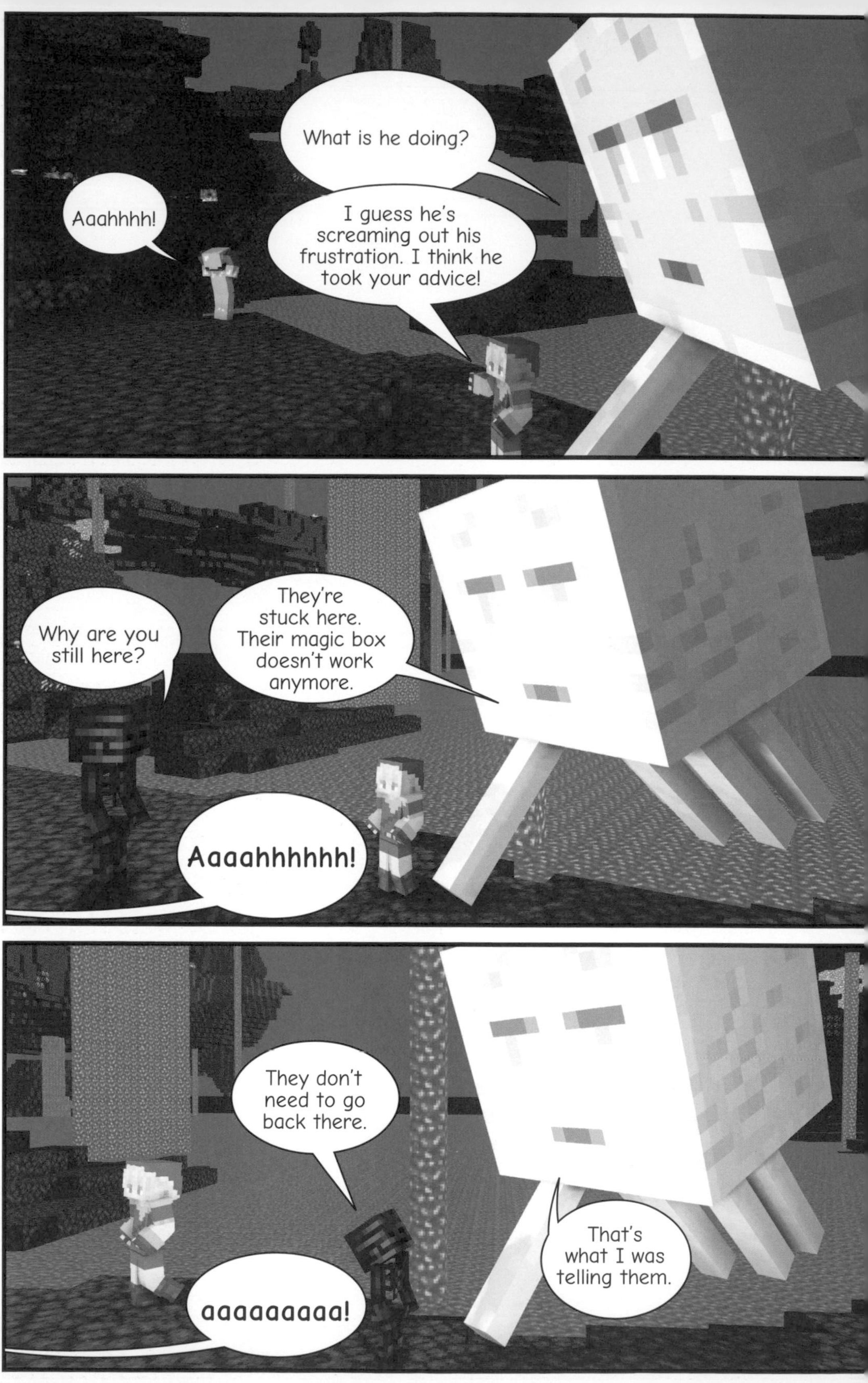
What is he doing?
Aaahhhh!
I guess he's screaming out his frustration. I think he took your advice!
Why are you still here?
They're stuck here. Their magic box doesn't work anymore.
Aaaahhhhhh!
They don't need to go back there.
That's what I was telling them.
aaaaaaaaa!

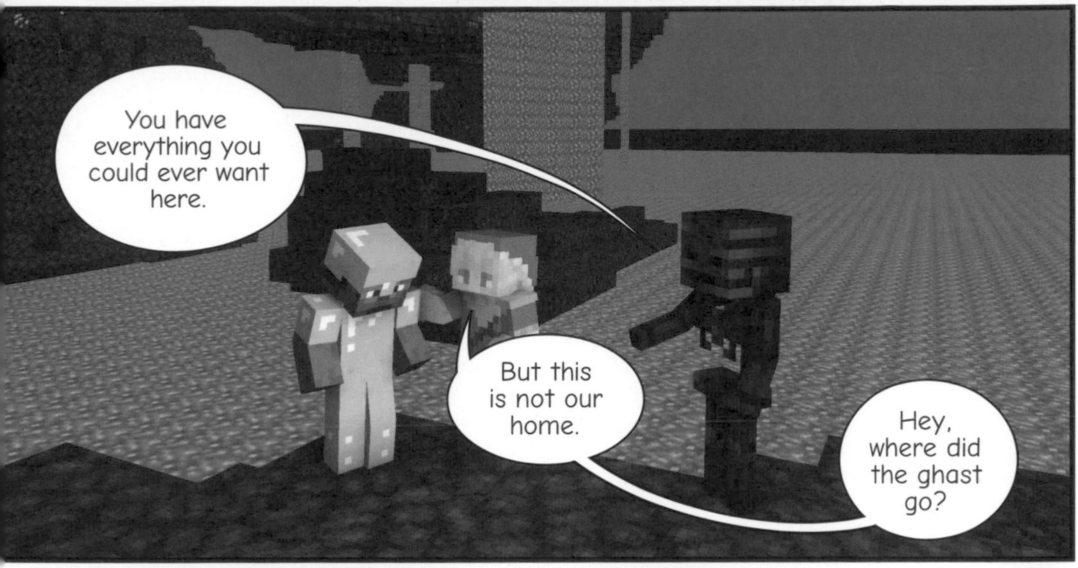
You have everything you could ever want here.
But this is not our home.
Hey, where did the ghast go?

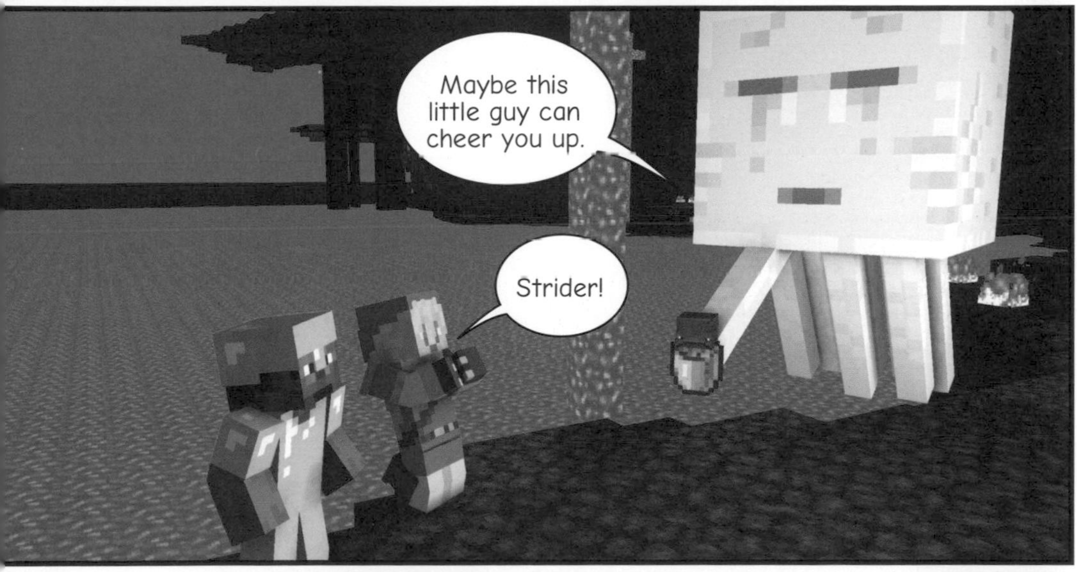
Maybe this little guy can cheer you up.
Strider!

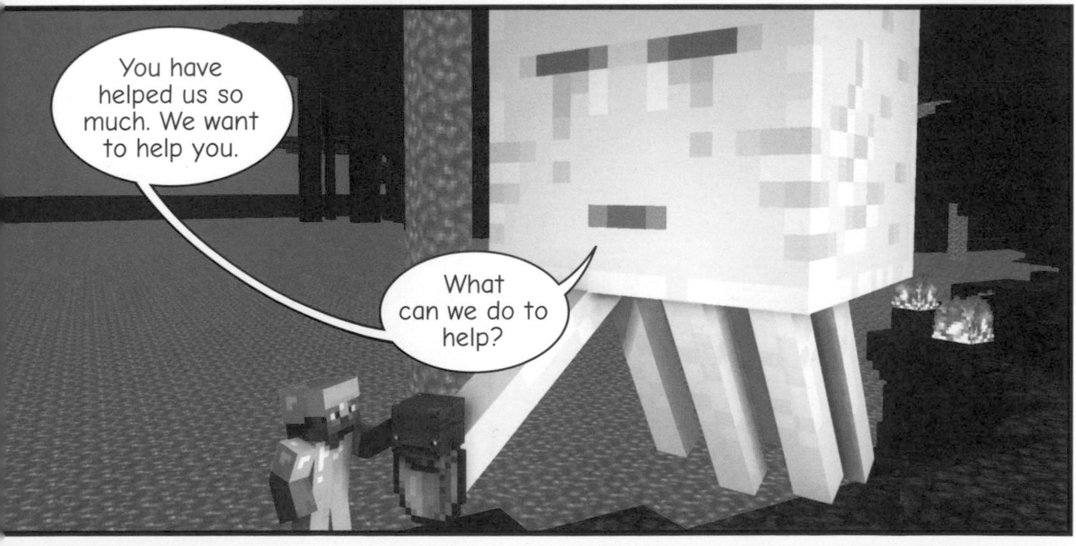
You have helped us so much. We want to help you.
What can we do to help?

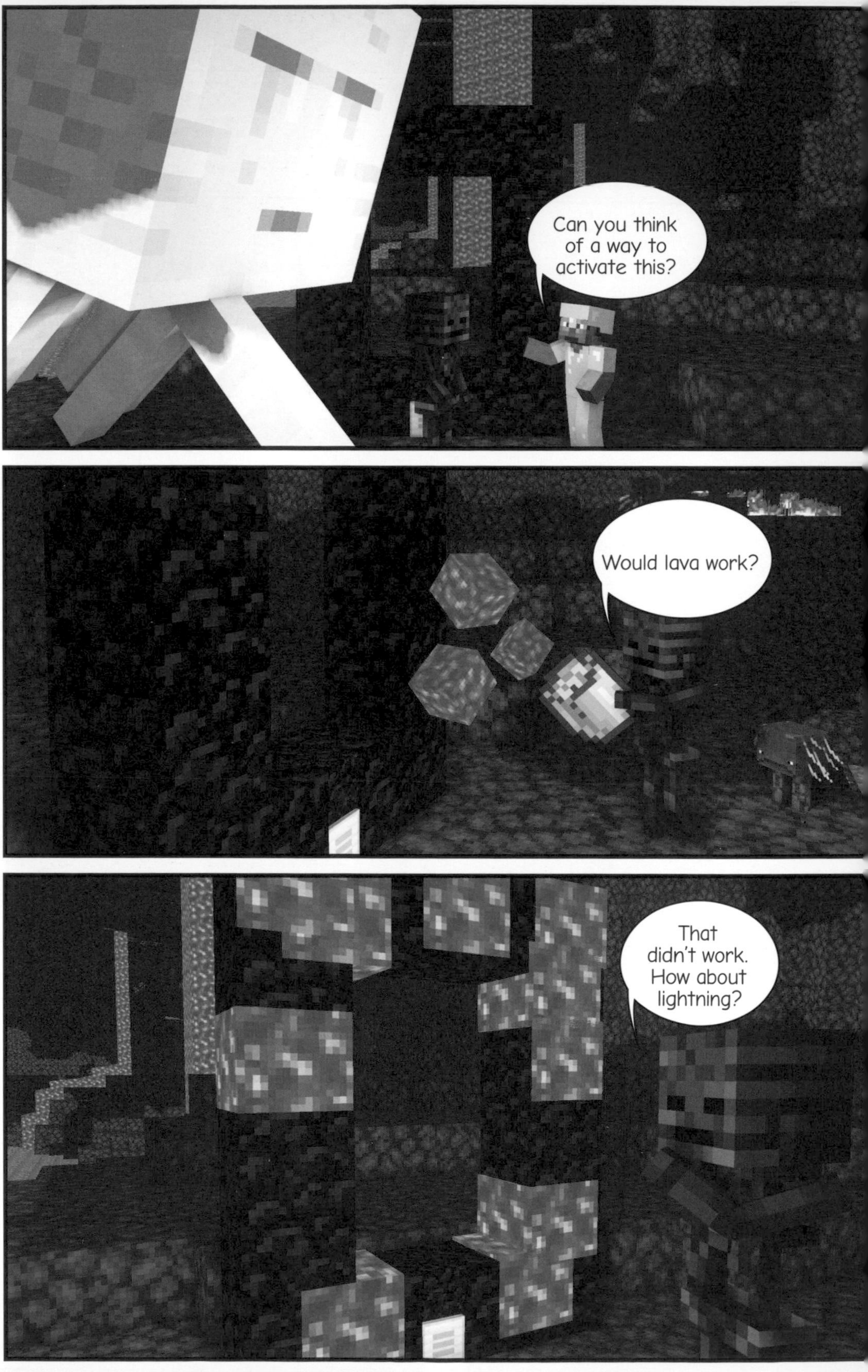
Can you think of a way to activate this?
Would lava work?
That didn't work. How about lightning?

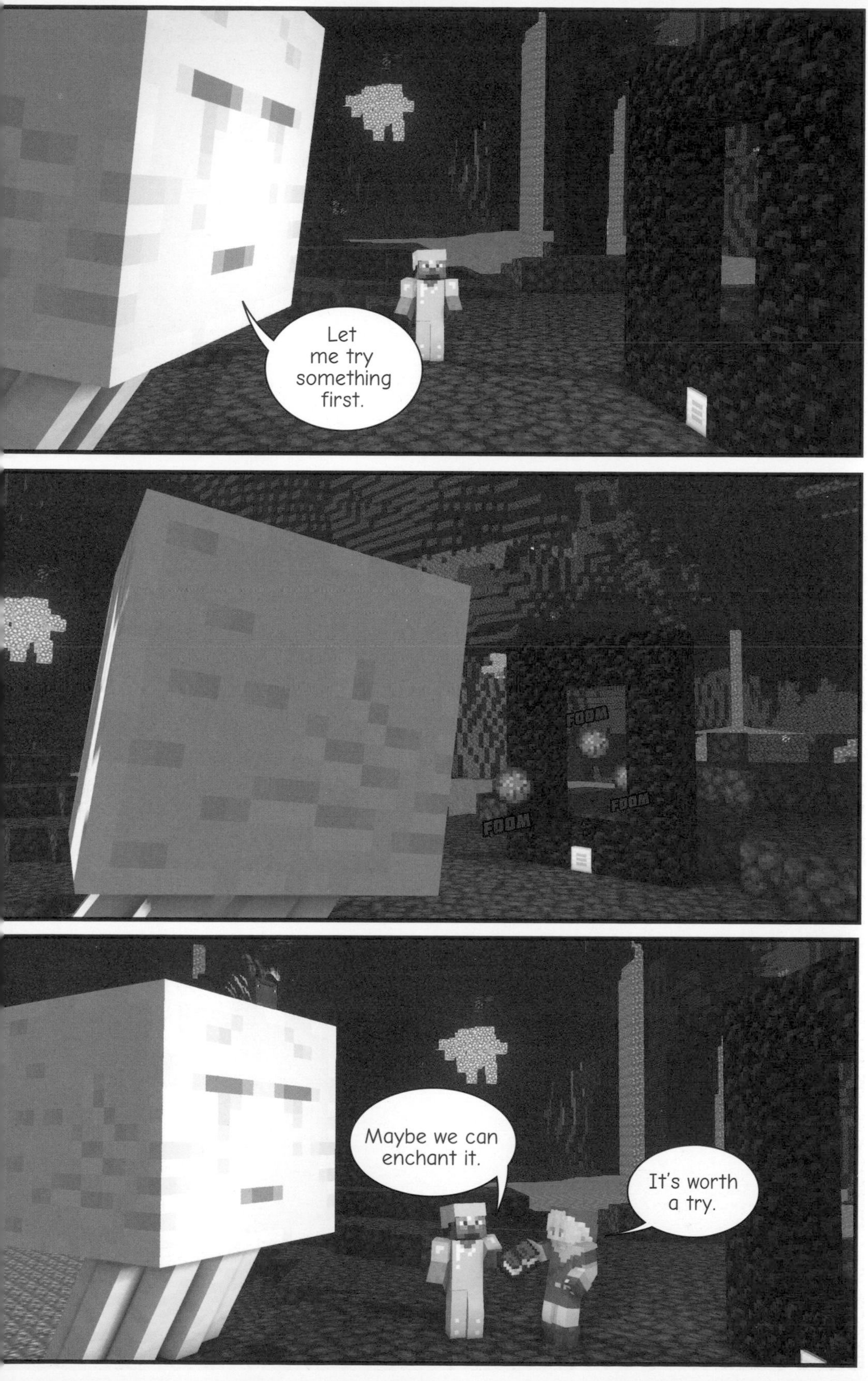
Let me try something first.
FOOM
FOOM
FOOM
Maybe we can enchant it.
It's worth a try.

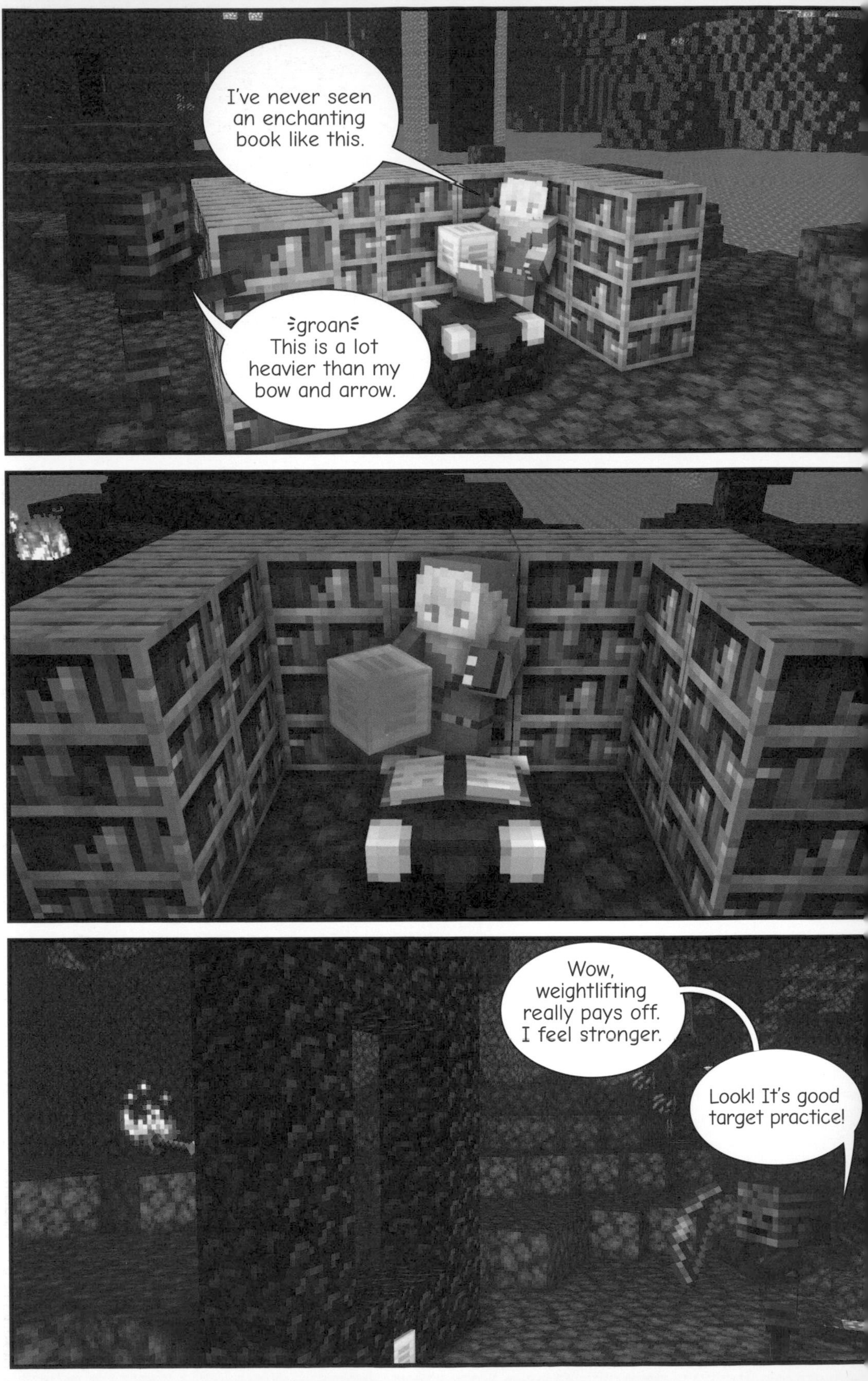
I've never seen an enchanting book like this.
groan This is a lot heavier than my bow and arrow.
Wow, weightlifting really pays off. I feel stronger.
Look! It's good target practice!

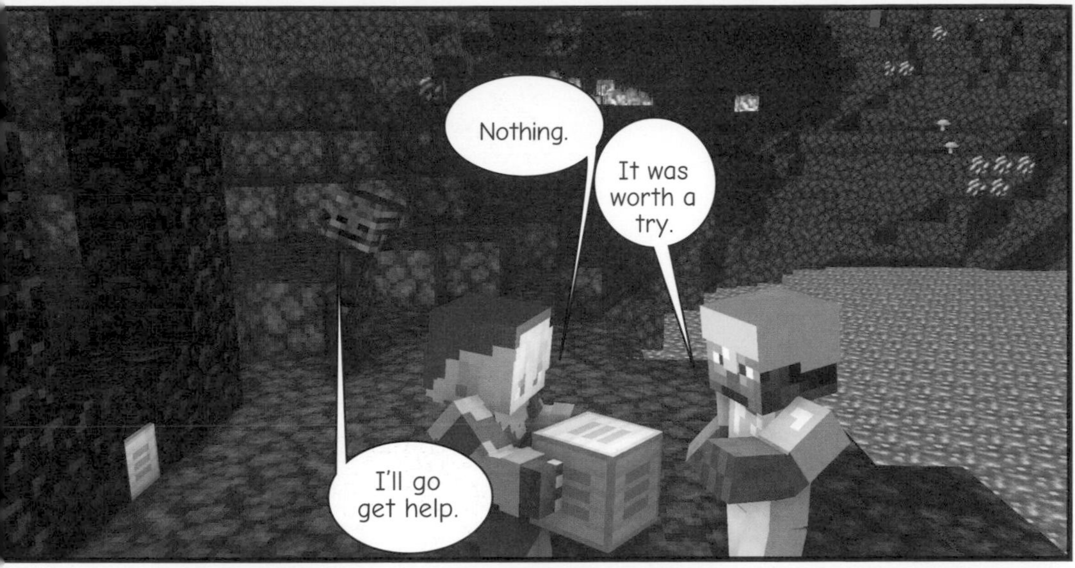
Nothing.
It was worth a try.
I'll go get help.

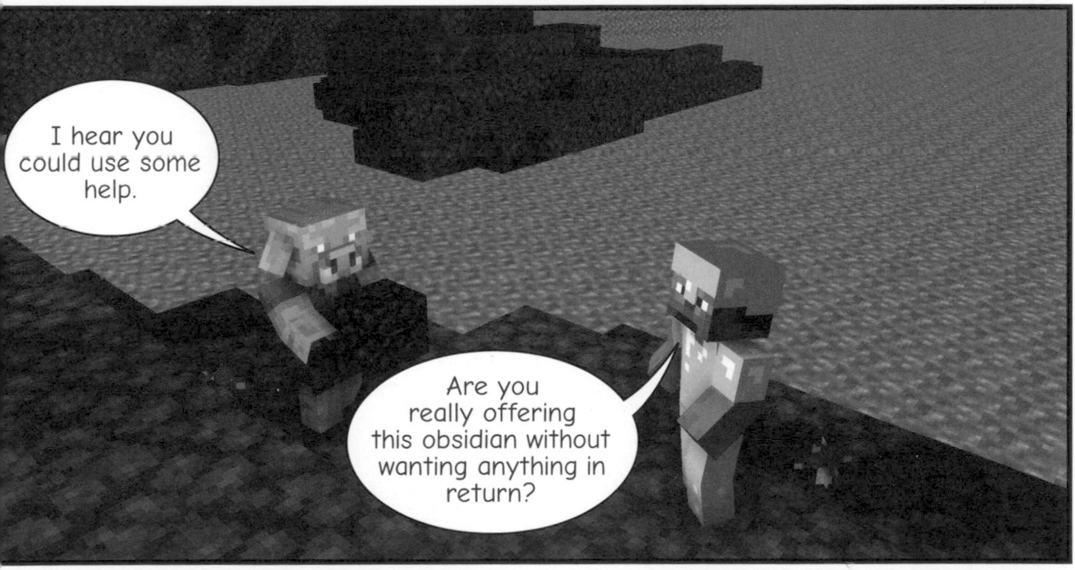
I hear you could use some help.
Are you really offering this obsidian without wanting anything in return?

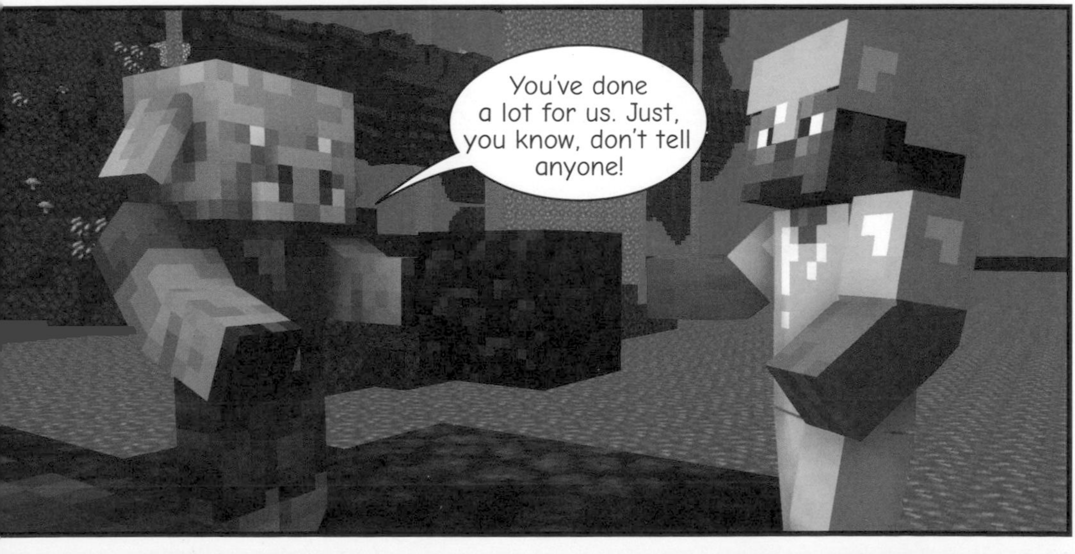
You've done a lot for us. Just, you know, don't tell anyone!

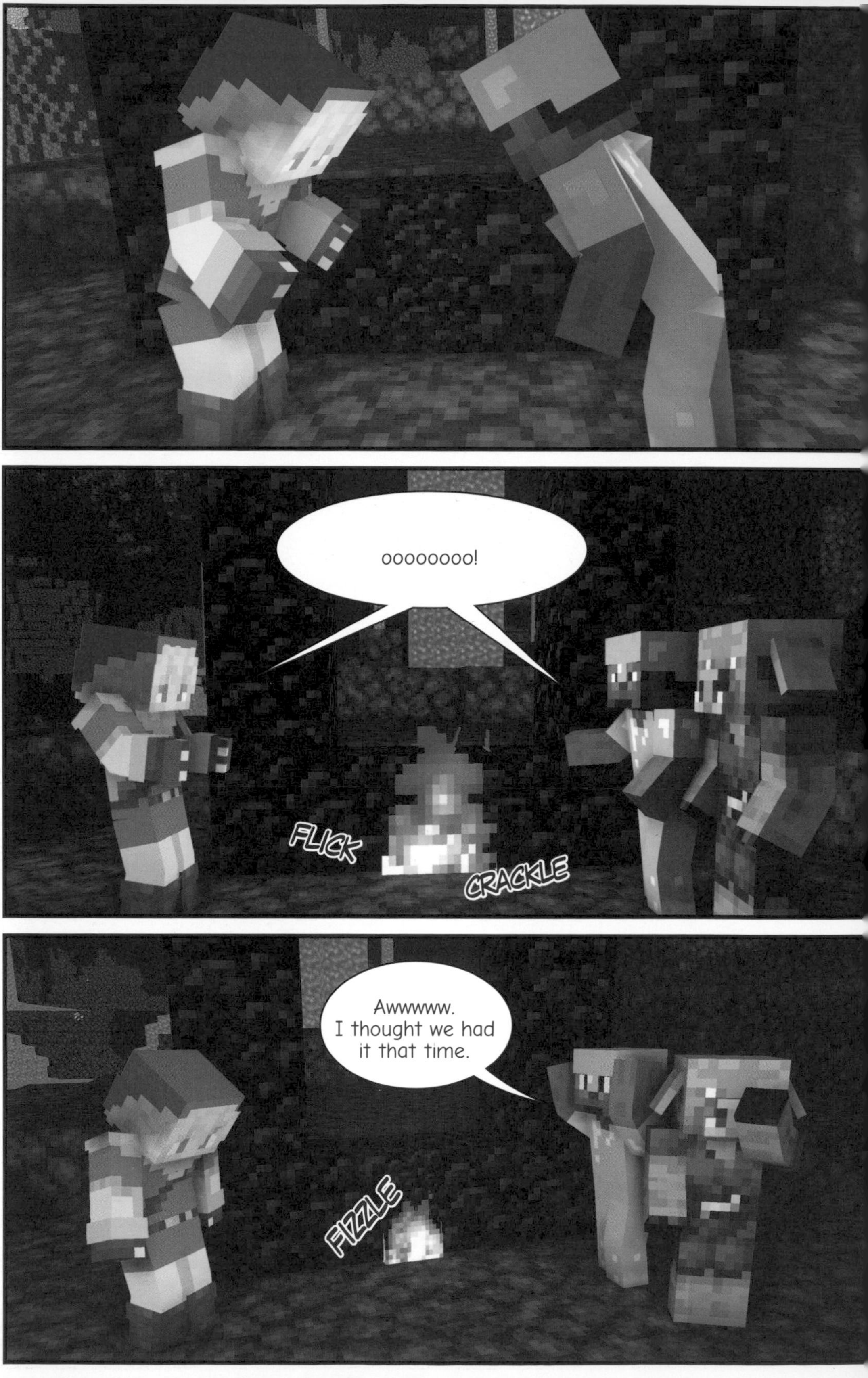
oooooooo!
FLICK
CRACKLE
Awwwww.
I thought we had
it that time.
FIZZLE

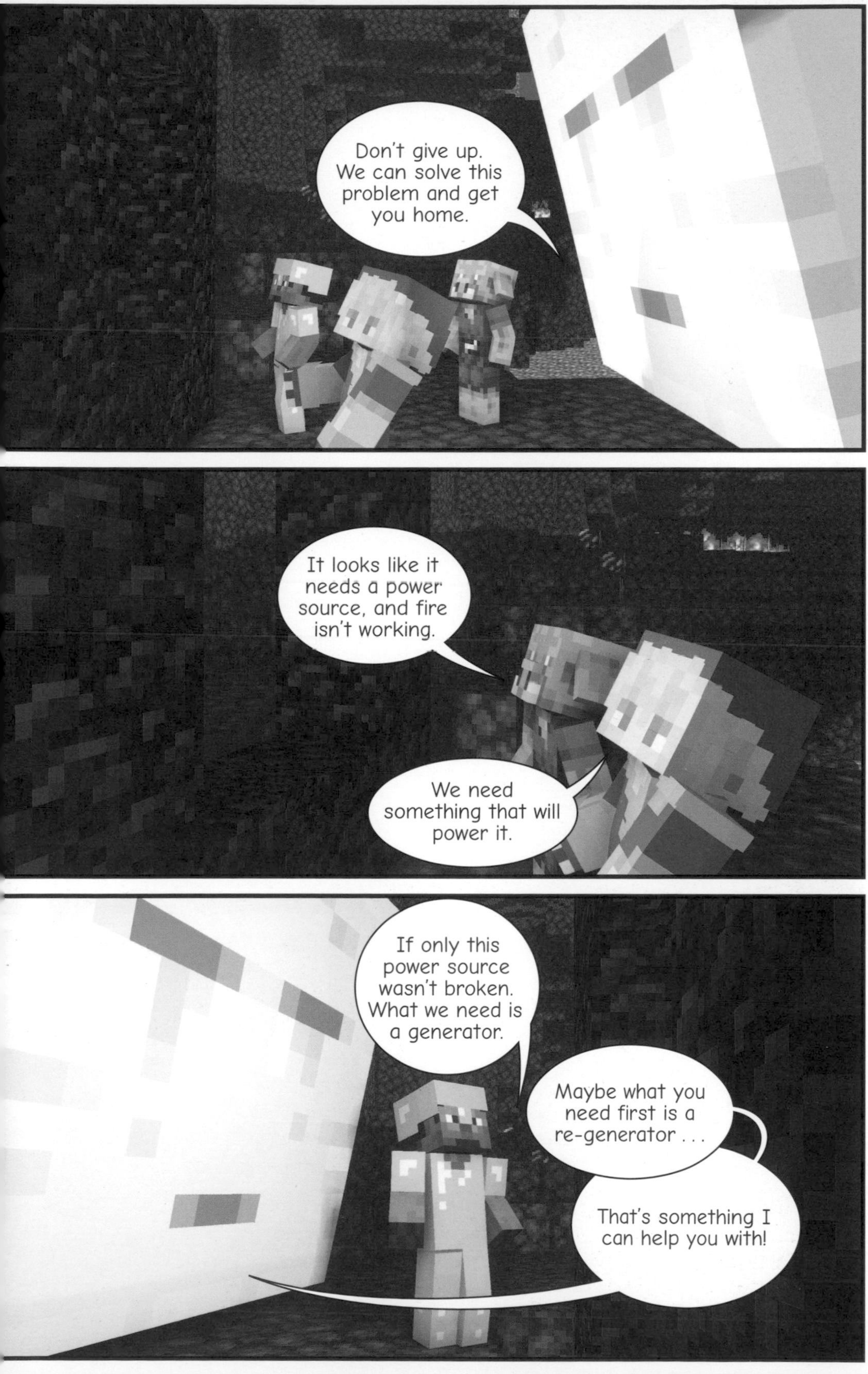
Don't give up. We can solve this problem and get you home.
It looks like it needs a power source, and fire isn't working.
We need something that will power it.
If only this power source wasn't broken. What we need is a generator.
Maybe what you need first is a re-generator . . .
That's something I can help you with!

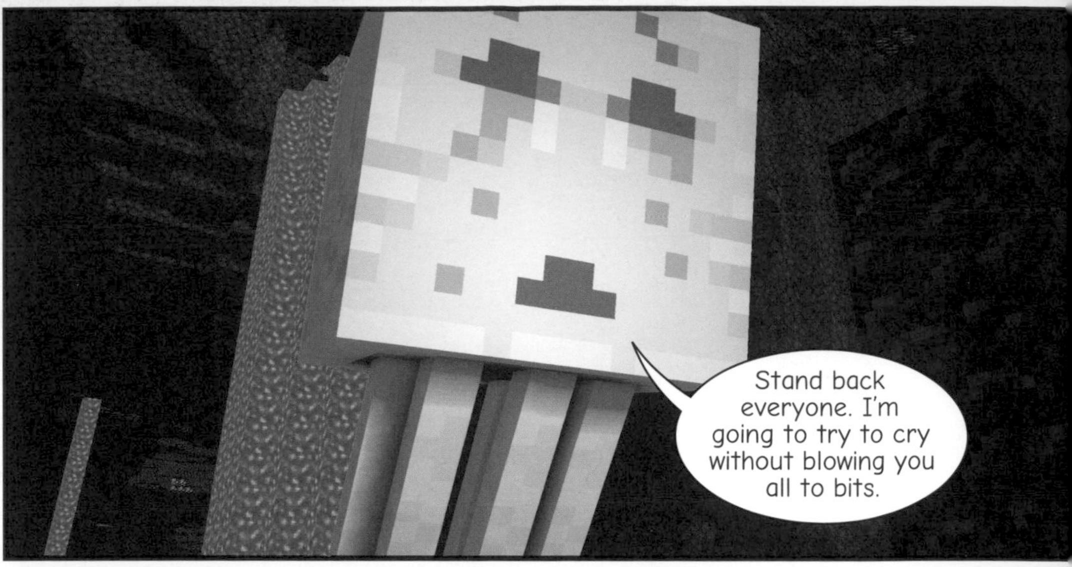
Stand back everyone. I'm going to try to cry without blowing you all to bits.
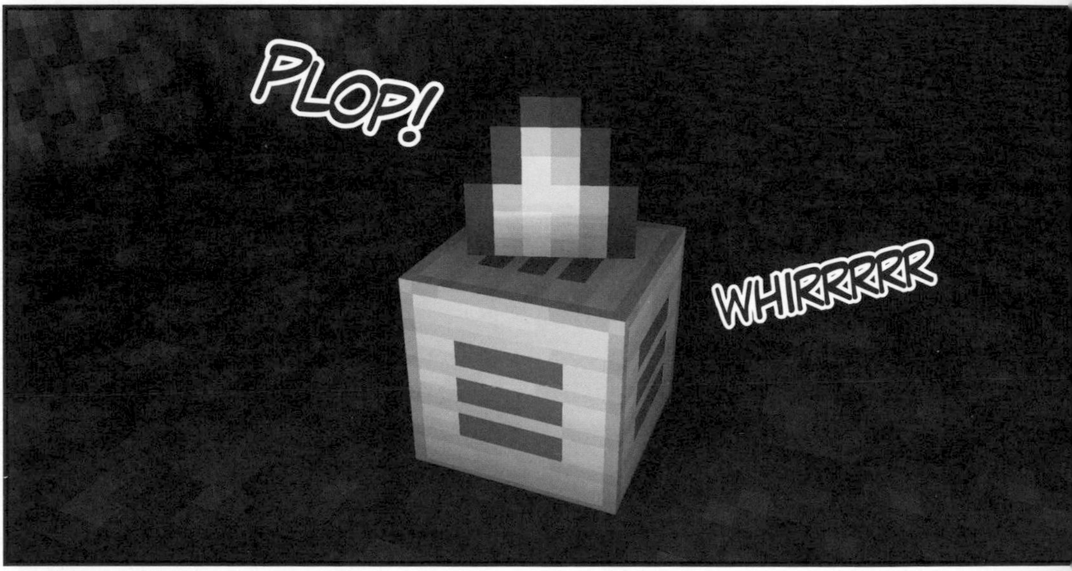
PLOP!
WHIRRRRR
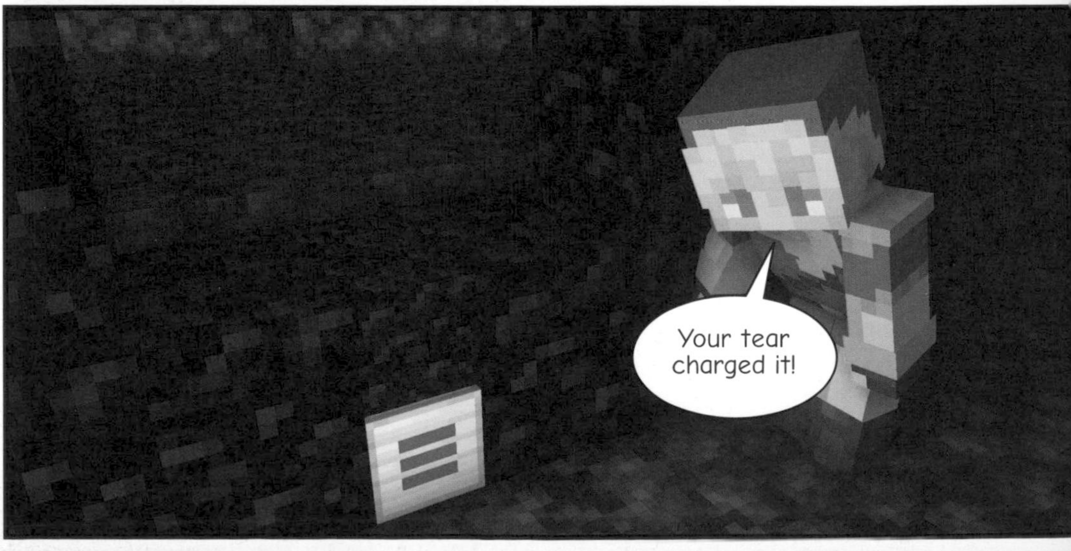
Your tear charged it!

Chapter 12
A Tearful
Goodbye

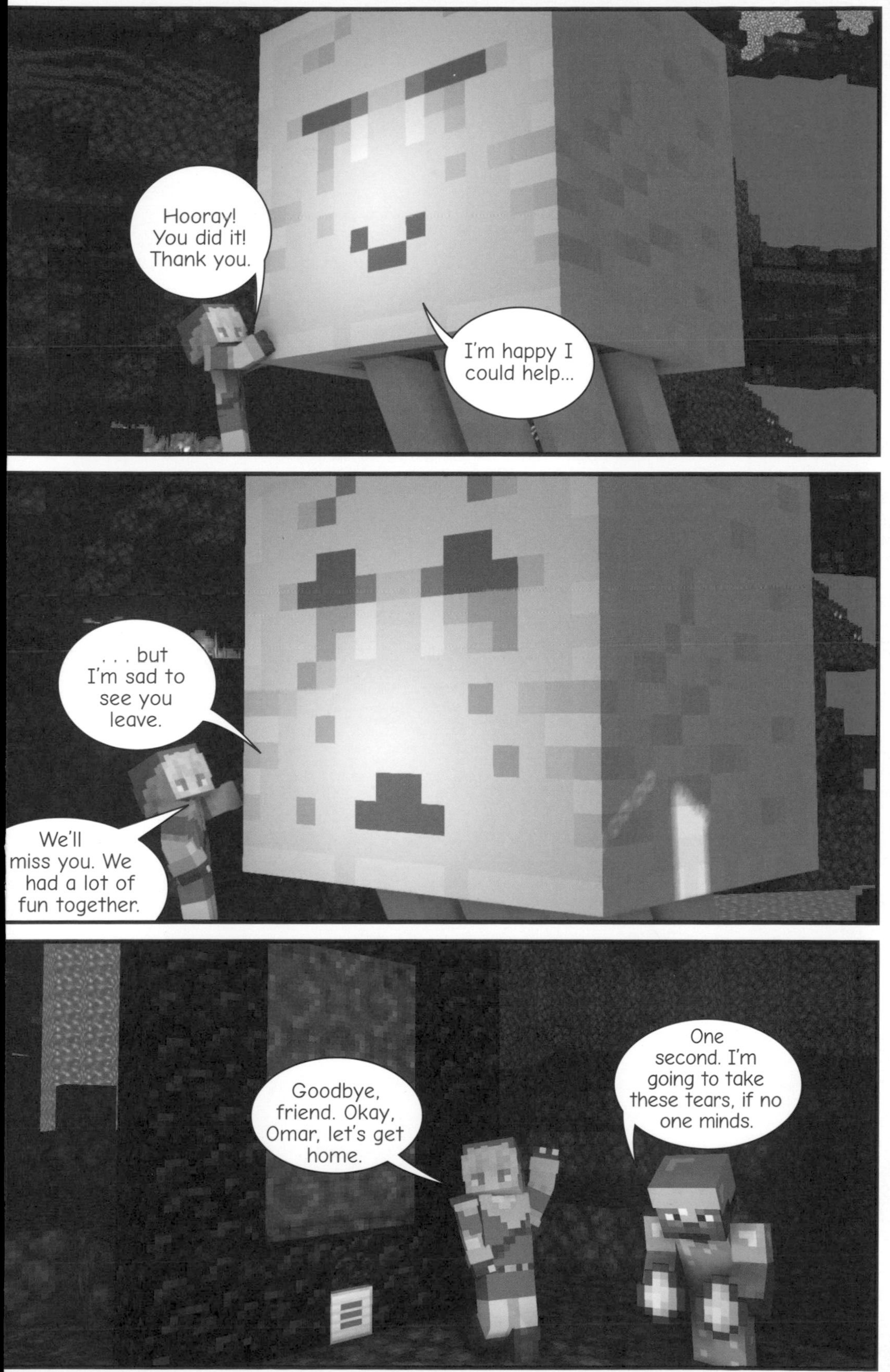
Hooray! You did it! Thank you.
I'm happy I could help...
. . . but I'm sad to see you leave.
We'll miss you. We had a lot of fun together.
Goodbye, friend. Okay, Omar, let's get home.
One second. I'm going to take these tears, if no one minds.

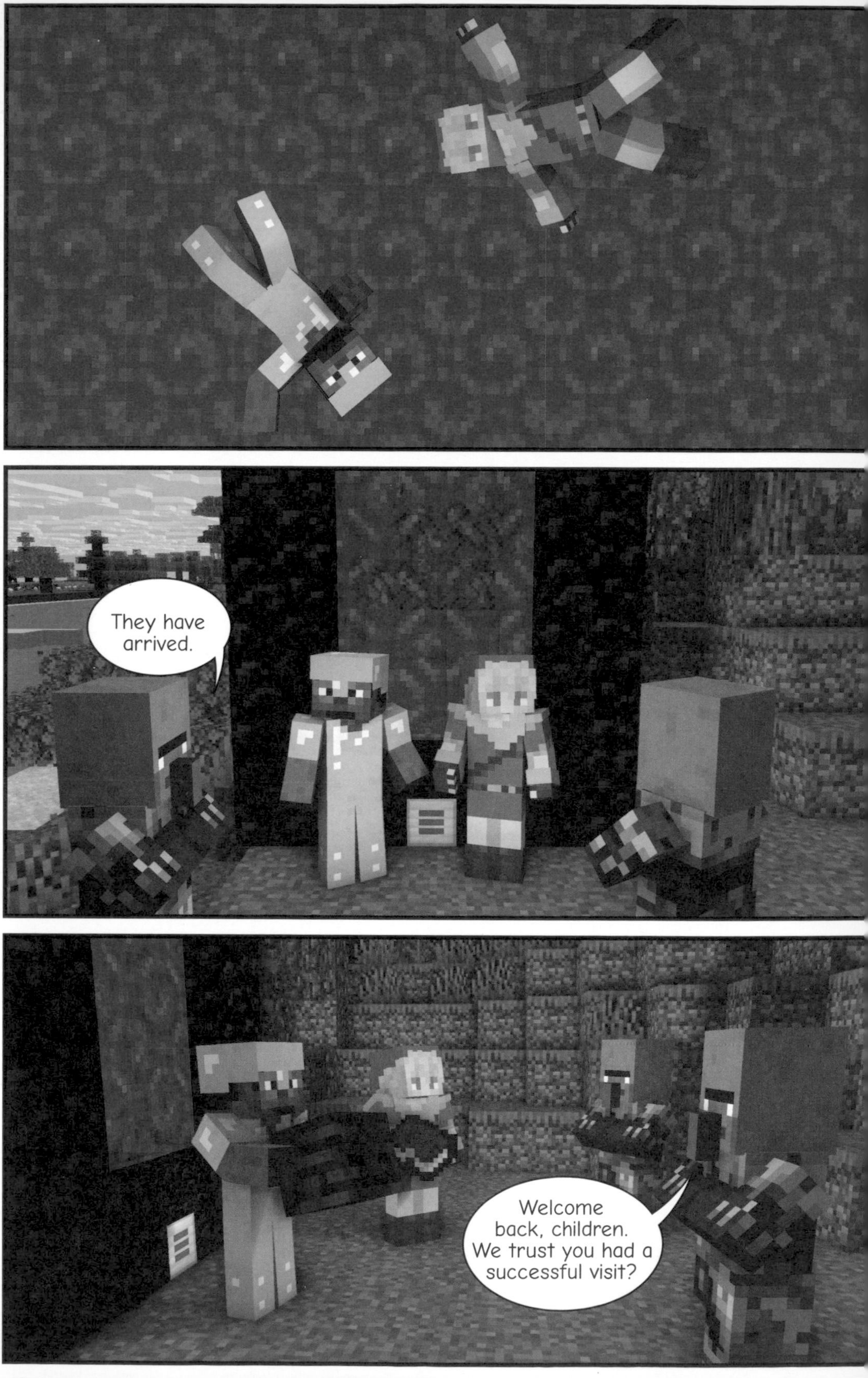
They have arrived.
Welcome back, children. We trust you had a successful visit?

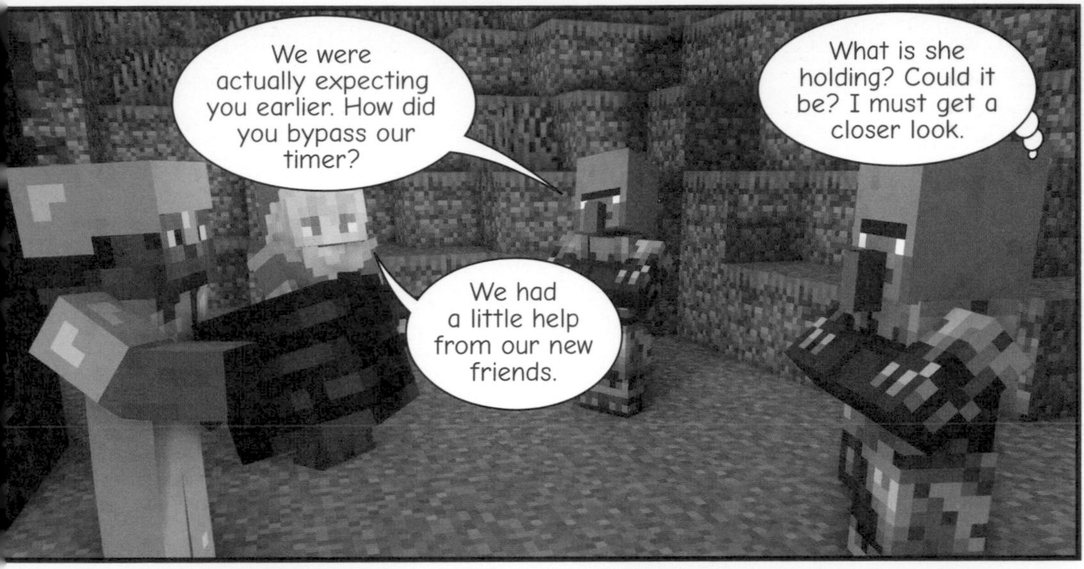
We were actually expecting you earlier. How did you bypass our timer?
What is she holding? Could it be? I must get a closer look.
We had a little help from our new friends.

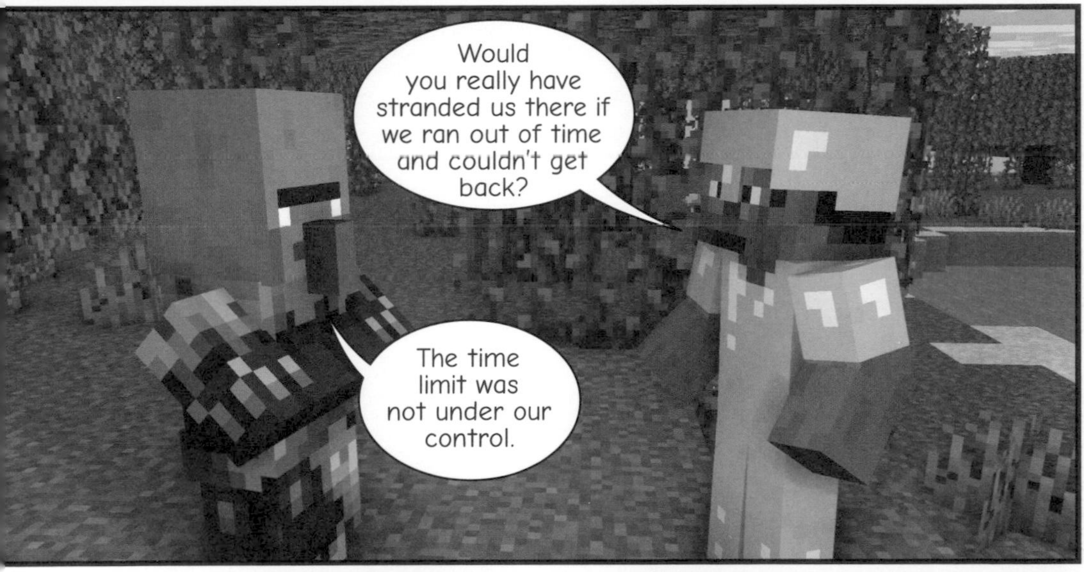
Would you really have stranded us there if we ran out of time and couldn't get back?
The time limit was not under our control.

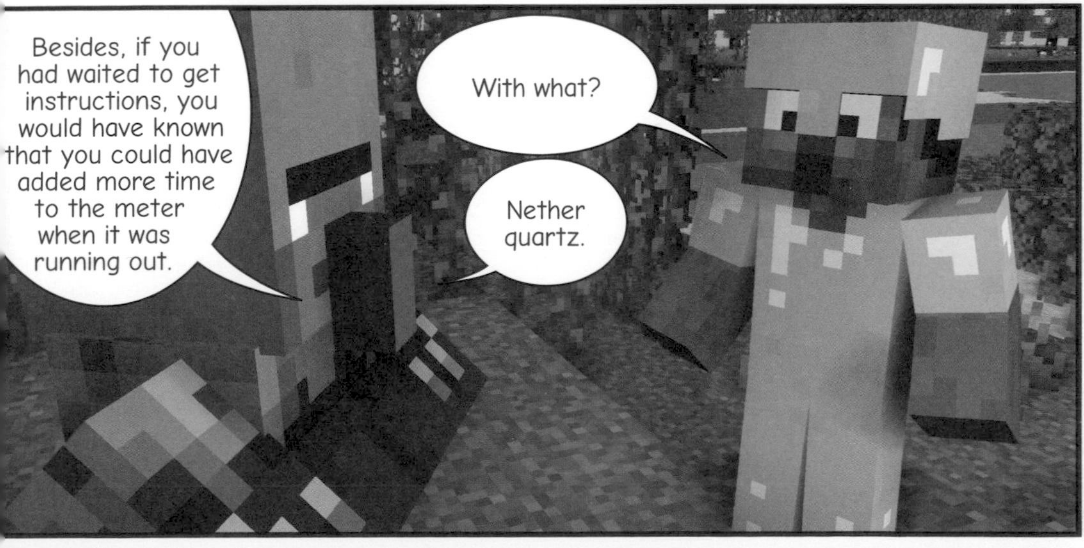
Besides, if you had waited to get instructions, you would have known that you could have added more time to the meter when it was running out.
With what?
Nether quartz.

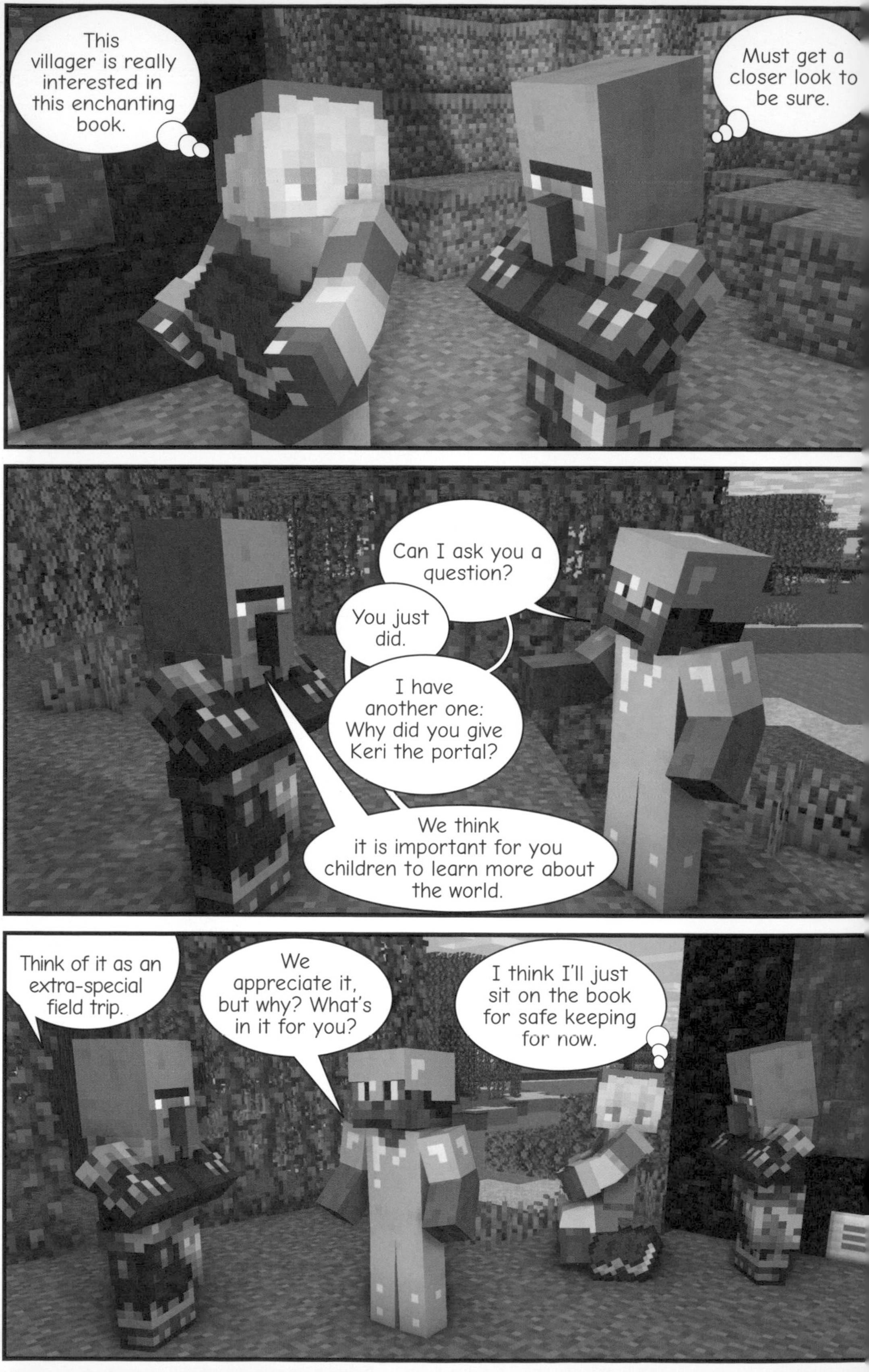
This villager is really interested in this enchanting book.
Must get a closer look to be sure.
Can I ask you a question?
You just did.
I have another one: Why did you give Keri the portal?
We think it is important for you children to learn more about the world.
Think of it as an extra-special field trip.
We appreciate it, but why? What's in it for you?
I think I'll just sit on the book for safe keeping for now.

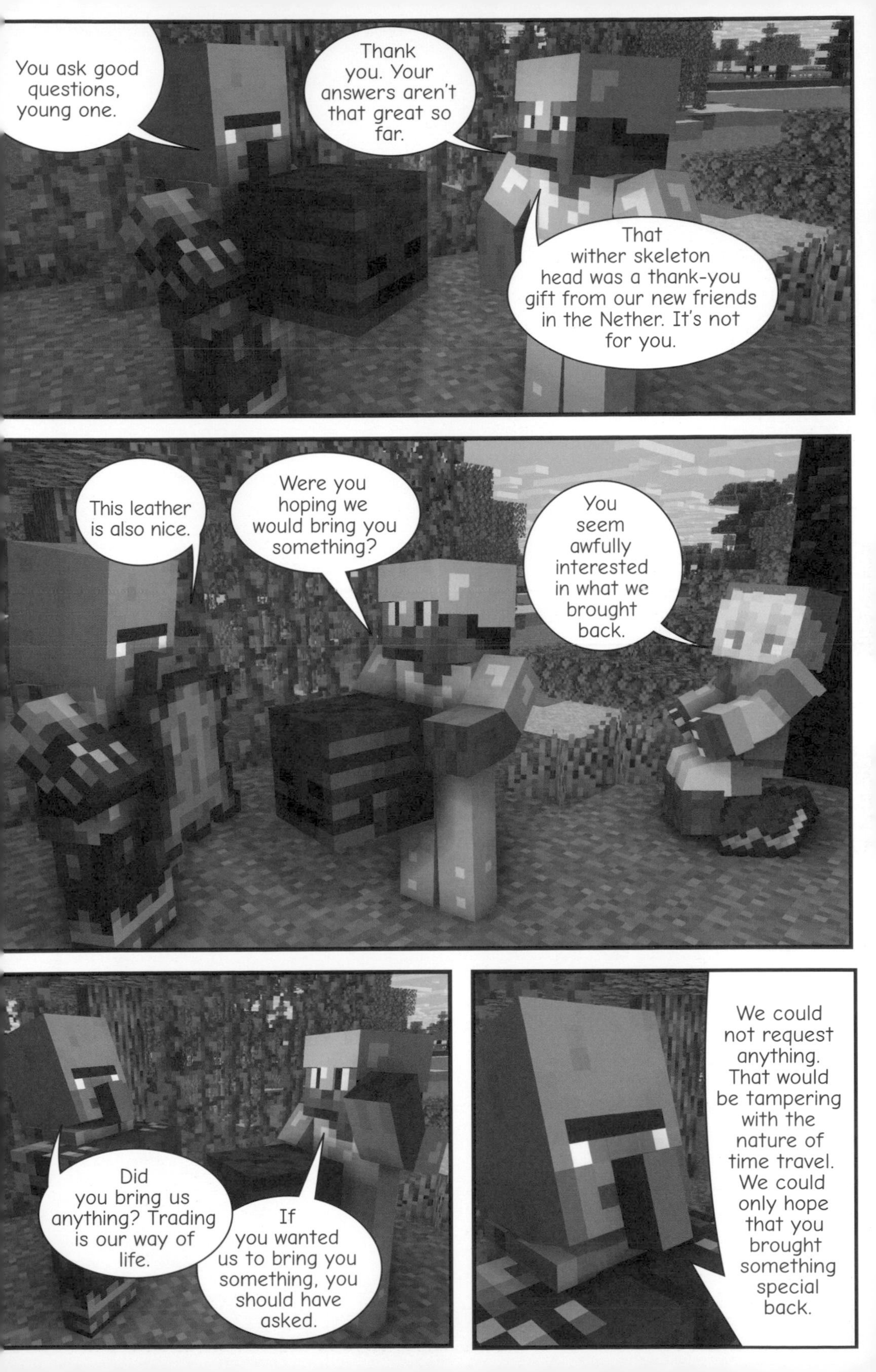
You ask good questions, young one.
Thank you. Your answers aren't that great so far.
That wither skeleton head was a thank-you gift from our new friends in the Nether. It's not for you.
This leather is also nice.
Were you hoping we would bring you something?
You seem awfully interested in what we brought back.
Did you bring us anything? Trading is our way of life.
If you wanted us to bring you something, you should have asked.
We could not request anything. That would be tampering with the nature of time travel. We could only hope that you brought something special back.

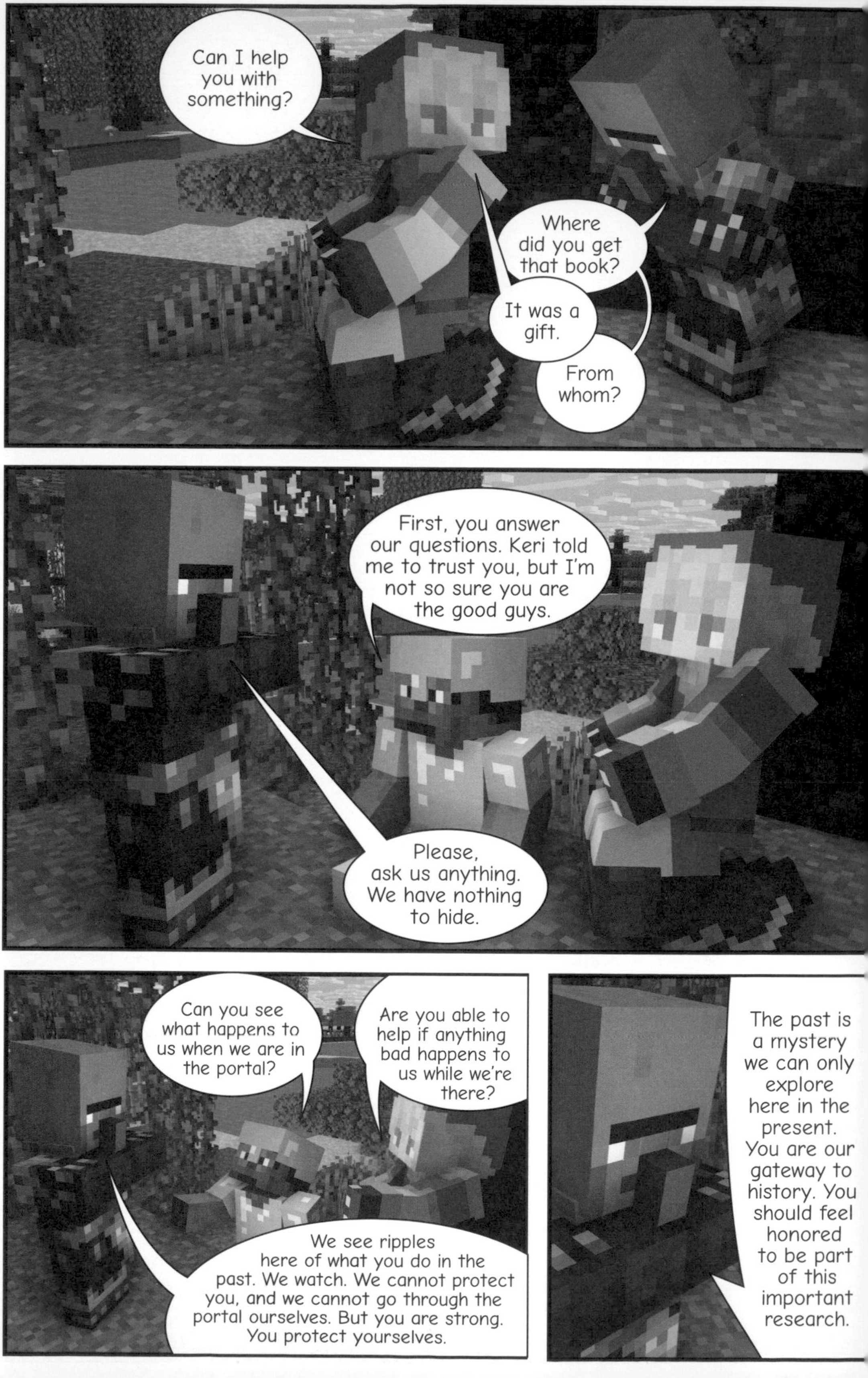
Can I help you with something?
Where did you get that book?
It was a gift.
From whom?
First, you answer our questions. Keri told me to trust you, but I'm not so sure you are the good guys.
Please, ask us anything. We have nothing to hide.
Can you see what happens to us when we are in the portal?
Are you able to help if anything bad happens to us while we're there?
We see ripples here of what you do in the past. We watch. We cannot protect you, and we cannot go through the portal ourselves. But you are strong. You protect yourselves.
The past is a mystery we can only explore here in the present. You are our gateway to history. You should feel honored to be part of this important research.

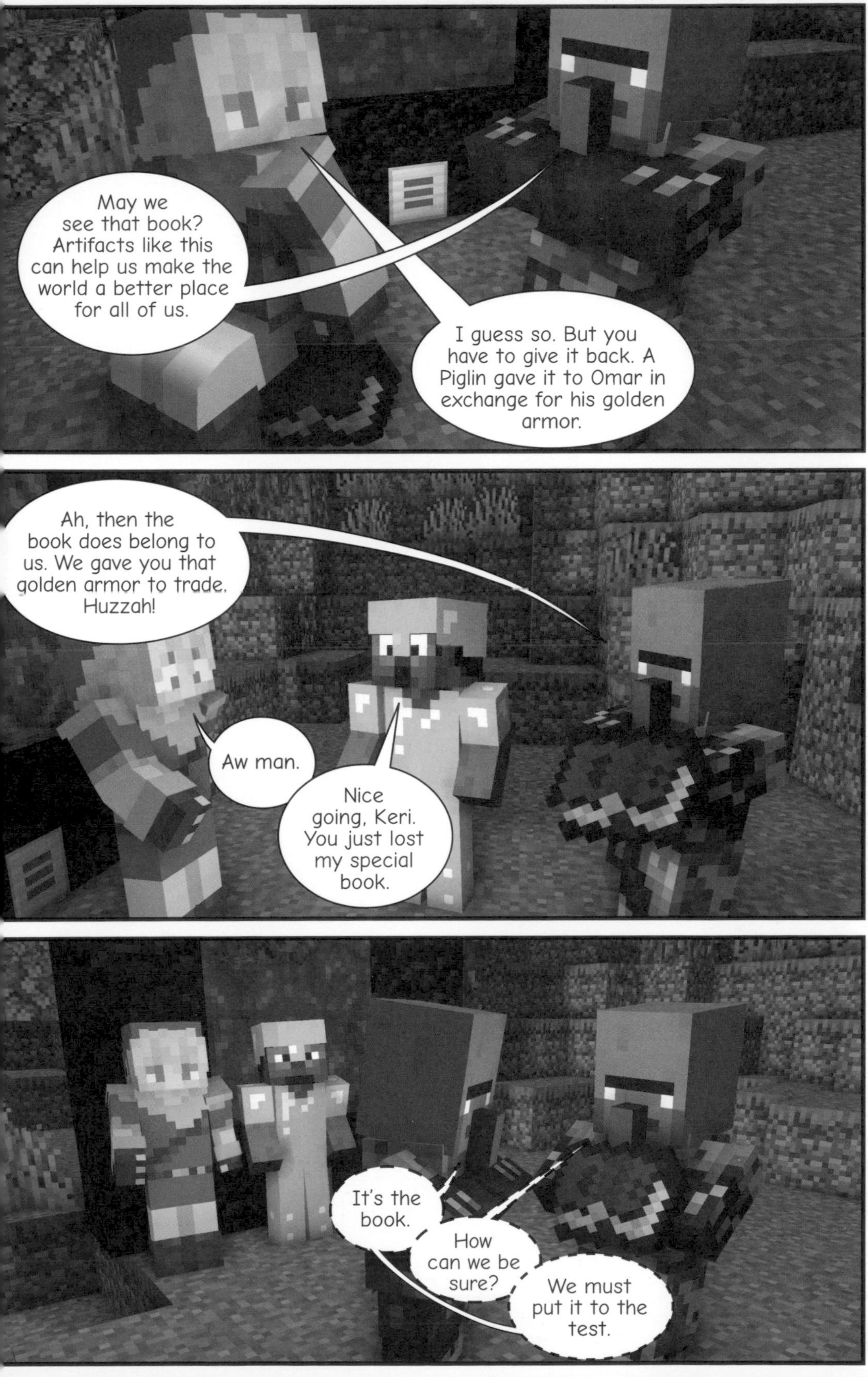
May we see that book? Artifacts like this can help us make the world a better place for all of us.
I guess so. But you have to give it back. A Piglin gave it to Omar in exchange for his golden armor.
Ah, then the book does belong to us. We gave you that golden armor to trade. Huzzah!
Aw man.
Nice going, Keri. You just lost my special book.
It's the book.
How can we be sure?
We must put it to the test.

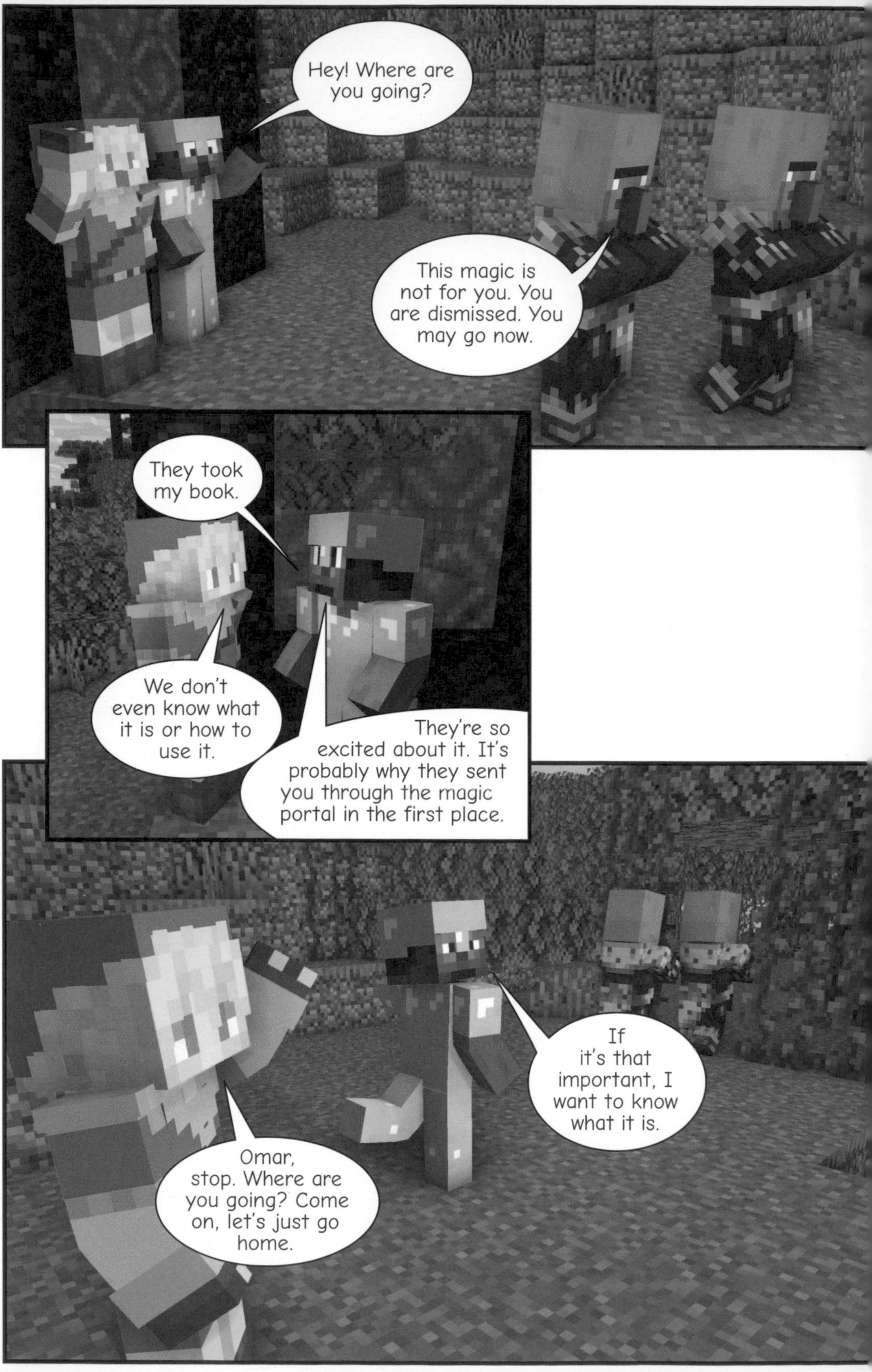
Hey! Where are you going?
This magic is not for you. You are dismissed. You may go now.
They took my book.
We don't even know what it is or how to use it.
They're so excited about it. It's probably why they sent you through the magic portal in the first place.
If it's that important, I want to know what it is.
Omar, stop. Where are you going? Come on, let's just go home.

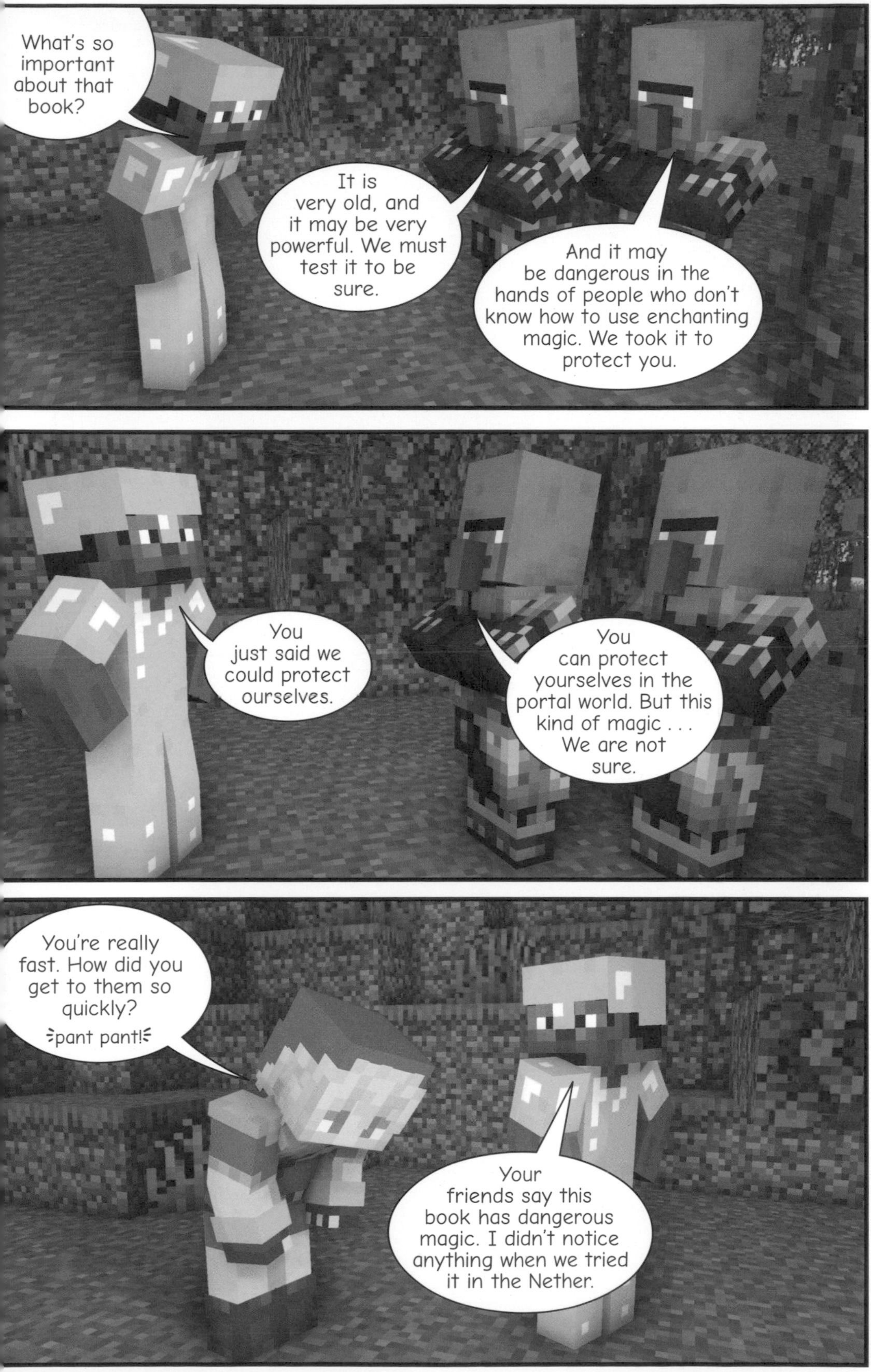
What's so important about that book?
It is very old, and it may be very powerful. We must test it to be sure.
And it may be dangerous in the hands of people who don't know how to use enchanting magic. We took it to protect you.
You just said we could protect ourselves.
You can protect yourselves in the portal world. But this kind of magic . . . We are not sure.
You're really fast. How did you get to them so quickly?
pant pant!
Your friends say this book has dangerous magic. I didn't notice anything when we tried it in the Nether.

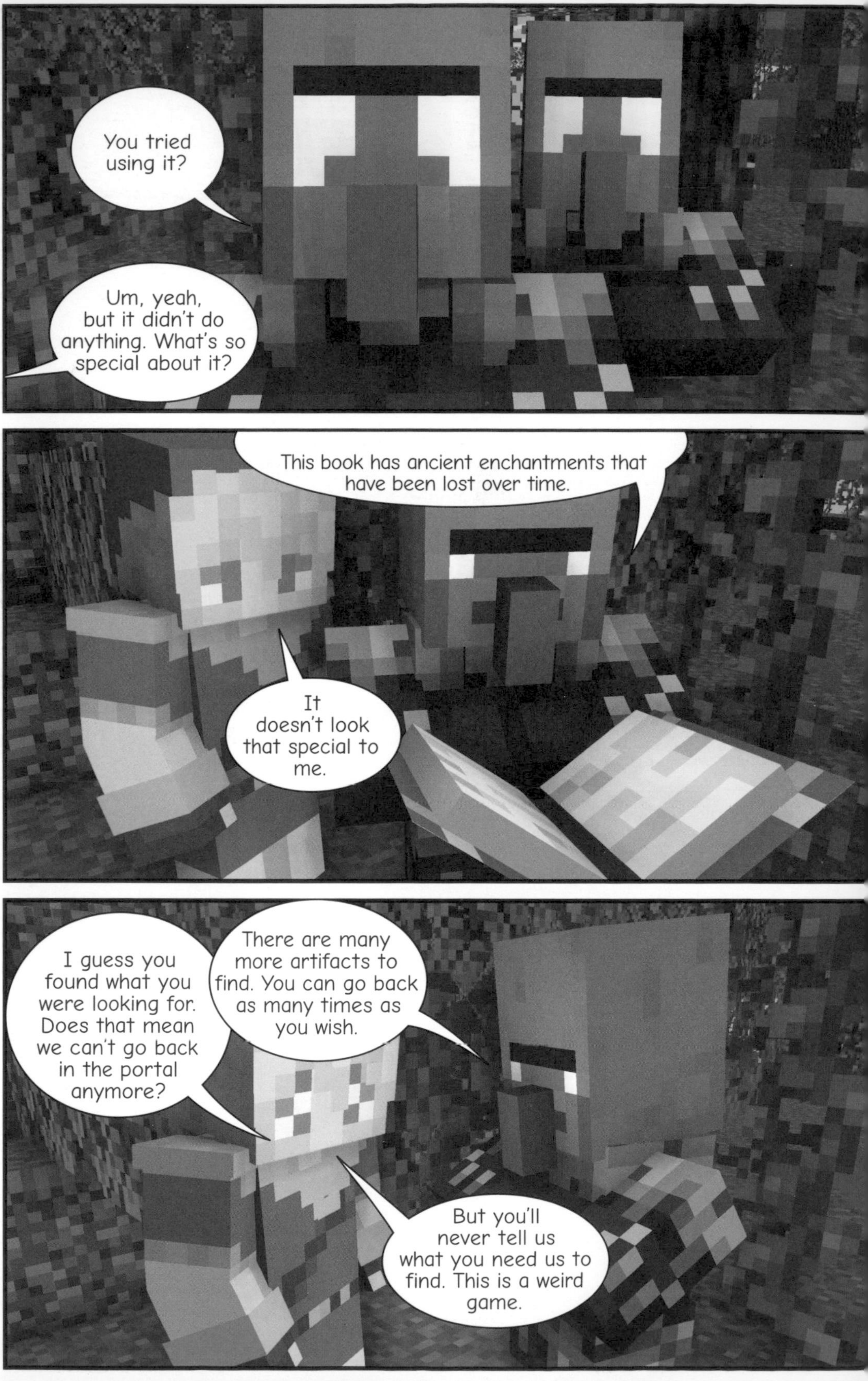
You tried using it?
Um, yeah, but it didn't do anything. What's so special about it?
This book has ancient enchantments that have been lost over time.
It doesn't look that special to me.
I guess you found what you were looking for. Does that mean we can't go back in the portal anymore?
There are many more artifacts to find. You can go back as many times as you wish.
But you'll never tell us what you need us to find. This is a weird game.

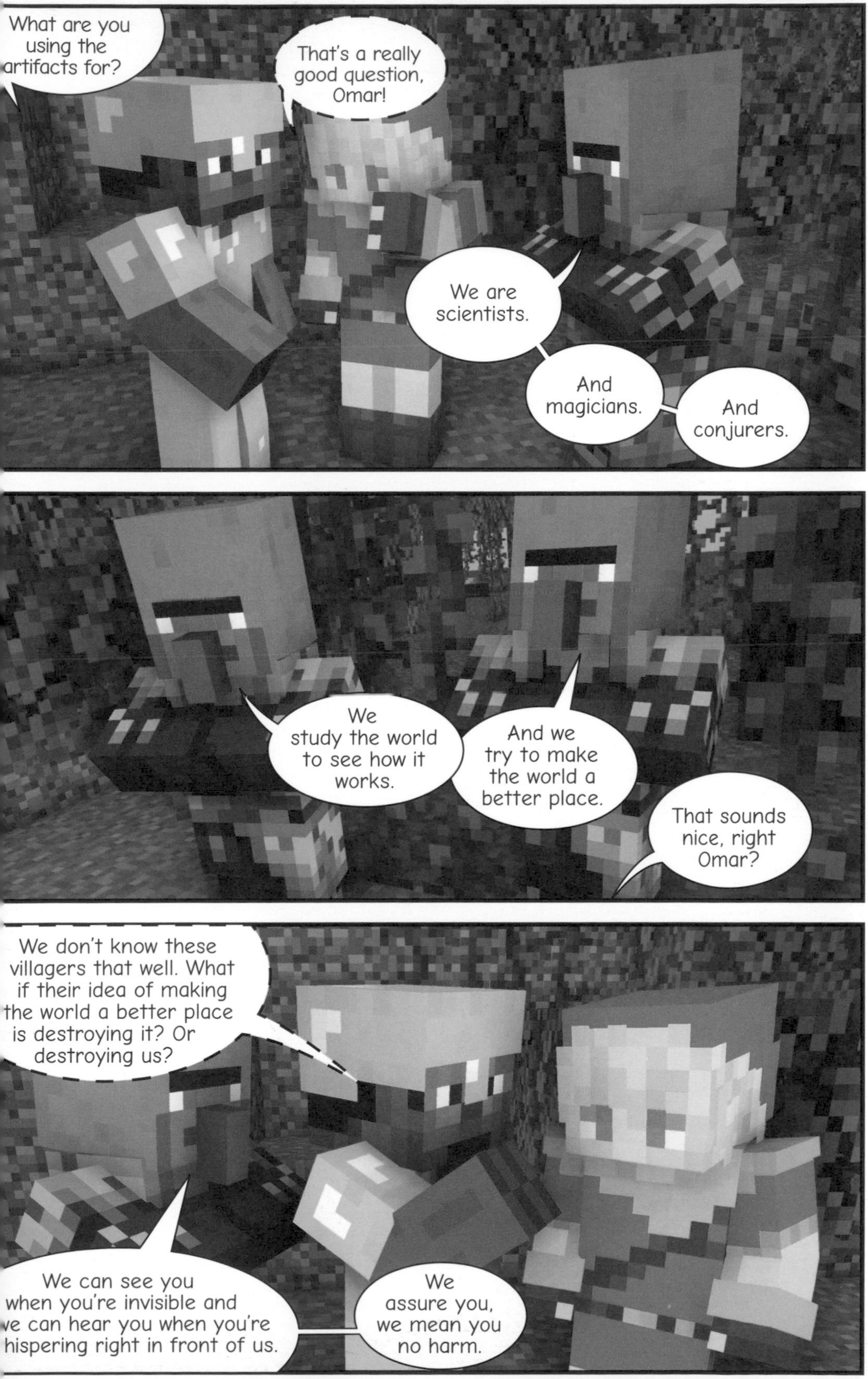
What are you using the artifacts for?
That's a really good question, Omar!
We are scientists.
And magicians.
And conjurers.
We study the world to see how it works.
And we try to make the world a better place.
That sounds nice, right Omar?
We don't know these villagers that well. What if their idea of making the world a better place is destroying it? Or destroying us?
We can see you when you're invisible and we can hear you when you're whispering right in front of us.
We assure you, we mean you no harm.

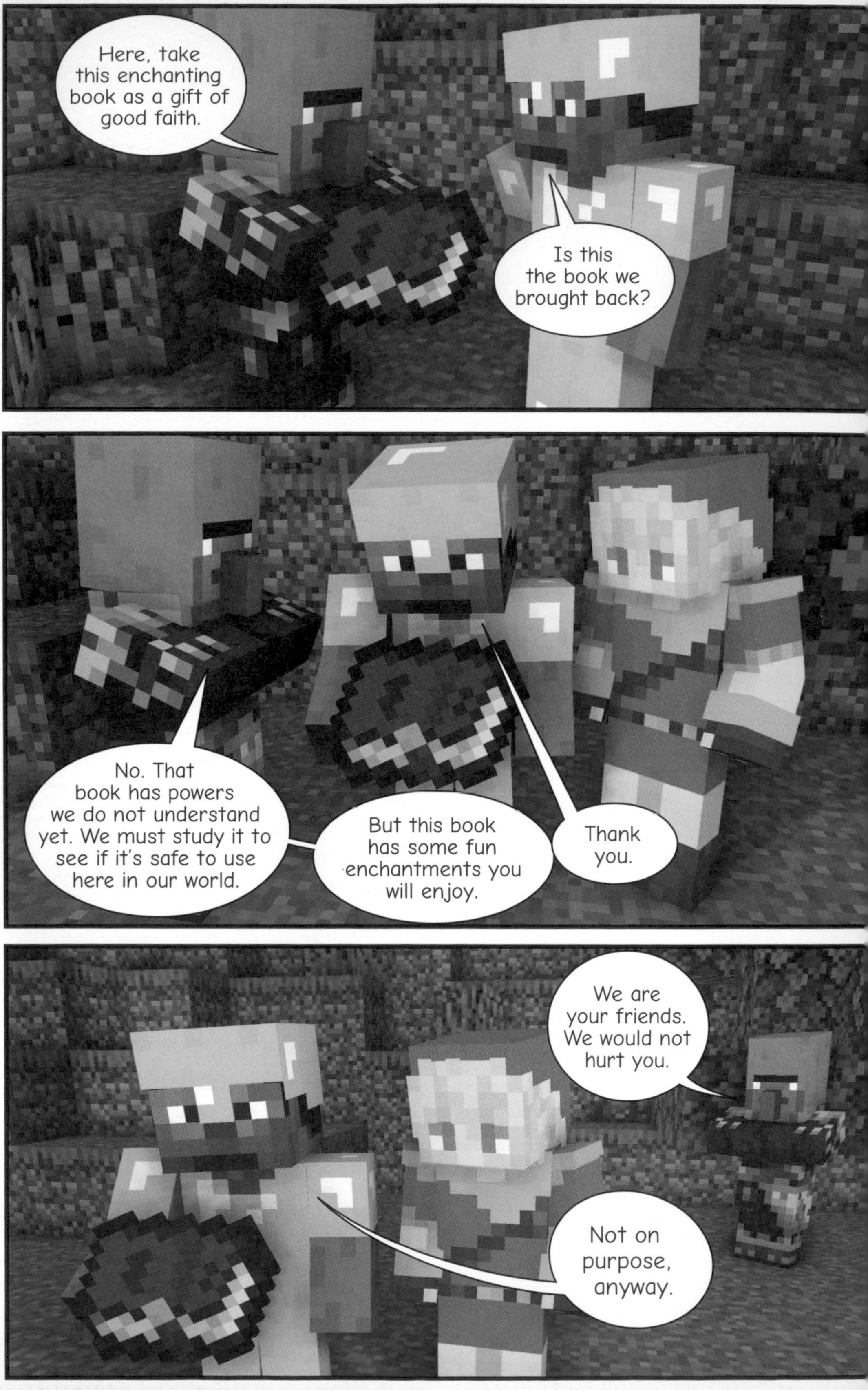
Here, take this enchanting book as a gift of good faith.
Is this the book we brought back?
No. That book has powers we do not understand yet. We must study it to see if it's safe to use here in our world.
But this book has some fun enchantments you will enjoy.
Thank you.
We are your friends. We would not hurt you.
Not on purpose, anyway.

Chapter 13
Trust

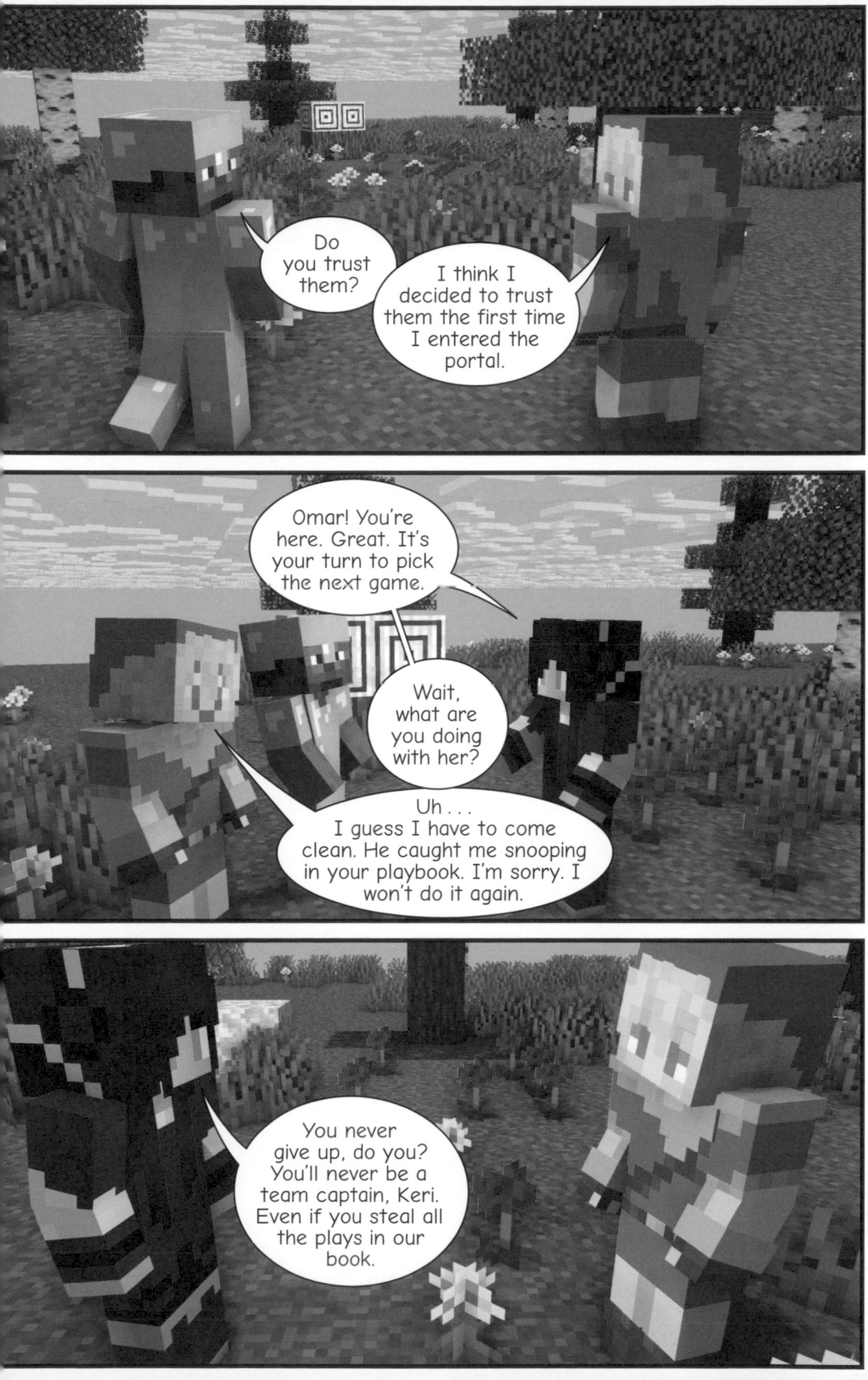
Do you trust them?
I think I decided to trust them the first time I entered the portal.
Omar! You're here. Great. It's your turn to pick the next game.
Wait, what are you doing with her?
Uh . . . I guess I have to come clean. He caught me snooping in your playbook. I'm sorry. I won't do it again.
You never give up, do you? You'll never be a team captain, Keri. Even if you steal all the plays in our book.

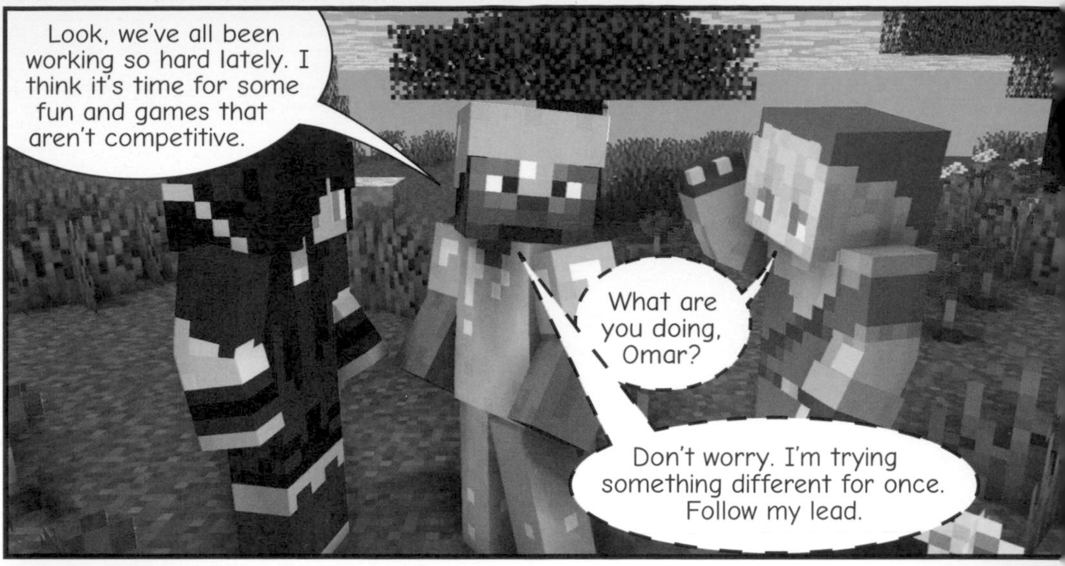
Look, we've all been working so hard lately. I think it's time for some fun and games that aren't competitive.
What are you doing, Omar?
Don't worry. I'm trying something different for once. Follow my lead.

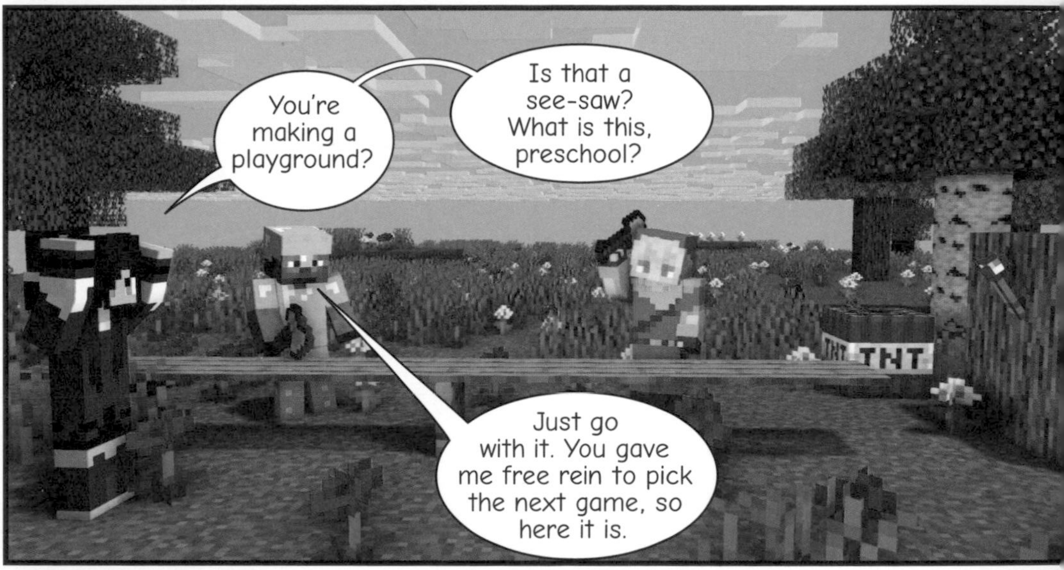
You're making a playground?
Is that a see-saw? What is this, preschool?
Just go with it. You gave me free rein to pick the next game, so here it is.

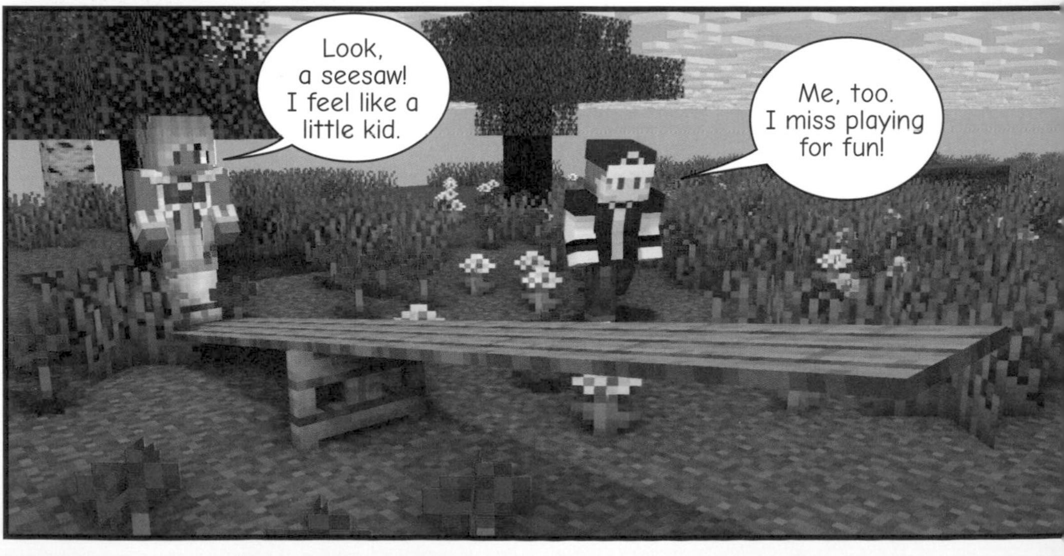
Look, a seesaw! I feel like a little kid.
Me, too. I miss playing for fun!

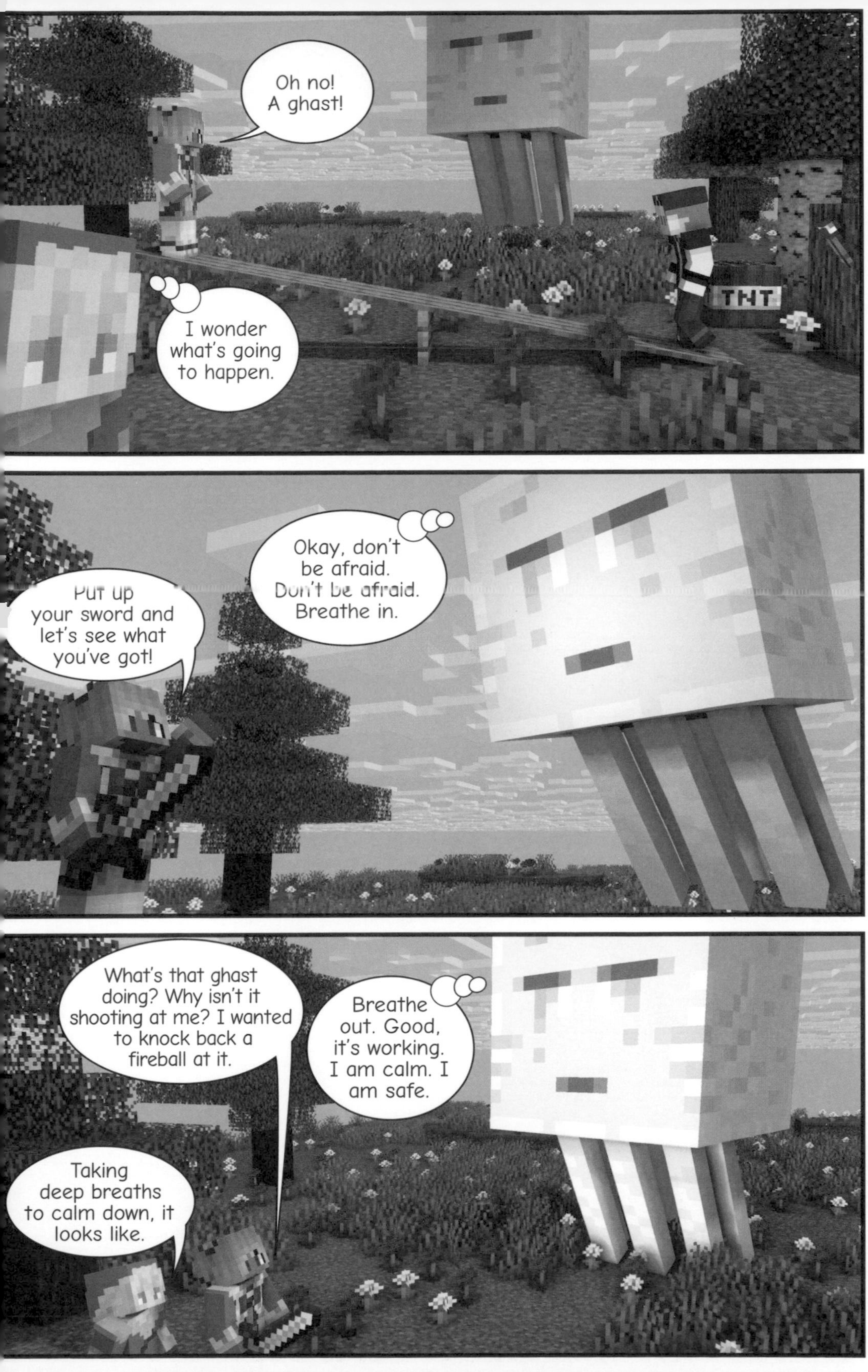
Oh no! A ghast!
I wonder what's going to happen.
Okay, don't be afraid. Don't be afraid. Breathe in.
Put up your sword and let's see what you've got!
What's that ghast doing? Why isn't it shooting at me? I wanted to knock back a fireball at it.
Breathe out. Good, it's working. I am calm. I am safe.
Taking deep breaths to calm down, it looks like.
TNT

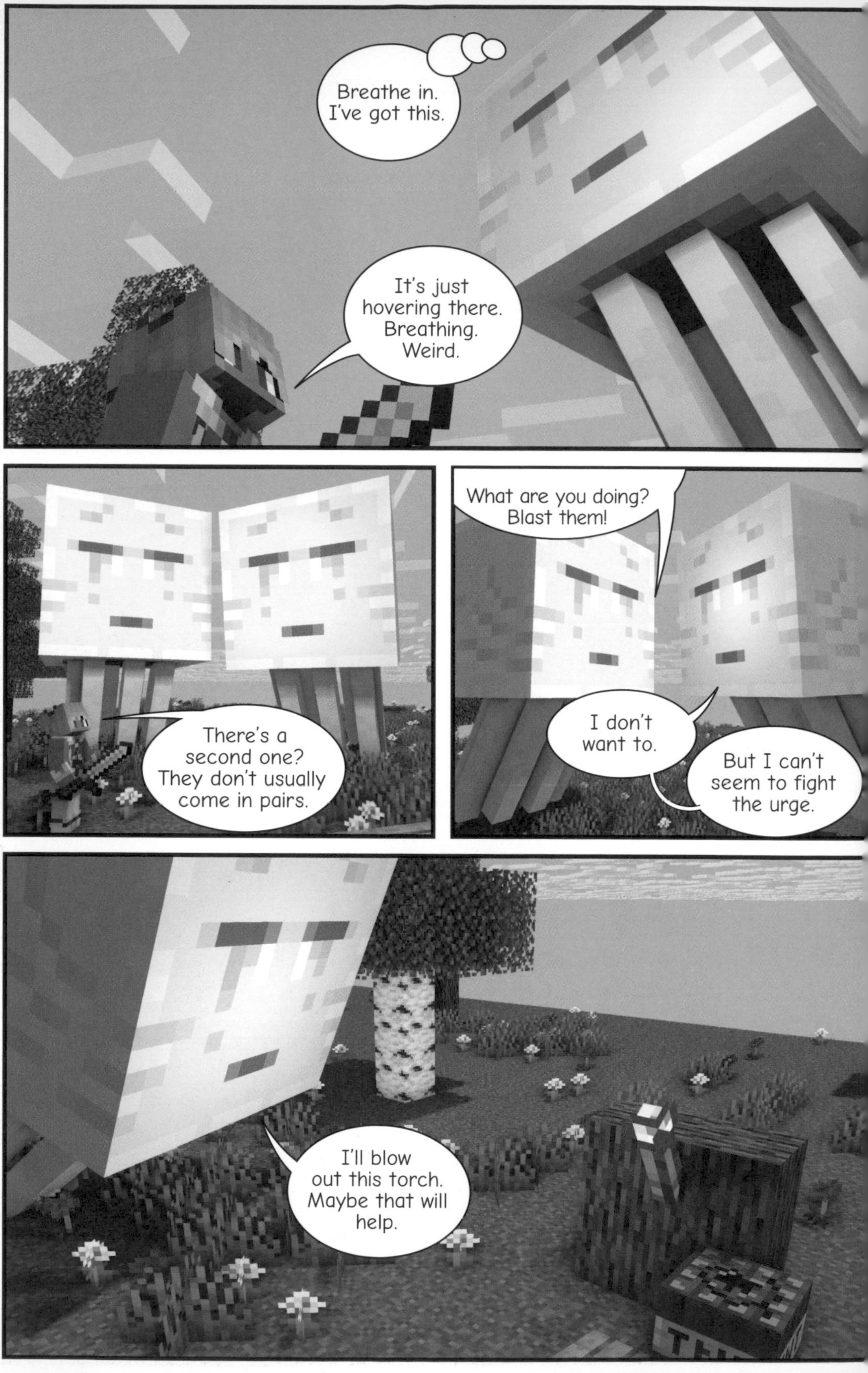
Breathe in. I've got this.
It's just hovering there. Breathing. Weird.
There's a second one? They don't usually come in pairs.
What are you doing? Blast them!
I don't want to.
But I can't seem to fight the urge.
I'll blow out this torch. Maybe that will help.

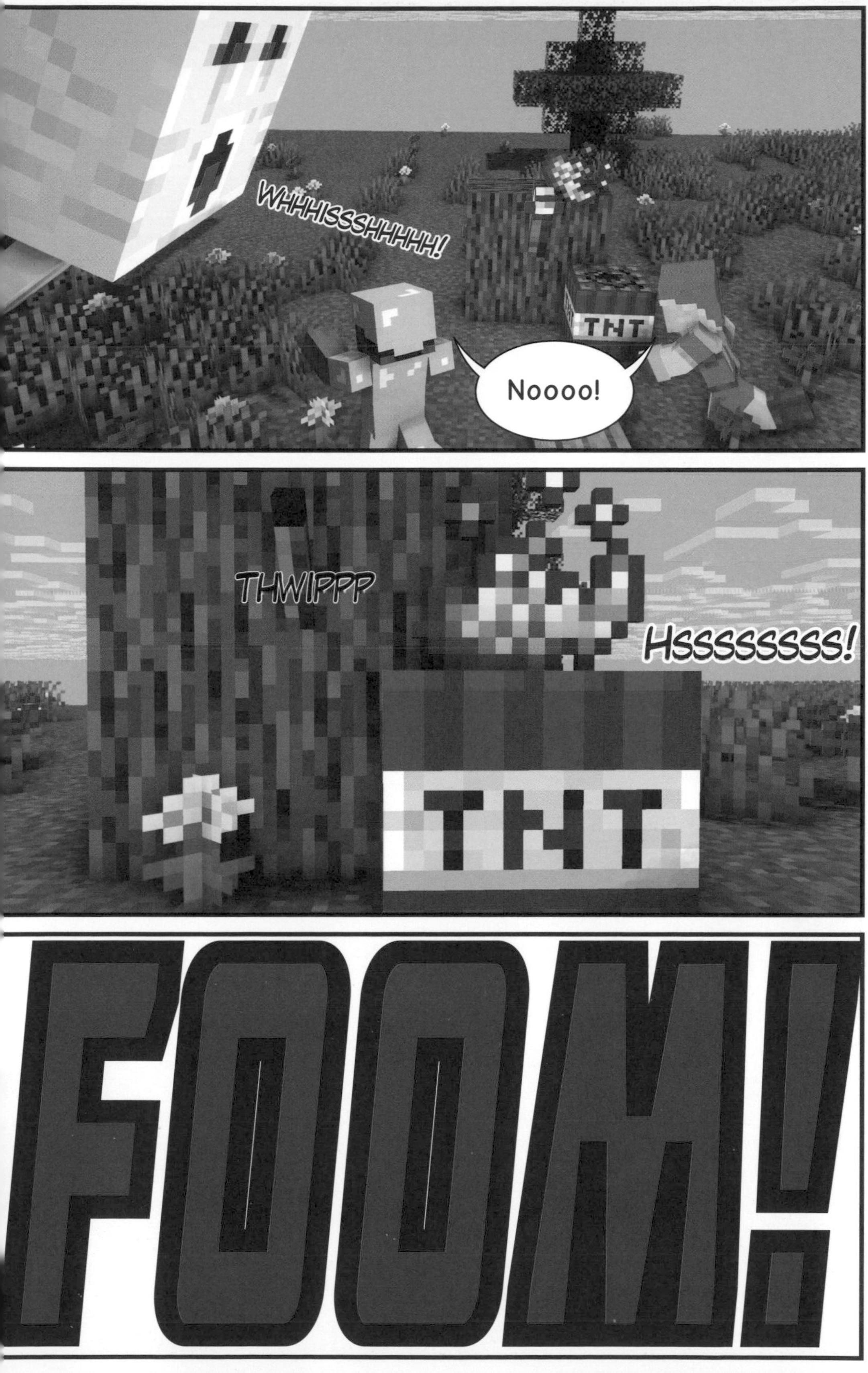

WHHHISSSHHHHH!
Noooo!
THWIPPP
Hssssssss!
FOOM!

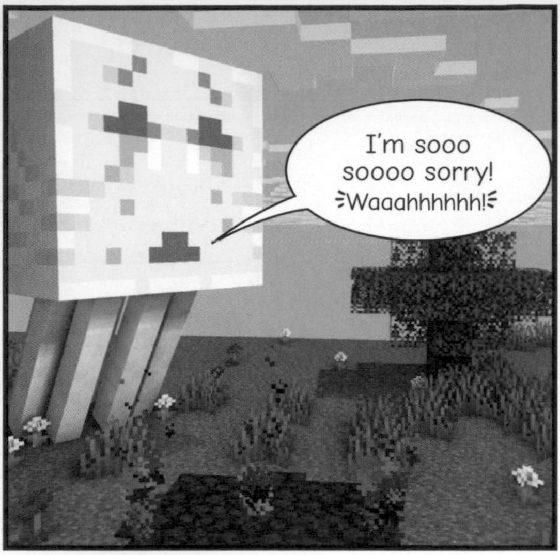
I'm sooo
soooo sorry!
Waaahhhhhh!

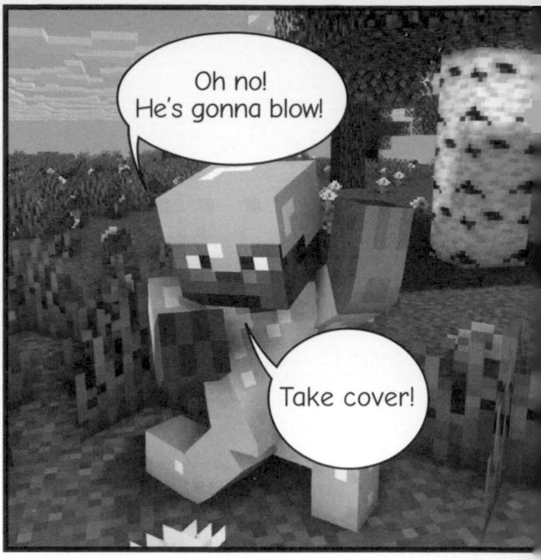
Oh no!
He's gonna blow!
Take cover!

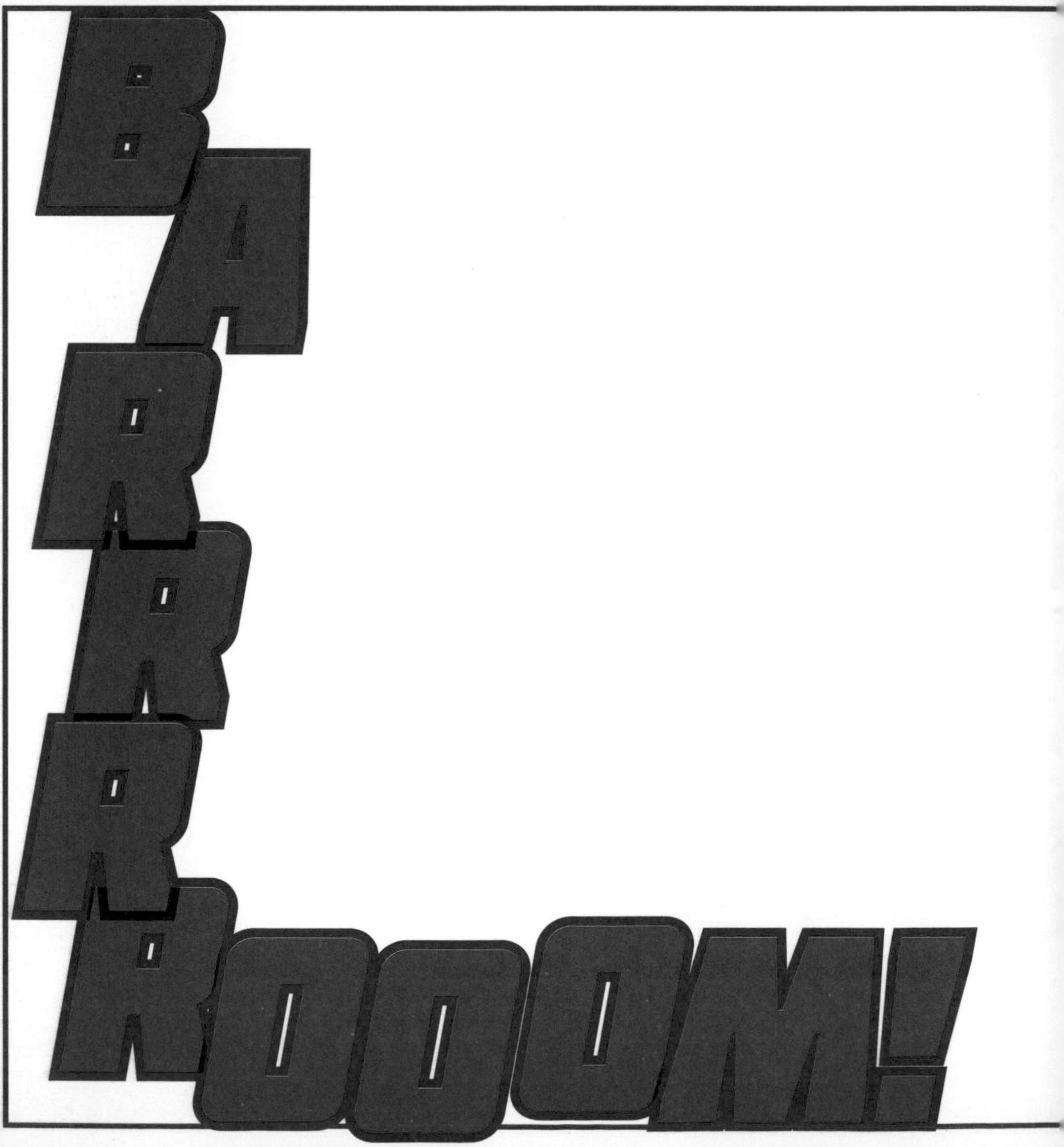
BARRRROOOM!

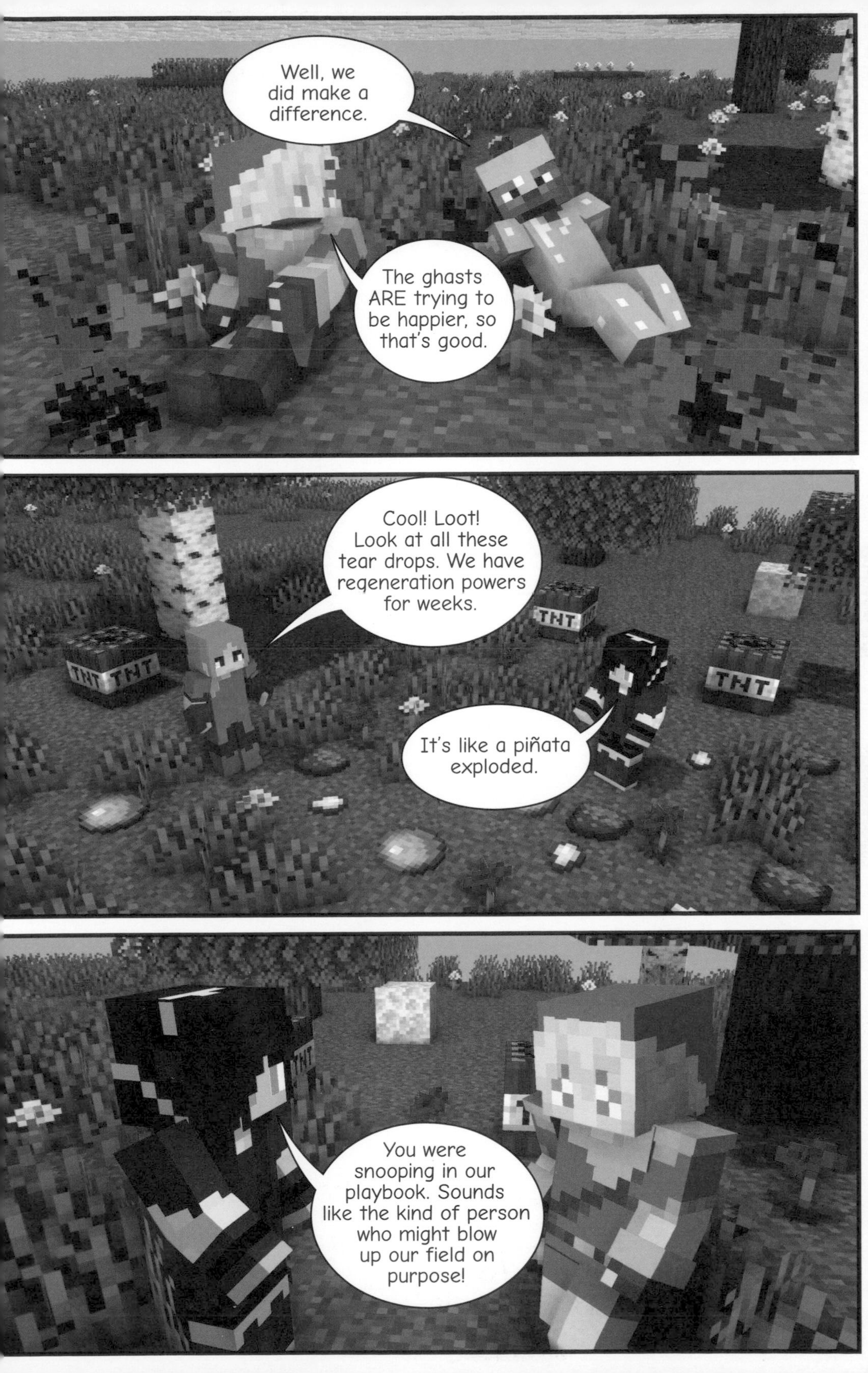
Well, we did make a difference.
The ghasts ARE trying to be happier, so that's good.
Cool! Loot! Look at all these tear drops. We have regeneration powers for weeks.
It's like a piñata exploded.
You were snooping in our playbook. Sounds like the kind of person who might blow up our field on purpose!

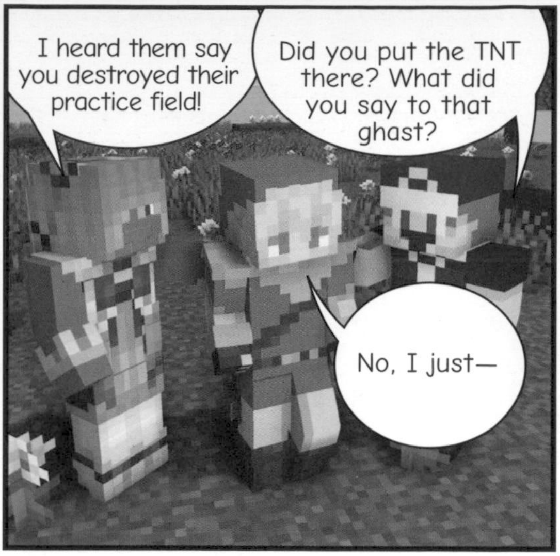
I heard them say you destroyed their practice field!
Did you put the TNT there? What did you say to that ghast?
No, I just—

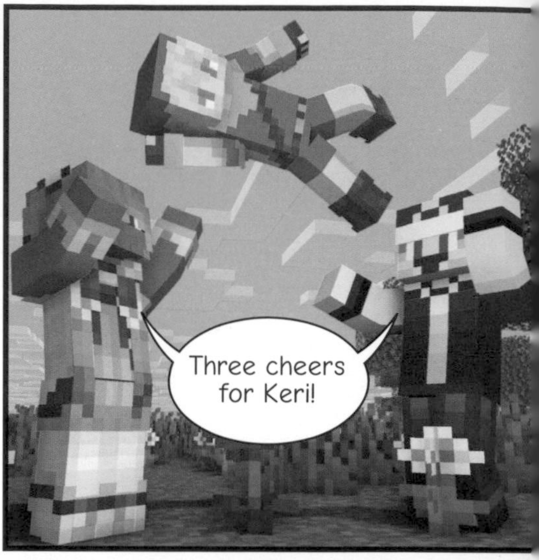
Three cheers for Keri!

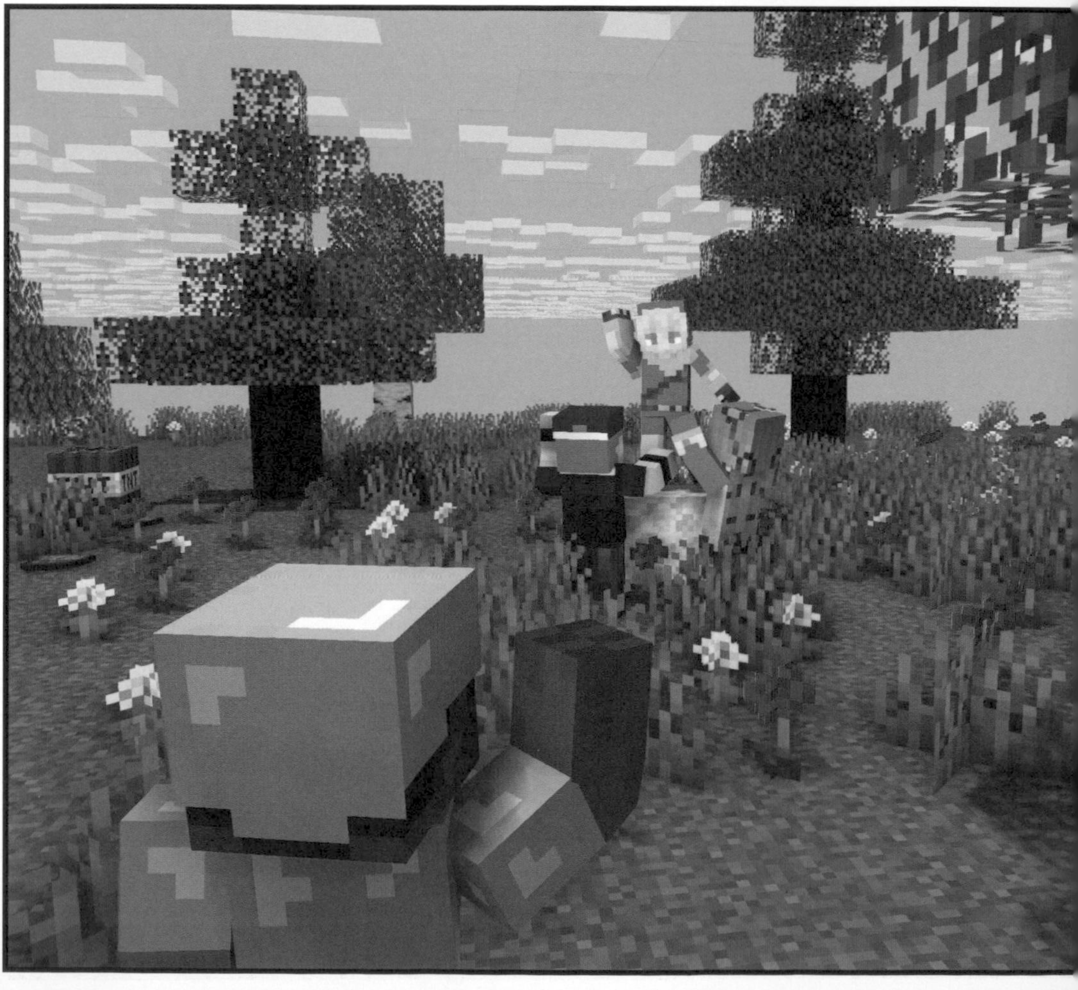
TNT

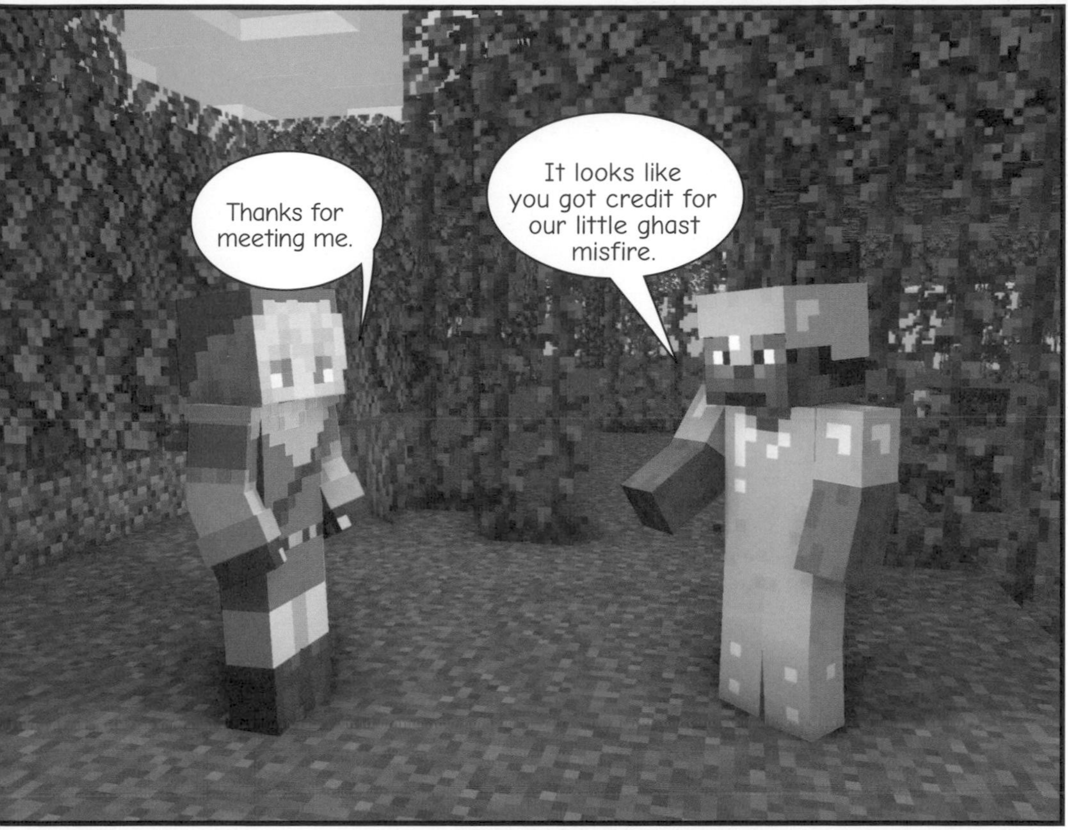
Thanks for meeting me.
It looks like you got credit for our little ghast misfire.

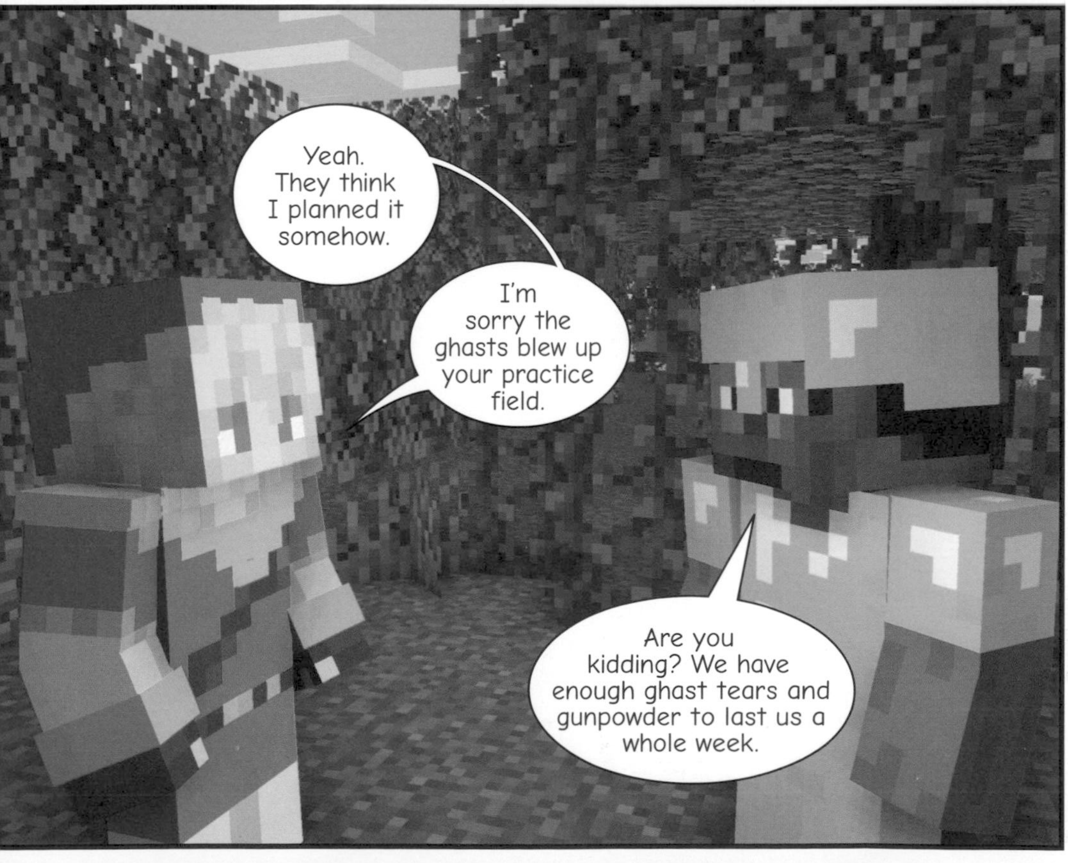
Yeah. They think I planned it somehow.
I'm sorry the ghasts blew up your practice field.
Are you kidding? We have enough ghast tears and gunpowder to last us a whole week.

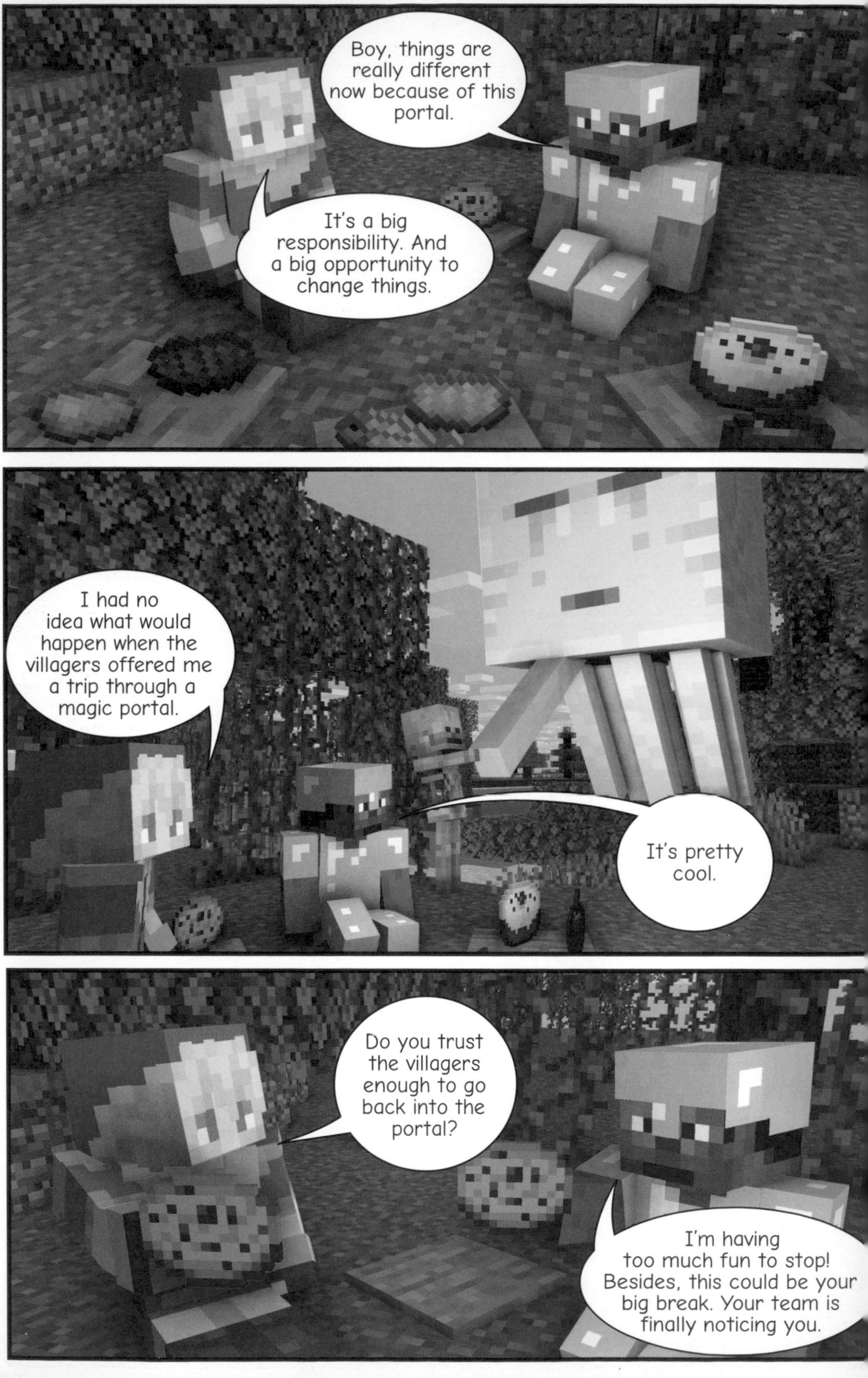
Boy, things are really different now because of this portal.
It's a big responsibility. And a big opportunity to change things.
I had no idea what would happen when the villagers offered me a trip through a magic portal.
It's pretty cool.
Do you trust the villagers enough to go back into the portal?
I'm having too much fun to stop! Besides, this could be your big break. Your team is finally noticing you.

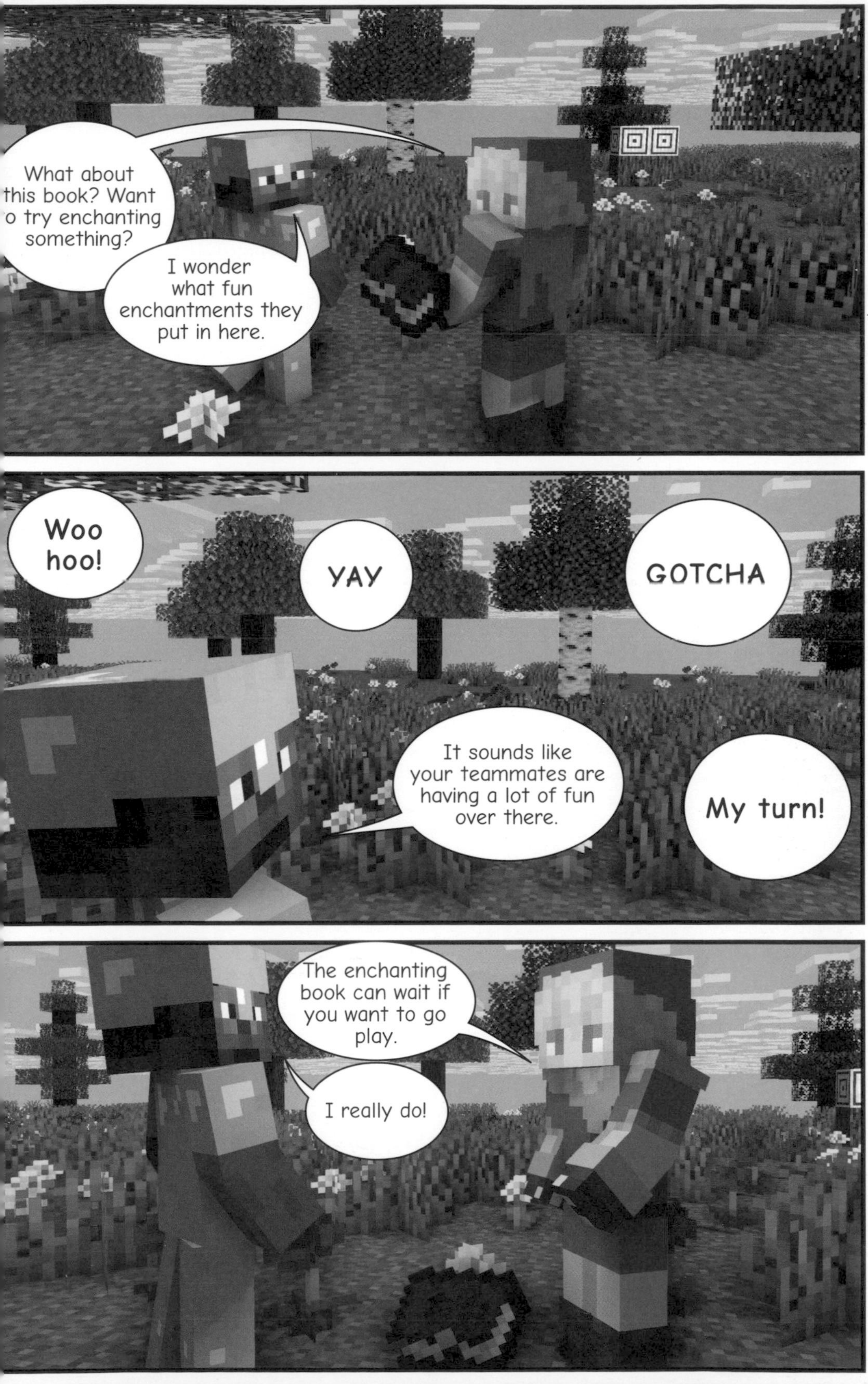
What about this book? Want to try enchanting something?
I wonder what fun enchantments they put in here.
Woo hoo!
YAY
GOTCHA
It sounds like your teammates are having a lot of fun over there.
My turn!
The enchanting book can wait if you want to go play.
I really do!

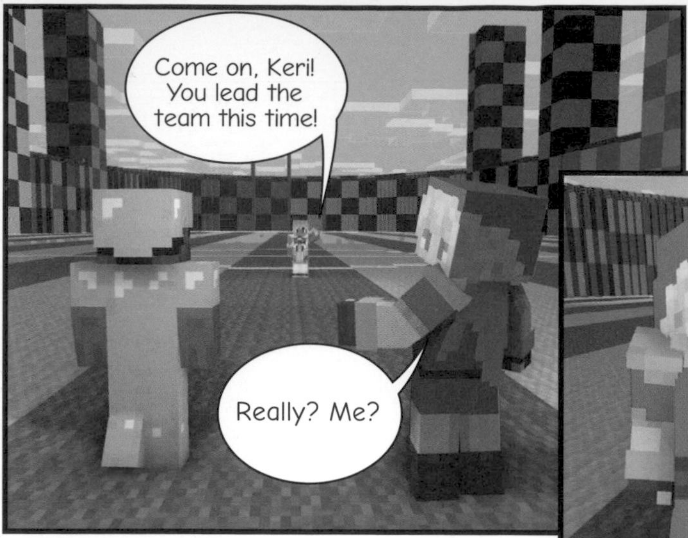
Come on, Keri! You lead the team this time!
Really? Me?
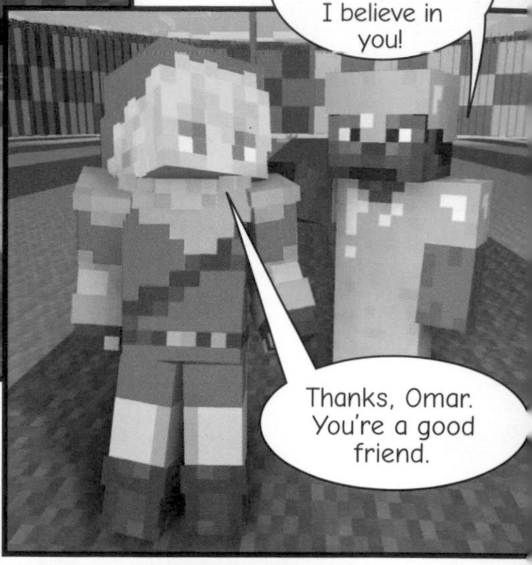
You'd better get in there. Good luck! I believe in you!
Thanks, Omar. You're a good friend.
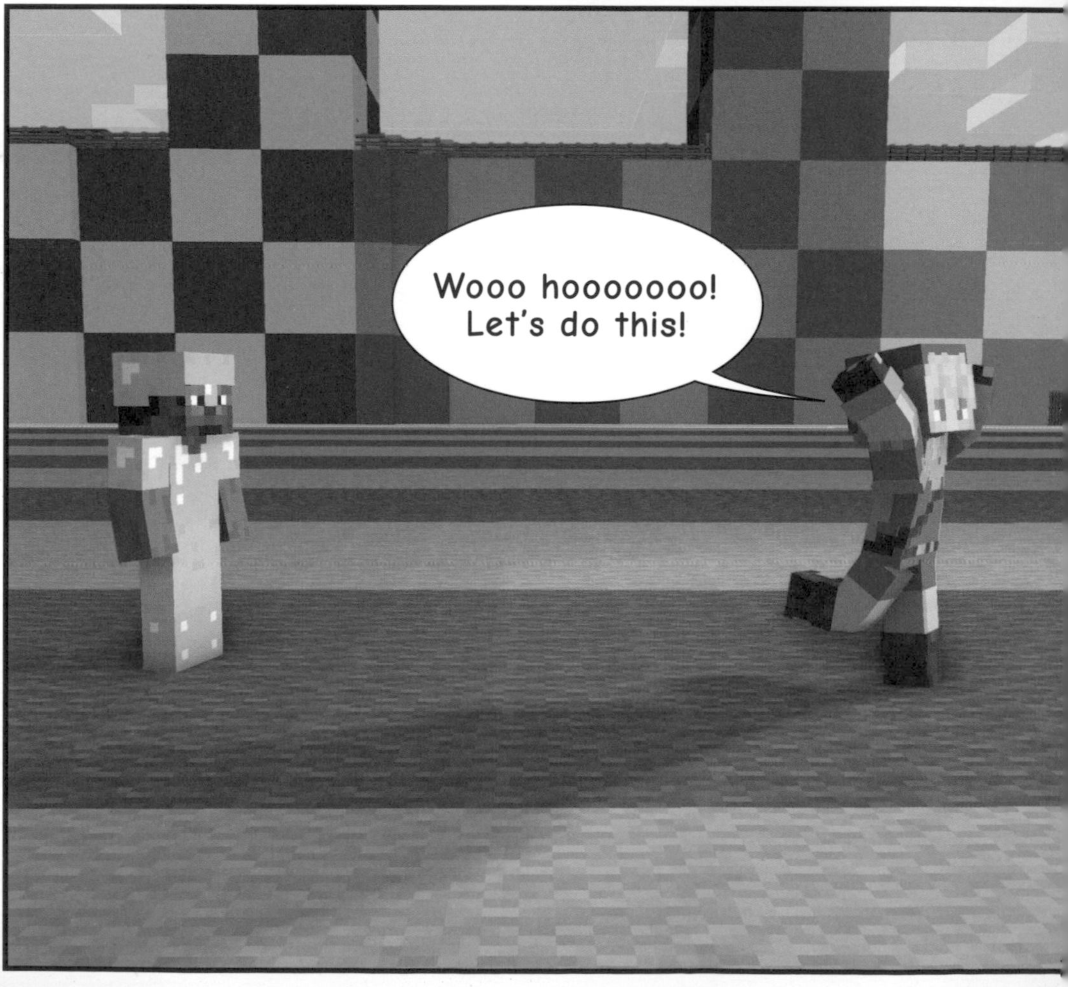
Wooo hooooooo! Let's do this!